THE SHADOW PALACE

❊ JANE STEEN ❊

THE SHADOW PALACE
Jane Steen

Copyright ©2016 by Jane Steen. All rights reserved. No part of this publication may be reproduced, stored in a retrieval system, or transmitted in any form or by any means—electronic, mechanical, photocopying, recording, or otherwise—without the prior written permission of the publisher, except for brief quotations in printed reviews and articles.

Published by Aspidistra Press

ISBN: 978-0-9857150-8-3

Cover photography by Steve Ledell
Cover design by Derek Moore
Print edition design by Derek Moore

This is a work of fiction. Names, characters, places, incidents, and dialogues are products of the author's imagination and are not to be construed as real. Any resemblance to actual events, locales, organizations, business establishments, or persons living or dead is entirely coincidental.

JANE STEEN

THE HOUSE OF CLOSED DOORS
SERIES

THE HOUSE OF CLOSED DOORS
ETERNAL DECEPTION
THE SHADOW PALACE

To Susan,
For helping me move back to England

THE SHADOW PALACE

By

JANE STEEN

ONE

"Are we in Chicago yet?"

"Not quite. Go back to sleep."

I sounded breathless, for good reason. The train had jolted and swayed alarmingly—as it had several times that morning, to be sure—but I hadn't been asleep and dreaming about the snow before. This time the sudden movement sent prickles of fear into my fingertips as I opened my eyes in panic. It was here—it—what had it been? Some terrible fate, looming out of a white blizzard.

"Ridiculous, Nell," I whispered. What I'd thought were snowflakes tickling my face must have been Sarah's wiry, copper-colored hair, already escaping from its braids. She had curled into a ball on my lap, her bony posterior and her boots making dents in my traveling dress, her head hot and heavy.

"Nasty, smelly train." Sarah delivered her pronouncement with conviction, but her eyes didn't open, and she only butted her head harder into the softer part of me just above the boning of my corset.

I swallowed hard, willing the anxiety coursing through me to subside. The other passengers were quiet. Only the preacher's wife was still reading, in the lowest of murmurs, from a seemingly endless book of sermons. Her husband had fixed a half smile of encouragement on his face, but his eyelids were drooping. We had all boarded the train, the last leg of our journey to Chicago, very early in the morning.

Across from me, Tess stirred and lifted her head, pushing her spectacles back up her nose.

"I'm thirsty."

"We must be almost there," I said. "We've already stopped at Joliet to let some passengers off. When we get to the Palmer House Hotel, we can drink tea and eat cakes to our hearts' content."

Tess licked her lips and smiled, settling back into her half-asleep contemplation of the rain-drenched, partially frozen landscape through which we rattled. Beneath the gray, cloud-laden sky, a repeating series of views passed before us—yellowed prairie, the thick brown clay of fields bristling with last year's corn stalks, and gray-brown trees gathered together in spindly, desolate clumps. Behind us in Kansas, the first green shoots were showing, but the only color in Chicago's hinterland was the occasional red-painted barn or whitewashed farmhouse.

Chicago. No doubt my fear that we were on a collision course with disaster had given rise to my dream of stumbling through the snow toward an unknown doom. Ever since we'd clambered aboard the cart that had taken us away from the Eternal Life Seminary, the dread that I'd made a horrible mistake had settled over my shoulders like a cold blanket.

I blamed Martin, of course. Well, to be fair, I was at fault too for giving in to his insistence that we come to Chicago. But wasn't it typical of him, that assumption that he could steer my life? The more so now that I knew—and *he* knew—I'd fallen in love with him. Perhaps women really were as weak as Judah Poulton had said.

Something inside me twanged like a harp string as the memory of Judah's broken body and his blood seeping into the snow intruded on my thoughts. I stiffened and Sarah stirred, making a sound between a snort and a moan. Two of the traveling salesmen who had boarded the train at Bloomington were moving through the carriage, and hearing the sound, they nodded an apology and trod more carefully. Their scents of pomade, sweat, and cigars lingered in the air after they passed, adding to the carriage's general mustiness.

"Drat Judah." I gritted my teeth. He was dead, after all, and no longer a threat to us. But he'd been right about one thing. I felt myself drawn to Martin like a moth to a flame, in danger of burning. Was *that* what Martin wanted after all? That I should become his mistress? He'd explained to me so carefully that as much as he wanted to divorce his wife, he couldn't do so without the risk of dragging my name, and Sarah's, in the mud. He had left me with little hope that he'd make the attempt.

"Leaves me in a pretty position, doesn't it, Martin?" I whispered in the direction of the window. The little farmhouses and sturdy barns were more frequent now. It was the landscape of my youth—we must be nearing Chicago. I imagined Martin climbing into his carriage with his glittering, faithless Lucetta while I stood at a distance, watching from the outer edge of his world.

Did he still entertain a spark of love for her? That question had pounded in my head to the rhythm of the train's progress. Martin had told me he was living in a hotel—did that mean he never saw her? Or did they appear together in society when the occasion demanded? Could I—we—even aspire to the sort of society Lucetta and Martin moved in?

"Is the Palmer House awful grand, Nell?" Tess's question was an odd echo of my own swirling thoughts. I realized she was gazing at me, her almond-shaped eyes magnified behind her spectacles.

"I think it is." I bit my lip but then straightened my shoulders. "We can afford it, Tess. We won't be out of place there."

"*You* won't." Tess looked doubtful.

"Neither will you. I promise." I smiled at Tess, finding my own courage in the effort to strengthen hers. I understood her fears. She'd led a retired life in Kansas while I'd at least had my dressmaking clients. I had attended many dinners and social events from which she'd been excluded. In Chicago, she would be under the scrutiny of many people, and I knew that daunted her. When I looked at Tess, I saw the sister of my heart; but we were both aware that strangers who saw her would have the word "imbecile" in their minds, and perhaps on their lips.

"Wouldn't it be nicer to have a little house of our own? You said we could afford one." The expression on Tess's face was almost pleading.

"I'd like nothing more." I sighed. "But it all depends on whether we can stay in Chicago."

"Why can't we? Martin's there."

I set my mouth into its most stubborn expression, hoping that might deter Tess from further remarks about Martin. She still wished that I might marry Martin despite the inconvenient existence of his wife. She never could see why the biblical patriarchs could have more than one wife and Martin couldn't. Intensely moral as she was, the idea of my being even remotely tempted to become Martin's mistress had never entered her head.

"And *I'm* from Chicago," Tess continued. "At least, that's where we lived when Ma and Da let the charity lady take me to the Poor Farm." Her mouth turned down at the corners. "I don't suppose they'd want to see me though."

"Oh, Tess." I felt the prickling of tears and wished I could hug her, but I couldn't move an inch without disturbing Sarah. "You'll always have a home with Sarah and me, whatever happens. Just give me a little time to look around and see what work I can do."

"But you're rich, Nell, and you're a lady. Rich ladies don't work. Except for being charity ladies and making sure that poor people behave themselves."

"I want to work. *Real* work, not committees." I kept my voice low—the preacher's wife's reading was faltering as she eavesdropped on our conversation. "I want to make beautiful dresses, like Martin's *couturières*."

And that was another thing. The one place in Chicago where I ached to work was permanently barred to me. I'd be a fool to put myself in temptation's way. I was a shareholder in Martin's store, but I could never truly become part of it. In some ways, the longing to do so was almost as strong as my longing for Martin himself.

Sarah's weight against my chest prevented a huge sigh from forcing its way out. There was no prospect of reconciling my conflicting desires, which all seemed to center on Chicago. I wanted my independence, I wanted Martin, and I wanted Tess and Sarah to be happy. I could neither marry Martin—which would have robbed me of my independence in any event—nor give in to my desires and condemn the three of us to a life of lies and potential disgrace.

"Hotel tickets, Madam?"

I'd been so preoccupied I hadn't seen the uniformed man approaching, but Sarah was awake in an instant.

"Are we in Chicago, Momma?"

"Very soon, I think. Could you move off my lap so I can look in my reticule?" I knew exactly where it was—the coins it contained had been pressing most uncomfortably into my hip for the last three hours. I gestured to the Parmalee agent to wait a moment.

"We're staying at the Palmer House." I fished out the slip of paper with one hand, steadying Sarah with the other.

The man jerked his chin toward the back of the carriage. "The Palmer House has its own carriage. The agent will be along in a minute."

Sarah giggled—every word the man spoke caused his abundant mustache to blow outward. I tightened my grip on her torso as a signal not to laugh, but after all she was only five years old. "Thank you," I said to the Parmalee agent.

"Don't forget the paper with the numbers of your trunks." The man moved on, his gait steady despite the train's rocking.

Sarah, clearly well rested, scrambled up onto the seat and pressed her hands and nose against the carriage window.

"Sarah, it's dirty. Don't do that." I tried to pull her away, but she resisted.

"Look—see that cart? It's coming toward us and going backward at the same time."

We'd been sitting with our backs to the engine, allowing Tess to face the direction of travel so she wouldn't get sick. We were passing through yet another small town clinging to the prairie with more stubbornness than sense, and Sarah was right. The bright yellow cart moving in the same direction was receding into the distance as the train's greater speed pulled us forward.

Just like my life, I reflected as I steeled myself for the task of getting my small family ready to disembark. We were moving forward all right, but my doubts and fears trailed me and would catch up with me as soon as I stood still. Worse, I was heading toward Martin, but every inch I moved in his direction seemed to increase the distance between us.

TWO

"Look at all the people! Why are some of them dressed so funny? And the buildings are so big. Momma, *look!*"

Sarah's hat, anchored by its ribbon, fell backward. I'd taken out her braids and brushed her hair once we'd descended from the train. It shone in crisp copper waves, ending in a cascade of ringlets. She wriggled around to get a better view from the window, and I saw her foot strike the well-dressed woman who sat next to her in the Palmer House carriage.

"I'm so sorry." I reached across Tess and seized my daughter's wiry midriff. "Tess, could you possibly move over so I can put her between us? Sarah, polite little girls sit still—no, you can't stand on the bench—oh, for goodness' sake. I'm sorry," I said again to the woman she'd kicked. "She's usually well behaved, but she had a long sleep on the train, and she's full of energy."

"And excitement, I imagine," the woman said, smiling. "It's quite all right. I have three grandchildren, although I don't see them nearly often enough." She was a sharp-eyed but not unpleasant-looking lady of around fifty, clearly well-to-do.

"Look at the buildings, Tess," Sarah crowed, oblivious to the fact that she was blocking Tess's view. "They're as high as the seminary—that one's higher. What's that smell?"

"The river," crowed the plump man sitting opposite, who had been grinning at my efforts to control Sarah. "You wait till summer, little lady," he continued as Sarah turned, a little startled by his loud tone. "It smells even worse in the warm weather, and if the wind's right, you can experience the perfume of the stockyards."

I wasn't at all sure what I could say to that. Besides, it didn't seem proper to be chatting to a gentleman, in a public carriage, without an introduction. I returned my gaze to the older lady, glad to see she'd fixed the plump man with a stony stare that indicated he was being too forward.

Outside the slowly moving carriage flowed a river of people. Sarah was right—many of them wore costumes that seemed outlandish, as if they belonged in the theater. The street *was* a theater, in many ways, thronged with peddlers, loungers, and groups of people through which a steady stream of purposeful-looking men and women threaded their way. In the roadway, carriages and horses seemed to be proceeding in random directions while pedestrians wove in and out of them. How there was not an accident every two minutes was a puzzle to me.

"Shops and shops and *shops*," breathed Sarah. "Where's Martin's shop? May we go shopping soon? Why aren't all the people inside the shops instead of walking by them? I want to look at *everything*."

"We'll have time for that." I made another effort to turn Sarah around into a more seemly position, and this time I succeeded.

"Are you joining your husband in Chicago?" the older lady asked in a kindly tone. As most of the other passengers were men, the exception being a couple who were plainly newlyweds and completely absorbed in each other, I supposed she was trying to shelter me from being importuned.

"I'm a widow," I said, hoping Sarah wasn't listening. I disliked having to lie in front of her. She was old enough to understand that my widowed state *was* a lie—and yet too young to grasp the need for deception.

"Oh, my dear, and so young." The older lady's gaze roamed over Tess. "And such responsibilities."

I bit back a retort, not wanting to embarrass Tess by explaining that she was an asset rather than a responsibility. People who knew her soon saw her potential. There was no point in defending her to people with whom I might only have a half hour's acquaintance.

"Have you stayed at the Palmer House before?" I asked by way of diversion.

"It is my home whenever I'm in the city." She had bright blue eyes, slightly shortsighted-looking but very shrewd. "I am Mrs. Parnell of Lake Forest," she continued, nodding affably. "I'm sorry we're too far apart to shake hands. You'll forgive my forwardness when I tell you that my youngest daughter is just about your age. She should already be at the hotel—my husband escorted her there this morning. We have a busy week of committees ahead of us."

"I see," I said. "I'm Mrs. Lillington, late of Kansas. This is Sarah." I smoothed down my daughter's hair. "And this is my dearest friend, Miss O'Dugan."

"Delighted to make your acquaintance," said Tess, beaming. "I understand our hotel's on State Street—could you please tell me if this is State Street, Mrs. Parnell? I can't imagine how Nell and I are going to find our way around such a big city."

"It *is* rather large, although not as large as Saint Louis—did you not board the train at Saint Louis? I thought I saw you at the station. And Chicago is a small city compared to New York, where my oldest daughter—the married one—lives. Were you staying at the Southern too? The Palmer House is much nicer, to my mind."

"Is it larger? I thought the Southern was quite big enough," replied Tess. "I want Nell to take a house, and I will run it." She spoke, of course, with her usual stutter, but I could see Mrs. Parnell revise her opinion of Tess on the spot. And Mrs. Parnell had spoken directly to Tess rather than to me. I decided I liked her.

"You'll be perfectly happy at the Palmer House while you look around you," said Mrs. Parnell kindly. "And we're almost there. To answer your first question, Miss O'Dugan, this is indeed State Street, which some call the Great Street. Although if you've seen New York, you won't think it so grand. Chicago is a practical city rather than a beautiful one as yet, I fear. I wonder," she continued, looking at me, "if you all might not take tea with me at four? In the Grand Parlor—just ask any of the hotel employees to show you the way.

I can introduce you to my daughter. Unless, that is, you have other acquaintances in Chicago you are eager to see."

"None I think are actually in Chicago at this moment." My last letter to Martin had gone unanswered, from which I'd surmised he was traveling. Time enough to ascertain his whereabouts once we'd settled in. Truth be told, I was a little nervous about our first meeting on his home ground. Would things have changed between us?

"I'd be delighted to take tea with you and meet your daughter," I said to Mrs. Parnell. "You're kind to take us under your wing."

The noises of the street diminished abruptly as the carriage pulled into some sort of sheltered courtyard. Sarah let out a squeak of excitement.

"Momma! Is this the hotel?"

"I think it must be." The other passengers had all begun to look around themselves for belongings in the manner of people who were ending a journey. Mrs. Parnell reached up to ensure her hat was in the right position, and as the carriage came to a halt, she stood, smiling down at Sarah.

"You've reached your new home, young lady. I hope you like it."

Sarah hopped nimbly down from the bench and looked Mrs. Parnell in the face for the first time. "I'm sorry I kicked you, ma'am," she said, making a small curtsey. "I guess I really am just too excited to stay still."

"That's quite understandable," Mrs. Parnell said. "And now, since fate appears to have put you, as Mrs. Lillington said, under my wing, come with me. I have my preferences among the concierges at the Palmer House and intend to put you in the hands of Mr. Harman. He'll make sure you have everything you need."

č

It was some twenty minutes before we saw our suite of rooms at the Palmer House, but they were a fruitful twenty minutes. I thanked Providence for Mrs. Parnell. She had, as she'd promised, found us a competent concierge. Observing that we had no maid with us, she suggested one of the hotel's *femmes de chambre* to help us unpack and perform any other services we might need. Last but not least, Mrs. Parnell challenged the concierge over the rooms they had designated for us. She insisted that they would receive odors from the kitchen and were quite unsuitable for ladies. The concierge agreed and secured us rooms that, he assured us, were the best to be had.

Having performed these valuable services, Mrs. Parnell—with her own femme de chambre, with whom she seemed well acquainted, hovering at her elbow—reminded us of our engagement for tea at four o'clock, and took her leave. Our concierge led us to the elevators—still a novelty to the three of us—and thus to the third floor. After a short walk along an ornately decorated corridor, he ushered us into our newly reserved suite.

"It's very grand," said Tess the moment the man had closed the door behind him, promising to send the femme de chambre up immediately.

"Land *sakes*, Momma, we're living in a palace," Sarah breathed. "Where are the beds?"

"We have a parlor and two bedrooms," I explained. "A large one with two beds and a smaller room with one. I thought Tess could have the small room, and you could be with me—" But Sarah had already broken away from me and was running around inspecting the furniture and opening doors.

In point of fact, our living space had just increased fourfold. At least. Our plainly furnished room in the Eternal Life Seminary was dwarfed by this richly appointed suite, all polished wood and red-and-brown plush upholstery. It cost the unthinkable sum of eight dollars and forty cents a day—precisely two weeks' worth of our original earnings at the seminary. And from the last accounting Martin had sent me, I knew we could easily afford it. The money I had made through my dressmaking business in Kansas alone would have bought us comfortable rooms and a little time to look about us, but thanks to Martin's management of my small inheritance, I was back in the world of affluence in which I'd been raised.

Sarah had disappeared and would presumably soon be back to tell us about the bedrooms. I crossed to the large mirror over the marble fireplace and located my hatpin, carefully separating hat from curls. Tess untied the strings of her hat—her hair was too fine for pins—and lifted it off her head.

We both jumped as a shriek—an oddly echoing shriek—sounded from somewhere close by.

"MOMMA! TESS!"

Tess bustled off in the direction of the shout, and I followed. We found ourselves in a room lined with blue-and-white tiles. My daughter was standing on a chair before a large porcelain basin, turning the faucet on and off. A bathroom with piped water, and only the three of us to use it. My spirits soared.

"And look at this—*much* nicer than the ones in the station or the other hotels." Sarah jumped down from the chair and pulled me into a much smaller room. A gleaming porcelain convenience, decorated in blue and white to match the tiles and surmounted by a sturdy oak seat, sat in splendor.

Tess grinned. "With a pull chain and everything—no more chamber pots, Sarah! And did you see we have gaslights? We're very grand now."

A knock on the door interrupted our admiration of our new facility, which Sarah had hastily decided she had to use, no doubt as a consequence of playing with the water faucets. The interruption was the femme de chambre, a pleasant Scotswoman named Alice, whom I liked immediately. And, miracle of miracles, Alice was followed by the trunk containing our afternoon dresses, which I had marked as for immediate use. The next forty minutes passed in washing and tidying ourselves and changing into the dresses. By half past three, I was sitting—in my combinations and petticoat so as not to crush my dress—before a mirror watching Alice work wonders with my hair.

"Such a fine head of hair." Alice pushed the last pin into the chignon she'd created. "You'll never need a switch to bulk it out." Her Scots accent had been a little difficult to understand at first, but I was attuned to it now. "Hold still, Madam."

I did as I was told as Alice retrieved the curling iron from the fireplace and persuaded my unruly curls into smooth ringlets that cascaded over my shoulders.

"Goodness, that's far more fashionable than anything I can achieve on my own." I looked up and saw Alice's mouth twitch as her eyes met mine in the mirror. "We must seem very countrified to you, I suppose."

"We get plenty of folks who've made a fortune on the frontier, Madam." Alice held out the skirt of my two-piece dress for me to step into. "Your clothes are lovely; you won't look out of place among the best in Chicago." She beamed at Sarah, who was twirling the skirt of her light blue dress, trimmed in white, looking fresh and dainty with a pale blue ribbon in her hair. "You'll all do fine. Miss O'Dugan, may I clean your spectacles?"

Tess removed her spectacles and peered at the glass. "I suppose they do need washing." She looked pretty in her pink and gray. Our dresses were perhaps a little lightweight for Chicago in March, but I'd guessed correctly that the hotel would be well heated. I wasn't intending to go anywhere else until we'd had a good rest.

"No, Sarah, you can't wash Tess's spectacles. You'll get your dress wet," I said, seeing my daughter look hopefully at Alice.

The task accomplished, I stood still as Alice buttoned the bodice of my silk dress. It was in two shades of blue and quite new, as were all our clothes. I had put a great deal of thought into our first steps in Chicago. We were heading into a completely new life and would undoubtedly make mistakes, but we had nothing to be ashamed of in terms of our manners, dress, or wealth. And money, if I had understood Martin well, counted for a great deal in Chicago. He had made me wealthy. Whatever happened between us, I would return the favor by making him proud of me.

THREE

Alice gave me precise instructions on how to find the Grand Parlor before she released us, intending to stay behind and await the arrival of the rest of our trunks. So we had leisure to appreciate the sheer size of the Palmer House's grand hall with its sweeping staircase. Alice had been adamant that we proceed downstairs by way of the staircase so that our dresses would show to best advantage. Below us, well-dressed people scurried between the columns that supported the heavily decorated ceiling.

"They look like mice in a cage," Sarah whispered as we began our descent. I was holding her hand fast, not from fear that she would fall—with her shorter skirts, she didn't have to hold the handrail as we both did—but to prevent her from scampering away from me.

"When have you seen mice in a cage?" I was often surprised by Sarah's astuteness. Growing up almost exclusively with people much older than her and being so fond of having books read to her, she had a vocabulary and imagination that would not shame a ten-year-old. She wasn't good with her hands and showed little talent in the simple drawing and needlework tasks I'd set her, but her thirst for learning was fast outstripping my abilities as a teacher.

"Mr. Boneham had some, remember? One of them bit my finger."

"Ah." Mr. Boneham had been one of the seminary's older students by the time we'd left, and his interest in the fauna of the plains consisted of trapping small animals and keeping them imprisoned until they died, no doubt of fear. I had not been fond of Mr. Boneham.

"The Grand Parlor must be over there." I looked round to ensure Tess was not left behind. The three of us proceeded unhurriedly in the direction of what turned out to be another excessively large room. This one was lit by many windows trimmed in scarlet drapes that ran from ceiling to floor. Thank heaven, the armchairs and tables were arranged into cozy groups, lending the overpowering room a more homey air.

"Do you see Mrs. Parnell?" I could see Sarah was itching to run up and down the expanse of figured carpet. I'd have to find a park for her to play in.

"This room is so big I can't see anyone," Tess replied. "The people all jumble up in my head."

"I feel the same way too," I admitted. "It's hard to become accustomed to so many people all at once. I suppose we should stroll between the tables until we spot her."

"I hope it's soon," Sarah piped up. "Because I could eat a whole hog. Oh, I wish I had some of Netta's cornbread and fried-up bacon right now."

My stomach agreed with a growl. Traveling involved meals at irregular hours, and our last one had been some time ago. I distracted myself by observing the bobbing hats and flounced skirts of the women seated in chattering groups. I noted new details of dress as I invariably did when my mind wasn't immediately occupied with something else.

"Mrs. Lillington?" The voice came from a group of armchairs we had just passed. I turned on my heel, blushing as I realized I'd completely missed seeing my new acquaintance.

"I'm so sorry—I didn't see you." I caught at Sarah's hand, turning her in the right direction as the two ladies rose gracefully to their feet.

"No reason why you should, my dear. It's always hard to spot a recent acquaintance in a crowd, especially when they've changed their dress. And talking of dress, you all look charming." She sounded quite sincere. "Now allow me to present my daughter, Elizabeth. Elizabeth, this is Mrs. Lillington, Sarah Lillington, and Miss O'Dugan, newly arrived from Kansas."

I held out my hand toward the younger woman, who was indeed about my age. Elizabeth Parnell had the same sharp blue eyes as her mother, but the resemblance stopped there. Where Mrs. Parnell's hair was mid-brown and her face and figure on the lean and angular side, Miss Parnell was a robust, buxom young woman with corn-blond hair and softly rounded cheeks. She looked like a pretty farmer's daughter, albeit one dressed in silk, with her up-tilted nose and fresh complexion glowing with healthy color. Her smile was cheerful and open, and she shook my hand with vigor.

"I'm the *unmarried* daughter," she said with emphasis. "I'll bet Mother has already referred to me as such."

"Don't be vulgar, my love. Ladies never bet." Mrs. Parnell waved us into the empty chairs, and we all seated ourselves, the Parnell ladies and I taking great care with our skirts.

"Such an enormous room," I remarked conventionally, and Miss Parnell took up the theme with gusto.

"Dreadful place, isn't it?" she said. "Like a factory for feeding and housing hens and turkey-cocks. I'm always telling Mother it would be better to take a house in Chicago, but she insists that wouldn't be thrifty. My mother's still living in the days when she and Father lived in a boardinghouse, I think." She gave her mother's arm an affectionate squeeze, at the same time signaling to a passing white-jacketed waiter. "Tea for five, please, with plenty of sandwiches and cakes."

"My dear girl," said Mrs. Parnell to her daughter, "the day you have to arrange to move a household of servants back and forth between one house and another is the day you'll understand what a bother two houses are. There's always so much complaining, and things always get lost. Here, I have my favorite femme de chambre at hand and can simply enjoy myself without having to worry about what to order for dinner or fret over two sets of household accounts."

Tess's eyes gleamed. "I would love the accounts. When Nell takes a house, I'm going to be in charge of the ledgers. I know how to do it."

"Do you, Miss O'Dugan? How clever of you." Miss Parnell turned to Tess with a smile. "Don't you find it a terrible bore?"

"I'm never bored." Tess's brow wrinkled. It was true—discontent was not one of Tess's failings.

"Sarah, darling, don't fidget so." I helped Sarah into a more comfortable position on her chair since her feet didn't touch the carpet. "I know you've had to sit still all day, but when you've eaten, you can go back to our rooms and play. And tomorrow we'll find a place where you can run around outdoors. Is there a park anywhere nearby?" I asked the ladies.

"Lake Park is just two blocks away," said Miss Parnell. "I'm sure Mother can spare me tomorrow morning—why don't I show you? It's not particularly pretty, of course."

"Chicago," said Mrs. Parnell in an arch tone, "is woefully devoid of anything but commerce. Such a beautiful blue lake, and what do they put in front of it? A railroad. The Great Fire gave us an excellent opportunity to set things right, but we let the businessmen rebuild as they liked and left out the public buildings altogether. If a few of us hadn't insisted, Lake Park wouldn't even exist."

"You've hit on one of Mother's hobbyhorses," said Miss Parnell cheerfully. "She's on all kinds of committees for providing the people of Chicago with culture and refinement. Of course, it's the same ladies who have the leisure to sit on committees who will benefit from the culture. I can't imagine that most of the ordinary people will go to the opera."

Tea arrived, and the diversion of cakes and sandwiches—quite good, I was glad to find—headed off what was clearly a well-rehearsed difference of opinion. Sarah hadn't been wrong in saying she could eat a whole hog; I'd taught her not to load her plate, but her visits to the tiered platters of food were stealthy and frequent. I noticed with amusement that Miss Parnell almost matched her pace.

"My grandmother lived in Chicago when it was little more than a trading post," I told the older lady. "She often told me about standing with my mother on her hip, watching the Indians perform their last dance before they left the town forever."

Mrs. Parnell's gaze sharpened. "You have Chicago antecedents? Mrs. Lillington, you're quite the enigma. Pray explain to me how you came to be in Kansas. Was it because of your husband?"

A qualm assailed me—was I never going to be rid of the specter of my imaginary late spouse? But fortunately Sarah was talking to Tess and hadn't heard.

"I was brought up in Victory. My grandparents moved there before the war," I explained. "In '72 I found myself alone and short of money. We went to Kansas so that I could take up a post as a seamstress in a seminary." I stared steadily at Mrs. Parnell as I made this admission, hoping she wasn't going to turn out to be a snob. But it seemed she had other questions on her mind.

"You must have prospered, to be staying at the Palmer House." Mrs. Parnell's brows knitted.

"I built up a dressmaking business when I wasn't busy with the seminary's work, and I did well," I said. "But mostly—Sarah, darling, it's rude to interrupt." A peremptory tug on my sleeve caused me to lose my train of thought.

"I need to be excused, Momma. And Tess would like to go back to our rooms too. May we?"

There were some departing courtesies to be got through, but Sarah was in a hurry and they were soon heading—fast—toward the door.

"I hope they won't get lost," said Mrs. Parnell, gazing after them. "Such a sweet little girl, and Miss O'Dugan is quite—well, I don't wish to sound unflattering, but quite unexpected. Is she a relative of yours?"

"A friend I met before my mother died," I said. "She has nobody else in the world, and she's been a godsend to me. As I was starting to tell you, I owe most of my wealth to an old childhood friend. I inherited a small capital, and he has multiplied it. It was his suggestion that we come to Chicago for a while, to get used to our new life and decide what we're going to do." I felt myself blush, just a little, but plowed ahead with determination. "When I went to Kansas, he was just starting out in Chicago as a merchant. Mr. Martin Rutherford, of Rutherford's store. Do you know it?"

"Every woman in Chicago knows Rutherford's," Miss Parnell said. "Mother prefers her own dressmaker, but she's kind enough to let me have my dresses made at Rutherford's. Her dear old Mrs. Chester doesn't know how to dress a young lady of fashion. And my sister, Frances, is great friends with Mrs. Grace Fairgrieve of New York, who was a schoolgirl friend of Mrs. Rutherford, so we have met Mr. Rutherford. He seems like a nice man, and Mrs. Rutherford is terribly well known in Chicago society. Mr. Rutherford made quite a catch by marrying the Gambarelli heiress."

"I'm surprised to hear you say that, Elizabeth." Mrs. Parnell nodded at the waiter who had come to clear away the tea things. "Considering your views on marriage."

"I'm not against marriage *per se*," said Miss Parnell. "Just against the imbalance of power between the man and the woman." She raised her eyebrows at her mother. "Having to wait for widowhood to take control of their own finances—oh, I'm sorry, Mrs. Lillington. Of course, you were most unfortunate to lose your husband so early. But in purely practical terms, having the former Miss Gambarelli as a wife must be a tremendous advantage for an ambitious man. Not," she dropped her voice to a near-whisper, "that I'd like to be related to any of the Gambarelli men, even by marriage. They have a reputation for ruthlessness and—well, you never see their wives. You'd think they're in purdah, like the Hindu women. How Miss Gambarelli—Mrs. Rutherford now, of course—got out into society at all is a mystery to me."

"She twists all those dreadful men around her little finger, which is a woman's true power." Mrs. Parnell gathered up her reticule, a signal that our conversation was coming to an end. "Now, Mrs. Lillington, is there any other way in which I can be of service to you? I must say, knowing that you're a friend of Mr. Rutherford's is a tremendous help as far as introductions are concerned."

"Well," I said and hesitated. There was one matter that had been on my mind as I'd dressed. The minor embarrassment of consulting Mrs. Parnell was preferable to talking to a concierge. "You see," I began again, "I don't know how to go about arranging for withdrawals of money from the bank. I need to pay the hotel, and I'll need spending money and all sorts of things. I have traveling money with me, but I'll need some more fairly soon."

Mrs. Parnell's blue eyes became sharp indeed. "Which bank?"

I named it, and Mrs. Parnell seemed to relax a little. "It's quite straightforward. I'll show you how to have a representative of the bank come to you here. That will spare you the unpleasantness of having to enter a men's domain, and of traveling alone through the streets of Chicago. Don't, by the way. There are mashers and pickpockets everywhere. If you need to go somewhere, have a concierge summon a hired carriage and avoid carrying too much money with you." She paused. "I have many more things I could tell you, but one lesson at a time. Shall we go find a concierge together?"

"And I'll retire to my room and read a novel," Miss Parnell said. "Mrs. Lillington, I'm looking forward to our outing tomorrow. I too have many things I can tell you." The last was said *sotto voce* behind her mother's back with an impish smile.

I followed Mrs. Parnell out of the Grand Parlor, feeling both apprehensive and excited. I was going to be in control of my wealth for the first time. Martin had made it clear to me in his letters that he'd given the bankers firm instructions in that respect, and that even if I sought his advice, I would have to make the decisions. This, then, was freedom—of action, at least, if not of the heart.

FOUR

Miss Parnell had been right—Lake Park was not particularly pretty. Especially in March when the sparse lawns were still yellow from the winter's rigors, with just a few green blades poking up here and there. But the morning was bright and sunny, even though the icy wind from the lake reddened our noses and kept our hands inside the fur muffs we both wore. Paths crisscrossed the park in a formal pattern, so we were able to walk around while Sarah bowled her hoop.

We spoke for a few minutes on conventional subjects—the weather, our journey, and the inexhaustible topic of railroad travel. The last was suggested by the black line of the railroad that marred our view of the lake, which would otherwise have been beautiful. Shifting like a wild animal at rest under its glittering blue-green surface, the vast stretch of water was populated with small dots that were no doubt boats leaving or arriving from nearby lakeside ports—it was too early in the year for large ships. To the north of us, the glass panes of the Exposition Building winked in the sunlight, its flags fluttering showily in the stiff breeze.

But our conversation didn't remain banal for long. I was beginning to learn that Miss Parnell's nature was frank and impulsive.

"You do realize, don't you," she said when our small talk flagged, "that Mother's motives for helping you with your banking aren't entirely altruistic? I thought I should give you fair warning."

"What do you mean?" The odd thought flitted through my mind that Mrs. Parnell would try to entice me into some unreliable investment scheme involving one of her committees. I repressed a smile.

"It's rather delicate." Miss Parnell's rounded cheeks, already pink from the wind, deepened in hue. "I do hope you won't be offended. There are so many people who arrive in Chicago claiming to have made a fortune on the frontier, you see."

Realization dawned. "You don't mean she thinks I could be some kind of confidence trickster? With Sarah and Tess part of the act?" I wasn't sure whether to be offended or amused.

"Well, no, she rather likes you—as do I—and thinks you couldn't possibly be up to something with a child and a—well, a feeble-minded person in tow, although Miss O'Dugan's mind seems to be in good working order as far as I can see. But not to the point where she could be anything other than honest. But you do see, Mrs. Lillington, that my mother, if she intends to introduce you a little to Chicago society, is duty bound to make sure—oh dear, I'm making a terrible mess of this." She gave a little stamp of her neatly booted foot. "You must think we're entirely lacking in Christian charity."

By now I was definitely amused. "I don't think it's at all wrong to not take strangers at face value. I've been too trusting myself in the past, and it's always ended badly for me. Your mother is a shrewd woman."

"Well, yes, she is. If only she weren't a woman, she would have been a formidable man of business. That's why she's in such demand with her committees and causes. And Father's a dear—he doesn't mind one bit what she does, and gives her free rein with his money. She, at least, doesn't have to wait for widowhood to be able to spend what she likes *when* she likes."

"Hmmm." I watched as Sarah rolled her hoop toward another little girl who belonged, I presumed, to the two women who sat huddled together on a bench. "I'm beginning to learn, Miss Parnell, that you're something of an advanced thinker. But I can give you my personal assurance that I'm no confidence trickster and that my money is all my own—and Miss O'Dugan's, of course, although for the time being our funds are in the same account."

"If the bank employee comes readily to your summons, Mother will have proof positive that you're in funds, so I shouldn't worry if I were you. And please don't say anything to Mother. She'll send me back to Lake Forest— she does that every time I show signs of independence." Miss Parnell sighed. "And I know we barely know each other, but would you call me Elizabeth? I disapprove on principle of all this Miss-ing and Mrs.-ing. I'm convinced it's de- signed to keep us in our place, to designate us as women rather than as people. Mother says I'm just being vulgar, but she has no notion of radical thought."

"I'll happily call you Elizabeth, and you may call me Nell," I replied, "but I don't think I'm nearly as radical as you are."

"You've not come here looking for a husband, have you?" Miss Parnell— Elizabeth—looked crestfallen.

Now it was my turn to blush, and I fervently hoped that my cheeks were also reddened by the wind. How could I answer *that* question?

"I've come here to decide what to do with my life," was my eventual reply. "It's not an easy decision, and I can't discuss all the ramifications of it on a day's acquaintance, if you'll forgive me for saying so. But marriage is not something I'm contemplating right now. What I really want to be is a dressmaker. What I really *don't* want to be is a society woman who spends her time paying and receiving calls and sitting on committees."

"Oh, hoorah!" Elizabeth's bright eyes flashed, and she clapped her hands, quite like a child. "Good for you, Nell. I find society to be an absolute shack- le. I'm condemned to spend far too much time sitting and chatting with silly women or enduring endless introductions to suitable young men. And chang- ing my dress four times a day *at least* when we're in the city and being perma- nently at Mother's beck and call. My only way out is marriage, and I—" She stopped short and stared at me. "I'm about to shock you inexpressibly, Nell."

"You are?"

Elizabeth widened her eyes into a comical expression of pure mischief. "We told you about my older sister, Frances, didn't we? The *married* one." She said the last phrase with a roll of her eyes. "Frances, since her marriage, has become a Feminist and is quite subverting Mother's plans for me. Frances has three children already and one on the way, and she's only been married six and a half years. She loves them dearly, of course, but she wishes they would not come *quite* so frequently. She smuggles copies of *Woodhull & Claflin's Weekly* to me. Victoria Woodhull, you know, writes that the notion of ownership of one person by another is quite wrong and the cause of many a tragedy. Don't you agree?"

I was beginning to feel as if I'd run into a patch of quicksand. Elizabeth's remarks were so pertinent to my own situation that I barely knew what to say. If my forthcoming separation from Martin were indeed a tragedy, his marriage was certainly the cause of it. But—

"I agree in principle," I said slowly, trying to feel my way through the question without running afoul of my emotions. "But in practice, when you love a man—and love *will* happen, you know, whether you want it or not—you're faced with the choice of marrying him and bearing his children, with all that entails, or letting someone else have him and feeling miserable about it. The third way is all very well, but the world sees it as immoral, and if there are children involved, the taint of immorality is laid on them. Do we have a right to make others suffer for our principles?"

Elizabeth leaned in a little closer. "Frances says there are ways of preventing children. Her Adolphus won't hear of it, but she says she's going to show me some books next time I visit New York. I'm absolutely agog."

I shook my head. "It still all sounds like a lot more fun for the men than for the women," I said. "I wouldn't like to spend my life worrying if my—precautions—had worked or not."

"This is why our society needs to evolve to embrace the principles of Free Love," was Elizabeth's rejoinder. "A true marriage is based on absolute freedom, not legal coercion, and is thus pure and generous. Where there is no possession by one of the other, there is no jealousy, no hatred, no deception, no unfaithfulness."

"Good heavens," I said. "It all sounds terribly theoretical and idealistic. It's my experience that matters are never clear-cut when it comes to the heart. Are you proposing that all married people dissolve their legal bonds and live with whom they please? There may not be deception and unfaithfulness in such an arrangement, but I'm doubtful whether there would be no jealousy or hatred."

"The common women manage it well enough," replied Elizabeth. "You read all sorts of things in the newspapers—well, the ones Mother doesn't want me to read, anyhow—about women married to one man and living with another, that kind of business. Mind you, they all seem to settle matters with knives and frying pans, and I can't imagine myself rolling up my sleeves and clouting my rivals with kitchen equipment."

"Could you recognize kitchen equipment?" I couldn't help asking. We both dissolved into laughter.

"Nell, you're the brightest spot in my whole week. I'm grateful for the prairie wind that blew you in, even if I never succeed in making a Feminist of you."

"What do you mean?" I asked, amused. "I'm perfectly in favor of women having a profession and making financial decisions alongside their men. I'm just not sure your Free Love schemes will work in practice, especially when there are children involved. And you can't tell me that men and women are going to avoid having children altogether."

I spoke lightly, but my mind was continually on Martin and Lucetta and the image of the gilded cage I had formed when Lucetta made it clear to me that she would hold on to Martin by any means at her disposal. And above it all, I could hear Mama's voice the day she and Hiram had discovered that I was to have a baby: "It is wrong in the eyes of the law and the Lord not to marry."

Sarah waved good-bye to her little friend, who skipped off hand in hand with one of the two ladies. She ran toward us, hitting her hoop as hard as she could with the stick.

"It's *cold*, Momma. Look, my hands are all red." She pulled off her mittens and wiggled her fingers in the air. "May we go indoors and have some hot chocolate?" Her cheeks were as red as her hands under her knitted hat, contrasting sharply with her naturally pale skin and brilliant copper hair. Her skirts seemed shorter than yesterday, as if she'd grown an inch or two overnight.

"We certainly may." Elizabeth held out a hand for Sarah's hoop and the other hand to my daughter, who took it willingly. "And I know just the right person to ask to get the biggest, creamiest cup of chocolate you'd ever want." She grinned at me. "I've had plenty of practice with my sister's offspring. Even if my advanced views end in my being an old maid, my principles won't stop me from playing with other people's children. Now, Sarah, let's see who can run to that tree the fastest."

I watched as Elizabeth, somewhat impeded by skirts and bustle and whooping like a hoyden, made a pretense of racing Sarah from one small tree to the next. Her enthusiasm for Free Love seemed to me to be part of her impulsive, youthful freshness, with no basis at all in reality. It was reality that held me in its grip and presented me with a simple choice. I could give in to my desire for Martin and bring misery and scandal down on all our heads, or I could run away and have my misery all to myself.

FIVE

I peered anxiously at Tess, who had made a nest of cushions in a large armchair. She lay with her eyes half-closed, her gaze fixed on the glowing embers in the fireplace.

"Are you sure you're all right? You were too tired to come with us to the park this morning, and now you're telling me you're still tired. Are you feverish? Are you getting a cold?"

I put out a hand, intending to lay it on Tess's forehead, but she forestalled me with a stern look over her spectacles.

"You don't have to mother me, Nell. I'm just tired. I don't have your energy, and we traveled an awfully long way yesterday. And Sarah needs someone to stay with her, not be dragged downstairs again to listen to grown-ups talk about money."

"But it's your money too. And I could get Alice to look in on Sarah. She fell so fast asleep that I don't suppose she'll wake till teatime."

"I'm Sarah's family, not Alice. And *not* your Miss Parnell."

I frowned. "You're not upset because we went out with Elizabeth, are you? I did ask you to come with us."

"Elizabeth." The word came out in a soft breath. "Your friend Elizabeth."

I opened my mouth to protest that we weren't exactly friends as yet, but Tess's eyes were already closed. As gently as I could, I removed her spectacles from her nose and placed them next to her Bible on the small side table. Doubtless she really was just tired and would be her usual cheerful self after a couple of days' rest.

By ten minutes to two, I was downstairs in the Grand Parlor, having informed a concierge that a representative of my bank would call on me at two o'clock. I felt a little self-conscious sitting on my own amid so many people, but it couldn't be helped. I didn't suppose that anyone would draw the wrong conclusions from seeing me sitting with a bank clerk anyway. Such persons were invariably dried-up, elderly men with shiny patches on the arms of their jackets from leaning on a counter.

It wasn't five minutes before the concierge coughed gently, pulling me out of a reverie, the topic of which was, naturally, Martin. I had sent a note to his store the previous day informing him of our arrival and had received no reply. He was traveling, no doubt. Yet I somehow expected, every moment, to see his tall, thin figure, easily distinguished from other men by his white-blond hair, proceeding toward me and saying—what? If he were absent, was there nobody he could send to the hotel with a message for me? He knew where we'd be staying. Drat the man.

I stood automatically, smiling my thanks at the concierge, and looked at the bank clerk. Far from the wizened, dusty functionary of my imagination, this was a fine physical specimen of around six feet and broad-shouldered in proportion to his height. His face walked the line between plain and handsome with one foot on the side of handsome, mostly due to a certain intelligence and openness in his expression and the smile that reached his light brown eyes.

"Mrs. Lillington? I'm happy to be at your service. My name is Fletcher."

We shook hands and sat down. Mr. Fletcher extracted a ledger from his attaché case, laid it on the table, and politely refused my offer of refreshment. These preliminaries over, he hesitated.

"I suppose you'd like to see some proof that I am who I say I am." I took a folded paper out of my reticule and laid it on the table beside the ledger. "This is the last accounting I had from Mr. Rutherford. And this is the notebook where I've kept track of all the figures he's sent me since I moved away from Victory in '72. Is that sufficient?"

"Almost." Mr. Fletcher pulled a slip of paper from the ledger and studied it, occasionally looking up at me. Then he grinned.

"Mr. Rutherford's description of you tallies exactly with the lady I see before me. To be absolutely sure, would you mind showing me your wedding ring?"

I pulled off my glove and held out my left hand so that he could see the ring. It was my stepfather Hiram's ring, bought for his first wife, Emmeline, but too large for her fingers. It was incised with a delicate pattern of leaves and flowers, a pretty thing that Hiram had given me to maintain the pretense of widowhood. No doubt he had intended to recover it from my body after he'd thrown Sarah into the river, knowing I would try to save her and probably drown.

"Do I pass muster?" I shoved the memory of Hiram into the back of my mind. He couldn't harm me now.

"Thank you for understanding. It's rather a large sum of money, and in fact the paper you gave me is a little out of date. Let's see—" He opened the ledger and indicated a recent page. "This is more accurate, although Mr. Rutherford never leaves capital idle, and your holdings increase daily. If it's at all helpful to you, I can summarize that you can comfortably expect an income of a little over seven thousand a year as things currently stand. Of course, that's without touching the portion that Mr. Rutherford has designated as available for your use should you wish to purchase a house."

"Of course," I echoed faintly. Seven thousand dollars a year! I always read the papers Martin sent to me, but I supposed I'd never really translated the figures into an income. Martin had once told me he'd worked to ensure I would be independent of him or any man, financially at least. He'd given me my freedom in no uncertain terms.

"I'm not sure whether I'll buy a house in Chicago or elsewhere. My plans are somewhat uncertain at this time." I tried to sound businesslike and brisk. "For the moment, I'm concerned about my current expenses—paying the hotel, money for meals and clothing, that sort of thing. I will need—"

How much exactly would I need? I had no idea how much I would spend by the week or month in Chicago. Fortunately, I had just spotted someone who would know.

"Miss Parnell!"

At my exclamation, Elizabeth, who had walked past us without seeing me because she'd been saying good-bye to two frilled and flounced acquaintances, turned and smiled broadly. I waggled my fingers to indicate she should come over. Mr. Fletcher rose to his feet, prudently shutting the ledger and slipping the paper back between its pages.

Elizabeth nodded graciously at the two of us as she approached, showing no surprise. Yet the gleam in her eyes suggested she was thinking of her mother's unfounded suspicions. She looked lovely in a dark blue dress so richly patterned with deep-red roses that the overall effect was more red than blue. Ivory lace at the neck and cuffs set off her fresh, creamy skin and emphasized the rosy tinge of her rounded cheeks, which were dimpled by the mischievous smile she was trying to repress.

"Miss Parnell, may I call on you for help?" I indicated the bank clerk. "This is Mr. Fletcher of Briggs Bank. I need to tell him how much I require for living expenses, and I realized I haven't the faintest idea. What does one need to live in Chicago? And there's the hotel, of course."

"Oh, the hotel's no trouble at all—you can either have the bill sent to you and send it on to the bank for payment, or you can even have them send it directly to the bank if you prefer. Mr. Fletcher can speak to them and arrange things according to your wishes, I presume?" She quirked an eyebrow at the young man, whose hand she had briefly shaken before seating herself beside me.

"I'm entirely at Mrs. Lillington's service," Mr. Fletcher replied, but he didn't sound at all subservient. There was something very pleasing about his air of confidence and quiet strength.

"That's excellent." Elizabeth's bright blue gaze focused on Mr. Fletcher with a sharper interest than before. "Now, Nell, the first decision is the hotel bill."

"Oh, anything from the hotel must be delivered to me first for review. My grandmother always lectured me on the inadvisability of letting tradesmen of any sort realize you were not scrutinizing their bills. And the larger the establishment, she said, the more careful one must be. My grandfather was a banker, you see. He and Grandmama were apparently in perfect agreement about money and made all their decisions as one."

And if Mama's illness had not made her rely too heavily on Hiram in money matters, I probably would never have had to go to Kansas. I still didn't know exactly where Mama's inheritance from her parents had disappeared to.

"That's settled, then," said Elizabeth. "Now do you want to live quietly or be fashionable? As far as dresses and so on are concerned, it's easy enough to open accounts in all of the larger stores. Mr. Fletcher can provide a note attesting to your bona fides." She looked at the young man, who nodded. His face was serious, as befitted his role, but there was a certain twinkle in his eyes that suggested he was thoroughly enjoying the conversation. I was also amused—I supposed it was typical for a lovely young woman's mind to go straight to articles of dress, but Elizabeth's enthusiasm rather belied her claims to be a Feminist of the deepest dye.

"If you have a yearning for gaiety and excitement," Elizabeth continued, "there'll be numerous expenses in the way of carriages, tickets to entertainments, and so on. And if you pay a lot of calls, you'll find yourself giving tips *everywhere* because people's servants are far less eager to hurry and fetch your manteau, hold an umbrella, or find a carriage if you don't grease their palms. That's the trouble with this town—absolutely everything is business."

"Do you have to grease the palms of the ladies you visit?" I couldn't help asking and was gratified when both Elizabeth and Mr. Fletcher burst into laughter.

"Very good, Mrs. Lillington," the banker said. "I see you understand Chicago completely."

"And in a way, you're correct." Elizabeth screwed her mouth to one side in a wry expression. "There are ladies—those who hold the key to certain society gatherings or whose husbands might help other husbands along in the way of business—who are known to be *so* much sweeter and more obliging if you bring them nosegays or bonbons or an adorable pair of gloves that you just *happened* to see in Field and Leiter's that made you think of them *straightaway*. They usually have the most rapacious maids too."

"Oh dear," I said, feeling a qualm at having to find my place in such a society. "Well, I don't care for paying calls and will make just as many as I need to avoid accusations that we're hermits. We may venture out to an entertainment two or three times a month, but not more than that—unless Tess and Sarah want to. Their happiness is of great importance to me." I looked at Mr. Fletcher. "You know about my daughter and friend, I suppose?"

He nodded. "Mr. Rutherford was most thorough with his instructions."

Of course he was, I thought. Martin was too conscientious by half. But I banished Martin—well, almost—from my mind and continued.

"I will need some money as soon as possible, for visiting the stores up and down State Street—Sarah and Tess are eager to buy a few gewgaws." I was equally eager to go to Rutherford's and make inquiries after Martin, but tomorrow was Saturday, and I knew Mr. Salazar, his general manager and the man I most wanted to speak to, did not work on Saturdays. "I was thinking of Monday for an expedition to the stores. Tess will be feeling more rested by then."

"If you could possibly wait until Tuesday, I could act as your guide." Elizabeth's face brightened at the thought, but then her mouth tightened. "Mother's gone and commandeered me for all of Monday morning, which means half the afternoon as well because she wants to introduce me to the son of a dear friend." She sighed dramatically. "He's just returned from Harvard University and is *most* charming. So we'll have to sit through at least an hour of our Mamas trying to find common ground between us, and then we'll eat luncheon together. After which, the matriarchs will suggest a stroll somewhere and positively *rush* ahead of us to allow the young people to get to know each other."

Mr. Fletcher interrupted with a small cough, passing his hand in front of his mouth a tad too late to hide the grin that was trying to break out on his face. "The sum of money?" he suggested.

Elizabeth glared at Mr. Fletcher but then smiled with the air of a queen addressing her subjects. "Thank you *so* much for recalling my silly female mind back to the business at hand." She was perched on the edge of her armchair, endeavoring not to crush the back of her gown, and gave a funny little bounce as she turned to fix the young man with a stony stare.

A lesser man might have blustered out an apology for his inadvertent rudeness, but Mr. Fletcher was clearly made of sterner stuff. He returned Elizabeth's stare with cool poise and said gravely: "I think you're anything but silly." He left it at that, allowing the silence to lengthen until Elizabeth let out her breath and gave an expressive shrug.

"Don't mind me," she said. "I do tend to rattle on, and I suppose you must have other clients beside Mrs. Lillington. So, Nell . . ."

And she proceeded to involve both Mr. Fletcher and me in a complex evaluation of what the coming days might bring in terms of expenditure, arriving at a sum with which the banker agreed with a certain degree of respect. I felt I was witnessing two persons getting the measure of each other and arriving at a pleasant equilibrium.

"I'll make all the arrangements with the hotel," Mr. Fletcher concluded. "And I'll have a sum large enough for the next few days brought confidentially to you in your suite—tomorrow morning?"

I agreed and supplied the number of the suite, which Mr. Fletcher wrote down in a small notebook. A general shaking of hands and a few pleasantries ensued, and Elizabeth and I were left alone.

"Well!" was her first remark, her eyes on Mr. Fletcher's back as he made his way through the Grand Parlor. "That kills two birds with one stone. I can reassure Mother that you're clearly a lady of some means—bank employees are never so obliging unless you have money. And you'll have more than enough for Tuesday's outing. Do you need to be fitted for a new dress?"

"Not at all," I replied. "I spent the last month or two in Kansas sewing everything we needed."

Elizabeth's gaze suddenly switched from the doorway through which Mr. Fletcher had passed to my dress. In cinnamon and pale gold silk taffeta, it set off my hair nicely. The skirt was heavily swagged and ruched, but the bodice was almost entirely unadorned, giving it a businesslike look I had thought suited to the occasion.

"Are you telling me you made that?" she asked. "And the pretty blue you wore at tea yesterday? *And* your walking dress?"

I nodded in the affirmative.

"Then you're far more fitted to be a dressmaker than frittering away your life paying calls. It would be a crime to waste such skill." She frowned. "Heavens, what a dilemma. It's positively an inconvenience to you to be rich."

We both laughed, but my amusement was tinged with a wry sense that yes, in some ways my wealth *would* be an inconvenience. The very suggestion of a wealthy woman having a profession would make any society belle laugh out loud.

"Did you find Mr. Fletcher impertinent?" I asked by way of diverting my thoughts from my own troubles. "You seemed out of sorts with him for a moment."

"Perhaps. No." Elizabeth's cheeks flushed a deeper shade of rose, almost matching her gown. "It was idiotic of me to take umbrage at him for simply trying to keep to the subject. I thought he was rather nice."

"I rather thought you did. And I thought that *he* thought—"

"Oh, heavens, Nell, you're not going to turn out to be one of those match-making women, are you?"

"Not in the least. Besides, your parents might object to a bank clerk as a potential son-in-law."

"But he's not a clerk, is he? Not if they let him loose to take instructions at the Palmer House. He must be doing quite well for his age." She hesitated for a moment. "How old do you think he is, anyway?"

"Twenty-five? Perhaps a year or two older. But not yet thirty."

"Hmmm. And besides, Mother and Father aren't insisting that I marry into money or anything. Not that it was marriage I was thinking of." She said the last part almost under her breath, and I sat up straighter.

"What? I mean, I beg your pardon? Elizabeth, you can't possibly mean what I think you mean."

Elizabeth's only answer was to rise to her feet, smoothing down her skirts. "I believe we've done a good day's work today, Nell. Thank you for trusting me for advice."

"I hope you'll trust me to give *you* good advice—when the time comes."

"Of course, if I feel I need it." Elizabeth widened her eyes into large, disarming blue circles and swept away into the main current of people departing and arriving in a ceaseless murmur of polite conversation, giving her skirts an expert twitch so that her train fell into place.

I followed her, but I wasn't fooled. I too had large blue eyes and knew how to use them to dissemble as well as attract. Elizabeth hadn't flirted with Mr. Fletcher, but she was definitely interested in him—and her head was full of nonsense about Free Love into the bargain. I supposed that if I'd heard about that scandalous topic back in my Victory days, I would have been fascinated by it too. But I had learned my lesson. I was very afraid that my impulsive new friend might turn out to be just as heedless at twenty-two as I'd been at sixteen.

SIX

On Saturday evening, something happened that erased all thoughts of Elizabeth's intentions from my mind. We were in the Palmer House's dining room, a cavernous space flagged in white marble inset with diamond-shaped pieces of a darker hue. Huge gasoliers—I counted twenty at least—lit the space with their brilliant hiss and flare, still much too bright to my eyes compared to oil lamps. The columns that marched down the room in regular rows were encrusted with leaves and flowers, a theme echoed by the overblown pink-and-blue frescoes. This was elegance of a sort, but elegance taken right up to the point of vulgarity, and I said so to Tess.

"I think it's pretty," was her response as she gazed at the bill of fare. This too was richly decorated with drawings of food of all kinds, and, rather alarmingly, proclaimed the Palmer House to be "thoroughly fire proof." Considering that the ovens in the kitchens were no doubt roaring at their full capacity somewhere below us, and that our dinner was lit by a highly inflammable gas, I doubted that was entirely true.

"Sarah, would you like baked trout or ham?" I asked as our white-jacketed waiter headed in our direction. There were numerous waiters present, some white, some black, all under the command of a headwaiter of, I guessed, German origin. They proceeded at a dignified pace between the tables amid a clatter of plates and silverware and a babble of voices in several different languages.

"I'm going to have sugar-cured ham," said Tess rather loudly. She had a tendency to be hard of hearing in large, noisy public spaces. "I don't like the way a fish's eyes look at me, and ham doesn't have skin and bones to worry about."

"I would like ham too, Momma, if you please," said Sarah daintily. She appeared to be enjoying herself, especially as several of the waiters—and the gentlemen and ladies they were serving—had smiled at her and made kind remarks about her bright hair and pretty manners. She wasn't exactly vain, but she did enjoy the attention that the contrast between her small size and nice behavior brought her, and always did her best to win people over. This tendency had begun with the servants at the seminary. Sarah was used to being admired and held up as a model child in a world composed mostly of adults.

"Then we shall all have ham," I said to the waiter and proceeded to order the rest of the dishes. We had spent Saturday resting quietly with just one short outing to the park for Sarah's benefit. With Alice's help, we had stowed our clothes and belongings in perfect order. I had celebrated the arrival of our money by consulting with Tess about her needs and allotting a small amount to Sarah, and we were all in good humor with one another.

As we chatted, the behavior of one of the waiters began to impinge upon my conscious mind. He was most definitely hovering. And that was strange because he was evidently assigned to another part of the room. Whenever he walked toward us on his way to the back of the restaurant, he spent three or four minutes dawdling while he scrutinized all three of us. His face, snub-nosed, serious, and plain, but not unfriendly, seemed vaguely familiar, but I couldn't place him from my years in Victory. I had begun glaring at him whenever he slowed his steps since I was starting to believe the focus of his attention was Tess, and I disliked it when people stared at her in public.

"I do like this hotel," Tess said. "Although it's not as nice as having our own house. But my bed is nice and comfortable, and I like having my own room—you get up so early, Nell, and Sary, you snore." Her almond eyes crinkled, signaling to us that she was in a teasing mood.

"I make very little snores," said Sarah with dignity. "And only when I have a cold."

The waiter had stopped again, his mouth hanging open. Really, this was too much. I didn't want to get the young man into trouble, but I was starting to feel distinctly uncomfortable.

"I can hear carriages in the street, but they sound far away, and they make me feel sleepy. Clip-clop, clip-clop." Tess's imitation of a horse set Sarah chanting "clip-clop, clip-clop," but very softly. Always ready to proclaim her opinions when we were alone, she knew that an important rule of polite society was that children should be seen and not heard.

I narrowed my eyes at the staring waiter and made a peremptory beckoning motion to leave him in no doubt that he was to approach us without delay.

"That's not our waiter, Momma." Sarah tugged at my sleeve. "Our waiter's over there. I've been watching which ones go to which tables."

"I know, darling. I just need to have a quiet word with this man." He had stopped to answer a question from a passing gentleman and was eyeing me nervously as he spoke, fidgeting his feet a little.

"Ma'am?" Freed, he approached me with a sideways glance to the other side of the room, where the headwaiter was busy. "Should I summon Charles for you?"

"I don't need anything except an explanation." I may have been little better than a servant myself for four years, but the training given to me by Grandmama and Mama sharpened my tongue to just the right degree. "It is unseemly to stare, and in your profession, I would think you'd have learned to accept that your customers come in all shapes and sizes. I feel you are giving one of our party unwarranted attention." I hoped Tess wouldn't realize I was talking about her. She was often nervous about going out into a world that was too ready to apply the words "imbecile" and "feeble-minded" to her.

"I'm so sorry, ma'am." The young waiter looked over his shoulder to see where the headwaiter had gotten to. Fortunately for him, his superior was engaged in a protracted trial of question and answer with a large, loud-voiced gentleman—and yet I had the impression that his eyes missed nothing.

"I'd never bother a customer in the normal way of things, sure I wouldn't." His speech revealed the trace of an Irish brogue, although in the main, his accents were the quick, brash tones of the native Chicagoan. "But a wonderful thing may have been revealed to me." He turned his gaze full on Tess with an odd, yearning look. "Ma'am—Miss—with no disrespect in the world— could your name possibly be O'Dugan?"

"It is," said Tess, beaming. "How funny you should guess that."

The waiter bit his lip, and the color mounted to his face. "I hardly dare ask—is your given name Theresa?"

I sat up straighter. Sarah opened her mouth, and I flapped a hand at her.

Tess's small teeth showed in a broad grin. "It *is* Theresa! You're very good at guessing. But I like Tess better."

The young man's face was now red to the roots of his light brown hair. "Mother of God," he breathed. "Could it ever be true?"

I was almost certain I understood what was happening and felt a bubble of joy mixed with apprehension surge through me. The apprehension was aided by the fact that the headwaiter had freed himself and was looming over the waiter with a look that boded no good for the young man.

"What do you think you're doing, William?" He looked as if for two pins he'd have grabbed William's ear, like a master punishing a naughty school-boy. "You know very well this is not your table. This is not what we expect at the Palmer House." He glanced at me. "I apologize profusely, Madam." As I'd expected, he had a German accent.

"No need to apologize," I said. "In fact, I think I must insist that you give William a few minutes' grace. I believe something remarkable is happening."

"I'm sorry, sir." William had gone from red to pale. "It truly is an exceptional circumstance. I had a sister, you see, sent away when I was no more than five years old. But I never forgot her face, and now here it is before me." He swayed a little and turned to address me. "If I faint, Madam, you'll not let them send me away, will you? I don't know in what relation you stand to our Tessie, but surely you must understand the feelings of my heart."

The situation was getting out of hand, and I decided to take charge. Sarah's face was pink, her obvious longing to fire off a volley of questions and observations at top volume competing with her desire to be well behaved. William really did look as if he were going to faint and would soon have to sit down in clear breach of professional etiquette. Tess was staring at him as if entranced. I stood up.

"Listen," I said to the headwaiter, "there's going to be a tremendous scene at any moment, and I don't suppose you want it happening in the middle of your dining room. Please show us immediately to a private room where we can make a great deal of noise, and kindly allow William the rest of the day off. I will be sure to mention your kindness to the hotel manager."

I began walking away from our table, assuming—correctly—that the others would follow.

"But, Momma," said Sarah, "what about our dinner?"

The headwaiter, who seemed to grasp the situation at last, heard her. "If I ask the kitchen to wait, say, twenty minutes?" He smiled ingratiatingly at me. "It's kind of you to think of the other diners. William, lead the way to the third private dining room—it is not currently in use." He steered the young man to the left with a firm hand on the small of his back. "And stand up straight, man."

Our sudden removal caused a few heads to turn, but it did spare the hotel the loud, chaotic, and tearful scene that followed once we reached the safety of a chilly, unlaid dining room. William—better known to Tess as Billy—did indeed sit down on the carpet and sob loudly.

"And here we are at the end of our twenty minutes and barely a word of our stories told," he remarked after thoroughly wiping his face and blowing his nose on an enormous red handkerchief. "You ladies had better get back for your supper, but may I beg the favor of waiting on you in your room later? Pardon the impertinence of asking for the room number, but they'll never let me stay if I'm seen sitting downstairs with our guests. As it is, I must go back to the dormitory and put on my own clothes or I'll get into trouble for walking on the guest floors."

"Of course you can come and see us, as soon as it's convenient to you." I scrabbled around in my reticule for a ticket stub and a pencil to write down our room number. "We'll expect you as soon as dinner's over."

"And you'll tell me all about the rest of the family, won't you?" Tess pleaded. She was standing still so that I could repin her hat and neaten her hair, which had started to come down from its bun when Billy had enveloped her in a bear hug. He was of a compact, muscular build, not terribly tall, but he still towered over Tess's small, plump form.

"I'll tell you all there is to know, Tessie," replied Billy, pocketing the slip of paper. "All the good—and the not so good." He stared at Tess for a moment as if he had more to say, but then shook himself. "I'll not be keeping you ladies from your food any longer."

With one last look at Tess, he darted toward a door at the back of the room, disappearing into the gloom—the headwaiter had lit only one gas lamp for us.

Tess shivered. "What does he mean, the not so good?" she asked.

I shook my head, not wanting to speculate. But I too wondered what the evening had in store for Tess.

❦

Billy's tentative knock sounded on our door at seven thirty that evening. Sarah's attempts to stay awake after an early start, an excursion to the park, and an afternoon spent looking out of the windows and exclaiming about everything that was happening on State Street had been in vain. I had carried her to bed and shucked her out of her clothes without waking her. Tess and I had remained in our evening dresses in honor of Billy's visit, and we had tidied our hair as well.

I was glad we'd made the effort when Billy sidled through the door. He was dressed in what was evidently his Sunday best, a fairly good suit of dark brown with highly polished boots and a well-brushed hat. When he removed the latter article, his hair gleamed in the gaslight. He had oiled and combed it meticulously so that not a single strand was out of place.

"You can't imagine what a ribbing I've been getting from the boys about going into the good rooms," was his first remark as he entered. He sounded nervous, but his smile was cheerful and his manner easy, if a touch deferential. "The men's dormitories are nothing like this, to be sure. And a suite of rooms too." He turned around in circles, inspecting the ornate design of the ceiling, the polished wood of the floor, and the thick Turkey carpet, before looking at the two of us.

"May I kiss you, Tessie?" His voice was tender. "If I'm not too much of a stranger to you."

By way of an answer, Tess rose to her feet and dashed over to him, holding out her arms. Billy gave her three smacking kisses, one on each cheek and one on her forehead, and she turned pink with pleasure.

"Ah, I can't think what's the greatest happiness—the joy of finding you or the thought of what I'm going to tell Ma and Da tomorrow," Billy said when he'd done hugging Tess and was holding her at arm's length, gazing at her face. I felt a sense of relief; I'd been worried that Billy was going to inform Tess that one or both of her parents was dead.

"Whose story are we going to hear first?" I asked, motioning for Billy to sit on the plush settee that faced the fireplace. Tess and I, more hampered by our dresses, perched on the two armchairs.

"I want to hear about Ma and Da and Mary, Georgie, Aileen, Deirdre, Joseph, and Janet," said Tess. I'd heard her enumeration of her brothers' and sisters' names often enough that they were familiar to me. Billy had been the youngest child when Tess was taken to the Poor Farm.

Billy settled himself more comfortably, placing his hat on the side table with a self-conscious air. "I'll start with Ma and Da, then, Tessie. They live in the Back of the Yards—that's by the stockyards, the Union Stockyard, that is. It's a ways south of here and reeks something dreadful in the summer, but their house is a sight nicer than the tenement we lived in before the fire."

"Does Mr. O'Dugan work in the stockyards?" I asked.

"No, ma'am. His back is terrible, and we had some bad years when he quit working." Billy reached over to pat Tess's hand. "But we pulled together somehow. Ma took in washing, and we all went out to work. By that time, Mary was married and could've been sitting easy since her husband's a clerk in the railroad, but she wouldn't hear of it. She came over every day and baked pies to sell while Da sat in his chair and minded the boys—she just had two then. It's not a man's place to mind children, but Da said if everyone else was making a sacrifice, he could too."

"Mary has boys?" Tess clapped her hands.

"Four lads now, all as alike as twins. And a handful they are. Aileen's married too, but no children." He shifted on his seat and rubbed his palms together, looking uneasy.

"What about Georgie?" Tess asked. "I remember that his hair was red and very curly. Is it short now?"

Billy looked down at his hands and sighed. "Tessie, our George has been in heaven these seven years." He looked up at her stricken face, his eyes moist. "And our Janet before that, of the scarlet fever. It was cholera that did for

Georgie, and the Lord took him quick. Janet went blind toward the end, so it was a blessing it didn't last too long after that." He cleared his throat. "But the rest of us is hale and hearty, God willing. Da walks with a stick, but he walks, and that's a wonderful thing."

A fat tear caught the edge of Tess's spectacles, spreading along the rim. She removed her glasses and blinked at me, her expression so lost and forlorn that it wrenched at something deep within me. "Nell . . ."

"I'm here." I crossed the space between us and knelt on the rug by her chair, putting my arms around her, feeling another of her hot tears slide down my neck. Billy came to stand awkwardly behind her, stroking her hair and whispering, "I'm sorry, darlin'. I'm sorry I had to be the bearer of bad news." His homely face bore an expression of deep sorrow, and I decided I liked him immensely.

We stayed like that until Tess drew a deep, shuddering breath. "Poor Ma and Da," she said, scrubbing at her face with her handkerchief. "And now there are only . . ." She thought for a moment. "Six of us. Or did Ma have any more babies after I left?" She looked hopeful.

"No." Billy gave an unsteady grin. "Da says the angels took one look at my serious mug and decided Ma had a good boy to take care of her. I was never one for mischief." He looked across at me and shrugged. "An old soul, so I am, Ma says."

"So Mary and Aileen are married. What about Deirdre and Joseph?" Tess was smiling again despite her reddened eyes.

"Ah, no, not even walking out." Billy grinned. "Deirdre's got a good position as a maid with a preacher's family out by Winnetka way, and she says she's not in a hurry to marry and leave such a pretty place. Joseph's apprenticed to a cabinet-maker in Joliet—he's good at the carving and the like. So we're all going up in the world, Tessie darlin'." He kissed her lightly on the cheek before resuming his seat on the sofa. "With all of us working and scraping up every penny we could manage, Ma and Da were able to start a tidy little saloon and live above it. It's a decent place, with no brawling—a good house where the steady men from the yards can take a pint to get the stink out of their throats. Ma does free bread and soup every Thursday, even for the ones who can't afford a drink."

"When can I see them?" Tess leaned forward in her chair. "Nell, could we go there tomorrow? Billy said he was going."

"I suppose I could ask the hotel to hire a carriage for us," I said. "But won't it be a terrible shock for your parents?"

Billy grinned. "I can prepare them for the shock of seeing Tessie if you let me walk ahead a little. I'm not sure if they'll be ready for a carriage though. But I suppose you fine ladies won't be wanting to ride the horse cars."

He glanced at the clock on the mantelpiece and stood up, looking alarmed. "I'll be in hot water if I'm not in the dormitory by nine. And I still haven't heard your story, Tessie, but it'll just have to wait. Can you be down at the Ladies' Entrance at two o'clock? They won't want me in the good rooms any more than I can help it, and the dormitory master won't let me leave till I've been to Mass twice."

I nodded. "We can certainly manage that, and no doubt the carriage too. Is there a good Episcopalian church nearby?"

"I hear Saint James is . . ." Billy's voice trailed into silence. "Wait a second. Tessie, are you not Catholic?"

Tess shook her head slowly, and Billy gave a long, low whistle. "They turned you Protestant? Ma's going to have conniptions." He looked at me. "Since Georgie died, Ma's been a terrible one for Mass. Georgie saw an angel standing at the foot of his deathbed, you see, and it did something to Ma. She swore she'd never lose another child if she did her duty as a Catholic, and she was right—she never did."

With another glance at the clock, Billy settled his hat on his head. "I'm warning you, she's not going to like Tessie being turned away from her faith," he said. "And she'll winkle that out of us straightaway." With a swift kiss on Tess's cheek and a tip of his hat to me, he hastened out of the room, leaving me and Tess staring at each other.

"Well!" I said.

"My head's hurting," said Tess. "I'm full of happy feelings, but there are sad ones too. And Ma won't really be cross at me for being a Protestant, will she?" Her hand strayed to her precious Bible, which sat on the table next to her armchair.

I put my arms around her and kissed the top of her head. "I'm sure she won't." But I wasn't sure, not entirely.

SEVEN

Tess's mother was a surprise. I had expected a woman of the stolid Irish type, bearing a resemblance to Billy's snub-nosed homeliness or Tess's round, pleasant face. A woman who ran a saloon, I'd decided, would be a muscular, unwavering-looking matron of a demeanor suited to dealing with laborers. As we waited in our hired carriage for Billy to walk ahead and break the news, attracting much attention from an increasingly large crowd of urchins and curious bystanders, I built up a picture in my head of this paragon of sturdy Celtic energy and hoped I'd like her.

In fact, Mrs. O'Dugan turned out to be a fragile-looking, bird-boned waif of a woman with a mass of wavy hair swept up into a topknot and huge gray eyes that wore a perpetual expression of anguish. There was no doubting her identity though. The moment we descended from the carriage, she flung herself out of the doorway of the neatly painted saloon and wrapped herself around Tess. The wild keening she set up, with much raising of her enormous eyes to heaven and wringing of her hands, seemed to alarm nobody, as if this were perfectly normal behavior. The process of greeting lasted so long that even Tess, who at first had hugged her mother tight and cried a good deal, began to look a little uncomfortable. Fortunately, the man who followed her outdoors finally succeeded in prying her loose with an injunction to "calm down now, Margaret." He greeted Tess in his turn with a hearty kiss on both cheeks. By the stick on which he leaned and his resemblance to Tess, I deduced he was Mr. O'Dugan.

Sarah and I stood a little apart from the reunion, taking in our surroundings. There seemed to be children everywhere, spilling out of the open doorways onto a street with neither trees nor grass. The houses huddled close together as if for warmth. We had come through several streets like this, punctuated by drifts of wasteland bordering the railroad or dominated by hulking brick buildings with a utilitarian air. A few men and a great many more women sat in doorways, hung from windows, or leaned against walls, talking in groups or simply watching. Smoke and the acrid tang of the stockyards tainted the air. Yet the place didn't seem unfriendly—it was so full of people that it had almost a carnival atmosphere. I caught the eye of one or two of the watching women and smiled. They smiled back and nodded at me as if it was quite the usual thing to have a lady in a carriage come to call.

After a few minutes, during which Tess quite disappeared, so great was the throng surrounding her, a detachment of people broke away from the crowd and came toward us. They introduced themselves so rapidly I had no hope of remembering who was who. I heard the word "cousin" a few times. The rest appeared to be friends of the family. I caught a hint of Irish brogue often, but also German and Slavic accents, sharper and less musical than the Irish.

The assembled people herded us inside the tavern. Someone explained that there would be no drink, it being the Sabbath, but they needed the extra space. Women's voices came from a room adjoining that where we all stood, and before too long, great platters of bread and butter and plain cake were passed around. These were soon accompanied by large cups of strong tea, liberally sweetened. The scents of perspiration and damp wool competed with the odors of tea, sawdust, scrubbing soap, and a faint tang of beer. From time to time, a man would spit noisily into one of the pots in the corners of the room, following the instructions of the notices that proclaimed, "Do not spit on the FLOOR—use the SPITOONS."

After a while, a portion of the crowd disappeared, having exhausted the bread and butter and cake. Two men brought in a wooden table and several chairs. Billy made an entrance with Tess and his parents, flanked by two women who turned out to be Mary and Aileen, Tess's older sisters. Mary resembled her father and was a tall, strapping, buxom woman with a prominent chin. Aileen had her mother's wild hair and a more slender build than Mary's. A permanent expression of narrow-eyed suspicion marred her otherwise attractive face.

There were a few minutes of flurry as introductions—or were they reintroductions?—took place. Then everyone seated themselves, with Mr. O'Dugan at the head of the table and Mrs. O'Dugan at the foot. A girl of around fourteen or so took Sarah outside to play, promising she'd keep an eye on her. The rest of the crowd drifted outside or busied themselves with clearing away the remnants of food and drink, and Mrs. O'Dugan let her gaze drift away from Tess and onto me.

"From what Tessie tells me, you've been quite the benefactor." She extended a bony hand and rested it on my arm, smiling in the closed-mouth way that people usually affected to hide bad teeth. Her enormous eyes were red-rimmed and a little puffy, but her gaze held my own in a hypnotically beseeching way that smacked a little of the fanatic. The row of gaudy pictures of saints on a shelf testified to her devotion to the faith and looked oddly out of place in their surroundings.

"I don't think of myself as a benefactor," I replied. "Tess and I are the best of friends and are each other's help and support. She shares in my fortunes most deservedly. I couldn't have worked and raised Sarah without her help."

There was much nodding around the table, and Mary spoke up.

"She shares in your fortunes? But there's a sum of money that's hers alone, isn't there?"

I was taken aback but replied readily. "Of course. I've kept careful records of everything Tess earned while we were in Kansas. It would be easy enough to calculate the increase of her capital as a proportion of my own." I left aside the fact that I had, for quite some time, been disbursing sums for clothing—and now room and board—for Tess out of my own funds. I had plenty of money to spare.

"Tess will never want for anything." I tried to sound as reassuring as I could. "I think of her as a sister, don't I, Tess?"

Tess beamed. "And now I have my family again, so I have *two* families."

I was happy for Tess, but I was also uneasy. It was wonderful that she had found her family again, but who were these people, really? I instinctively liked Mr. O'Dugan, who largely sat silent and let his womenfolk do the talking, but Tess's mother was disconcerting. Aileen spoke less than Mary, but she never took her eyes off me. Still, although the neighborhood was poor, the saloon itself was spotlessly clean and looked highly respectable.

"I never imagined a saloon could look so fresh and inviting," I said by way of a compliment. "I've never set foot in one before." Indeed, I could have gone my whole life without ever seeing a taproom. These were not places where a respectable lady would venture. It didn't do to say so, of course.

"Cleanliness is next to godliness. It's not only the Evangelicals who think that, you know." Aileen's voice was oddly girlish with a nasal twang to it. Mr. O'Dugan made a wry face and smiled at me.

"Don't listen to Mother Aileen of the Sacred Heart, now. She likes to stick the needle in as often as she can find the opportunity. Aileen, remember that Mrs. Lillington has stuck by our Tessie and been a friend to her and treated her like a lady. And a lady she is, and I'm right proud of her for that." He nodded gravely at Tess in approbation. Now that I could study him more closely, his resemblance to Tess was a matter of nose and chin more than anything else. In other respects, he looked most like Billy, who had sat at his left hand after making sure his father was comfortable and then lapsed into a respectful silence.

"Yes, Da," said Aileen. "I just find it so strange that our Tess isn't Catholic. I don't remember the charity lady saying anything about such matters."

"No more she did, and if you'll remember, neither did we." Mr. O'Dugan pulled an empty pipe from his pocket and regarded it thoughtfully. "We weren't such good Catholics ourselves in those days."

Mrs. O'Dugan looked about to burst into tears at any moment, but she took a deep, shuddering breath. "We were almost as bad as heathens, and look what happened." She clutched at Tess. "I can go to my grave easy now that I have your forgiveness, but God let you be turned away from the true church as a punishment, of that I'm sure." She twisted her fingers together nervously. "Although I was never right in myself after I had Billy, and with eight children, it was a desperate hard thing to feed and clothe us all. If the girls hadn't gone into service, I don't know what I would have done, what with the war and all. They were hard times, Mrs. Lillington."

"And yet you've prospered." I tried to sound cheerful. "You've all worked hard and achieved something to be proud of."

There were general nods at this, and Mary, who had been comforting her mother with a solid, round arm, reseated herself. "But the Poor Farm was a good place, just like the charity lady said, Ma," she said with the confident authority of the eldest child. "It was a dry roof over Tessie's head and food in her belly when we had neither, and country air instead of the stink of cattle." She looked at me, her head tilted to one side. "You've not told us, Mrs. Lillington, how you came to meet Tess, and I'm that curious. She said it was at the Poor Farm—were you a charity visitor? Or a patron of some sort?"

I took a deep breath. I had come to Chicago ready to lie to society to preserve Sarah's good name, but somehow I couldn't lie to Tess's family.

"I was an inmate," I said steadily. "I got myself in the family way, and my stepfather sent me to the Poor Farm to have Sarah there. He wanted her adopted, but I kept her."

"Your family sent you to the Poor Farm?" Billy looked astonished. "Didn't you have a sister or cousin who could have pretended the baby was hers?" He looked at Aileen, whose mouth tucked into tight folds as she glared back at him. She pushed back her chair noisily, rose to her feet, and stalked out of the door that led to the yard and outhouse.

"What was that about?" I asked.

"Aileen made a mistake too, and shame on our Billy for hinting around it in company." Mary sniffed loudly. "She's sensitive enough that she had no more children after that." Seeing my puzzled look, she explained. "I would have taken Aileen's baby gladly, only she was born blue, poor little mite. I always wanted a little girl. And then Aileen up and married the father anyway when he took the pledge and stopped hanging around the taverns."

"It's a judgment," Mrs. O'Dugan said dolefully.

They seemed to have completely disregarded the truth about Sarah, accepted it as if it were quite in the normal way of things to bear a child out of wedlock. I breathed a soft sigh of relief, only to wince as a loud clattering of boots announced the entrance of a gaggle of muddy, breathless, and runny-nosed boys. Mary bounced to her feet with more lightness than I'd expected and grabbed the collar of the filthiest.

"Out, the lot of you," she bellowed, turning her captive around and giving all the children small shoves in the back. "You'll be the death of me with the state you get yourselves in." She gave the smallest boy's nose a quick wipe with the corner of her own handkerchief as she herded them back out of the saloon. Four of them, I noticed, had identical heads of strawberry-blond hair, including the little fellow who'd had his nose wiped. I deduced they were Mary's brood.

It was another forty minutes before I was able to extricate the three of us from our visit, and by the time we climbed into our carriage, it was growing dark. The driver, instructed to stay where he was as I hadn't known how long we'd be there, had clearly had a hard time of it. He set up a continual muttering that didn't abate until we had covered a good six blocks.

I too was out of sorts and exhausted. What with Aileen's sharp looks and pointed remarks and Mrs. O'Dugan's general air of tragedy, the visit had been trying. A day of being stared at had left me feeling like an exhibit in a zoological garden. Tess was happy, and I was glad for her—but I hoped I wouldn't be called upon to visit the O'Dugans too often.

EIGHT

I spent most of Monday prostrate on the sofa, suffering from a headache. This was highly unusual for me, but the nervous energy from our long journey to Chicago had drained away and left me feeling somehow depressed. It didn't help that there was absolutely no sign of Martin. I would, after all, have to go to his store and inquire after him like a tradesperson, or at best a mere acquaintance. So, naturally, I was cross with him.

When Tuesday dawned, my low spirits had converted themselves into something resembling a feverish state. I snapped repeatedly at Sarah, who had decided to master the skill of buttoning *all* of her buttons, including those on her boots. This procedure threatened, to my overheated mind, to take all morning. I ground my teeth at Tess's slowness in eating breakfast and wondered if it were possible for someone to chew toast so many times. I responded to Alice's remark that there was a curl coming loose from my hair with a glare and a hasty poke at my chignon. This disarranged more than it remedied, so she had to take my hair down and do it up again—during which time I glared at her reflection in the mirror some more.

By the time we met Elizabeth in the hotel lobby, Tess and Sarah were communicating with each other through rollings of the eyes and significant glances that did nothing to improve my temper. But here, at last, was Elizabeth, and our outing to State Street could commence. My bad temper evaporated.

I had agreed to Elizabeth's proposal to start with Gambarelli's and The Fair, then proceed north to Field and Leiter's before doubling back toward Rutherford's. This, we felt, would be quite enough excitement for a small child in a single day. It would leave out several other stores of interest, but as Elizabeth said, there was plenty of time for the others.

"And Rutherford's has a tea room," Elizabeth explained, "which will be an excellent place for Tess and Sarah to rest and refresh themselves."

"I bow to your superior knowledge." I smiled, but my insides were in turmoil. What would I have done if I'd been on my own? Probably run straight to Rutherford's and made a fool of myself. Better to start with Gambarelli's.

ℰ

"I told you it was vulgar." Elizabeth made a slight motion of her head toward the milling crowd of shoppers on the main floor of the Gambarelli store.

"It's—overwhelming." In the center of the expansive space, a modestly clad marble nymph raised her eyes to the heavens while the cornucopia she carried shed water into a large basin. Other statues of a classical bent were ranged in niches along the walls. Plaster cherubs decorated a ceiling hung with baskets, from which overflowed a profusion of silk flowers in colors never seen in nature.

"It's beautiful," said Tess, gazing, rapt, at the flowers. "Look at all the people, and look at all the things we can try on and not have to get measured for. Do you think we can find a pink hat for me?"

"That says, 'artist's supplies.'" Sarah spelled out the words on one of the many signs. "Does that mean paper, Momma? I need some paper to write on." She was exceedingly fond of writing, which consisted of spelling out the words she knew and inserting much gibberish in between.

"I suppose there's a place where you can buy paper. There seems to be a— well, I suppose you'd call it a department—for everything." The signs were ornately lettered and hung from every vantage point, as if guiding a traveler through some fantastic voyage. The effect was quite overpowering.

"I heard Mr. Gambarelli senior started out by buying anything that was cheap and could be resold for a little profit." Elizabeth nodded her thanks at a pair of roughly dressed women who stepped back to allow us to progress through the crowd. "Every time he laid his hand on some new wares, he started a fresh department. When he runs out of room, he finds a way to buy the next adjacent building. That's why this place is such a warren once you get out of the main hall."

"Look at the women," I said under my breath, watching a gaggle of middle-aged housewives argue vociferously about the relative merits of a range of petticoats. "You could almost imagine that shopping is some kind of entertainment for them, like going to a play."

"Well, why not?" Elizabeth grinned at Tess, who had come to a dead stop in front of a massive display of parasols, her eyes as round as saucers. "Many of these women can't afford well-cut clothes. Here they can buy gimcrack articles that fall apart after the tenth round with the mangle but which are within their reach for now. *Now*, as the journalists remind us, is the American obsession."

All around us was the hiss, buzz, and trill of many different languages. I could hear a great deal of German, Italian, and a language that seemed to contain many iterations of the letter *Z*—Polish, perhaps? The women talked and laughed, and I felt a brief stab of envy at how purposeful they seemed. For them, shopping was the whole point of their day.

"Do come along, Nell." Elizabeth's voice recalled me to reality. "There's plenty more to see."

So this was Lucetta's world. Did she too find it vulgar? The gowns I'd seen her wearing couldn't possibly have come from this vast bazaar of cheap articles. Did Lucetta simply accept her father's emporium as the source of her wealth? Did she walk through it as a princess walks through the city that lies outside her palace walls?

A shiver ran through me as I imagined meeting Lucetta Rutherford here, in the midst of her inheritance, with me gawking like a visitor from the country. I saw her in my mind's eye, proceeding through the crowd with Martin a step or two behind her. A rush of anticipatory mortification sent the blood to my cheeks, and I almost demanded that we exit the store that instant.

Except that Elizabeth had turned away from me and was smiling politely at a man who had stepped up to her.

"Miss Parnell, what a pleasure." His smile didn't reach his eyes, which were as black as midnight. He was a vigorous-looking man with an abundant black beard. His excellent tailoring enhanced rather than disguised his prize-fighter's physique, broad-shouldered and barrel-chested. His voice was low and pleasant, but the sensation I experienced as he turned his impenetrable gaze on me was fear. This man, my instincts declared, was dangerous.

"Mr. Gambarelli." Elizabeth nodded graciously, but there was no warmth in her voice.

"I hope you and your friends are finding what you're looking for." He raised his eyebrows at Sarah. "If the young lady would like a new doll, we have a wonderful selection on the second floor."

Sarah glanced at me before replying, uncertain as to whether he'd addressed her directly or not. "If you please," she said, hesitating a little, "I don't much care for dolls. Do you have any books?"

Elizabeth was now clearly in a position where introductions were obligatory. "This is Mr. Alessandro Gambarelli," she explained to us. "Mr. Gambarelli, allow me to present Mrs. Lillington, Miss O'Dugan, and Miss Lillington."

Mr. Gambarelli bowed, but I had the impression he barely registered our names. "Our book department is on the third floor," he said, speaking more to Elizabeth than anyone else. "I hope the young lady will enjoy our selection."

He bowed again and then, seeing a clerk trying to get his attention, made his excuses and left us alone.

"I don't like him," said Elizabeth into my ear as we turned in the direction of the steam elevators.

"He seemed to be making a point of paying attention to you," I said.

Elizabeth shrugged. "We have money and a position in Chicago society—at least, Mother and Father have money. And for some unaccountable reason, my sister, Frances, likes Gambarelli's. She's dragged me in here often enough."

"A dangerous-looking man."

"Hmmm." Elizabeth watched Tess and Sarah confer about what kind of book they should buy. "He has a reputation for ruthlessness, although I've never been able to find out why. Father knows far more about him than he lets on, I think. It's one of the drawbacks of womanhood—men so often don't *tell* you things, as if you'd break in half with the strain of knowing the truth."

That was an interesting thought, and one I would have liked to pursue. But the elevator had arrived, and Sarah had run back to tug at my hand.

By the time we were done with Gambarelli's and were about to leave the store, I could sense a change in the atmosphere. It had changed in the literal sense—the gasoliers had been lit because the sky outside had darkened, with drifts of somber clouds sliding under higher banks of grayish-white.

"I do hope we won't be outdoors when the storm breaks," I said to Elizabeth.

"Oh, the weather doesn't count for much on State Street," she replied cheerfully. "You just buy more, that's all."

"We've bought enough already. Thank goodness you insisted on everything being sent."

"It's going to be like Christmas tomorrow." Tess grinned with glee. "A new book, marbles, and paper and pencils for Sarah, new handkerchiefs for me. If I'd just found a hat I liked, it would have been perfect. A nice pink one with ribbons."

"I think you should buy a straw hat with pink flowers," said Sarah. "The kind that looks like a plate and you pin it to your front hair."

"I don't have much front hair," Tess replied. "I want a bonnet I can pin to my topknot. But I'd like pink flowers and a big pink satin ribbon hanging down the back."

I listened to her with half an ear, distracted by the behavior of the shopgirls and clerks. They barely seemed to be paying any attention to their customers. I watched a clerk, better dressed than most, shoot through the crowd of shoppers like an arrow loosed from the bow. He landed in the middle of a knot of shopgirls, scattering them with a few terse phrases. I could have sworn one of the girls was in tears.

"Elizabeth, look at that." I turned back to the others only to find that they had gotten ahead of me. I found them by looking for Elizabeth's hat, which was now close to the entrance door.

Struggling through the throng in an attempt to catch up with them, I passed another group of clerks. They separated politely to allow me to pass, but not before I'd heard one of them say something about closing the store.

"Why would you close the store?" I addressed the question to the whole group, not knowing which one of them had spoken. "Is something wrong?"

For a moment, the men stared at me in blank astonishment, as if I'd suddenly appeared from nowhere. Then one of them, recalling that I was a customer, stretched an ingratiating smile across his face.

"We were referring to the weather, Madam. That we would instruct the doormen to keep the doors closed when the storm arrives. There is nothing wrong at all."

This was so patently untrue that the eyebrows of one or two of the men rose—but after all, wasn't I being rather nosy? I decided to accept the explanation at face value. What had Gambarelli's to do with me? With a small shrug, I plunged back into the mass of women in an attempt to catch up with the others.

NINE

I stepped out onto the street, shielding my eyes against the damp, chilly wind that had begun to swirl the dust and tug at the ruffles on my dress. The scents of horse manure and people greeted me as I hastened to rejoin my friends, although there was definitely less human and horse-drawn traffic than before. Near to us, a blue-coated policeman moved on an itinerant peddler from whose cart rose an appetizing smell of roast meat.

"I think we'll leave the Fair for another day." Elizabeth held up her hand to shield her face from the grit stirred up by a passing horse car. "Let's go to Field's and then to Rutherford's. The Fair's a lot like Gambarelli's anyway."

We began walking, occasionally glancing up at the sky. Scores of soberly suited clerks and shopgirls passed us, moving rapidly with their heads bent against the wind. Most of the women were in groups of twos or threes, but some were on their own, a sight that cheered me. Despite Mrs. Parnell's warnings, it looked as if an unchaperoned woman would be safe enough on State Street in daylight.

"We won't spend too long in Field's," Elizabeth said with a glance at Tess, who had looped her arm through mine. Elizabeth, who seemed to have a way with children, was holding Sarah's hand. "Tess, you'll find the best hats at Rutherford's. Are you happy just to have a quick look at Field's?"

"Oh yes." Tess had cheered up since Elizabeth had insisted they be on first-name terms too. "I'm sure Martin's store is the best one."

"It's my favorite, mostly because it doesn't try to sell you absolutely everything." Elizabeth removed a piece of grit from the corner of her lips. "Rutherford's is just modes—everything a woman needs. And it's elegant, like a *grand magasin* in Paris."

"A what?" Sarah nearly had to shout to make herself heard.

Elizabeth gave Sarah's hand a little shake. "A big shop, nosy-posy. Little girls aren't supposed to interrupt all the time, you know. Or issue decided edicts about what their elders and betters should be wearing."

Sarah grinned.

"She's too much with adults." I sighed. "I'm going to have to find a little school of some kind for her so she can make friends of her own age." And then, returning to my own preoccupations, "Do you mean that Rutherford's looks French?"

"Not French, exactly." Elizabeth wrinkled her nose. "But not exactly American either. A perfect paradise for women. You can wander around all day unchaperoned, and nobody bothers you unless you actually need their advice. If you do, the modistes know an awful lot. They have absolutely every single journal of women's fashion available to peruse in a little reading room, even the French and English ones."

I smiled to myself, remembering Martin's house in Victory, which had been full of delights—clippings of newspaper advertisements, folded quarters of fabric, samples of lace and ribbon, and jars of different buttons. And, naturally, journals. Many men would doubtless find it odd that Martin could be so fascinated with women's furbelows, not seeing that this was his way of worshipping the female sex—by truly noticing what they wore and what they cared about.

I swallowed, trying to rid myself of the warm feeling such thoughts gave me. I could see his store from across the busy street, dominating its corner, which stuck out a little into the intersection as if the streets were somehow uneven. The building was faced with pale stone banded with white marble. Its corner entrance was surmounted by a sort of canopy, but I couldn't see any details. Lights gleamed in the windows, the awnings raised because of the darkness of the day and the gusting wind.

"Just half a block to Field and Leiter's." Elizabeth's voice fought against the rumble of yet another horse car. "Then we'll turn back to Rutherford's and have a nice rest. We should get there before it starts raining."

※

"That was quite the largest and grandest store I've ever seen," I remarked to Elizabeth as we stepped out of Field and Leiter's doors onto a sidewalk spotted with rain. Above us, the clouds hung dark and heavy, and there were fewer people than before.

"My boots are pinching my toes," remarked Sarah. "Are we going to eat something now?"

"As soon as we get to Rutherford's." I wasn't surprised that she was tired—I was too. It was odd that I could walk miles across the prairie and still feel fresh at the end of the ramble, but just a few blocks in Chicago had left me feeling quite worn out.

"I suppose we'll have to find a good boot-maker for Sarah too." And the dress that I'd made for her just six weeks ago, a pretty sky blue with a matching hat trimmed in white fur, looked a little short—clearly she'd grown again. Still, I had put growth pleats into the length and the arms, so it would be easy to let out. "We should be able to find blue boots to match that dress instead of those gray ones. Does Rutherford's have dresses for little girls?" I asked Elizabeth.

"My dear, they'll make you anything you wish. Rutherford's has ready-made underthings, petticoats, hats, and so on, but the dresses are almost always bespoke. Mr. Rutherford has been known to say that a woman is most becoming in clothing that fits her form exactly. But do you know, his people will fit a servant for a new dress just as readily as they do a wealthy woman. Or a—well, a woman of ill repute. There's one who—Nell, dear, you're not listening."

"I'm sorry." My heart had begun to skip against my ribs. "I guess I'm just excited to see Mr. Rutherford's store at long last. I've heard so much about it." I had indeed been the recipient of many of Martin's worries and triumphs as the store he had held in his heart for so many years at last became reality. I'd been his confidante until Lucetta Gambarelli entered his life and his letters became more impersonal. I realized now that Martin could not square his conscience with the presence of two women in his heart and mind. He would either choose me or Lucetta. Or perhaps he would be forced to cleave to Lucetta, who was, after all, his lawfully wedded wife.

I could see Martin's store clearly now, dominating the noisy intersection of State and Madison, where two horse car lines crossed. The traffic, both horse-drawn and pedestrian, was so dense at this spot that it required the efforts of four blue-coated policemen, all shouting and waving energetically, to bring it into some kind of order. The pale stone of Rutherford's, culminating in its prominent awning on the corner, looked like the prow of a ship at sea from this distance.

"Look at all the people outside Martin's store." Tess was panting from trying to keep up with me. "Are they all waiting to get in? Something exciting must be happening."

I glanced back at Elizabeth, who shrugged. "New merchandise? Something new from Paris, perhaps. They're certainly attracting a crowd. I do hope the tea room won't be full."

I stared hard at the distant scene, trying to make sense of it. Behind me, I could hear Elizabeth telling Sarah about a trip to Paris she'd made when she was much younger, but her words no longer made sense to me.

"There's something wrong." I put out a hand to stem the flow of talk behind me. There was something about the way the people in the crowd were moving that alerted me. At this distance, their faces were mere pale ovals, the odd light cast by the approaching storm making hollows and shadows. I couldn't read their expressions—so why did I feel such a sense of dread?

As we approached the street corner, I suddenly realized what had been bothering me.

"The doors are shut." I swung round to face Elizabeth. "And the lights are out. I'll run ahead and see what's happening. Tess, please take Elizabeth's arm."

I abandoned Tess and plunged toward the edge of the sidewalk, dodging fast through the foot traffic and collecting a few epithets from people I jostled in my headlong flight. I could see the heavy wooden doors clearly now, inset with large panels of glass engraved with the peacock feather that had become familiar to me, incorporated as it was into the letterhead that graced most of Martin's letters. They were closed tight. Behind the panes of frosted glass loomed waiting shadows, as if there were people guarding the entrance.

What were all the people saying? I crossed State Street as fast as I could, dodging horse droppings and moving carefully over the horse car rails. The stones that paved the street were covered with a layer of grit, churned up by the traffic of wheels and feet into fine ridges, dampened by the large raindrops that occasionally hit me in the face.

I was now on the northwest corner of State and Madison, with only Madison Street to cross. A knot of pedestrians, too tightly packed to push through, was in front of me. People spilled off the sidewalk on either side of a waiting landau, whose driver glared and twitched his whip as his horses fidgeted nervously.

The people in front of me moved forward, and I pushed as far as I could into the crowd, enveloped by the scents of sweat and damp clothing. I gained the edge of the sidewalk only to find that a horse car had halted to let off passengers, and all hope of crossing the street was gone. I could hear the crowd outside Rutherford's now, a subdued roar of angry voices.

"Look at that." The tall, fat gentleman next to me, made even taller by his silk hat, pulled at his companion's arm and pointed west along Madison Street. Where Martin's store ended and the next building began, the two separated by a narrow alley, a heavy black vehicle, windowless, had arrived from the west. It steered in close to the alleyway, and one of the uniformed men on the driver's bench jumped down. The other waved his arms vigorously, apparently in an attempt to clear the area of onlookers. His efforts had the opposite effect. The crowd surged toward the vehicle, the women's voices rising above the general hubbub in a single, repeated note that I could not understand, so great was the noise of the street.

Another horse car, this time heading west on Madison Street, blocked my view as it rumbled past, the tired horses straining at their task. Now, surely, I could cross.

I put a foot into the road—both feet—and then jumped back. I had not realized that the black vehicle had made an about-turn. It was heading straight at me, clearly attempting to pass the horse car before the latter reached a line of stationary drays. Its glossy, painted side rocked perilously close to me as it completed its turn and then it righted itself to proceed on its journey at speed. Only one of the uniformed men remained on the bench.

Seizing my chance, I plunged into the road, ignoring the shout of anger from the policeman directing the traffic. I reached the crowd outside Rutherford's, which had turned back on itself and seemed to have lost its sense of purpose.

I scanned the women's faces. Who would be the best person to ask for information? I grasped the sleeve of a plump, middle-aged woman with a sensible, intelligent face.

"I'm sorry to bother you." I let go of her sleeve and stepped back a pace. "I just need to know why the doors are closed. Please."

The woman looked at me and pursed her lips, visibly hesitant to satisfy what must have looked like mere vulgar curiosity. A gust of wind eddied up the street from the south, and we both clutched at our hats and squinted against the dust blown up from the road.

"I'm new to Chicago," I said. "I was supposed to meet a friend at Rutherford's, and now I can't get in." I could see Elizabeth, Tess, and Sarah waiting to cross Madison Street and gestured toward them. "What am I supposed to tell my family?"

"I shouldn't think they'll open those doors again today." Her voice had a faint Southern drawl, the syllables longer and more languorous than the brash Chicago speech. "They pushed us all out here and locked up. My parcels are still inside. I'll have to send the girl round tomorrow, although I declare I'm in half a mind never to come back again after what's happened."

"What *has* happened?" I heard the edge of frustration and impatience in my voice. I could see my companions picking their way across the street amid a crowd of gawping pedestrians. "Tell me quick, please. My little girl will be here any second, and I need to know whether I must take her away."

She followed the direction of my gaze and nodded. "You'll not want to keep her hanging around here to hear things she shouldn't. Murder's been done, and there's always a few men want to get up a lynching."

The word "murder" sent my heart plummeting into my boots. Not here, in Chicago, in Martin's store. I could picture Martin sitting across the table from me on our last day together in Kansas, hear our laughter as he told me he'd disown me if I mixed myself up with yet another murderer.

"Murder's been done? Who's been murdered?" Stay calm, I ordered my-self. Why should this have anything to do with me? But the woman's next words robbed me of that hope.

"Mrs. Rutherford's had her throat slit. By her own husband." The word "husband" lingered on her lips, the last syllable pulled out into two musical notes. "She lies there still, inside the store. They've taken Mr. Rutherford away."

TEN

I realized I couldn't feel my hands or feet. I wondered for a fleeting moment whether I would faint, but I fought back the darkness that threatened to cover my eyes. I wasn't the fainting kind of woman, I told myself sternly.

The phrase "Mrs. Rutherford's had her throat slit by her husband" arranged itself with perfect clarity in my mind, along with an oddly vivid image of the windowless black carriage that had nearly run me down. In my mind's eye, I could see the shine of its black paint, the long vertical scratch on that paint near the rear, the louvered slits under its roof. That must be for ventilation, the detached part of my brain helpfully supplied. I could see again the stout bolts on the double door at the back of the carriage and the large padlock that had banged heavily against the door as the vehicle bounced on its springs.

How could it have been Martin inside that carriage? That was what the woman's words seemed to suggest. But Martin wasn't in Chicago—I had been certain of that fact up till that moment. Why else had I not heard from him? He would surely have replied to the notes I sent him. At least, the Martin who had kissed me that last day together in Kansas would have.

"I hope you find your friend." The woman's lips twitched upward into a brief smile, and she moved away south along State Street, her ample hips rolling, one hand raised to protect her face from the wind-blown dust.

"Nell, what's happening? Why have they shut the doors?"

I turned to find Elizabeth behind me, still holding Sarah's hand. Tess trailed behind her, looking as if she'd had quite enough of the day.

"Momma, I'm so hungry. Can't we eat now?"

I grabbed Elizabeth's hand and squeezed it hard, leaning in to hiss into her ear: "Don't ask again." She looked puzzled but made the tiniest of nods to indicate she'd understood.

"I think we should visit Rutherford's later." I fixed a smile on my face. "I think something went wrong with their lights, and they had to ask the customers to step outside." I was surprised how calm and normal my voice sounded. "Let's all go back to the Palmer House—we know we can get an excellent luncheon there. We can always go to Rutherford's another day, and it's going to rain."

I turned my back on Martin's store, proceeding south, knowing the others would follow. I walked with as firm a step as possible, praying that my legs would stop trembling. The news would be everywhere soon. Lucetta—dead—her throat slit. Martin taken—but taken where? How *could* he be implicated in his wife's murder? He surely wouldn't—couldn't—

But Martin was given to moments of violent rage, I knew that well enough. If Lucetta had goaded him, if she had somehow broken through to that dark core of himself that he was not always able to hide . . . "She lies there still, inside the store." No, I told myself, he couldn't kill a woman. But Lucetta was dead, her throat slit . . . I clenched my fists and swallowed hard. I was categorically *not* going to be sick.

"Momma, wait for us." Sarah's high voice sounded from behind me. "Why are you walking so fast?"

I turned and tried to smile, holding out my hand so that Sarah could run to me. "I guess I'm just in a hurry to eat. Aren't you?"

"Your hand is sweaty, right through your glove."

"Maybe I'm walking too fast." I made a deliberate effort to proceed at a stately pace. "Aren't I silly?"

The hotel was only a block away, but it seemed like the longest walk of my life. I could have sworn that the corner dome and Greek pediments of the Palmer House were moving away from us as we walked.

At last, we reached the Ladies' Entrance, and I stood back to let Tess and Sarah precede me, nodding at the smiling doorman.

"What's wrong?" Elizabeth spoke into my ear, grasping my upper arm to stop me from entering the building. I stepped back from the door, motioning to the doorman to shut it.

"Please don't ask me. Not just yet. And not in front of Sarah."

Elizabeth gave me a hard stare. "Very well. We'd better go in—they're waiting for us. But you have to explain soon."

It was pure agony to sit down and try to make conversation when I felt like I wanted to scream. I sipped a little water and tried a bite of the luncheon I'd ordered. The water I could stomach, but the food tasted like ashes in my mouth, and I abandoned it after one bite. Thank heaven for Elizabeth, who kept the flow of conversation going so I could sit silently and brood over Martin.

But there was no fooling Tess. "Is something wrong, Nell?" she asked after she'd satisfied her hunger. "You're not eating. When you don't eat, that means you're upset."

I shook my head at her, directing my eyes to Sarah. "I'm fine. I'm not upset."

Tess opened her mouth to protest but shut it again with a glance at Elizabeth, who was distracting Sarah with a funny story about a puppy one of her brothers had owned. She leaned forward and narrowed her eyes.

"Yes, you are," she hissed in her loud version of a whisper. "I can see Miss Parnell knows. Why don't you tell *me*?" She banged one small foot against the leg of her chair.

"I haven't—I can't—" I was babbling, not knowing what to answer, feeling perilously close to tears. "Tess, please don't ask me." I swallowed. "I haven't said anything to Elizabeth—"

"Is that so?" Tess stuck out her lower lip. "Well, *Elizabeth* can put up with your moods today. I'm not going to."

She wiped her mouth with her napkin and stood up, holding out a hand to Sarah. "Come on, Sary. Momma has secrets again. She won't tell you and me, but she can tell her new friend all about it." Sticking her small nose in the air, Tess marched away from us with my daughter in tow. Sarah was full and tired and didn't protest.

I should have gone after Tess, but I couldn't move. I stared at my plate, trying to summon up some strength.

"Nell." Elizabeth's voice cut into my thoughts. "It's something to do with that scene at Rutherford's, I'm sure. I wasn't going to say it in front of Sarah, but I heard a man say—'murderer.'" Her voice dropped to a low breath of sound. "Was somebody murdered? Was that Black Maria taking the murderer away?"

I fought for composure, setting my jaw so firmly that it hurt. I squeezed my eyes shut, but I couldn't stop the tears. "They took Mar—Mr. Rutherford away. They said he murdered his wife. Elizabeth, what am I going to *do*?" I turned my back on the room and fumbled in my reticule for a handkerchief.

Elizabeth let out her breath in a great rush. "So that's what it was." She frowned. "What do you mean, what are *you* going to do? There's nothing you can do except pray, I suppose, if you're the praying kind. If Mr. Rutherford didn't murder his wife they'll let him go free—or do you think he did?"

My despair gave way to instant fury, heat coursing through my veins. "How dare you even suggest he might have? Of course he didn't." My anger was all the more violent because of the sudden image of Martin's white face as he hit Judah Poulton, blind with the desire to kill.

"Hush." Elizabeth flapped her hand. "Do you want the entire room to hear you? I'm sorry for saying it. Mother says I have a knack for making precisely the remark I shouldn't."

"You said what everyone will say." I sniffed and stared at the long windows, through which I could see the rain falling in sheets. "It's what everyone will think. But I *can't* think it." Of course it wasn't possible.

Elizabeth seemed about to reply when her face assumed an expression of mild curiosity. Turning round to look in the same direction, I saw a gentleman of slim build and medium height, very correctly dressed in top hat and frock coat, following with his eyes the direction in which a waiter was pointing—directly at me.

"I do believe there's someone looking for you," she murmured. "He looks familiar somehow."

"Not to me. I've never seen him before in my life." I stared at the gentleman, who was making his unhurried way through the groups of tables and chairs. He was definitely heading in our direction.

"Mrs. Lillington?" He reached our table and bowed. He removed his silk hat to reveal neatly dressed dark hair streaked lightly with gray. His face was thin with heavily lidded eyes and a strong, mobile mouth bracketed by two deep creases that deepened as he gave me the ghost of a smile.

"My name is Salazar," he said as he held my hand for a moment. "You may know the name."

"Oh, of course." Elizabeth rolled her eyes up to the ceiling, gesturing with her hands. "You're the general manager at—at Rutherford's, aren't you?" She suddenly became conscious of what she'd said. "You had a tragedy today—Mrs. Rutherford—" She swayed a little and grasped my hand. "Oh, Nell, it's just come home to me. Lucetta Rutherford, *dead*? All that beauty, that *voice*—" She looked up at Mr. Salazar. "How did she die?" she asked, a grim expression on her face.

Mr. Salazar hesitated for a moment. "Her murderer . . . cut her throat," he said finally. "You may as well know—it'll be in this evening's papers."

"Dear God." Elizabeth's normally pink cheeks were pale, waxen-looking in the gaslight. "My sister knows her," she said to Mr. Salazar.

"I'm sorry." And he genuinely looked it.

I didn't want to talk about Lucetta anymore. The only person on my mind was Martin.

"Where's Mr. Rutherford?" I asked. "I must go see him immediately."

"That's precisely what he doesn't want," Mr. Salazar said, an expression of sympathy in his brown eyes.

And that, I realized, was precisely the answer I had already half-consciously anticipated. "Did he tell you that?"

"He wasn't free to give me explicit instructions, but yes, his meaning was clear. When they arrested him, they emptied his pockets, but fortunately those were prison guards and not detectives. They made a note that he had a bundle of correspondence in one pocket, not noticing that most of the letters were from you."

I felt a little dizzy. The phrase "*cherchez la femme*" sprang to my mind from the crime reports in the newspapers. I realized how close I had come to figuring prominently in a police investigation. "Did they keep them?" I asked.

Mr. Salazar seemed unable to repress a smile. "Martin asked if he could have the contents of his pockets back once they'd made a note of them. He shoved the bundle of letters at me and said, 'Salazar, you're going to have to deal with my mail. I want it made quite clear that I want no visitors except yourself. None at all.' He knew I'd understand. I've already made a memorandum of the private correspondence on his desk, with the exception of your letters, should a more astute policeman ask me about it."

I could see Elizabeth watching me closely, but she kept silent. She, undoubtedly, would be more intelligent than a prison guard, and I wasn't at all sure how I could answer her questions. But this was not the matter uppermost in my mind.

"Where is he?" I asked. "If you can't tell me, Mr. Salazar, I'll have to make inquiries. And it will be in the newspapers later today anyway, I suppose."

Mr. Salazar's shoulders slumped, and I almost felt sorry for the man. "They took him to the county courthouse," he said. "On Hubbard Street, north of the river." He looked anguished. "He'll be in the jail behind the courthouse by now, I'm sure. You won't be able to see him."

"I have to do *something*. And the rain's easing."

"You'll have to take a carriage," suggested Elizabeth. "How far is it?"

"Nine or ten blocks via the LaSalle Street Tunnel." Mr. Salazar swallowed hard. "But you can't possibly turn up at the courthouse in a carriage. It's swarming with journalists, and any attempt to see Martin will draw attention to you. Can't you see that's what he doesn't want?"

I could feel my nails digging into my palms as I balled my fists. "But I have to go."

"Can't you take her?" Elizabeth asked Mr. Salazar.

"I'm known to the press, and even coming here is a risky business. Please, Mrs. Lillington."

Elizabeth clutched my arm. "Nell, if I walk there with you so that you can see the place, will that be enough?" She looked up at Mr. Salazar. "We won't do anything to draw attention to ourselves."

He let out a groan. "Martin will be furious if he finds out."

"So don't tell him."

❦

I had to return to our rooms to refresh myself before the journey, and that meant encountering Tess's reproving glare. But explanations would have taken time, so I merely did what I needed to do and was back in the lobby ten minutes later to meet Elizabeth.

She was silent as we headed along Monroe Street and turned north onto LaSalle. I was a fast walker—especially in the circumstances—yet Elizabeth easily matched my steps. But as we neared the entrance to the river tunnel, she grasped my arm.

"Tell me what this is about. What, exactly, is Mr. Rutherford to you?"

"I told you. He's an old friend of mine. I've known him since we were children."

"That *might* explain why you're as white as a sheet and ready to throw yourself into the path of the journalists. I should tell you that Chicago newspapermen are a hungry lot. If they catch a whiff of any possible scandal, they'll invade the Palmer House and probably find their way into your rooms. Do you realize that? But it *doesn't* explain why Mr. Salazar—and, clearly, Mr. Rutherford—are so eager to keep any connection between you and Mr. Rutherford out of the papers."

She was silent for a few moments and then blurted out, "Mother doesn't believe there's a Mr. Lillington. Nell, before you get me entangled in this, I need to know—is Sarah Mr. Rutherford's child?"

We were on the steep slope of the tunnel's mouth, and I stopped so abruptly I nearly pitched forward. The man behind me said something very rude, and Elizabeth turned to glare at him before grabbing my arm and propelling me onward into the gaslit tunnel. She pulled me to the side so that the impatient man could go ahead of us.

"Well? I'd hate it if Mother was right yet again."

"Sarah's not Martin's—Mr. Rutherford's child." I bit my lip. "But your mother is right—there was never a Mr. Lillington. I suppose that means you won't be able to see me now."

Elizabeth shrugged. "Mother's less of a prude than you'd think. She believes you may have been wronged. She doesn't think you're what she calls 'that sort of woman.' But this business with Mr. Rutherford may force her to change her mind, so I'm going to have to be severe with you. Is there anything improper between you?"

We were talking in whispers as the tunnel's rounded walls made our voices echo alarmingly. I shook my head but felt a qualm. "I can't help my feelings for Martin. But I won't do anything wrong, for Sarah's sake. And for mine. Yes, I was wronged—I suppose. And I did wrong. I was young and stupid, and I'll not do anything of the sort again. I came to Chicago because it was the only place I knew to go to after Kansas—my time there had come to an end. I know I can't stay here in Chicago forever, and Martin knows it too. He won't wrong his wife either." I swallowed hard. "If I hadn't made my mistake, I suppose Martin and I might have married eventually. But it's too late now."

"That depends on how you look at it." Elizabeth took my arm again as we climbed the slope out of the tunnel, blinking at the daylight, which seemed much brighter now. "He's a widower, don't forget."

"That's not funny." I lengthened my stride, but Elizabeth kept hold of my arm.

"I'm not trying to be funny. If he's innocent, and for your sake I hope he is, things may have changed considerably for you."

"Or they might be ruined forever."

"You don't believe he did it, do you?"

I wished I could break into a run to get away from Elizabeth's questions, which were altogether too like the ones my own mind was putting to itself. "No, I don't." I hoped I sounded certain. "I don't believe Martin could kill any woman, let alone his wife." That was the truth, and the realization that I really did think that made me feel better.

"But—and you'll forgive me for being frank—from the way Mr. Salazar is behaving, there's enough between the two of you to run the risk of making you the object of journalistic, and even detective, attention."

I took a deep breath before replying. "Yes. At least there's enough to give the impression that things are otherwise than they are. Martin's afraid that people will come to the conclusion that I'm his mistress—which I'm not."

"That's quite a mess, my dear." Elizabeth gave me a sympathetic glance before squinting shortsightedly at a street sign. "We'll need to turn east when we reach Hubbard Street. We're doubling back on ourselves a little, but the LaSalle Street Tunnel was the best way to go. And Mr. Salazar's quite right. Making any attempt to see Mr. Rutherford would draw attention to you most unpleasantly."

The fast walking had burned off some of the nervous energy that had made it impossible to stay in the hotel, and I was beginning to recover my senses. "You're correct, of course, and for his sake I won't try to see him. But—"

"But you need to know. Very well, we'll pretend to be sightseers. There'll be plenty of those."

There were. A large crowd milled around the entrance of the huge courthouse building, a new-looking edifice of pale brick and stone with impressive rows of arched windows.

"I believe that's the jail behind the courthouse," Elizabeth said into my ear. "He'll be in one building or the other. Try not to look too anxious. Pretend you're here out of curiosity."

She held my arm tight, forcing me to walk at a slow, ambling pace. Most of the people in the crowd wore dingy clothing, but here and there was a well-dressed lady or gentleman. Elizabeth kept well away from them. A large party of men with notebooks in their hands represented the gentlemen of the press. Not far away from them, a group of unpleasant-looking men stood silently watching the entrances to the buildings.

"See them?" A man standing near us nudged his wife, pointing to the silent men. "There's trouble."

"What kind of trouble? Harry, my feet hurt. Do we have to stay here?"

"I don't suppose there'll be much to see. Unless they bring him outside—that lot look like they'll tear him to pieces." The man called Harry nodded toward the group of men. "They do that on the frontier, I've heard. Grab the guilty parties and string 'em up—no need to bother with the judge."

"He's safer inside, then." The woman gave a short, neighing laugh. "Just shows you, doesn't it? These rich men aren't so different."

"Safer, all right. They search everyone who enters the jail, right down to the skin. Women too. And you have to write down who you are and what your business is."

The woman shuddered. "Fancy searching women. That's disgusting."

"Stands to reason." Harry chewed on one end of his mustache. "A woman might have a bomb or a metal file hidden in her drawers."

That remark made his wife break out into high, nervous laughter. The two of them moved away to get a better look at the courthouse, leaving me feeling thoroughly sick.

"We'd better go," Elizabeth said into my ear.

"Five more minutes." I stared at the jail building, wondering if Martin was somewhere in there looking out of one of the windows. Or was he in a windowless cell? It was horrible not knowing what was happening. I knew I should leave, but I couldn't tear my eyes away from where Martin must be, undergoing heaven only knew what indignities and discomforts.

"Your best hope is Mr. Salazar." Elizabeth tugged at my sleeve. "He can legitimately gain access to Mr. Rutherford, can't he? He was quite right, you can't stay here. In fact, there's almost nothing you can do."

There wasn't. All coming to the jail had done for me was demonstrate the futility of my situation. I couldn't help Martin in any way, and my impulsivity might indeed harm his interests. *Cherchez la femme*—if the police found out that Martin was in love with me, wouldn't that provide a clear motive for murder? The best thing I could do for Martin was to behave as if nothing had happened.

"Let's go away." Defeated, I turned my back on the massive building, feeling my shoulders slump. We had walked almost all day, and my feet were beginning to ache. I was hollow inside—quite literally, as it was several hours since I'd eaten.

"If Sarah's illegitimate," Elizabeth began after we'd walked in silence for several minutes, "you'd better not put her into a school. Some kind of nurse-maid or governess for her might be a good idea though. You already have plenty to think about."

I nodded, knowing she meant it kindly, but despair surged through me. I could hardly leave Chicago now, with Martin in jail. But staying in Chicago would mean staying in the shadows for the time being, at least until I knew what was going to happen. The more people I met, the more I would have to explain myself, so society was effectively barred to me. Besides, society was full of sharp-eyed, skeptical Mrs. Parnells, wasn't it? I would have to tread very carefully.

And yet none of that mattered compared to the enormity of Martin's situation. He was in jail—I couldn't imagine what that was like. And Lucetta, the bejeweled, beautiful obstacle to our happiness, had by somebody's hand been transformed into a mutilated corpse. At that moment, the future looked blacker than I'd ever known it to look.

ELEVEN

By the time Elizabeth and I walked into the lobby of the Palmer House, I ached from head to toe. I must have been holding my neck, shoulders, and back stiffly during my rapid, impatient walk to the courthouse, and now they throbbed in pain. My impulsiveness had gotten me precisely nowhere and could have harmed Martin. Why hadn't I listened to his wishes?

The sight that greeted us as we walked in through the Ladies' Entrance was not cheering. Mrs. Parnell was ensconced in an armchair strategically placed so that she could see whomever passed through the door. She rose to her feet as she saw us.

"Oh, glory," I heard Elizabeth murmur behind me. And then, in a louder voice, "Hello, Mother."

Mrs. Parnell's smile was frosty. "I was looking all over for you, dear. I brought Mrs. Balke-Stockman to see you since you'd been quite certain you'd be back by four. May I point out that it is now six o'clock, that you have been walking around Chicago in the near dark, and that by the time you've dressed for dinner, we'll be quite late? I had to apologize profusely to Mrs.

Balke-Stockman, who got quite the wrong impression of you, and that's a pity because her son is somebody you definitely should meet."

"It's my fault," I said hastily. "I made Elizabeth come with me on a fool's errand. I'm terribly sorry." Knowing Mrs. Parnell was already on the *qui vive* over my lack of a husband and now had even more reason to disapprove of me made me feel like I was a small child again, waiting for Mama's housekeeper, Bet, to scold me over some misdemeanor.

Mrs. Parnell turned her attention to me, and her blue glare actually softened a little. "You look quite done in, Mrs. Lillington. I accept your apology. I've heard the terrible news about your friends, the Rutherfords."

"Yes. Thank you. I must dress for dinner too." I turned to Elizabeth and gave her arm a squeeze. "I'm sorry. It was stupid of me to think only of myself."

"Oh, I daresay I'll survive," Elizabeth said, smiling. "And Mother, I *have* met Augustus Balke-Stockman, remember? He was that fat boy with the dirty neck who dropped his ice cream on my skirts at Grace's coming-out party. He's quite horrid. And you don't even like the Balke-Stockmans. You said once that Mrs. Balke-Stockman found fault with everything."

Mrs. Parnell's stern gaze wavered a little, and the edges of her mouth twitched, but she held firm. "Time to dress for dinner, Elizabeth," she insisted.

Knowing that Tess and Sarah would be waiting for me, I made a few more conventional remarks and fled to our rooms. I wondered if I would find Tess asleep, but she was very much awake—and in a bad mood.

"I'm awful cross with you," was her opening salvo. "Alice told me about Mrs. Rutherford and about Martin being taken to jail. Why did I have to hear it from Alice and not from *you*?" Her face crumpled.

I sat down in the nearest chair, heedless of my dress, feeling that if I didn't rest I would simply fall over. I looked up at Tess, who was sobbing angrily.

"You're always doing this to me," she said before I could formulate a reply. "You treat me like a child, as if I'm not worthy of knowing your secrets. I'm Martin's friend too, remember? He said I was his friend. I don't even know where you went, but I suppose it had something to do with Martin. And you took Miss Parnell, and not *me*." She stamped a foot down hard on the carpet.

"I'm sorry." I reflected that I was spending the whole of the dinner-hour apologizing. "But it was Sarah I didn't want to know—"

"I'm not going to listen to you," Tess said, her chin sticking out. "I asked

Alice to order me a carriage for tomorrow at ten, and I'm going to spend the day with my family. And speaking of Sarah, you're going to have to look after your own child for a change and not leave her with me whenever you're off doing something important with friends who aren't *imbeciles*."

"I've *never* called you an im—"

"But you *treat* me like one." Tess was positively yelling. "I should have been the *first* person you told about Martin, not the last." She took off her glasses and dragged her handkerchief over her eyes and mouth. "And now I'm going to bed because I've about had enough of you. I had Alice bring us up some sandwiches, so we've both eaten, and Sarah's already asleep. You're going to have to shift for yourself for dinner, and see how you like it."

She stalked off toward her bedroom. She didn't slam the door, no doubt for fear of waking Sarah, but the glare she gave me as she turned to close it told me she'd have liked to.

I put my face in my hands, but I was too exhausted to cry. It occurred to me that this should have been the day I saw Martin again. I didn't know when he had returned, but if he'd been carrying my letters, he had clearly wanted to communicate with me in some way. In my mind's eye I reimagined our arrival at Rutherford's, with its doors flung wide open, brightly lit and full of women. Martin would have greeted me, and we would have met as friends—but I would have seen by the warmth in his eyes that he loved me. He would have shown me around his store, and I would have enjoyed his pride in his creation and showered him with admiring remarks. We would have sat down together and had tea. Sarah would have climbed on Martin's lap, and Tess would have laughed at his jokes and beamed at him in the way she always did.

I jerked upright, realizing that my daydream of happiness was threatening to become an actual dream as I drifted off into the merciful release of sleep. But I couldn't risk Sarah waking up and finding our bedroom empty and me asleep in an armchair, fully dressed. Groaning, I heaved myself to my feet and lurched unsteadily toward the bell. The day was ruined—gone—broken—and I seemed to have injured everyone around me, but I would start again tomorrow.

TWELVE

It was Alice who woke me the next day, to inform me that it was twenty minutes to ten and that Miss O'Dugan had already gone downstairs to wait for her carriage. She had dressed Sarah, and when the two of them had returned from breakfast, she had "popped in" again. Now, she told me, Sarah was playing with her marbles.

"But I won't be able to come in and out all day, Madam," she continued. "I have other duties to perform as well as taking care of you, you see. If you'll pardon me for saying so, I think your little girl needs a nursemaid."

"Or a governess, perhaps?" I teased the lace out of my left cuff so that it fell onto my forearm properly. "She's keen on learning."

Alice paused, hairbrush in hand. "She's still very small—but I suppose you could find a woman who's happy to work with such a young child and doesn't mind taking on tasks such as helping her dress. She's an independent wee thing, anyway. She buttoned her boots almost all the way up to the top and only asked me for help with the last two or three." She rolled a section of my hair into place with a deft movement and pinned it.

"I may have to hire someone if Miss O'Dugan spends more time with her family." I closed my eyes for a moment, trying to think of the steps I'd need to take to find some help with Sarah—without reinforcing Tess's impression that she had become surplus to requirements. But all I could see in my mind's eye was Martin. What kind of night had he spent?

We both turned our heads as a knock sounded on the outer door of the suite, and Alice laid down the brush. "I'll get it." She hurried out of my bedroom, and I heard her addressing a remark to Sarah as she passed through the parlor. She returned a few moments later.

"The gentleman from Briggs Bank sends his compliments, Madam, and would you please read his note?" She handed me a folded piece of paper.

"Momma, are you awake now? Tess said not to disturb you until you were dressed and in a good temper." Sarah appeared at the door, looking hesitant.

I took the piece of paper with one hand and held out the other arm to Sarah, who laid her head against my shoulder and presented her forehead to be kissed. "I'm feeling much better," I told her. "I was so busy yesterday that I became very tired, that's all."

Sarah pushed her brow more firmly into my shoulder and held up a marble for my inspection. The small ceramic sphere was glazed in an interesting pattern of yellow, blue, and white blotches.

"It's very pretty." I kissed her again. "You are being careful not to leave them anyplace where you or someone else will step on them, aren't you?"

"Will they break if we step on them?" Sarah looked interested, as if she'd like to try the experiment.

"They may not break, but they'll probably chip. And you know, if someone steps on several at once, their feet will go right out from under them, and they'll land with a bang."

"I mostly play with them in the corner under the funny painting of the lady with a dog." Sarah looked thoughtful.

"That should be all right because nobody walks back there. But do put them back in their box when you're done, won't you? And don't leave any where people walk."

"What are we doing today?" Sarah asked. "Are we going to the park?"

I was unfolding the piece of paper as she spoke and now looked up at Alice. "Tell the messenger I'll be down in five minutes." And then to Sarah: "I have to go downstairs and see the nice gentleman from the bank. You'll have to come with me because Tess isn't here. Can you read your book while I talk?"

"May I do writing? I have my new paper, remember."

A few moments' negotiations ended with my fabricating a small book by folding, refolding, and then cutting a sheet of Sarah's paper to make the leaves, then using a piece of string to tie them together at the fold. While I did this, Alice expertly finished my hair, then ordered me to stand while she inspected my dress.

It was ten minutes later when we arrived at the Grand Parlor to be greeted by the sight of Mr. Fletcher and Elizabeth seated together in a tête-à-tête. They were so absorbed in each other that they didn't notice me until I stood directly in front of them and coughed. Mr. Fletcher stood up immediately. Elizabeth, fetchingly attired in a dress the exact color of her bright blue eyes, rose slowly and graciously to her feet and placed a hand on my arm.

"I seem to be monopolizing your visitor, Nell. We've discovered a shared interest in the poems of Arthur Rimbaud." Elizabeth grinned. "Do you know him? He leads a deliciously ill-regulated life, I've heard."

"I have little interest in poetry, I regret to say. How are you, Mr. Fletcher?" I shook the young man's hand.

"I'll leave you to your business discussions." Elizabeth glanced at Mr. Fletcher and blushed charmingly, bringing a look of open admiration to his face. And yet there was a certain reserve in his manner that told me that, although he liked her, he was not the sort of man to rush headlong into wooing.

"Oh, and I should tell you before I go," Elizabeth said, "that Mother's being quite understanding—about *everything*." She squeezed my arm. "If there's one thing you should know about my mother, it's that her bark is worse than her bite." Nodding at Mr. Fletcher, she swept away, the train of her bright blue gown contrasting sharply with the muted tones of the carpet.

I introduced Sarah to Mr. Fletcher, who went down on one knee so that his face was level with Sarah's and asked her a series of questions about her impressions of Chicago. Within five minutes, Sarah was chatting with him nonstop about every toy, dress, hat, and pair of boots she owned.

"You may get more than you wished for, encouraging her to rattle on like that." I smiled at my daughter.

"Nonsense." Mr. Fletcher rose easily to his feet and looked down at Sarah. "I've never believed that children shouldn't be heard. And in my job, I hardly see any, so I'm taking advantage of the opportunity. What are you going to do while I talk to your mother about boring old figures?" he asked her.

"I'm going to write a dictionary," said Sarah gravely, holding up my improvised book and only slightly stumbling over the long word. "With illustrations." Her missing teeth made her lisp the last word charmingly.

"Well, you're going to need to sit at a proper table." A large round table had just been vacated by an elderly lady in a bath chair, wheeled away by a disdainful attendant. Mr. Fletcher led Sarah to it and helped her into a chair, assisted her in arranging her pencils, and returned to where we were sitting.

"You're very kind," I said. "I'm sure you're exceeding the obligations of your job."

He smiled. "I have nieces and nephews. And my job is to be at the beck and call of our wealthier clients—and you are a woman of some means, Mrs. Lillington. Moreover, Mr. Rutherford instructed us that you were to be given every facility." His eyes held mine for a moment, his expression sympathetic. "I'm so terribly sorry about the tragedy at Rutherford's," he said, dropping his voice. "For what it's worth, I don't believe for a moment that Mr. Rutherford had any involvement in his wife's death. None of us do."

"Neither do I." I cleared my throat against the rise of emotion, and we were both silent. Not an awkward silence though. Mr. Fletcher may have been young, but there was nothing awkward about him. His manner was easy and confident without being impertinent.

"I am here," he continued after a few moments, "to give you a more thorough picture of how your capital is invested. I would like to put some questions to you about how you wish those investments to proceed in Mr. Rutherford's absence. He has been in regular communication with us and no doubt will be again, but we feel it would be imprudent not to do everything we can to get specific instructions."

"Very well," I replied. "Will you be able to explain to me how the overall sum is shared between myself and Miss O'Dugan? The question has arisen, and I would like to have a better idea of what she owns."

"That will be no difficulty."

The next forty minutes were absorbed by a detailed discussion, held in low voices and with occasional reference to a notebook in which Mr. Fletcher had noted the important points of my investments in a similar manner to the one Martin employed. I was a little daunted at the outset, but Mr. Fletcher's explanations were clear. He put questions to me in a way that required common sense rather than arcane financial knowledge to answer. He then patiently sat through Sarah's explanation of her dictionary, which consisted of words she knew how to write followed by a page of squiggles which represented the definition, and a drawing that generally resembled nothing at all.

I spent the rest of the day alone with Sarah. This was such a delight, in so many ways, that I was sorry I couldn't wholeheartedly enter into her little world. But my mind couldn't help straying to Martin, and I wondered how I could summon Mr. Salazar to the hotel without drawing attention to myself.

I was able to look at the newspapers in the reading room later that afternoon while Sarah looked at a picture book, but the accounts were contradictory. Martin had been found with a knife in his hand; or prostrate with grief, sobbing above his wife's butchered body; or cold and unemotional when questioned by the police.

The facts that I gleaned by noting when they appeared in all of the reports were that he had returned from Saint Louis, where he had been meeting with his business partner, Mr. Fassbinder, on Tuesday morning. Lucetta had been waiting for him for some time in a large room on the fourth floor that held the props for window-dressing. This odd location was frequently remarked upon, but no clear explanation was given. Martin had arrived and was told of his wife's presence in the building. He had spent a few minutes sorting through his mail, had visited the washroom, and had proceeded upstairs. That was the point at which accounts had become confused and unclear except for one detail—the blood. There had been a great deal of blood.

By the time we went up to our rooms to dress for dinner, the exhaustion of the previous day was threatening to creep back. Alice had finished with me and taken her leave when Tess walked in, looking no less tired than I felt. We stared at each other, a little wary, but I felt it was incumbent upon me to make the first move.

"Did you have a pleasant day?" That seemed like a safe enough question.

Tess hesitated for a moment before speaking. "I'm sorry I was cross with you, Nell."

I swallowed hard. "I'm sorry I didn't confide in you. I was beside my-self—and somehow the opportunity to speak with you without Sarah hearing passed me by."

I stood up and went to Tess, embracing her warmly. She returned the hug. "You look very pretty." She touched the lace on my dress.

I sniffed back a threatening tear. "Shall I call Alice back to help you dress? You could wear the pale lilac-and-white dinner dress you haven't worn yet."

"Would you help me?" Tess gave a tentative half smile. "I'd rather you did."

She emerged from the bathroom a few minutes later smelling of lavender soap, and I helped her into her dress and redid her fine, flyaway hair. Sarah emerged from our bedroom when she heard the running water in the bath-room and greeted Tess with joy before returning to her game.

"I'm still a little cross with you." Tess looked at me over her spectacles as I pinned an arrangement of feathers and flowers onto her topknot.

"I'm sorry to hear that." I tried to sound neutral. "If there's anything I can do to make you less cross with me, please let me know."

Tess was silent while I finished dressing her hair. "You could let me know how much money I have," she said eventually.

I had been half expecting her question, and had the figures to hand thanks to my morning's work with Mr. Fletcher.

"You have just over three thousand dollars," I said. "That's a great deal of money, but not enough income to live the way we do. At the moment, it's producing around one hundred and fifty dollars a year, which is added back to the capital. I've not touched it for over two years since I had plenty enough for our joint expenses in Kansas."

Tess looked blank, as I'd expected she would. She loved her ledgers but had no real grasp of the value of money. "I suppose Mary would know if that was enough," she said.

"Enough for what?"

"Mary says I should go and live with them. She needs help with her boys, and she says if I have money, they could find a bigger house and give Ma and Da more comforts. Only I'll have to be a Catholic because Ma will want me to go to church with them and she won't step foot in a Protestant church." Tess gave me a level stare. "Mary says I should be with my real family because you don't need me anymore. They're grateful for the help you gave me, but I earned my money fair and square, and I should be able to do what I want with it. Mary says."

"Of course I need you." I was sure I sounded as dismayed as I felt.

"But we don't work together anymore," Tess said. "I liked it at the seminary when we were sewing things for the boys, and you did some work and I did other work. And sometimes I helped with your dresses, although you did most of that."

"I liked it too." I was caught somewhere between exasperation and sorrow and barely knew how to express what was in my heart. The notion that Tess might want to leave me—leave *us*—had never crossed my mind before coming to Chicago. Since I had taken her from the Poor Farm to live with us, we had depended on each other. She needed my ability to order our lives and supervise her work while I depended on her for help with that work and raising Sarah.

"What about Sarah?" I asked. "You'd be leaving her too, and you're a second mother to her. Doesn't she need you?" I had dropped my voice—we were in Tess's bedroom, and I was fairly sure Sarah couldn't hear us, but her young ears were sharp.

The corners of Tess's mouth turned down. "I'd miss Sary," she admitted. "But Sary's a little girl now, and when she gets bigger, she may not need me either. Although she's not as much work as Mary's boys. They're awful noisy. They run up and down the stairs until Mary tells them to go outside and not show their faces till dinner. And one of them will be sure to rip something or cut their arms or legs or get a great bruise on their head. They're little imps, so they are."

In other circumstances, I might have been amused at Tess's imitation of her family's slight brogue. But there was nothing amusing about the prospect of Tess leaving us. Quite apart from anything else, I would be worried for her health if she were to spend her days looking after Mary's house and children—Tess tired easily. And yet the enforced idleness of a lady didn't suit her either, no more than it suited me. No wonder we were at odds with each other. And far more than I did, Tess needed stability and a place to belong.

"Must you make a decision just yet?" I asked.

"Oh no, not at all." Tess suddenly sounded far more like her usual self. "I told Mary and Aileen that I would have to think very carefully." She frowned. "And I don't really want to have to be a Catholic. I like worshipping God the way I do already."

"Please don't be hasty. You're the best friend I have in the world. Elizabeth isn't going to replace you." I found the reticule I had sewn to match Tess's dress and handed it to her with a glance at the small clock on her bedroom mantelpiece. "We'd better go down to dinner. I'll fetch Sarah."

The corners of Tess's mouth compressed into an expression that was half-rueful, half-apologetic. "I'll get her," she said. "And I'll make sure she uses the lavatory and washes her hands and face again before she goes downstairs."

She walked to the door and then looked at me over her shoulder.

"You don't have to feel bad about asking me to look after Sary. I was cross with you when I said that."

I heard her call for Sarah, and I crossed to her mirror to make sure my hair was in place. Tess had said I looked very pretty. Well, I had to admit, Alice was able to achieve a far more elegant effect with my hair than I ever could. She had tamed my rebellious curls into smooth reddish-bronze waves, caught up at the back by a large enameled comb onto which she had attached pale green silk flowers to match my dress. A cascade of silken ringlets fell from the comb down below my shoulders, gleaming with vitality. For the first time in my life, I rather liked my hair.

But the moment of vanity—of normal thought—passed as quickly as it came, and the eyes reflected back to me by the mirror were shadowed. What did my hair matter if Martin couldn't see it?

Mr. Fletcher's visit had been prompted by the possibility that Martin might not be able to oversee my finances. The implications of his assumption were only gradually dawning on me. I had arrived in Chicago torn by the desire to be with Martin and the necessity of leaving him, but at least the future had seemed full of possibilities. Now I felt rudderless, a small boat in a stormy sea, and I had absolutely no idea what to do.

THIRTEEN

"So you've seen Rutherford's at last." Elizabeth nodded her thanks to the smartly uniformed waitress. We were sitting in Rutherford's tea room, a harmonious, intimate space of soothing blues and greens that appeared to be highly popular with a very elegant set of ladies. There were gentlemen too, in morning suits and silk hats, and that surprised me. I said so to Elizabeth.

"Men are not entirely banished from Rutherford's." Dimples appeared in Elizabeth's rounded cheeks. "They are positively encouraged to linger while their wives roam the store. Do you see that door over there? It leads to a short corridor with a thick baize door at the end. Beyond that is a smoking room and gentleman's retiring room. The whole thing is arranged so that not one wisp of smoke finds its way into the store itself. Did you know that Mr. Rutherford will not employ clerks who smoke because the odor lingers on their fingers?"

"I hadn't known that." I smiled. "But it sounds like Martin. He's not given to vices."

A pang much like grief went through me, as it so often did when I spoke or thought of Martin's life as it had been before Lucetta's murder. He had been in prison for five days, and I had heard nothing of him. The papers had report-ed that Lucetta's body had been released into her family's care. She would be buried in a family plot in Wilmette, next to the mother who had died when Lucetta was a child. After my futile attempt to do something on the day of Martin's arrest, I was determined to follow his instructions and keep away, but I was in a ferment of worry and impatience. To be sitting here, in his store, sipping coffee and pretending to be unconcerned—

"Stop that." Elizabeth's voice broke in on my thoughts. "He's probably safer in jail than he would be out here anyway. I've been hearing rumors about the Gambarelli brothers over the last couple of days—"

"What kind of rumors?" My heart gave a lurch.

"They have a reputation," Elizabeth said carefully, her eyes on my face, "for being involved somehow in the underworld. People are afraid of them."

"Afraid? You don't think they could have killed Mrs. Rutherford, do you?" As soon as I said it, I knew it was a ridiculous idea. Besides, hadn't we been talking to Alessandro Gambarelli at just about the very moment Lucetta was killed? The thought made me shudder.

"By all accounts, every man in the Gambarelli family worshipped at Mrs. Rutherford's feet," said Elizabeth. "If anything, I think her killer should be most afraid. They're Sicilian after all, and unless it's a myth that their race pursues vengeance to their last breath . . ." She shrugged expressively.

I didn't at all like what she was suggesting. "You don't mean that Martin would have cause to fear his brothers-in-law?"

"I mean that if Mr. Rutherford *did* murder his wife, hanging would be a better end."

I pushed back the small chair on which I'd been sitting so hard that it fell backward as I rose to my feet. "This conversation is at an end," I said icily. "And our acquaintance too—"

"Nell." Elizabeth held up her hands. "This isn't my opinion I'm recount-ing to you, it's the world's. I thought it would be better for you to hear it from me, and you should know I'm not good at hiding things."

"Thank you," I said automatically to the gentleman behind me who had picked up my chair. "Elizabeth, a little tact—"

"Given the circumstances," said a familiar voice behind me. "I beg your pardon for intruding, Mrs. Lillington."

It was, of all people, Mr. Fletcher of Briggs Bank.

I probably sounded as surprised as I felt. "I wouldn't have expected to see you here," I said. Indeed, I'd gained the impression that Mr. Fletcher was a bachelor.

"*I* would have," said Elizabeth. "I invited him. Mr. Fletcher, would you be a dear and walk around a little while I finish my conversation with Mrs. Lillington?"

Mr. Fletcher complied with a wry smile, and as soon as he had left the tearoom, I rounded on Elizabeth.

"You invited him here? Elizabeth, are you mad? One does not invite—"

Elizabeth's cheeks dimpled. "Oh, Nell, you're not going to be a bore, are you? It's perfectly delicious to do something shocking. Mr. Fletcher *was* shocked, but I explained I would be in the company of a respectable widow—that's you, leaving aside the unrespectable bits, which are nobody's business, really—who was well enough acquainted with him to make our meeting quite acceptable."

"If you were going to cast me in the role of go-between, you might have asked me first," I said. "I would have said no. Couldn't you have thought of a way to meet Mr. Fletcher that didn't involve me?"

"To be honest, no," said Elizabeth. "I did give the matter quite a lot of consideration."

I put a hand to my forehead. "What will he think of me?"

"Nothing at all," replied Elizabeth. "He knows perfectly well this is my idea. Are you appalled?"

"I am, rather. I could see that you liked Mr. Fletcher, but I didn't imagine you'd gone so far as to see him as a prospective husband."

"Who said anything about marriage?"

❧

It took some considerable persuasion on Elizabeth's part for me to do what she wanted, which was to wait until Mr. Fletcher returned and then make an excuse to leave the two of them together for a few minutes. Had it not been such a public place, I would never have complied, and I said so after I'd returned to our table and Mr. Fletcher had taken his leave.

"It's fortunate for you that he's clearly the steady type," I said. "Do you think he was fooled by your subterfuge?"

"I don't think he's fooled by anything. That's why I like him—he has such an air of confidence combined with modesty. Confident men are usually arrogant, and modest men are usually timid. Mr. Fletcher is neither arrogant nor timid."

"And what on earth did you mean, that you weren't thinking of marriage?" I felt I was beginning to sound like Mrs. Parnell, but in truth, Elizabeth's carelessness of her reputation worried me. I had been like that myself once, so I had good reason to be worried.

"I'm thinking of seduction." Elizabeth leaned in close to me and dropped her voice to a whisper. "If one is to espouse a principle, one must be prepared to carry it out. And I have thoroughly espoused the principles of Free Love."

"Merciful heaven." I closed my eyes and tipped my head back, dumbfounded. "You're thinking of enticing him—Elizabeth, supposing there's a child? Believe me, much as I love Sarah, I don't recommend the consequences of bearing a child out of wedlock. You'll be forsaking the company of respectable people—of your own class—your family—forever."

"*You're* still received by respectable people," said Elizabeth shortly. "Besides, there are ways to avoid children. My sister has sent me her useful little book."

"For heaven's sake—"

"I really don't see why you're so against the idea," Elizabeth said. "I gained the distinct impression that you were no more keen to put yourself into the hands of a man, financially and practically speaking, than I was."

"Look." I leaned forward in my chair. "You have no idea just how you put yourself into people's power by making them—well, morally superior to you. Because of Sarah, because of what I did, I almost ended up in the clutches of a man who would have held me in utter bondage for the rest of my life. Who would probably have sent Sarah and Tess away from me. Who offered me respectability in return for—well, just about everything I had. But I have a feeling I wouldn't have liked it. Why would you do something that might make you miserable for the sake of a principle?"

"Do you know how many mistresses there are in this town?" asked Elizabeth, her cheeks red. "Hundreds, probably thousands. There's barely any rich man in Chicago who doesn't have some kind of rumor attached to him. And behind every one of those men is a woman who has both love and freedom."

"But is it freedom? If I were sure of that, I'd choose it myself."

"I *am* sure. Free love is the future of mankind, Nell, and if you can't see it, I can. It is my fixed intention to embark on the seduction of Mr. Fletcher, and you can't dissuade me."

༭

By the time Elizabeth and I gathered up our possessions and made our way to the door of the tearoom, my head was spinning. I understood one thing—Elizabeth was every bit as stubborn as I was despite her peaches-and-cream prettiness and open, insouciant way of speaking. At least, she was as stubborn as I'd been at sixteen, before I'd had Sarah and Tess to think of. Those responsibilities had taught me that my actions had consequences, often unintended. I had learned that circumspection, if boring, was sometimes necessary to avoid disaster.

My own resolve was tested almost straightaway. As Elizabeth and I proceeded toward the main entrance, I spotted Mr. Salazar making his way toward us. My heart soared—this was exactly the person I'd been waiting to see. I had forced myself to remain discreet with regard to Martin, but the effort was killing me. If I didn't have word of him soon, I'd not be able to stop myself from banging on the courtroom doors. Here, at least, was someone I could consult.

"May I have a few minutes of your time?" Mr. Salazar asked.

I looked at Elizabeth, who grinned. "It's perfectly acceptable for a lady to walk one block down State Street without a chaperone, and I will avail myself of that glorious opportunity. You will have to do the same, Nell."

Mr. Salazar waited until Elizabeth had passed through the entrance doors before speaking. "Would you like to visit the silk department?" he asked formally.

"I would indeed." Elizabeth and I had made a brief tour of Rutherford's sales floors, and I was longing to revisit them. I knew that there was far more to see. Several rooms were available to welcome women who had progressed beyond the mere idea to the reality of getting a dress made. Elizabeth said there were even parlors large enough to receive a whole group of women who could sit and encourage each other into ever greater excesses of expenditure, fueled by bonbons and ratafia if they wished.

The silk department was at the center of the store—a huge, hexagonal room of simple white marble with a frieze that incorporated the Rutherford's peacock feather motif. Bolts of silk were arranged by hue and weave, from the finest pale gauzes to heavy, sumptuous raw silk dyed in the colors of jewels—sapphire, emerald, ruby, and some shades not encountered in nature but somehow not at all gaudy. The effect was rich and overwhelming without losing one iota of elegance. In the center of the hexagon, a pedestal spilled out silks of all colors, which should have clashed but didn't. The effect was to excite the eye rather than offend it, and I said so to Mr. Salazar.

"Martin has built something quite extraordinary." I looked toward the ceiling, where a row of windows set high up in the towering walls allowed in the sunlight without letting it touch the silks.

"I'm glad you can see it. The designs of many of the rooms were Martin's ideas—he relishes the possibilities of architecture."

"I'm not sure if I know the man who built all this." It was a feeling that had been growing on me all day. I knew Martin's past, I knew him as a friend, and I knew him as the love of my life. But looking at this incredible edifice, with its busy clerks, its skillful shopgirls, its promises of a wardrobe to suit any woman, its simple motto "Dress well"—this was a bolder and more confident Martin than anything I had known. "I'm not sure if I know this side of him at all."

"The showman? The palace-builder? The manufacturer of dreams?" Mr. Salazar smiled at me. "Perhaps you don't. I'm not sure if Martin knew the extent of his abilities until he began putting them to the test."

"That was what he wanted to do." I remembered him telling me back in Victory, before I left for Kansas, that he aspired to manliness, to risking all that he had in pursuit of his venture. He had done it—and was it to be taken from him?

"Did you see . . . Mrs. Rutherford?" Somewhere in the building above our heads was the place where Lucetta had lain. When I had found the bodies of Johanna Mauer and her baby at the Poor Farm, there had been a stain like a shadow on the floor where they had lain for so long. Even after the floor was cleaned, the shadow worked its way up again. And now Martin's marble palace also had a shadow on it, a history hidden behind a closed door, but never to be forgotten.

"I did."

Something in Mr. Salazar's tone of voice made me look up at him. "How bad was it?"

"Bad enough. I served in the infantry during the war, and I've seen my fair share of butchery." He looked sideways at me. "But I've never seen carnage dressed in silks and lace. She fought, Mrs. Lillington. Hard, and over a period of several minutes' duration, if I'm any judge. She saw her death coming— she must have felt her life flowing out of her, even as she fought for it." He shook his head. "No rational man could have thought Martin had done that if he'd seen the blood. There was blood only on Martin's hands, and on the knees of his trousers where he'd knelt down. If he'd killed her, he would have been covered in it."

"But then they must free him," I exclaimed. "As you say, it's not rational to do otherwise."

"His attorneys are requesting that he be released to the Grand Pacific Hotel, where he has rooms, even if he remains under arrest." Mr. Salazar shrugged his shoulders. "The Gambarellis are pushing for a bond so high that even Martin couldn't pay it, and against all reason, the judge and grand jury appear to be leaning in that direction. Which means, of course, that there's corruption."

"You mean that the judge and jury have been bought?"

"Either that or some threat has been made against them." Mr. Salazar sighed. "This is Chicago, Mrs. Lillington. Criminals go free, and the innocent pay for crimes they didn't commit. It happens so often that it's considered a normal occurrence. Have you noticed how the newspapers are vague about the details of the court procedure and the indictment? They have no doubt been bought too, or they're afraid to criticize the proceedings too openly."

"I had no idea that this was happening," I whispered. "How are Martin's spirits?"

"Better than I'd hoped." Mr. Salazar laid a hand briefly on my arm. "He is, in several ways, numb with the shock of it all, but he copes by concentrating on practical matters. He asked me today about—" He stopped with a quirk of the mouth that might have been a wince. "I'm sorry, that's not a subject I should even have thought of introducing."

"Don't spare me, please," I said. "Nothing you can tell me can be worse than my imagination. And I need to know how he lives. What he eats. What he says. I torture myself hourly, picturing it all."

"All I can tell you is what I've gleaned from my visits, but yes, I understand." I had barely noticed where Mr. Salazar had been leading me as we spoke but now found that we were in a room furnished with a grouping of chairs arranged in front of a curtain. Potted palms gave it an intimate air. Mr. Salazar motioned for me to sit down in one of the chairs and seated himself in another. For a moment, he said nothing, and I realized he was trying to bring some order to his thoughts so that he could give me the details I so desperately wanted.

"In the county jail," he began, "they bring all the men who have visitors into one large room and bring the visitors to the other side of the bars. So all of our conversations have taken place in public, amid the pandemonium of the visiting cell, and have consequently lacked—well, a certain depth, I suppose. But I have also spoken with his attorneys and the police detectives. I have been to speak with the Pinkerton Detective Agency to see what light they can shed on the progress of such a case and if there is anything we can do privately." He smiled. "That's why I haven't been to see you, and I apologize for making you wait. I don't want to leave Martin in the county jail for any longer than I possibly can."

I nodded. "I understand," I said. "But please give me every tiny detail. It's costing me a great deal to pretend to live my life while he's behind bars."

"All right." Mr. Salazar closed his heavy-lidded eyes and thought for a moment. "In purely practical, bodily terms, it's not as dreadful as you'd think. Martin told me that he generally has one cellmate, but who that is changes almost daily. This, I presume, is because their cases are proceeding in the normal fashion, and they don't have armies of lawyers to slow the process down. The food is beans and coffee." He grinned. "I lived on a similar regime at intervals during the war. It won't kill him, but he has asked me to bring in food when I visit. He is suffering from a lack of sleep brought about by his surroundings and, presumably, by everything that's happened. The first question he asked me, the first time I visited him, was whether I understood there should be no visitors. That means you. He visibly relaxed when I told him that the party most anxious to contact him fully understood the situation. I didn't tell him about your walk to the courthouse."

I sighed. "I admit that was stupid." Then my mind, roving over what he had said so far, fixed on one point. "What was it that Martin wanted to know, that you thought was too delicate a matter for me?" I stared at him steadily.

Mr. Salazar hesitated, then seemed to reach some kind of decision. "He was concerned about what was happening to Mrs. Rutherford's . . . remains. He was almost as fixated upon that question as he was on the matter of you staying away from him."

That was unexpected and left an unpleasant taste in my mouth. But why should it? I asked myself. Martin had a strong sense of what was proper, and the idea of Lucetta's body left splayed out on the floor amid her congealing blood must have been upsetting to him. And he didn't hate her, whatever she had done to him—I knew that somehow.

"She's already been buried, hasn't she?" I asked.

"She has. Her corpse was taken to the Cook County morgue, presumably so that the police detectives could examine it again. The cause of death was clear, of course, but there might have been some indications to help with the identification of the murderer." He frowned. "Except that the Gambarellis, by all accounts, put considerable pressure on the morgue to release her body for burial, and she has already been interred, as I gather you have read in the newspapers. The report of the forensic examination shows nothing that would not have been expected."

"Have you told Martin that?"

"Martin is kept informed by his attorneys of everything the police know," Mr. Salazar said quietly. "And of everything that is printed in the newspapers. When he was told of Mrs. Rutherford's burial, he simply said, 'Poor Lucetta.'"

The pang of something like distaste went through me again. But how could I expect Martin to disregard the burial of the woman he had married? It wouldn't have been like him. No doubt I was in the wrong, to let Martin's words of sympathy for his dead wife irk me. But they did irk me, all the same.

FOURTEEN

After another three futile days of worrying about Martin, I sought relief in my usual remedy—practical action. After all, I reasoned, if I couldn't control the progress of Martin's case, I could at least control my own circumstances to a certain degree.

It had occurred to me more than once that I was courting danger by remaining at the Palmer House. I thought I could trust Elizabeth and Mrs. Parnell to remain silent on the matter of my relationship with Martin, but what about Sarah and Tess? Inevitably, as our stay at the Palmer House lengthened, we were beginning to make acquaintances among the other guests. It was only a matter of time before the Rutherford case came up in a conversation. I was a bad dissembler myself, and Tess was worse—and it was ridiculous to expect a five-year-old child to remember what she should or shouldn't say.

And with so many emotions coursing through my body, I was beginning to wish I could endure my inner turmoil in a more private location. I said as much to Elizabeth.

"So move." Elizabeth shrugged. "Take a furnished house. You can find offers in the papers from people who are traveling and wish to rent out their house for the duration. You'll need references, of course, but Mr. Fletcher can supply a strong one. And I daresay Mother could be prevailed upon to issue her opinion that you're a good risk." She grinned. "People move all the time, you know. You wait till moving day, which is the first of May. I swear a full third of Chicago's citizens move house, like a great game of musical chairs."

I took her advice by spending an hour or two in the hotel's reading room searching the personal advertisements in the papers and sent off half a dozen letters of inquiry. I received three replies. Two were clearly unsuitable, but one looked promising. I saw no harm in taking it to Mrs. Parnell since she seemed to know half of Chicago. I knew nobody else in Chicago with such an extensive circle of acquaintances—except possibly Martin.

"Their name is Katzenmeier." I showed Mrs. Parnell the letter, which bore an address in Aldine Square. "They say they have to spend six months in Düsseldorf and would like someone to take on not only their house, but their cook and carriage driver. Both servants are on the elderly side and disinclined to change. I might have to hire other help for cleaning, of course." I caught Tess looking askance at me and added hastily, "Although I could think of no better housekeeper than Tess, if that's still her wish."

I had been careful to include Tess in my search for a house. Her visits to her family seemed to be settling down into a twice-weekly pattern, but she inevitably returned home in a state of discontent unusual for her. I could only imagine what Mary and Aileen might be saying about me. I had to admit the idea of enticing Tess to stay by fulfilling her long-held dream was also in my mind as I contemplated leaving the Palmer House. She would have something to do, but I would make sure her duties were not so onerous that her family could accuse me of taking advantage of her.

Mrs. Parnell smiled at Tess and tapped the letter with a fingernail. "The Katzenmeiers are related to the Krupp family—steel, you know. The address is hardly Prairie Avenue, but in the circumstances, that might be just as well." She then made it quite clear to what circumstances she referred by saying, "And where is little Sarah?"

"With Alice, our femme de chambre." I sighed. "She'll oblige with a little minding from time to time, but I also feel the need for some sort of nurse-maid-governess for Sarah."

It occurred to me that I was contemplating hiring rather a lot of staff all at once, but I could, after all, afford it. So I returned to the original point of our conversation by asking, "Where is Aldine Square?"

"Off Thirty-Ninth Street, or is it Thirty-Seventh? East of the stockyards, you'll understand, but well away from them in social terms. It's fashionable among socially prominent people with an industrial or professional background. It's quite new and has a pretty sort of park in the middle."

"Yes, they say so in their letter." I indicated the place with my finger. "I thought it would be excellent for Sarah, particularly if we had someone to take her there every day, even if Tess and I are busy." At what I could possibly be busy was beyond me at that moment, but I was going to have to do something other than moon about over Martin or I'd go mad.

"The Katzenmeiers say they will include the use of the carriage in the rent, but they've named no figure. Should I go prepared to make an offer? And what should it be?"

Mrs. Parnell tilted her head to one side, thinking. "Land prices have fallen shockingly in Chicago since the Panic of '73. They're still falling, and it can be very hard to find good tenants for any house over one hundred dollars a month. For a fashionable address, they'll be hoping to get over two hundred a month. So I suggest you offer them one hundred and ninety with the carriage thrown in. You'll have to pay for servants, food, fuel, and all the rest of it, but I doubt you'll come out worse than staying at the Palmer House—and you'll have far more room. I personally find a hotel more convenient, but then our family has dwindled to so small a number and will no doubt soon dwindle some more."

She gave Elizabeth a hopeful glance, to which Elizabeth returned an innocent, wide-eyed blue stare. She had hinted to me that her campaign to seduce Mr. Fletcher was ongoing, but she had not yet achieved success. Of course, success would be hard to achieve under her mother's watchful eye, and I wondered exactly what Elizabeth was up to.

I had come to a decision. "I'll write back to the Katzenmeiers today, asking to see the house. And I've already asked Alice about reputable agencies for finding the right sort of woman for Sarah. She recommended one agency in particular, and I intend to write to them too."

℃

It was surprising how easily matters fell into place once I took action. All three of us liked the house at Aldine Square. Although I fretted inwardly that it was so far away from Martin, I knew I had made a sound decision based on rationality rather than emotion. I shook the hands of Mr. and Mrs. Katzenmeier over a small glass of celebratory cordial while Tess and Sarah explored the park. We settled on two hundred and seven dollars and eighty cents a month, all-inclusive, with a gardener thrown in.

I thus took possession, figuratively speaking, of an Irish cook named Mrs. Abigail Power. Her dried-up appearance, with her black dress hanging off her bony shoulders, did not bespeak a great interest in food. Still, her pantry was immaculate, and what food she presented to me as evidence of her skill seemed well cooked. The Katzenmeiers introduced me to their—temporarily my—carriage driver, an elderly man called Arthur Nutt, whom the Katzenmeiers assured me had the strength of a young man when it came to his job.

And then I had a tremendous stroke of luck. Upon hearing of our plans to move, Alice, our femme de chambre, immediately offered herself as my lady's maid and a sort of assistant housekeeper for Tess. This would, as she pointed out, allow Tess to visit her family without throwing the management of the house into disorder. She promised to help me find a young and inexpensive maid-of-all-work to do any cleaning or other tasks that didn't fall under the purview of the other staff.

"It's a good thing Alice will be there to help me," said Tess, who had clearly not thought through the implications of taking on a job that usually required a near-constant presence in the house. "Mary says I should go stay with them for a while, to see how nice it is to be a family again."

I bit my lip. I was rather tired of hearing "Mary says." Moreover, this phrase was often followed by "Aileen says." What Aileen had to say was mostly on the theme of Tess receiving instruction from their parish priest. Mrs. O'Dugan was reportedly racked with guilt at having allowed Tess to be steered away from the Holy Roman Church. She would burst into tears on a regular basis and cry to heaven to bring Tess back into the fold, a performance that impressed Tess tremendously.

Personally, it didn't much bother me whether Tess was Catholic or Protestant except that this seemed to be another ploy to drive a wedge between me and Tess. The worst thing was that I sympathized with them to a certain degree. Perhaps they were, after all, just trying to give Tess that sense of belonging she so clearly craved.

On the other matter that kept me mercifully busy, I did not have the success that I'd had with Aldine Square. Sarah made it quite clear that she didn't like a single one of the candidates I interviewed for the post of nursemaid-governess, and there had been several. I gained the impression that times were even harder than I'd realized. The prospect of working for a widow with just one child, at the rate of pay suggested by the agency, was plainly an enticing one. I even went so far as to suspect the agency of suggesting overly generous wages. I was sure they realized I was without experience in the matter of domestics.

Without any helpful sign from Sarah, I had to rely entirely on my instincts. I chose an Englishwoman called Miss Patricia Baker. She was young—around my age—and able to talk intelligently on a wide variety of subjects. Her youth recommended itself to me, in light of the number of middle-aged women with very decided views I saw. I didn't want to end up being dominated by the hired help. And I thought it would be more amusing for Sarah to be with someone same age as her mother. Besides, I could never resist an English accent. I was sure Sarah would grow to like Miss Baker over time.

With these arrangements completed, I allowed myself to feel that I had done my best for my small family in terms of settling down into our new life in Chicago. All I had to do was get my family to agree with me on that point.

FIFTEEN

Given the care shown by Mr. Salazar not to be seen with me, it was hard to get the firsthand news of Martin that I craved. The secondhand news reported by the newspapers was not encouraging, and I suspected it was highly biased against Martin. Two long articles in particular suggested a certain lack of impartiality. One was headlined "A Father's Grief" and described a broken-hearted Domenico Gambarelli at his daughter's funeral. The other depicted Lucetta's death in grisly detail and painted a nasty picture of Martin rising to his feet, his hands dripping blood.

I mentioned those pieces to Mr. Salazar when we at last met again. He eventually took the enormous risk of visiting me in our rooms at the Palmer House at eight o'clock in the evening.

"We believe the journalists have been bought," was his response. "Every article of that sort that they print makes it harder for us to have Martin released. And yet it's perfectly clear to the police by now that Martin could not have done the deed. When our attorneys protest, the Gambarellis' representatives claim that Martin could have had his wife killed by someone else. They claim he deliberately went up to the storeroom to raise the alarm and act the part of the grieving husband. It's pure conjecture without a shred of evidence.

Yet somehow the judge has found a hundred different ways of using such arguments—and others—to prevent Martin's release. We're bringing a writ of habeas corpus, but my guess is that we could again be beaten back by the judge's procedural delays."

"And if they find out about me, that would give them even more ammunition to use against Martin."

Mr. Salazar nodded. "As you say."

"I'm moving into a house on Aldine Square—here's my new address." I held out a piece of folded paper. "Not, of course, that it would be hard to track you there if anyone's watching, but it's a little less public than the Palmer House."

"Thank you." Mr. Salazar copied the address into a small notebook he kept in an inner pocket.

"What I don't understand," I said, "is why the Gambarellis continue to believe Martin killed Lucetta in the face of all the evidence to the contrary. Do they hate him that much?"

"I'm not sure if it's a matter of hatred, exactly. They're beside themselves. Their adoration of Lucetta went almost to the point of idolatry, particularly in the case of Alessandro and Gianbattista, her oldest brothers. Samuele, the youngest, is not nearly so attached. Did you know he is still working for Rutherford's?"

"I didn't know. In fact, I didn't know he existed until this moment. The newspaper articles mention Alex and Jacky Gambarelli, but no Samuele."

"He has remained in New York," Mr. Salazar said. "He's been working as a buyer for Martin's business enterprise on the frontier. He couldn't possibly have returned in time for Lucetta's funeral, so apparently he didn't try. I was surprised they buried her so quickly, come to that. Young Sam's an artist and would rather not have to work at all. But his father won't allow him to live as he pleases, so Lucetta pleaded with Martin for a place for him. Apparently, he does his work fairly well. There's also a cousin, John Powell, who works for Martin as a business prospector and construction manager on the frontier. Another ne'er-do-well, but he seems to have a knack for finding good locations for the new stores and creating enthusiasm among the towns where they'll be sited. He was there for Lucetta's funeral, completely drunk. That fact did not make its way into the newspapers, but I have a few sources of my own."

"John Powell doesn't sound like a particularly Italian name."

Mr. Salazar smiled wryly. "His father was an Irishman. Only tolerated by the Gambarelli family because he had the good grace to die soon after marrying Powell's mother. That left the boy to be brought up in Domenico's household, where he was known as Giancarlo."

"I tend to forget that you worked in the Gambarelli store," I remarked. "You must know them all quite well."

"I do. Alex and Jacky are as fine a pair of Sicilians as you'd wish to find. And yet for all their connections, they never realized that Lucetta had taken a lover right under their noses, in the store itself."

That made me sit up straighter. "You knew about Lucetta's—peccadilloes." I also noted that he had used her given name rather than refer to her as Mrs. Rutherford.

"Yes, I did. I was the general manager of the store, and not much escaped me. I wish I'd known Martin better before he met Lucetta because I'd have warned him off her—but it took us a while to become friends. My wife says Martin's the sort of man who reveals himself to you in layers, each more interesting than the last."

She was right about that. "I'm sorry. I didn't know you had a wife. And here you are risking your good name and deserting your home for my sake. Do you have children?"

He smiled, and the transformation of his face from its usual saturnine watchfulness was so dramatic I couldn't help smiling in return. "Two girls and a boy. They and my Leah are everything to me."

"She must be an understanding woman," I said. "I don't suppose you get home much, what with the store and the investigation."

"She likes Martin." He shrugged. "He's an enlightened and generous employer, and free of the usual prejudices about Jews. I did not encounter such respect and consideration at Gambarelli's."

"Who was Lucetta's lover there?"

"One François Godin, a Frenchman, as you'd guess by the name. Only he calls himself Frank Gorton at work. He's the chief buyer and, as such, travels frequently. His mastery of European languages makes him valuable to the Gambarellis, and besides, he's a talented man." Mr. Salazar's heavily lidded eyes held a trace of irony. "And if you're going to ask whether I think he killed

Lucetta, I doubt it. I got the distinct impression that his, let us say, *friendship* with Lucetta was based on mutual pleasure rather than passionate love. One does not murder a mistress when she makes few demands, and Lucetta had no intention of leaving Martin. I can't be sure, of course. Gorton was—is—exceptionally discreet."

"Not discreet enough to escape your notice," I remarked.

Mr. Salazar looked smug. "I have excellent people working for me."

"Excellent people? Do you mean spies?"

His mouth twisted. "I suppose I do. The world of the Chicago department stores is a small one, and we all employ, ahem, assistants to keep an eye on each other. We also employ people to be our eyes and ears within our own stores. Of course, we're usually looking for thieves and the spies of our competitors rather than for love affairs and murderers."

"It sounds like a dirty business when you put it that way," I said. "Not at all like Martin."

"Even Martin can't afford to be above employing a spy or two or paying protection money against arsonists and the like. This is Chicago, after all."

"This is Chicago," I echoed. "You know, Mr. Salazar, I sometimes have the impression that Lucetta has more power over Martin now than she did when she was alive. I feel as if I'm fighting against a ghost, a memory."

"Don't think that," he said gently. "It's not Lucetta who's your antagonist now."

"Isn't it?" I asked, my own voice grating on my ear. "She told me—not in so many words, but she made it plain—that she would do everything she could to keep Martin. What was it she wanted to tell him that was so important she waited two hours at the store for his return? Would she have succeeded if she'd lived? If we find out the truth, might it not be even more destructive than Lucetta's death? I'm afraid Martin may lose his fight against the noose, Mr. Salazar, but part of me is also afraid of what we may learn if he wins."

℘

I shut the door gently behind Mr. Salazar and made the circuit of the parlor, extinguishing the gaslights on the wall one by one. I felt I should call Alice to help me undress, but that would mean disturbing Sarah, and I could manage by myself. I had expected Tess to come out of her room during Mr. Salazar's visit, and I opened the door to wish her a good night. The room was dark and silent, from which I deduced she had already fallen asleep.

The servant who had lit the gaslights before Mr. Salazar's visit had also drawn the drapes. I pushed aside one of the heavy velvet panels and looked out into the street. The panes of glass were streaked with rain. April's whips of wet, windy weather were lashing at Chicago again, not yet the storms that ushered in the warmer days, but the icy remnants of winter, raw and unpleasant. On the prairies of Kansas, where I had spent the last four years, there would be verdant growth and a few flowers, but here all I could see was mud and puddles.

The lights of the street, both moving and stationary, winked at the wet flagstones of the sidewalk. They flashed on the leather hoods of carriages and the umbrellas of the few passersby who had reason to frequent State Street on this Sabbath day. Streaks of light glittered on the churned grit that overlay the pavement, only to be obliterated and reformed by each passing carriage. A horse car rumbled past, gouts of wet mud spraying outward from under the horses' hooves as they labored for a footing in the murk.

I stared blindly at the rain-soaked street. A tear tracked down my cheek and then another, patterning themselves on the raindrops that slid slowly down the windowpanes.

"Don't waste your time on tears," I told myself. "They won't help Martin."

And yet for a few minutes, I allowed myself the luxury of despair, wracked with half-suppressed sobs that did little to bring me relief.

SIXTEEN

"Why can't I learn things by myself?"

Sarah stabbed her buttonhook through one of the buttonholes on her boots, a rebellious scowl on her face. "Why do I have to have lessons with Miss Baker if I don't feel like having lessons? Maybe I'll be tired today, or maybe I'll want to play instead. You let me play when I'm too tired to do lessons. Why do I have to have a nasty old governess?"

My fingers were itching to grab the buttonhook and fasten Sarah's boots myself, but I knew there was no point in offering help. "She's not nasty, and she's not old," I said. "And you won't have that many lessons. Miss Baker says that a child your age should spend more time in play than in sitting in a chair. And she's friends with lots of other governesses and nursemaids. They meet up in a park together sometimes so that their children can play together. They organize games for them."

"I don't like ornized—organized games." Sarah's face was red from her efforts to hook the difficult top button. "I like playing games by myself."

"You like running around with other children in the park."

"That's different. They do everything I tell them to."

I sighed. Sarah was much too used to getting her own way. There had been a time when our day was carefully divided into learning time and playtime, but that routine had been dropped before Martin and Lucetta had visited us in September. And then there had been Martin—and Judah—and all the arrangements needed to move our lives to Chicago. Somehow I had found myself making more and more concessions to Sarah's wishes. After all, she was only a little girl and I, her mother, had not lived up to my own ideals of an ordered life.

"You'll like Miss Baker's games. Isn't it nice that she's English?"

"Why can't I have an *American* governess?" Sarah stood up and looked critically at her buttoned boots. "Americans are better than foreigners."

"Well, she's English-American. She's an American citizen."

"She talks funny. I don't like the way she talks."

"You'll get used to her. Now are you ready? Let me brush your hair again. You want to make a good impression for your first day of lessons."

Sarah narrowed her jade-green eyes at me but then thought better of whatever it was she was about to say. Good children did not talk back to their elders and betters. "My hair is fine, thank you, Momma," she said with icy dignity.

ℰ

With Sarah settled—depending how you looked at it—and Tess visiting her family yet again, I was free to take coffee with Elizabeth and regale her with my woes.

"If you'd seen Sarah this morning, pretending not to know arithmetic she mastered months ago, you'd have more sympathy." I bit into a petit four from the plate Elizabeth had insisted on ordering. "She seemed to have lost all her wits and some of her manners."

"She's doing it on purpose," Elizabeth said airily, stirring cream and sugar into her coffee. "It's not generally easy to settle a child in with a governess, especially a small child."

"I'm not sure if a governess is quite American," I mused. "It seems so undemocratic not to send her to a school. I never had governesses. I went to a dame school when Grandmama wasn't teaching me, and then to a young ladies' academy." And spent much of my time looking out of the window when I wasn't in danger of the teacher seeing me and hitting my hand with a ruler.

"You know very well why it's not a good idea to send Sarah to school." Elizabeth picked up a tiny cake dusted with cocoa powder and disposed of it in three elegant bites, her eyes gleaming. She had rather a sweet tooth. "So stop fretting about your choice. Your anxieties are communicating themselves to your child and making her nervous and mischievous. Have you spoken to her about Mr. Rutherford?"

"Of course not." I took too large a sip of my black coffee, which burned my tongue. "She's far too young to understand."

"But old enough to know that you're worried about something, so she'll be worried too. I imagine you hovered over her when Miss Baker arrived, didn't you?"

I thought back over the events of the morning. "I imagine I did, just a little."

"Well, then. Mother always turned her back on me the moment anyone arrived to take charge of me. When I was not much older than Sarah, she put me in the care of a Frenchwoman and ordered her to speak only French to me. As soon as I saw her, I would begin to cry and scream, but Mother would leave the room. Naturally, I calmed down once I had no audience. Except for the time when I put a cicada in Mademoiselle Néry's pocket and she whipped me, we got on quite well in the end. My French is excellent."

"But to leave her alone with a stranger, and Tess not there either." I sighed. "I've been Tess's sister in practice for so long that I can't get over her having real sisters—ones who want to see her all the time."

"Poor Nell." Elizabeth selected a petit four covered in pink icing and put it on my plate. "Try that—they're the best ones. You're feeling bereft, aren't you? But don't worry. Your little birds will come home to roost once you've made your nest at Aldine Square."

"It's too pink." I put the cake on Elizabeth's plate and watched as she ate it. "Besides, I promised Sarah we would eat luncheon together as a treat after her morning with Miss Baker."

Elizabeth put her hand to her head in mock exasperation. "Really, Nell, you indulge that child far too much."

❦

Elizabeth and I compensated for the petits fours with a brisk walk in Lake Park. By the time I returned to our rooms, I was looking forward to my luncheon with Sarah. I was sure Elizabeth was right. Sarah—who was generally at ease with grown-ups—would be chatting away to Miss Baker as she always did.

I was wrong. I knew I was wrong the moment I opened the door and Sarah, red-eyed and runny-nosed, catapulted out of her chair and came to a halt in front of me. Behind her, Miss Baker rose to her feet more slowly.

"I want milk and ham, Momma. She says I can't have any."

A qualm assailed me. Had Miss Baker whipped Sarah? Was she planning to deprive my child of food? I glared at her. She was a brown-haired, brown-eyed young woman with no particular beauty to recommend her, but I'd found her appearance pleasing. Now I looked for signs of incipient cruelty.

Still, Sarah was not to get away with being impolite. "Is Sarah in trouble?" I asked Miss Baker, and to my daughter I said, "Don't say 'she,' darling. That's rude. Kindly address or refer to your governess as Miss Baker."

"Will you tell your Mama what you did?" Miss Baker rubbed a region on the anterior part of her anatomy.

Sarah's mouth clamped into a straight line. "My mother is not my Ma-MAH. She's my *Momma*. She's American, like me."

I was beginning to suspect that the fault may not all lie on Miss Baker's side and fixed my daughter with a stern eye. "You are being insolent, Sarah Amelia Lillington. It's not your place to criticize Miss Baker's speech. And kindly don't try to divert my attention away from yourself."

"Yes, Momma." Sarah's rosebud mouth pinched itself into a tight button of resentment.

"And tell me why Miss Baker is proposing you do without your luncheon." I darted forward and wiped Sarah's nose with my handkerchief, then nodded at her to speak.

Sarah turned toward Miss Baker and dropped a half curtsey. "I'm sorry for critishing your speech, Miss Baker." She turned back to me, and her face, still mutinous as she looked at the governess, transformed into the very picture of wide-eyed innocence.

"I just left some marbles on the floor by accident, Momma. I forgotted them. I didn't even *think* Miss Baker would slip on them."

Her tongue sought the side of her mouth, pushing out the skin of her cheek in a prominent bump. I knew that bump. It meant she was lying. On the few occasions when Sarah told an untruth, her tongue inevitably gave her away. I'd never troubled to inform her of that useful piece of knowledge. A mother had to have *some* advantages.

"That's a lie, isn't it?" I asked her, keeping my voice even. "Don't try to tell me otherwise, young lady."

I turned to face the governess. "So going without luncheon is her punishment?"

"I had bread and water in mind, Mrs. Lillington. I don't generally make a young child go hungry, nor do I use the switch on children under eight."

I nodded. "It's an eminently fair punishment. And those marbles are to be locked in my bureau until further notice."

Ignoring the trembling of Sarah's lower lip, which had a slightly theatrical quality to it, I retired to my bedroom and rang the bell for Alice. I now had nobody to eat luncheon with, but I should change out of my walking dress anyway. I unpinned my hat, and then I sat down on my bed and put my face in my hands.

Elizabeth was undoubtedly right. Sarah must have some idea that something was wrong in my life, and that was enough to shake the foundations of a small child's world. And Tess was frequently absent and not her usual, cheerful self much of the time. Was Sarah's prank—I couldn't believe a five-year-old child would deliberately set out to hurt someone—a result of her sensitivity to my moods?

However I tried to excuse her though, some small and selfish part of me saw Sarah's rebellion as yet another desertion. A well-deserved one, perhaps. A memory surfaced of my workroom in Kansas. The day Martin had come back from riding across the plains, we had all been so happy and comfortable together. But just minutes later, my world had turned upside-down with the realization that I loved Martin Rutherford. Nothing had been the same ever since. The train of events that would lead me to Chicago was put in place. This collision course was due largely to my selfish stupidity when I was a spoiled, flirtatious girl with no thought for the future.

And now I was separated from Martin by the walls of a jail. I was divided from Tess by her competing loyalties. And I was trying to steer the right course with a child too young to understand the social consequences of her illegitimacy and the preoccupations of her adults. The allies of the last six years were drawing away from me, and for a moment I felt that the whole world was ranged on one side of a divide, with me on the other.

SEVENTEEN

Miss Baker was not a live-in governess. She lived with several women friends in a house near Bridgeport and preferred to keep her independence. It seemed a little unusual—but who was I to deprive another woman of her freedom? So she viewed our move to Aldine Square with equanimity and, despite the incident with the marbles, told me she'd like to persevere with Sarah.

The move to our own home buoyed my uncertain spirits. For the first time in almost five years, I was the mistress of my own household again. That household included a smart green rockaway with carmine wheels, which Tess instantly commandeered for a visit to Mary. I could only imagine what an impression her regular appearance in a carriage was making in the Back of the Yards.

"How is Mary?" was my tentative question when she returned.

"She says I shouldn't be your housekeeper." Tess was never one to dwell on polite nothings.

"You know I'd be happy for you to do nothing at all," I pointed out. "It's entirely up to you to arrange matters with Alice."

"Why would I want to be idle?" Tess's scanty eyebrows rose above her round spectacles. "'A little sleep, a little slumber, a little folding of the hands to sleep: so shall thy poverty come as one that traveleth, and thy want as an armed man.' That's in Proverbs, and it means we shouldn't be lazy. *You're* never lazy."

"Well, that's true, I suppose." Tess's biblical certainties always left me nonplussed. "Of course, we wouldn't be poor even if we did nothing. Martin's arranged things so well that we can easily afford this house and our daily expenditures."

I indicated the parlor in which we were busy arranging our belongings. It was pleasantly furnished with the Katzenmeiers' heavy but not overwhelming armchairs and tables. A profusion of walnut trim gave the room a fashionable solidity, but the walls were painted cream rather than festooned with the usual patterned wallpaper. The velvet drapes were an attractive dark green color. We faced north across the central gardens of the square, so our view would soon be of burgeoning leaves and bright flowers.

"It's a nice house." Tess found her Bible and placed it on the table near the armchair she had selected as her own. "My bedroom is comfortable, and imagine—Sary has her own little room to sleep in! You don't think she'll be afraid, do you?"

"I'll be close by." We had, in fact, designated the dressing room off the largest bedroom—where I slept—to hold a small bed, soon to be delivered. That seemed preferable to putting such a little girl upstairs in the nursery-schoolroom. Sarah felt mightily grown-up to have a room of her own.

"I thought Sarah seemed a touch less sulky this morning," I observed. "She let Miss Baker show her how to make a paper boat and helped her arrange the schoolroom. And she likes the pond in the garden." A momentary image of Sarah somehow ensuring that Miss Baker fell into the pond entered my mind, and I firmly kicked it out of doors.

"Sary's really a good little girl," Tess said. "She's just being naughty because she doesn't like things to change."

"I don't much like all the upheaval either. But I think our new house is a change for the better."

The change I liked best of all was that a box room on the north side of the house had been cleared so that I could use it as a sewing room. I planned to spend as much money as I wanted on getting it fitted out with shelves, a cutting table, a pressing table, and a brand new sewing machine. Had I not been so worried about Martin, the excitement of such a project—and the prospect of useful occupation—might have consumed my days.

"If Martin were free, you'd be quite happy, wouldn't you, Nell?" Tess's words broke into my thoughts with uncanny aptness.

"If none of this had happened, we might be making plans to leave Chicago." I was arranging Sarah's picture books and Tess's novels in a neat row on a shelf by the fireplace and kept my head turned away from Tess. "But what's the use of talking about might-have-beens?"

I furtively wiped away a tear and turned to smile at Tess, who returned my look with sympathy in her eyes. We still hadn't talked openly about my relationship with Martin, but I was aware that somehow Tess knew. I swallowed.

"I've made a mess of things, Tess."

"You're not responsible for everything that happens." Sometimes Tess had more sense than any of us. "Besides, when we make a mess we can clean it up, can't we, Nell? Is there anything you can do?"

Again, she had hit on something that lurked in my mind, where I thought nobody else could find it. Now the notion resurfaced from somewhere deep down. I reached into my workbasket and pulled out a scrap of newsprint.

"It's a ridiculous idea, I know, but—look at this."

Tess read the advertisement slowly and carefully. "Young women of clean and neat appearance, with good English and of ready address, are invited to apply to Gambarelli's Emporium for employment on the sales floor. Terms and conditions upon application."

She read it again, silently this time, her lips moving. Then she looked at me.

"If you worked at Gambarelli's, you could find out things. And you wouldn't fret so much."

I let out my breath. "Precisely. It would mean being away from home a lot."

"And you'd have to pretend to be the sort of woman who needs money." Tess wrinkled her brow. "That shouldn't be too hard. You still have some of the clothes you wore when you worked as a seamstress, don't you? You couldn't go into Gambarelli's dressed like a rich lady."

"You're very clever." I couldn't help smiling. "I'd have to take the horse car along State Street all by myself. But working women do that, don't they?" Somehow the idea of freedom from the rules and regulations appertaining to society women more than made up for any slight danger or unpleasantness.

Tess pursed her lips. "I shouldn't tell our servants what you're doing—except maybe Alice. We can tell the others you're busy doing charity work." She glanced at my face and sniffed. "If you don't think I can keep a secret, you're wrong. When you ran away from the Poor Farm, I had to pretend I didn't know where you were going, and I did know, didn't I?"

I left what I was doing and went to hug Tess. "I know I can trust you absolutely."

"And I'll try not to go to the Back of the Yards too often so that Sary doesn't get lonely." Tess attempted a severe expression. "But that doesn't mean I'm staying with you forever."

EIGHTEEN

It was Good Friday, and we'd been to church twice. That was my daily limit. Tess had been spirited away by Aileen for an afternoon Mass to counteract our two visits to Saint James's. I had nothing to do except sit by the fire and fret over my forthcoming application in person to Gambarelli's.

"Momma, can't you ring for Zofia to put the lights on? I like hearing them pop, and it's nearly dark."

Sarah lifted her head from her game, which involved the creation of an entire society made out of people cut from old fashion plates. Every one of them had names Sarah had made up, and she told herself stories about "her people" in a continuous monologue as she played.

"Go and push the button," I said. "And don't slide along the floor in your stockinged feet."

A swishing sound informed me that Sarah had ignored the latter injunction. Fortunately, Miss Baker didn't mind darning stockings. Zofia was a very young Polish woman Alice had found as a maid-of-all-work. She was pale and thin, but her capacity for work was impressive.

"You look tired, Momma." Sarah abandoned her game and climbed into my lap.

"I'm not, really. I just don't like days like today when you're supposed to do nothing. And I really can't read one more sermon." I smoothed a hand over her braids. "It's not so much fun for you either."

"Oh, I don't mind." Sarah laid her head against my chest, seeking the position in which she could best hear my heartbeat. "Church was sad, but I'm glad I have no lessons today."

"Is Miss Baker really so dreadful?" For a moment, I almost weakened and told Sarah I would dismiss her.

"She *does* tell me interesting things," Sarah admitted. "Did you know, Momma, that most people work all day?"

"I worked all day in Kansas." I grinned and dropped a kiss on her hair.

"But you *liked* it. Most people have to work for a long, long time, even if their work's really hard. Like cutting up meat and hitting—I can't remember the word. How you make big pieces of metal stay together."

"Rivets?"

Sarah nodded. "They make them very hot so that they're soft, and then they hit them. I would think it would be hard to do that for ten or twelve hours. And they can't stop and play with their little girls like you did in Kansas."

Satisfied that my heart was still beating, Sarah straightened up and began to run a finger along the ruffles on the front of my dress. "Miss Baker says I'm streemly clever," she observed. "She says I'm too clever by half." Her jade-green eyes glowed in the firelight. "She says if I were in school, I'd have to be in a class with bigger girls."

"Would you like that?"

"No." Sarah shook her head. "Big girls try to tell little girls what to do. A big girl in the park told me not to climb the tree."

This was news to me. "You were climbing trees?"

"Miss Baker said I'd tear my dress, and the trees are too little anyway. She says that when we find some really nice trees, she'll put me in old clothes and teach me how to climb up safely."

I watched as Zofia entered and lit a taper from the fire, then visited each light in turn. Sarah followed her, staying at a safe distance from the popping noise the lights made. As she no doubt had known would happen, Zofia—

who ate a great deal despite or perhaps because of her slenderness—suggested a visit to the kitchen to try Mrs. Power's popovers, and I was left to my musing. Or was it moping?

It would be two days before Mr. Salazar could visit again. Did they celebrate Easter at the county jail? Would Martin receive some variation in his diet of beans and coffee? I knew his attorneys were meeting with the judge next week, but little else about what was happening to him. Mr. Salazar continued to visit him every day except Saturdays.

I sank into my chair, eyeing the paper people Sarah had spread out on the carpet, unable to help noticing details of outmoded styles. Zofia had closed the drapes, but I could hear the rain beating on the windows. The bad weather made the parlor seem even more snug and warm by comparison, and I thought of Martin for the thousandth time that day. Was he warm?

The clang of the doorbell a floor below startled me out of my reverie. I looked at the clock—it was almost Sarah's bedtime. Nobody could possibly be calling on me on Good Friday, especially at this hour. I crossed to the door in six strides and yanked it open.

"Mr. Salazar." Ignoring etiquette, I ran down the stairs to where Zofia was helping Mr. Salazar out of a coat so wet it was dripping all over the marble floor. He had told me once he had to be home early on Friday nights to celebrate the beginning of the Sabbath. Fear coursed through me.

"What's wrong?"

Mr. Salazar paused, and in the silence, Sarah's high-pitched giggle could be heard from the kitchen. Arthur Nutt, who was a great friend of Mrs. Power's, had probably dropped by to drink tea with her and was even now telling Sarah funny stories.

"May we go upstairs?"

"Zofia, please put Mr. Salazar's coat near the fire to dry." I eyed the fine wool coat with its Astrakhan collar, from which a steady stream of drips was still cascading. "And take Miss Sarah up to her room when she's done eating. I'll come up soon."

"Come up and warm yourself by the parlor fire," I said to Mr. Salazar. I led the way, trying to behave normally despite the thudding of my heart. "And whatever it is, don't spare me."

It only took a minute or so to get Mr. Salazar settled in the chair nearest the fire and put a fresh log onto the embers. But it seemed like a long minute before I could ask the question that was uppermost in my mind.

"Is Martin all right?"

"For now." Mr. Salazar held out his hands to the fire. "He's in quarantine. I tried to see him earlier, but they don't allow visitors on Good Friday, and besides, they may not allow anyone in now."

My shoulders had slumped a little in relief at his initial words, but the word "quarantine" sent pins and needles into my hands. "Quarantine for what?"

"His cellmate has typhus, and four more cases were diagnosed in the jail today. They think it was brought in by a new prisoner who hadn't been deloused thoroughly enough."

I shuddered. "Can't they move him?"

"For now, he's quarantined with half a dozen men who may also have been exposed, and they've boiled their clothes and burned their bedding. Prisons are used to typhus." He grimaced. "I will go to the jail tomorrow and try to bring him nourishing foods and tonics. I just hope my womenfolk will understand—my mother-in-law in particular."

I could feel my hands forming themselves into fists. "He should not be in there."

"No. And believe me, his attorneys will make much of this. We brought in a new lawyer, a most argumentative fellow whose specialty is arguing for the release of the prisoner. He's well connected politically, and we're hoping he can bring some kind of action against the judge."

"If you see Martin, let him know I'm thinking of him."

With a rueful look at the cheerful fire, Mr. Salazar rose to his feet. "I will. And now I must absolutely get back."

"But your coat—the rain—you'll make yourself ill. And you have so many people depending on you."

"I'll be all right." Again, the smile that transformed his lean, solemn face. "I'll be thoroughly scolded, but my Leah will fill me with broth and cover me with blankets. We men are nothing without our good women."

By the time I had said good night to him, it was I who was shivering violently. I wasn't cold—I was scared half to death. Martin was a strong man, but typhus was a dangerous disease.

C

I'd done my best to make Easter morning bright and cheerful with cards and papier-maché boxes at each of our breakfast places. I arranged an Easter egg hunt through our new domain for all of us, family and servants. There was church, of course, and a large luncheon of roast leg of lamb, which Mrs. Power did exceptionally well. We could eat cold roast lamb in the evening, so I was able to give all the servants the rest of the day off. For a few hours, there were just the three of us again. I made every effort to push Martin out of my mind as we played games and walked in the square's garden together, exchanging greetings with various other residents. For a day, we could be an ordinary family.

I played my part well, but I was exhausted by the time we'd eaten our cold supper and settled down in front of the fire. Exhausted and yet unable to sleep. Tess and I put Sarah to bed once she started yawning and then returned to our armchairs. I had copies of *Peterson's Magazine* and a new French journal, *Le Salon de la Mode*, which I had discovered for sale in a small shop on State Street. Tess had bought a piece of open-weave fabric and an embroidery hoop. She was trying to learn cross-stitch by filling in a simple flower I had drawn for her on the fabric.

I was carefully studying a "Cerisse bodice for a miss of sixteen," adapting it in my mind's eye into a more sophisticated version, when I heard the bell. Fortunately, it was a loud one since none of the servants had yet returned. I knew who it would be and was out of my chair and running down the stairs in a moment.

"He's all right," said Mr. Salazar as he stepped over the threshold. The rain had cleared away with the dawn of Easter morning, and his coat and silk hat were dry and well brushed. In front of my house, a smart landau waited, the driver having climbed down to talk to the horses.

I invited Mr. Salazar up to the parlor, and he shook Tess's hand. He refused my offer of refreshment—just as well since I didn't know my way around my own kitchen—and explained he intended to stay only a few minutes.

"I came here tonight because I believe I can at last find you an opportunity to speak with Martin," he said. "It would have to be very early tomorrow morning, before the press realizes that he's been moved."

"Moved?" My heart lurched with excitement and fear. I would see him—I would actually see him at last.

"To Harrison Street Jail. It's a filthy hole, but it's not infected with typhus. Two of the men in quarantine with Martin went down with the illness, and our lawyer kicked up the devil of a fuss. He's managed to get the judge removed on suspicion of taking bribes, which he clearly was, and the new judge seems ready to listen to the petition. Given the typhus, he also agreed that it would be best to put Martin somewhere else while he listens to the facts of the case and deliberates. He realizes they'd hear no end of it if they allow an innocent man to contract a dangerous disease. So Martin's probably even now undergoing a second delousing. He'll be moved tonight under conditions of strict secrecy. Harrison Street is a lockup for petty crimes, and you can visit there with far less formality than at the county jail."

"What time tomorrow?" I asked.

"Would five o'clock in the morning be too early to call?" asked Mr. Salazar. He nodded as I shook my head to indicate no, it would not be too early. I would have walked to the jail in bare feet at midnight if necessary.

"Then I'll be waiting for you outside—you saw my carriage."

I felt a momentary pleasure at knowing Martin paid this loyal man enough to buy him the splendid landau I'd seen. But there was another important question to ask.

"Does Martin know?"

Mr. Salazar shook his head slowly. "I have no way of informing him without risking the disclosure he's been trying so hard to avoid. Even now I'm taking a huge risk. The only assurance I have is that the move to Harrison Street will be undertaken secretly. They're still nervous about lynch mobs or—well, connections of the Gambarellis."

I looked at Tess, uncertain whether she would insist on coming with us. She wasn't as robust as I was and caught colds and such easily. The thought of taking her into a jail where disease of all kinds must run rife was alarming. But all she said was, "You'll tell Martin I pray for him every day, won't you? And give him all kinds of good wishes."

I nodded, relieved, and smiled at Mr. Salazar. He didn't return the smile, but leaned forward, resting his elbows on his knees.

"I have to warn you that Martin may not thank me for this. He may also not seem very pleased to see you. His spirits have been very low lately. To be honest, I'm proposing this visit more for his sake than yours. I'm hoping that you'll be able to comfort him in some way—or at least provoke him out of his mood. He said once that you'd probably find a way to see him contrary to all sense and propriety. I wonder, sometimes, if his refusal to let you near him doesn't contain a seed of hope that it'll have the opposite effect."

"I'm going to take this chance to see him whatever he thinks," I said.

"Yes," said Mr. Salazar, smiling at last. "I thought you would."

NINETEEN

The guard at the Harrison Street jail was dressed neatly enough. His coat and collar were buttoned, the wool of the coat carefully brushed. Yet the smell of confinement was on him, and I could see that areas of his coat were stiff with repeated perfusions of sweat. I wrinkled my nose at the sour, musty aroma as he accompanied Mr. Salazar and me to a barred door and turned the key in the lock.

It was six thirty in the morning. Mr. Salazar's driver had, at his behest, stopped the landau at Taylor Street so that we could walk the rest of the distance to the Harrison Street police station. Mr. Salazar had a large canvas bag in one hand. We were joined halfway along by a keen-eyed man who didn't introduce himself nor ask who I was. He did most of the talking as Mr. Salazar and I stood in a bare, dismal room inside the enormous station building while the official behind the desk argued that no visitors were allowed at this hour.

I couldn't be sure that money had changed hands, but at some point in the proceedings, the flow of argument seemed to die down and the keen-eyed man melted away. Mr. Salazar and I were led through a maze of corridors, each more depressing than the last. Eventually, we came to the lockup. The official spoke to the guard on duty, who had been sitting in a rocking chair opposite a row of barred cells, dozing. He searched the canvas bag Mr. Salazar held but otherwise didn't seem all that concerned about our presence.

The smell increased in intensity as we stepped into the area of the holding cells. The guard caught the look on my face and grinned.

"Bad, ain't it? You should try it when it's cold out and we let the bums sleep down here. Hoowee, sweetheart, you'd hold your pretty nose then." His chins folded down onto his coat front as he leered at me. I was wearing my plainest clothes from Kansas, not wishing to draw attention to myself, but I couldn't do anything about the color of my hair. I fervently hoped there'd be no journalist later inquiring about visitors. People tended to remember my hair.

"That'll do," said Mr. Salazar quietly to the man. "The lady doesn't need to hear your chatter."

"Lady." The guard snorted in derision and gave Mr. Salazar a long, hard stare. "She's not too fussy about the company she keeps, Jew-boy."

With that insult, he turned his back on us and went back to the lockup's barred door to talk with another uniformed man through the bars.

"How do you put up with that?" I asked Mr. Salazar, who shrugged one well-dressed shoulder.

"He's an ignorant Irish clown. Chicago's full of them."

I followed him down the corridor, reflecting that prejudice was a two-sided affair. But my heart had begun to beat in rapid, heavy thumps. I barely took in the men who sat or lounged on the bare benches that served as both seat and bed. One man, incongruously wearing a curly brimmed bowler, tipped it at me with the grave courtesy of a gentleman receiving a polite introduction. I took a deep breath of the fetid air to steady my nerves and then wished I hadn't.

"Whore!"

I jumped and stepped back a pace. We had come close to the bars of one of the cages. A dark, lean man directed the word at me from his position of watchfulness, his forehead jammed against the metal in a most uncomfortable-looking fashion. He reached a hand through the bars to make an obscene gesture and spewed forth a descriptive account of me in such disgustingly lurid language that I only understood one word in three.

"Leave her alone." The words were spoken quietly, but the man pulled away from the bars and let his cellmate guide him back to his bench.

"For God's sake, Salazar, why did you bring her here?" The second man turned back to us, and I realized it was Martin. Unlike the other men, who wore street clothes, he was wearing a uniform of coarse striped cotton, presumably from the county jail. His hair had been cropped all over his head to around a quarter of an inch. A three-day stubble of near-white hairs stippled his cheeks and chin. But he was in one piece, and not sick as far as I could see. My heart did a whole series of somersaults as his eyes met mine despite the unwelcoming sternness of his face.

"He brought me here because I've been fretting over you every day for the best part of a month, and he's a merciful man. Don't be angry at him." I moved forward with the impulse to wrap my arms around him, bars or no bars—but he moved a step back. The small rejection stung, but I refused to allow him to see that.

"I know you don't want me here," I said as steadily as I could. "I understand your reasons. But I can't bear leading a normal life as if you weren't sitting in a cell."

Martin said nothing, and I couldn't read his expression. He was able to do that—shut himself off from all hope of being able to penetrate his thoughts—while my every emotion showed on my face.

Mr. Salazar broke the silence, opening up the bag he carried. "Cheese, eggs, apples," he said, passing each item through the bars. "The apples are old, of course, but you need some fresh food. And Leah sends you mandelbrot." He waited until Martin had taken hold of the paper-wrapped cake and then passed the bag itself through to him. "I was told they'd be far more lax here," he said to me with a smile.

The dark-haired man had risen from his bench at the sight of the bag and edged toward us. Spotting me as if for the first time, he spat a word—the same word, repeated several times—in my direction. I thought I knew what that one meant.

"I'll give you something later if you'll shut up," said Martin, glancing briefly at him. "If you keep insulting the lady, I'll eat the lot while you watch." He didn't sound angry or even surprised. His cellmate, with another glance at me followed by one at the food, merely let a little saliva dribble down his chin before returning to his bench.

"I don't think I can get this through the bars," Mr. Salazar said, indicating the stoppered bottle he held in his hand. "It's cold tea. Can you manage?"

Martin's eyes lit up as he watched Mr. Salazar flip the stopper out of the bottle's neck. He reached through the bars to hold the bottle, swallowing thirstily. "Now this you can bring plenty more of," he said with a slight gasp after a few gulps. "Tea, lemonade, anything that's not coffee. I don't trust the water."

I'd been staring at Martin as if I were dying of thirst myself and he was a fountain. I hadn't seen him in four months, and every change in him mattered. The leanness of his throat and the way his Adam's apple bobbed as he drank, the shadows under his eyes, the slight greasiness of skin that didn't get enough soap and water, the dirt under his normally clean fingernails. He eventually caught my eye, finished drinking, and wiped his mouth with the back of his hand.

"I didn't kill her," he said in an undertone.

I felt faintly indignant. "I *had* managed to come to that conclusion myself."

"How's Aldine Square?" There was a beseeching look in his eyes. Satisfied that I was sure of his innocence, he clearly didn't want to talk about Lucetta.

"We all love it. Thank you for making it possible," I said.

He swallowed hard, and a corner of his mouth quirked up in the nearest thing to a smile I'd yet seen. "Thank you for saying that."

The heaviness on my heart lifted a little, but then Martin looked over me at Mr. Salazar. "Don't bring her again, Joe."

"Honestly, Martin." I made myself sound crosser than I was so as not to betray how sorry I felt for him. "Anybody would think you weren't pleased to see me."

Martin considered that last remark for a moment, a small line deepening between his eyes. When he spoke, his voice might, to the casual observer, have held a note of levity. To anyone, that is, who didn't know him well enough to hear the desperation that lay behind his carefully ironic phrasing.

"You know, Nell, I was looking forward to welcoming you to Chicago, despite the . . . circumstances. I anticipated with pleasure the immense impression I would make, a man bestriding the empire he'd built with his own hands. Strange to say, I'm hardly edified by being obliged to receive the woman I love in a jail cell, with a madman for company. You'll excuse me if I'm unable to express delight at your visit."

His cellmate chose that moment to lift the lid from the enameled bucket in the far corner of the cell—its eye-watering reek did not improve the air—and relieve himself into it with a loud groan of satisfaction. Martin moved his body between me and the sight, coming closer to the bars, and I reached out to touch his hand. But he anticipated the movement, folding his arms, a look of raw distress in his eyes even as he kept his face carefully immobile.

"I'm sorry." I looked down at my boots, not wanting to see Martin's eyes anymore. "You're right, maybe I shouldn't have come. This doesn't seem to be helping you. I just—I wanted to see you so much." The last words came out in a hoarse whisper, and I blinked hard, willing myself not to cry.

"Nellie." The word was spoken in a tone that made the ever-considerate Mr. Salazar remove himself instantly from my side and turn his back on us, pretending to inspect the strip of sky visible through the high, barred window across the passageway. I looked up at Martin, my jaw clenched.

"Don't think I haven't been longing to see you, even as I've dreaded the inevitable moment when you arrived," Martin said. "I didn't imagine that even a jail cell, a murder charge, and my express wishes would keep you away forever."

At last, he reached his hands out to me between the bars, and I noticed that Mr. Salazar's position also blocked the turnkey's view of us. I took his hands, feeling his long, warm fingers wrap around mine, the solid smoothness of his palm under my thumb. "I'm frightened for you," I said.

"I'm frightened for myself at times," Martin admitted. "Not as to the outcome of my case, although that last judge was clearly hostile. I did wonder for a while if he would hang me for the size of my bank account."

"Then what are you frightened of?"

"Of not being able to forget. Of spending the rest of my life dreaming of that room. Of the press getting hold of the idea that I have a mistress for whom the removal of my wife is highly convenient, and hounding you to death." The words came out in a rapid torrent, and Martin shook his head as he took a breath, as if to rid himself of his thoughts. "You won't come and see me again, will you? Unless—well, if things should happen to go badly for me, I'd like you at my side then." He let go of my hands and moved back.

"Don't talk such nonsense." I dug my fingernails into my palms. "You won't—they won't hang an innocent man."

"There's a gallows at the county jail, did you know that?" The words rushed out of him, and I bit back my retort. If it helped Martin to share the burdens of the last month, I could put up with the horrors of such thoughts too.

Mr. Salazar moved back toward us, his back still turned. "Fatty's shaking his keys at me in a significant manner," he said. "We'll have to go."

I knew it was no use trying to touch Martin's hand again. I could see it by the way he held himself, as if warding off contact. I tried hard to control my voice.

"I can't bear to leave you here."

"We don't have much choice, do we?" It was almost humor. "I'm sorry I can't offer you more optimism, Nellie. I seem to have lost it somewhere."

"You need some work to do," Mr. Salazar said to him, taking my arm. "I'll try to oblige you with a long list of questions about the running of the store."

"Bribe the jail keeper not to mention your visit," was Martin's only re-joinder. He turned away from us and picked up the canvas bag, placing the foodstuffs he'd laid on his bench into it under the watchful eye of the madman.

Mr. Salazar and I were silent as we followed a younger man back through the corridors and out of the building. The Chicago air, redolent of soot, horse dung, and onions, if not worse aromas, seemed ambrosial after the jail.

"I'm not his mistress," I eventually said as we turned south again. "You do know that, don't you?"

"I didn't ask, but I've never believed Martin to be the kind of man who would keep a mistress. I knew that he loved you though. He's never said a word about you, but a man doesn't constantly reread the letters of a mere friend." Mr. Salazar's smile lit his face.

I tried to smile, but it wasn't a very successful attempt. "I don't know what you must think of us, Mr. Salazar."

"I think that . . ." Mr. Salazar hesitated and then shook his head. "Our lives cannot be always ordered as we wish them. I think Martin's a good man. And—would you call me Joe?"

I said nothing while he guided me expertly through the puddles and horse apples as we crossed Clark Street, looking at his face in profile. "Joe," I said at last, this time really smiling. "Martin couldn't have a better ally—or friend."

Please call me Nell, and thank you for looking after me as well as Martin. And his store—I suppose you find time to do that."

He grinned. "Oddly enough, the store is the least of our worries. The customers are still coming in, and the takings are even slightly up. Besides, Martin makes more money out of his private investments than he does from the store, as you know. The store fulfills some other part of his nature than the need to make money—his creative side, I suppose. But I'm glad enough to be a part of it."

"Do you think I'll lose him?" Somehow Joe's words had freed the question that had been waiting to be asked. He let the silence stretch out between us for a few moments as we walked on, bathed in a sudden onset of sunshine that felt almost springlike. He didn't protest that Martin would be released from jail soon or point out that Martin had, in the end, admitted he wanted to see me. He knew what I meant. He saw the same danger that I did.

"Not if you have the patience to wait for him to find himself again."

But how long would that take?

TWENTY

"You did *what?*" Joe Salazar had looked surprised enough when I presented myself at his office door a few days later, once more in the everyday clothing of a woman of lesser means. Now his eyebrows rose toward his crisp, dark hair.

"I obtained a post at Gambarelli's this morning as a junior assistant in the millinery department," I repeated. "It was surprisingly easy." I motioned for Joe to sit down, as he had risen to his feet when I entered. "I employed a minor subterfuge to see you. I said I was a friend of your wife's family and wanted to give you this for her."

I held out a small parcel wrapped in brown paper. "It's hat trimmings— the best I could find, as I'd be happy for her to use them. I bought them at Gambarelli's, of course."

"The lady who's fond of putting herself in danger," Joe murmured. "Martin returned from Kansas in December telling me he'd had to rescue such a lady from the clutches of an adventurer. I quickly put two and two together and deduced the lady was the Mrs. Lillington of the letters. He seemed so happy upon his return that I deduced other things—but the happiness didn't last."

He was speaking in a hushed tone since his door was open, and I dropped my voice to match his. "He realized that he couldn't divorce Lucetta without dragging my name into it, and he wouldn't do that."

"And yet you came to Chicago."

"Because Martin wanted me to. He felt that he could at least help me start a new life."

Joe stared steadily at me for a moment, and I felt the heat rise to my cheeks. "I'm almost certain I could have started that life. And besides, I didn't know where else to go after Kansas." I hesitated but then plunged on. "I'm not sure if this job at Gambarelli's isn't as much for myself as for Martin. I don't know as much about millinery as I do about dressmaking, but at least I'll have something to do."

Joe smiled. "I'm trying to imagine my Leah wishing to do anything other than run the house and raise the children—and do good for other people. She loves to bake, even though we have a cook. She visits the poorer Jewish communities three times a week to deliver her cakes and bread. The visits allow her to indulge her other passion, which is binding up small wounds, literally and figuratively. She combines a little physicking with finding solutions to the other small problems of life."

"She sounds quite saintly." I couldn't help grinning, and Joe smiled back.

"She's bossy and talks too much, as do her mother and mine. I accept those faults in return for never having to lift a finger the moment I walk through my door. We all have to make compromises in love, especially when we're tied together for life."

"I feel that remark was directed at me," I said.

Joe shrugged his shoulders. "Martin has his demons. You'll have to make peace with them, especially now."

I squared my shoulders, conscious of the noises in the corridor that reminded me we were not talking in private. "Just one thing before I go," I said. "At Gambarelli's, my name is Amelia Harvey, and you had better adopt that name if I have reason to come to you here again."

Joe nodded, but a small frown furrowed his brow. "Be careful how you step at Gambarelli's. Don't ask too many questions. Martin doesn't need the extra worry of knowing you're risking your skin for him."

℃

By the time I'd worked my first two weeks at Gambarelli's, I'd come to the conclusion that my main danger might be boredom. Either that or exhaustion. I'd never realized before how tiring a shopgirl's life was.

But it wasn't the physical exertion or long hours that made me aware this job could only be a temporary expedient. I had taken off my wedding ring when I applied for the position, knowing many employers disapproved of married women working, and found, to my dismay, that I was expected to live in a mansard room within the store itself. There was row after row of them, all furnished exactly the same with a narrow bed, a chest of drawers, and a small dressing table. I would only see Tess and Sarah on Sunday afternoon, after I had attended the Sunday morning service. This was held for all unmarried employees in the basement room where, on all other days of the week, goods not taken immediately were parceled up and sent out to their purchasers.

Explaining to Sarah that her mother would be absent for the entire week was hard enough. But Sarah was, it seemed, becoming accustomed to Miss Baker, who was at her side from breakfast to her evening meal except for Wednesday afternoons and Saturdays. Tess staunchly asserted that she would visit her family only when Miss Baker was there and be at home otherwise.

Yet it was Tess who rounded on me as soon as we were alone. She shut the door carefully, waited until the sound of footsteps told us that Sarah and Miss Baker had ascended to the schoolroom, and then stuck her bottom lip out as far as it would go.

"Nell, I said it would be all right if you worked at Gambarelli's to find out things. I even said I would lie for you. But I say it's all wrong to pretend to be a spinster when you have a child. A little white lie to help people is not a sin, but this is a big lie. 'Conceiving and uttering from the heart words of falsehood.' This is pretending Sarah doesn't exist."

"It's the only way I thought I could get the job. Tess, if we didn't have the money Martin made for us—if we'd come to Chicago with just our savings from Kansas and I'd had to go out to work—wouldn't you have understood if I had to lie? And this is to save Martin."

"Why is Martin more important than Sary?" Tess's eyebrows contracted into a frown so fierce that her spectacles slid down her nose, and she pushed them back with a huff of annoyance.

"He's not. But he is important to me—and he's in great trouble, as you know. I thought you'd understand that. Didn't you always want me to marry him?"

"I'm not so sure about that now." Tess crossed to her chair and dropped down into it, grabbing her Bible and holding it on her lap. "Maybe if you marry him, you won't have time for us anymore. You don't have time for us now."

"You're being unreasonable."

Tess rocked herself forward so that her feet hit the ground and stood up. "No, *you're* being unreasonable. We'd just started being a real family again, and now we're not even going to see you. And supposing you marry Martin and he says, 'Let's send Sarah to school and Tess to the Poor Farm again?'" She stalked to the door, still clutching her Bible.

"He won't." Of that I was absolutely sure. "Martin loves both of you."

Tess sniffed. "Martin is a merchant prince—I saw it in the newspapers. Merchant princes spend all their time working or amusing themselves with society ladies in salons. Their wives spend all their time going to balls and dinners and paying visits and traveling to their country homes. So where does that leave me and Sary?"

I opened my mouth to speak but shut it again. I was finding it hard to counter Tess's insecurities since I honestly had no idea what kind of a life Martin *did* lead, under normal circumstances. I knew he traveled—his early letters had talked about restaurants and amusements. I knew he hunted and rode, sometimes with his merchant friends, sometimes without. I knew he worked hard. But did he, in point of fact, have any notion of a family life into which Sarah and Tess could fit?

"Hmph." Tess saw my indecision and gave a small, abrupt nod of the head. "And now you're working too, which you always like the best. In Kansas, we were together when we worked, but we can't be if you're at Gambarelli's and I'm here running the house. Think about that. Maybe you hired Miss Baker so you don't have to be Sary's Momma anymore, and Alice so you don't have to look after me. Sary may have to stay and put up with you being out all the time, but I won't."

TWENTY-ONE

My mornings at Gambarelli's began at five thirty so that I could be in the basement refectory by six. After breakfast and a brief morning service, the shopgirls all had to be on the floor at seven. By the time the earliest customers arrived, we had taken the covers off all the merchandise, fetched replacement items from the surplus store, and dusted, fluffed, and straightened the goods so that they looked as appealing as possible. At the end of our long day, we had to tidy every counter, polish the glass, and clean the wood trim so no fingerprints or marks showed.

But in between were endless hours of standing with only short breaks every three hours for the washroom or a hastily gulped cup of coffee, and half an hour for luncheon. I was a good walker—could go for miles without fatigue—but I had never known that my feet could ache as they now did. Sometimes the ache became a burning sensation that was extremely hard to relieve.

"You get used to it," said Miss Sweeny, one of the other three millinery assistants, when I finally remarked on the pain in my feet. "I thought you said you'd been employed in Kansas?"

"As a seamstress. I could sit down whenever I wanted." I leaned for a fraction of a second against the counter to soothe the various aches that assailed my body.

"Well, weren't you the lucky one." Miss Sweeny grinned, showing a chipped front tooth. "And if Mrs. Crowford catches you leaning on the counter, she'll deduct twenty cents, so if I were you, I'd remember how grateful you are to have a job at all."

Mrs. Crowford was the head of millinery. I understood that the "Mrs." was a courtesy title only, there being no Mr. Crowford. The heads of department wore their own clothes, while the rest of us were clad in simple dark gray dresses that were not as well cut as I would have liked. Still, they had quite nice overskirts, swept back into a knot and supported underneath with a ruffled pad of ticking, far more comfortable for working than a bustle cage.

"Best way to relieve your feet is to stand on one leg, if you can manage it." This advice came from Miss Dowling, pale and willowy, always pinching her cheeks to give herself more color. No shopgirl would dare wear rouge. Our third colleague, Miss Green, had succumbed to a toothache so bad she was going to have to get the tooth pulled, and had gone to her room crying.

Apart from the physical drawbacks, I was enjoying myself. Hats weren't my passion, but at least I could spend time talking about modes with other women. Being the junior and new to millinery, I wasn't given many chances to make a sale. My role was mostly to stand by while Miss Sweeny or Miss Dowling—usually Miss Sweeny—chatted volubly with the ladies who stopped by to try on hats, snapping her fingers at me when she needed an item fetched. I received wages, but no percentage on sales until I advanced to full assistant.

From afar, I'd seen Domenico Gambarelli, a man in his late sixties with a thick-necked, compact build and bushy gray beard flecked with black below bristling black eyebrows. He was usually flanked by his two sons, whom I soon learned to call Mr. Alessandro and Mr. Gianbattista. It seemed that their American names, Alex and Jacky, were only used by intimates.

I knew Alessandro Gambarelli, even from a distance, by his barrel chest and jutting black beard. His brother Gianbattista, by contrast, was tall and thin to the point of emaciation. He was the most feared and disliked by the employees, I soon found out. This was due to his habit of making sarcastic or critical remarks about almost everything his inferiors said, an unpleasant ordeal when you couldn't answer back. Alessandro, at least, was appreciated for getting to the point. He had no tolerance for poor work, my colleagues told me, but if you did your job well and were polite, he'd give you no trouble. So it seemed his ruthlessness was held in check in the store.

I hadn't expected to learn much in two weeks, and I'd been right. We all wore black crape armbands for Lucetta, but the employees rarely talked about her except to sigh over her beauty, her dresses, or her voice. Those, of course, were no news to me, and I felt a strange pang every time she was praised in such ways.

"Do try this one." I was snapped out of my thoughts by a brisk lift of the chin directed at me by Miss Sweeny, who was now talking to a customer. "Miss Harvey, do you have a longer pin?"

I crossed to one of the many drawers at the back of the counter and selected a four-inch pin topped with a green glass pearl. Miss Sweeny was holding out a hat of the virulent shade called Paris green. It was decorated with bunches of yellow and pink flowers that peeped from under the brim and bristled on the crown. I handed the customer the pin, and we both watched as she carefully fixed the hat to her front hair. That hair wasn't a false front, and the silly bunch of flowers didn't look nearly so bad under the arching curve of the hat atop her abundant, natural, dark curls. She was a good-looking woman, somewhere in her mid-thirties, with large, flashing dark eyes that reminded me somewhat of Lucetta.

"A little vulgar, isn't it?" She had a pleasant, low-pitched voice and seemed very sure of herself. "What do you think, Crabb?"

A man detached himself from an ornamental pillar where he'd been lounging. He strolled up to the customer to inspect the hat, assessing us with bold eyes as he approached. He was of imposing height and breadth of shoulder with close-cropped, sandy hair and a fine, bushy mustache that curled over the edge of sensual, nicely delineated lips.

"Makes you look like a flower-seller's cart, Lizzie, my love. That color lights you up though."

Behind his back, I nodded significantly at Miss Sweeny and then at a dark green hat trimmed in bright ribbon. The flowers peeping from under the brim of this one were silk violets. She understood my glance and nodded briefly.

She was too good a saleswoman to object to my interference. She held out her hand for the hat, and I passed it to her.

"This one, perhaps, Madam? A little less gaudy."

"Rutherford's would have better." The man, who was definitely younger than his companion, lifted the head of his cane to brush his lips. The gesture drew attention to their fine shape, and I was sure he often employed it. He had the cocksure bearing of a handsome man used to being admired.

"I'm cross with Rutherford's. They sold me exactly the same hat as Carrie Watson's, and hanged if I didn't turn up at Simon's looking like her twin." She looked slyly out of the corners of her eyes as she took off the Paris green hat. "What has Field's got?"

The young man's cheeks colored. "We're not going there."

"Of course not." The woman lifted her eyebrows at him and widened her eyes, as if they were sharing a great joke.

"Should've ordered bespoke at Rutherford's." The man made an obvious effort to regain control of the conversation. "Why buy ready-made when you can afford otherwise?"

The woman grinned. "True enough. Has Mr. Rutherford been jerked to Jesus yet? The store might not last long if they find him guilty. We'd better hurry."

The man's expression darkened. "I'll take you there another day. C'mon, Lizzie, this one's not so bad."

"The dark green looks nice against your hair, Madam." Miss Sweeny had been listening to their conversation, but her well-trained expression suggested that hats were the only thing on her mind. "And the violets are most appropriate for May."

"Very well. Miss Allen's account, and have it delivered." The customer removed the hat, replacing it with her own dark brown one. "Come along, Crabb, I could do with a drink."

"Do you know who that was?" Miss Dowling asked me when the pair had departed.

"I gathered her name was Miss Lizzie Allen, but that means nothing to me."

"That's Lizzie Allen all right, although 'Miss' is a bit of a laugh." Miss Sweeny's good-natured face broke into a broad smile. "She's a famous chippie."

"She wouldn't thank you for calling her a chippie," Miss Dowling said. "She owns her place."

"She's not bad looking," Miss Sweeny mused. "I wouldn't say she's the finest-looking woman in Chicago, like they say she is though. A little coarse around the mouth." She pursed her own lips, which were full and soft.

"What's a chippie?" I asked, puzzled.

"You *are* green." Miss Dowling laughed, though not unpleasantly. "A streetwalker, dearie. That's why Lizzie wouldn't like to hear herself called a chippie. She has her own parlor-house, with a good reputation for clean girls and nobody getting robbed."

"Such women shop here?" I felt curiosity rather than shock. After all, in the eyes of the world, I was no better than a prostitute.

"This is Chicago," Miss Sweeny said. "If you've got money, the stores will take it. You heard her mention Carrie Watson. Well, she's regularly seen at Field and Leiter's and Rutherford's. She buys the best silks and has diamonds for the evening." She looked down at her own uniform dress with a sigh.

"Don't think I'm not tempted too," said Miss Dowling. "It's a hard thing on a girl, being respectable. On your feet all day and a garret room to look forward to at the end of it, and a fine if you're caught with so much as a whiff of beer on your breath." She sighed too and then brightened. "Shouldn't complain though. It's better than living with my ma in Kenosha and getting knocked down by my stepfather every time I express an opinion. And I'll catch myself a husband here, see if I don't."

"Carrie Watson," said Miss Sweeny, ignoring Miss Dowling's interruption, "has a white carriage with yellow wheels. Horses as black as coal and a coachman who's even blacker. You can earn more in a day on your back than you can get in a week in a place like this." She rummaged in a drawer for one of our soft brushes and carefully whisked a few specks of dust from the pink and yellow flowers on the bright green hat. "I'll sell this thing today, I swear to both of you. I can't look at those colors anymore. Miss Harvey, next time a customer comes around, you stay well away from that hat. It doesn't look right next to your hair."

"It's not a good color hair for millinery," Miss Dowling agreed. "You're elegant looking and you speak well, and I suppose that's why they hired you. But I think you're in the wrong department."

"Who was the rooster?" Miss Sweeny's mind was still on Lizzie Allen and her companion.

"He looks familiar." Miss Dowling waved me back from the display as a pair of elderly women approached, arguing volubly in a Slavic language. "Pretty thing, ain't he? Almost as pretty as our Mr. Gorton."

❦

An opportunity to judge the good looks of Mr. Frank Gorton finally came once I'd been at Gambarelli's for three weeks. Of all the people at Gambarelli's, he was the one I most wanted to see. He was Lucetta's lover and the only man I could think of who might have a motive for killing her, even if Joe Salazar didn't think it likely. I envisaged a sudden access of passion over a new lover—although why Gorton would have tracked Lucetta down in a storeroom at Rutherford's was something I couldn't explain. The location of the crime, and the fact that the killer must inevitably have been covered in blood, were the most puzzling aspects of the whole affair.

Mr. Gorton, of course, was too exalted to speak to the shopgirls. However, he did come to speak to Mrs. Crowford. She, as well as being the head of millinery, was responsible for hat trimmings, umbrellas, muffs, and gloves.

I knew who he must be as soon as I saw him, but I affected otherwise. "My goodness," I said in an undertone to Miss Sweeny, "I don't think I've ever seen such a handsome man."

This wasn't strictly true. Judah Poulton, my erstwhile almost-fiancé, had been as beautiful as a painting of an angel. Yet Mr. Gorton came close with his thick shock of straight black hair and large hazel eyes with lashes as long as a girl's. He wore a black armband like the rest of us, but I could discern no signs of grief. His manner was brisk and businesslike as he leaned in to inspect Mrs. Crowford's books, one hand stroking his neatly trimmed beard.

"Don't get any ideas, Miss Harvey." Miss Sweeny surreptitiously stuck her elbow into my side. "He's never so much as looked at a shopgirl. Never heard of him being seen with a woman, come to that."

Which answered one of my questions. Frank Gorton was clearly well versed in the art of discretion.

I moved along the counter with a dusting cloth, pretending to have spotted some smears on the glass. Mrs. Crowford, with remarkably clear recall, was regaling Mr. Gorton with details of the hats sold in the last two weeks.

"And the shantung ribbon? I was not sure about it, if you remember. Has it sold well?" He had a strong French accent, the letter *R* a deep purr.

"It holds a bow very well." Mrs. Crowford looked around and caught sight of me. "Miss Harvey? The inventory for those broad Chinese ribbons, please."

I hastened to bring her the book where we noted the sales of trimmings. "The pale lilac has done particularly well for quarter mourning," I ventured, opening the book to the last set of totals.

"Hmm." Mr. Gorton's gaze flicked indifferently over me. "Hair a bad color for millinery," he remarked to Mrs. Crowford.

"She's fairly skilled at selling and speaks well." Mrs. Crowford was kind enough to defend me. "Elegant in her person and clean."

"Hmm." Mr. Gorton's eyes were on the book, but I felt an opportunity looming.

"I'm a dressmaker by profession," I said. "But I understand hats well enough. If I could be allowed to ask—with the little pointed collar so in demand, could we not have more of those hats that come to a peak over the forehead? There's such a lack of balance when the rounder brim is chosen."

Mrs. Crowford looked annoyed for a moment, but then she shrugged. She was essentially a fair woman. "It's not such a bad suggestion, at that."

Mr. Gorton withdrew a notebook and pencil from his pocket, licking the point of the pencil.

"Any particular color is desired?"

"Chocolate and mid-brown have been doing well, surprisingly so for spring—if they can be trimmed right. Green is popular," I said promptly. "Of course, as soon as it gets warm, they'll be wanting lighter shades."

"*Bien.* Very well. Thank you, Miss—"

"Harvey. Thank you, sir. Mrs. Crowford." I picked up my dusting cloth again, stepping aside to let the two of them pass. Mrs. Crowford gave me a regal nod and resumed her enumeration of sales figures.

"You've got a nerve," said Miss Sweeny when Mrs. Crowford and Mr. Gorton were safely out of earshot. "Hasn't she, Miss Green?"

The third assistant nodded morosely. She had been miserable all week owing to the fact that the troublesome tooth had been located in the front. Now her smile was ruined and her job possibly threatened. "You'd better make sure the peaked models sell, Miss Harvey. He'll remember who suggested them if we have to send them to the basement in July."

"They'll sell." I said it with as much assurance as I could muster.

"I'd say you won't be here anyway," said Miss Dowling. "I heard that remark about being a dressmaker, and your hair is quite wrong for millinery. You should look for a position in ladies' modes. The best way in is by selling unmentionables."

I was beginning to suspect Miss Dowling regarded me as something of a rival, but I didn't mind that. "You were trying to attract Mr. Gorton's attention, weren't you?" she continued.

"Only in the professional sense."

I had been watching Mr. Gorton as he took his leave of Mrs. Crowford and crossed to the counter selling perfume bottles. We were in the largest sales area of the store, the room with the fountain, and the flow of customers was steady at that time of day. I saw a man enter the store and cross to the same counter, engaging Mr. Gorton in conversation. The ostensible topic of their exchange was the perfume bottles, but something about them piqued my curiosity.

"That's the chap who was with Lizzie Allen," I said, nudging Miss Dowling. "Talking with Mr. Gorton. See him?"

"You've got good eyes. I can't make him out, but it doesn't surprise me." She peered shortsightedly. "He works at Field and Leiter's, and I've seen him come in here alone a few times. He's probably a spy."

She said it so casually that I thought I might have misheard. "A what?"

Miss Green, who had been listening to our conversation, sidled closer, cheering up a little. "Don't you know? All the department stores have people who inform on what the competition is doing. And he's a funny one, anyhow. With a funny name—Christopher Columbus Crabb."

"That was it." Miss Dowling looked pleased. "I knew I'd seen him before, and now you say the name I remember it. I've seen him coming out of Mr. Gorton's office."

My fingers tingled as my heart rate increased. I moved toward a pretty young woman who was looking hard at a boater-style hat trimmed with a cascade of ribbons and silk daisies, pretending more interest in my job than in the gossip about Mr. Crabb. But even as we discussed the merits of the hat and I invited her to try it on, my mind was working furiously. Had I stumbled on something significant? Probably not. The only person likely to have any real information about Lucetta's affair with Mr. Gorton was the man himself, and he would not speak to me. But it might be worth keeping an eye on Christopher Columbus Crabb.

TWENTY-TWO

"Mrs. Lillington!"

I turned around in alarm at hearing my real name called. I had just stepped off the horse car on my way back to Gambarelli's, and my mind had been occupied with Sarah, with whom I'd spent a precious three hours. State Street wasn't busy since all the stores were closed. I felt less safe with fewer people around than I usually did amid the vast crush of weekday traffic. I had become adept at riding the horse car, learning to sit near other women and to avoid any man who smelled of alcohol—as most did.

"Billy." I was relieved to see Billy O'Dugan's open yet shrewd face. "Please don't call me by my name—there are good reasons why not, if you'll trust me."

He stared at me, taking in my plain clothing. "But you're all right, aren't you? Not in any kind of trouble?" He held out his arm to me. "Gave me quite a turn, seeing you step off the State Street car. We've all been wondering about you since Tessie won't tell a word about your doings. Naturally, Ma and the others ask questions about you sometimes, just to be friendly. Our Tess is acting mighty mysterious in your regard."

I sighed. Clearly, Tess's idea of keeping a secret was presenting some challenges. "I'm quite all right. I'll have to be mysterious too, but it's all in a good cause."

"And you've not been at home, we understood that much. Tessie's been complaining she's in charge of Sarah all the time."

I bristled. "Miss Baker's there for most of the day. Does Tess really find it a great burden to put Sarah to bed? She never did before."

"If you ask me, it's Aileen and Mary who are putting her up to complaining," Billy said. "Are you going any farther? I'm on my way up to the Palmer House, but I'm not due there for another half hour. I can walk you safely to wherever you like."

Something occurred to me. "Have you walked all the way from the Back of the Yards?" I asked.

"Sure I have," said Billy with a grin. "I like the exercise, and it saves me the fare." He gestured at the sky, which was a pale blue tinged with pink as the sun began its journey downward. "And it's a fine day for a walk."

I nodded. "I wish I could walk from Aldine Square, but I don't suppose I should do that unaccompanied. What do you mean by saying that Aileen and Mary have been encouraging Tess to complain?"

Billy stopped short, so I had to stop too, and faced me. "I've been wondering whether I should come and see you about it," he said, "only I wasn't sure where I could find you. I don't think it's right, all this business about Tessie coming to live with Mary. You know they'll be after all the money she has." A range of emotions passed across his homely face. "They mean well, that's the worst of it. They've convinced themselves they're doing the best for Tessie and providing for Ma and Da. They'd take Tess in if she didn't have a penny in the world—but it's more money than they can ever spare themselves, and it's the devil of a temptation."

I shook my head, exasperated at what I was hearing. "If it's money they want—"

"They won't take yours," said Billy. "Matter of pride, see? And they wouldn't take Tessie's all at once. It'd be a matter of share and share alike, all prettied up with notions about how they're taking care of Tess and giving her a place in the world where she belongs. And Aileen would be after giving more to the church for the good they're doing in the parish. I wouldn't have anything to say against that if it was just her husband's money."

"Do you think Tess would be better off living with them though?" I had to ask the question, although I dreaded the answer.

"I do not." Billy took my arm and began walking again. "Mary goes on about how you're taking advantage, how you're keeping Tess near you for the help she gives you, but doesn't Tess get help from you too? And isn't that what a friendship is, after all?"

"Tess doesn't have to lift a finger in my house if she doesn't want to," I said.

"I know it. I reckon you're the best thing that ever happened to our Tessie, an angel of God sent to look after her."

"I wouldn't go that far." But I smiled all the same.

"I'll do my best to speak up for you," Billy said. "But I'm warning you to keep an eye on my sisters. If you want Tess to stay by your side, you might have to put up a bit of a fight."

☙

When I saw Tess the next Sunday, my hopes lifted a little. I had sent a note asking Mr. Nutt, our driver, to wait for me a block west and south of Gambarelli's, where the horse car did not run. With a little thought, I was able to ensure nobody saw me heading in that direction. Having the carriage available saved me a great deal of time. I was home early enough to derive the utmost advantage from the piece of roast beef Mrs. Power had cooked for us.

"I'll have to wait a good hour before I can even move," I groaned, patting the location where my full stomach strained against my bodice. "You can't imagine how good it is to be able to rest after eating."

Tess had also eaten well and now pulled a small footrest to her armchair and settled herself with a pleased smile. "There's nothing cozier than a Sunday afternoon with nothing to do."

"But you will take me to South Park later, won't you?" piped up a small voice from behind my chair, where Sarah was laying out her paper people in preparation for a game. "I want to see the sheep."

"We'll certainly go out later," I promised. "Just give me a little time to recover from luncheon." I stretched my aching feet out, luxuriating in the feel

❧ 145 ❧

of the soft plush of the armchair against my back. The great advantage of less elaborate dresses was that they allowed one to actually sit instead of perch.

I never got enough sleep at Gambarelli's so before long I was dozing, listening to Sarah's constant babble as she invented adventures for her paper people. The sounds of children playing in the gardens filtered through from outside while Tess's soft snores soothed rather than irritated me. The various noises were blending in my near-sleeping brain into a harmonious symphony when the doorbell rang. I half listened to Zofia's voice and her footsteps on the stairs, only to sit bolt upright when she announced the visitor.

"Mr. Salazar, Madam."

"Joe." Ignoring Sarah and Tess's stares and regardless of etiquette, I was out in the hall in a flash and had shut the door behind me.

"Is Martin all right?" was my inevitable question. I knew by now that Joe would only call if he had important news.

"He's quite all right." Joe's lean face split in a smile. "It's good news. They've released him to his suite at the Grand Pacific. They walked him up there at four o'clock this morning, and so far the newspapermen haven't gotten wind of it. We've had Pinkerton agents watching for signs of journalists, but for now—nothing."

"Which means I can see him. Give me five minutes."

"Nell?" Tess called from the parlor. "Who is it?"

I opened the door. "Mr. Salazar," I said, and Joe raised his hand in greeting. "I have to go out. Now." I crossed the room and dropped to my knees next to Sarah. "I'm sorry, darling."

"But, Momma—" Sarah wasn't given to crying or whining when plans were changed, but now there was a distinct tremor to her lower lip.

"I'll make it up to you." I looked over at Tess, whose face was thunderous. "And you, Tess."

"You're leaving me behind again."

"I know, but—" I gestured desperately in the direction of where Sarah sat behind my armchair. "Please, Tess. I'll explain it all when I can."

Five minutes later, I was climbing into Joe's landau. "They're both upset with me now," I said. "But I can hardly take them with me, can I?"

"I wouldn't risk it. It'll be difficult enough ensuring the press don't find out about you," Joe agreed. "They'll understand."

"Maybe." The landau was a much more lively vehicle than the Katzenmeiers' rockaway and moved forward at a good clip, smooth and comfortable. I tried to relax into the velvet upholstery of the open carriage and enjoy the sunshine, but my mind was on both the scene I'd left behind me and the practical details of the scene ahead.

"Do we have to go in at the front of the hotel?" I asked Joe.

"I've arranged to use the same way by which Martin was brought in," he said. "Martin's been at the Grand Pacific ever since he returned from Kansas, and the management is most cooperative."

I nodded. "So tell me why he's been let out so suddenly."

"We found evidence that's made it impossible for even the most corrupt of judges to hold him any longer. Our biggest problem is that it may not be possible to publicize the evidence we have, for reasons I'll explain to you."

"What evidence?"

"For one thing, a good thirty of the witness statements we've gathered, read together, make it impossible for him to have murdered Mrs. Rutherford with such a protracted struggle as clearly took place. Simply as a matter of timing, you see. He was seen entering the washroom; he was seen leaving it; he was seen ascending the staircase; and he was seen kneeling by his wife's body. Once we worked out a system for reading the various statements together, it was clear that the timing absolved him. Then there's the evidence of the blood."

"You told me about that. There was blood on Martin's hands and the knees of his trousers, but nowhere else."

"Precisely. And yes, as the newspapers reported, he was holding the knife that killed Mrs. Rutherford. But all of the witness statements agree he was holding it by the *tip*. He said he had some idea of looking to see if he recognized it as belonging to someone in the store. But really he was so shocked by the sight of his wife's body that he was acting like an automaton. And more importantly still—" Joe looked at me cautiously.

"Yes?"

"You may not want to hear it. It's rather grisly."

"I've told you before, Joe. Don't spare me."

Joe took a deep breath. "More importantly still, the pool of blood in which the knife lay—undoubtedly the gush of blood from the final, fatal cut—had already begun to form into clots. Which means it hadn't just happened. The murderer had a few minutes to get away."

"But you must have realized that right from the beginning. Why wasn't Martin's innocence established earlier?"

Joe leaned forward so that I could hear him better over the street noises. "We'd had no idea how the killer could have gotten away, which muddied the waters considerably. As soon as the realization dawned that a murder had taken place, we cleared out the customers and shut the doors. The police searched the building from top to bottom and took the names and addresses of every employee who remained in the store. Then the employees were sent to search the store again, with the exception of the murder room. A detective came and took photographic plates of that and recorded all the contents."

"And nobody was found with any blood on them."

"No. It's taken a while to get statements from every single employee in the store. Not to mention checking them one against the other and going back to the witnesses to clear up some discrepancies that might be important. And we contacted every customer we could identify from the accounts as having been in the store that day. It wasn't till the new attorney started plotting every statement against all the others—and mapped them out on a huge grid—that we realized the killer must have headed directly downstairs, either via the elevators or the main staircase. And that all the elevators and the staircase were busy at that point, and that the murderer should have been seen. A man with blood—quite a bit of blood—on his clothing would be hard to miss."

"But he wasn't seen."

"And wouldn't have gotten out any other way unless he could make himself invisible." Joe's eyes gleamed. "And the way to make himself invisible—"

"—would be to have no blood on his clothes. He changed his clothes." I was catching Joe's excitement, my heart beating rapidly. "But how?"

"The room where Lucetta was killed was the room that held the props for window-dressing," Joe said. "Those props included men's clothing. We sometimes use it to set off the dresses. All he had to do was to find a suitable suit of clothes, and change right where he was."

I stared at Joe, dumbfounded. "And nobody thought of this before?"

"The rack of clothing was splashed with blood, as was everything else in the vicinity of the struggle," Joe said. "We were lucky we locked the entire contents of the room in the basement instead of putting it all in the furnace. We scrubbed down the room, you see, after five days—when the detectives were satisfied they'd recorded all the evidence. As soon as we had the theory of the change of clothes, we searched through the pile. We found a jacket with its right sleeve stiff with dried blood. It was that and several hours of explaining to the new judge the whole business about the witness statements that got Martin freed."

"So the case against him is dismissed?" I asked. "His name is cleared?"

Joe's face fell. "It's not being made public." He held up a hand to check my exclamation. "For good reason, Nell. If the murderer simply walked out of the store with the other customers, he may think he's safe. He may still be in Chicago. If the story of the facts as they're now understood is released, he could disappear forever." He looked down at his hands. "Unless the real killer is caught, Martin's always going to be under suspicion, at least with the general public. Almost certainly with the Gambarellis. None of us want that."

"I suppose not." The sense of dismay I felt was smothering, extinguishing my excitement of a few minutes ago like a blanket thrown over a fire. The thought of Martin's name being cleared had given me a momentary, selfish hope that my own undistinguished career as a private investigator could be brought to a speedy end. I thought I could go back to a normal life—a life that now included Martin. But now, I realized as the landau rolled northward, Martin could be in even greater danger than before without the prison walls to protect him. I would have to return to Gambarelli's that evening and stay there until I'd found something that would help the man I loved.

TWENTY-THREE

Getting into the Grand Pacific without being seen was surprisingly easy. A hotel employee led us by a circuitous route along utilitarian corridors and stairways. We eventually emerged into a hushed, elegant corridor. The soft hiss of the gilded gaslights was the only sound as we walked, our feet sinking into the deep pile of the carpet.

Joe opened one of the doors without knocking, and we stepped into a small vestibule. "I'll be in the sitting room," Joe said, gesturing toward one of the doors. "I'll walk you back to Gambarelli's."

I shook my head. "No, you won't. Much too risky. But I'd appreciate your help in getting out of the hotel unseen."

He opened the door to the sitting room, and I hesitated, looking at the other closed door. Oddly enough, I felt reluctant to intrude on Martin's privacy now that he had some. I remembered his bitter words in the jail, his wounded pride that I had to see him at his lowest ebb. Had I once more been too impulsive in insisting on seeing him?

Joe caught my look. "It'll be all right," he said softly. "It's better than letting him brood alone."

I wasn't so sure, but I took a deep breath and opened the door, hearing Joe retreat into the sitting room behind me.

Martin was standing by the window, lit by the afternoon sun. He was staring avidly into the street as if he couldn't get enough of the sight of it, ignoring the sounds I made as I entered. His arms were braced against the window frame. He was wearing an ordinary sack coat, which hung off him a little as if he'd lost weight. His stance revealed the tenseness of his muscles, the sharp lines of his shoulder blades appearing for a moment as he shifted his position.

Not until I clicked the door into its latch did he turn to face me. He was clean-shaven, but the air of the cage hung about him in his cropped hair, the shadows under his eyes, and the set of his mouth. For the first time I had ever known, he reminded me of my distant memories of his father. This was the closed, impenetrable stare of a beast that could attack at any moment.

"Nellie." His expression relaxed slightly.

I was determined not to "make a fuss," as Grandmama would have said, so I smiled as if it were a perfectly ordinary day and said, "It's good to see you."

Something moved behind his eyes, but his words were as conventional as mine. "Won't you sit down?"

He handed me to a chair as if I were a visiting acquaintance, punctiliously ensuring I was comfortable before seating himself opposite me. He was definitely thinner—the light picked out hollows under his cheekbones that hadn't been there before.

"I'm so glad you're free at last," I said after a few moments of silence while I racked my brains for something to say to him. I wanted, I supposed, a grand scene of reunion, of passionate kisses—I particularly wanted the kisses—but after the jail, I was prepared for this stiff, awkward interview. "I couldn't bear seeing you behind bars."

"And yet you came."

I tried to smile. "I couldn't stay away."

Another long moment of silence while Martin looked at his hands. They were scrupulously clean, the nails manicured, if I were any judge. A ray of sunlight made his thick stubble of short hair glow, and there was a rawness to his skin. Had he been scrubbing it?

"Joe told me that they've managed to prove your innocence on the basis of the evidence," I said at last.

He looked up at me, one corner of his mouth twisted upward in a cynical half smile. "Proof is a relative term, I'm finding. I've received the distinct impression over the last few weeks that evidence counts for very little. Nor does an impeccable record of respectable living, nor do powerful friends—most of whom haven't come near me."

"None of them?"

He shrugged. "Potter Palmer came to visit me at the county jail. He's a decent old stick. And Marsh Field has gone on record as saying he's sure I'm innocent. But for most people, I fear, nothing I can do or say will prevent them from attaching 'wife-murderer' to my name unless we can come up with proof of someone else's guilt. Perhaps even then. Martin Rutherford, wife-murderer. If I were you, I'd run in the opposite direction."

"Stop it." My sorrow on Martin's behalf was quickly transforming itself into strengthening anger. "What good does that kind of talk do? Especially when you aim it at me. I know you're innocent of any crime, and I certainly don't need you to offer me anything except yourself."

"*Myself*?" Martin croaked the word, rising from his chair in a jerky motion. "I've spent the last six years building *myself* into something worthwhile." He pushed the chair he'd just vacated back with such force that I heard the wood crack. "I thought I'd rid myself of Rutherford the draper—the man who wouldn't fight—for good and all. I thought I'd gained an empire. But it's all worthless."

He lifted one foot and brought it down hard on the corner of the chair. The leg splintered with a loud crack and the whole chair sagged sideways, tumbling off the rug onto the parquet floor.

"Further evidence that I'm a man of violence," said Martin curtly, gesturing at the ruin of the chair. He returned to the window and leaned against the frame, his back to me, his left hand squeezed tight into a fist.

"Don't be ridiculous." I was next to him in an instant, wrenching at his arm to turn him to face me. "Stop feeling sorry for yourself. Your business is thriving, and you're alive. Your good name, if that's what matters so much to you, can be rebuilt."

"Perhaps," he muttered, turning back to the window.

A memory surfaced, unbidden. "You leave him his dignity." The voice was that of Bet Bratt, Mama's housekeeper, and I was seven years old. I was glaring at her because she'd dragged me down to the kitchen and given me a good spanking with a large, solid hand. She'd caught me spying through the keyhole of the parlor door, which Mama had closed.

"You leave him his dignity," Bet told me as I stood before her, stubbornly determined not to rub my sore posterior. "The poor lad's got little else he can count on."

The sight I had been forbidden to see was Martin, then a raw-boned lad of eighteen, thin and gangly and anxious to be seen as a man and not a boy. He had been sobbing in my mother's arms—for what reason I didn't know, but I could guess it had something to do with his father. How could I restore a shred of dignity to him now? And then I knew.

"What's happening to that poor madman who was in Harrison Street with you?" I asked.

He frowned, turning to look at me blankly. "Poole?"

"Is that his name? What will they do with him?"

"Send him to Dunning, I suppose. I heard them talking about a hearing." Martin straightened up. "God, what a fate."

"What's Dunning? And what did he do? They didn't lock him up just for being insane, did they?"

My tactic was working. Martin had lost his frozen look, a spark of interest returning to his eyes.

"He'd been making a nuisance of himself around women. You heard the language he used to you—that, it seems, is fairly typical. With no women around, he becomes a mild enough sort, although his habits are disgusting and his personal hygiene nonexistent. Dunning's the insane asylum—it's got a reputation." He frowned. "They frighten children with the name."

"Does he have to go to Dunning?" For a moment, I too was taken out of myself, thinking of the fate that could be in store for the man. I'd heard bad things about insane asylums. "Martin, couldn't you do something for him?"

"Like what?"

"Find him a private arrangement of some kind. You could easily afford it. If, as you say, all he needs is to be kept away from women . . . you could at least try."

"I could, at that. I'll get Joe to look into it." Martin caught my look and smiled—a genuine smile this time. "I know—I'm heaping a great deal onto poor Joe's shoulders. Where is he, by the way?" He looked around the room as if expecting to see Joe Salazar lurking in a corner.

"In the sitting room, waiting to take me back to Gambarelli's. You know about that, don't you?"

I held my breath, but Martin only nodded.

"You're working there." He said it in a flat tone, as if the matter were of no interest at all. Under normal circumstances, he would have been angry or at least exasperated with me, told me I was putting myself into danger. But these were not normal circumstances, and Martin was not himself. I needed to remember that.

We were standing close enough that either one of us could have reached out and pulled the other in. I could feel the warmth radiating from his body, see the rise and fall of his chest. If I stretched out my hand, I would be able to feel the regular thud of his heartbeat. Ceding to the temptation, I lifted my arm—and then noticed, with a faint sense of shock, that he wore a black crape armband on his sleeve.

"You're in mourning for Lucetta." I slid my hand up his arm to the band of material, feeling its slight roughness under the tips of my fingers.

He shrugged his arm slightly, and I withdrew my hand. "And I will continue to be in mourning for an appropriate length of time. She was my wife. My faithless tormentor, but my wife."

I hoped my face didn't betray the dismay I felt. I let a long moment of silence stretch between us before saying, "I'm sorry for your loss." The conventional phrase was all that came to mind, but to me it had layers of meaning behind it. I felt a deep sense of irreversible change, a future that seemed to be turning its back on me—on us.

He pivoted away from me again, his gaze fixed on the street below. I realized that he was shaking, just a slight tremor of the arms and shoulders.

"He took her voice." When he spoke at last, his own voice had a strangled sound. He cleared his throat before continuing. "Do you think he thought about what he was destroying? Her stupendous voice. It was the one thing I could still—"

He didn't finish, and the shaking intensified. I wrapped my arms around his rigid back and laid my head against his shoulder. What else could I do? What could I say to him? Below us, the life of Chicago flowed in an endless tide, heedless to the agony of the man beside me.

We must have stayed like that for three minutes before he finally turned within the circle of my arms and buried his face in my neck. He hadn't made a sound, but I could feel the wetness of his tears against my skin.

Leave him his dignity. I said nothing—made no attempt to stroke his hair, to comfort him as I would Sarah—but merely brushed my lips against the short white-blond bristles, my own eyes squeezed shut to deny my tears.

After a few more minutes, he drew a deep, shuddering breath and spoke in a more normal voice into my shoulder.

"I wish to God I hadn't seen her. She haunts my dreams, staring up at the ceiling with that awful look on her face. What kind of a man could do such a thing?"

"Not you." My arms tightened around his shoulders, but he hunched them and drew himself gently out of my embrace, dragging his sleeve across his eyes.

"I never hit her." The words came out with a sort of proud insistence. "She used to goad me, did I tell you that? Not alluding to her lovers in any direct way, but hinting. As if she were daring me to lose my temper."

"And you never did."

"No. I suppose I passed that test, at least." Martin gave the ghost of a smile, but it disappeared in an instant. "She waited for me half the morning," he said. "She was trying to get me back."

"Are you certain?"

"She'd tried—hard—soon after I returned from Kansas. She visited me at the hotel—talked me into having dinner sent up. She tried to seduce me." His tone was again flat.

"And couldn't." A momentary surge of joy went through me. But it wasn't the real Lucetta who bothered me now—it was her memory and the legacy of pain she'd left behind her.

"Not even when she tried to make me angry by taunting me about her lovers, more openly this time. I told her that I knew about them and was sorry

I hadn't made her happy enough to abandon them. That I took the responsibility on myself."

"You weren't responsible for Lucetta's behavior."

"Wasn't I? I was wrong to marry her when I was in love with you. I played a considerable part in the wreck of our marriage." His tone was bitter. "Lucetta didn't want to be loved in a halfhearted way. She was desperate to be worshipped utterly—for someone who would never despise her or cast her off, no matter what she did. Perhaps her affairs were a way of testing me, and I failed."

"You married her because she told you she was having your child, and that was a lie. She knew she couldn't have children." I could hear the anger in my voice. "You can't bear the responsibility for her deception of you."

I wasn't sure if Martin had even heard me. "She knew about you before I even did, I believe," he said, his eyes seeing something far-off. "How do women know these things?" His gaze snapped back to me, his gray eyes like the sky before a storm. "It was in my power to save her, and I didn't."

I wanted to scream at him in frustration. It was Lucetta's fault that things had worked out the way they had, not his. Or perhaps it was mine—for not being strong enough to tell Martin to go away, for coming to Chicago when I knew I shouldn't. I clenched my fists, casting around for a way to turn the conversation away from Martin's sense of his own guilt.

"Was that the last time you saw her?" I asked.

"No." I could almost see the memory behind Martin's eyes. "She asked me to do one thing for her after that. To attend Domenico Gambarelli's Santo Stefano gathering with her to avoid gossip that we were separated."

"When was that?" Jealousy reared its head inside me, and I stamped on it. They had appeared together socially as man and wife, after all. Martin had connived with the deception Lucetta had elaborated, perpetuated it for her sake.

"Santo Stefano is the day after Christmas. Papa—Domenico—spends Christmas Day very quietly, as his wife died during the Christmas season. But on Santo Stefano, he holds a huge feast—a sort of symbolic rejection of mourning, I suppose. He invites every last relative and acquaintance, even some of his more senior employees. Lucetta sang, as she often does—did—at parties." His eyes had the distant look again. "She wore a gold dress, and even with three hundred or more people in the house, I seemed to see her constantly. She shone under the lights like—like treasure." He shook his head, a bemused look on his face. "Gold and diamonds, amethysts and rubies. Everyone turned to look at her as she passed."

I had to know. "Did you go home with her?" That "Papa" had hurt more than I could have anticipated, and my voice was small, mean sounding. Martin looked directly at me.

"I left early and alone," he said shortly. "I never saw her alive again."

I dropped my eyes, feeling the blood mount to my cheeks. "I'm sorry."

"I understand."

There seemed to be nothing I could say that would steer us in the right direction. Perhaps there *was* no right direction. So I resorted to practicalities, a thought prompted by Martin's description of a gold dress.

"Lucetta's maid—was that still Trudy? The one who came to Kansas?" Trudy had been well aware of Lucetta's affairs and might prove useful.

"Trudy left Lucetta just after we returned to Chicago. I didn't meet the maid she hired after that as I'd already moved to this hotel. It was some Italian girl—the police have tried to find her, but she's nowhere to be found."

"Don't you think that's significant? That she's disappeared?"

Martin turned his head to look out of the window yet again, and I wanted to shake him. Or kick him. Or kiss him. But the sky outside was darkening, and Joe's discreet knock sounded on the door.

"Come in." Martin crossed to the center of the room, brushing past me as if I were a passerby on the sidewalk.

Joe's eyes flicked to the broken chair and then to me. I gave a tiny shake of the head to indicate there was nothing drastically wrong, and his mouth relaxed.

"You'll make sure she gets back safely." Again, the flat, expressionless tone. In the twilight of the unlit room, only Martin's face, hair, and hands stood out. The black of his armband was absorbed into the gloom, invisible against the black fabric of his jacket, as if mourning had become a seamless part of him.

I didn't remember how I got out of the building and barely registered what I was doing as I made my way back to my garret room at Gambarelli's. My whole being was concentrated on one man, who perhaps was still standing in the darkness, looking out of the window. A free man—but not, by any stretch of the imagination, truly free.

TWENTY-FOUR

With only Sunday afternoons off, and devoting those to Sarah and Tess, I didn't see Martin. The newspapers—which, I remembered, were probably in the Gambarellis' pockets—continued to cast doubt on his innocence. I grew tired of reading such articles. I didn't know what, if any, progress he was making with the case himself. Had he hired men from the Pinkerton Agency, or was he concentrating on his business? I understood the need to stay away from Martin, for both our sakes, but it was wearing on my nerves. I felt more shut off from him than I had in my early days in Kansas, when we had corresponded regularly.

I was becoming accustomed to life at Gambarelli's, from the whirl of activity when the store was crowded with customers to the periods of boredom and endless tidying and arranging when it wasn't. Mrs. Crowford and the millinery assistants gradually allowed me greater freedom to make recommendations and suggestions to customers. When we were busy, I was able to make some sales on commission. I would feign delight in those few cents and buy such small supplies and gewgaws as a young woman with not much thought for the future—except for the exciting possibility of finding a husband—might wish for.

I missed Sarah and Tess, and my mind was far too often on Martin, but I also found myself longing for my dressmaking business. I used my increasing influence over customers to make recommendations on their entire ensemble. If I had a few minutes to spare, I would wander through the dress goods department, familiarizing myself with Gambarelli's stock of wools and linens, silks and satins.

Today had been busy, and at four o'clock in the afternoon, we were all taking advantage of a slower period to put our counter in order. I had one of the ribbon drawers open and was checking through and straightening the spools of bright color, my lower back complaining about the position in which I was standing. Miss Green quietly said, "Crowford" and I felt rather than saw the activity around me increase in pace and intensity.

"Is Mr. Gorton on the floor?" Mrs. Crowford hove into view with the speed of an arriving locomotive. She was a brisk, dried-up woman who did not hold with vague answers or slowness and rarely bothered to greet her subordinates. I rather liked her directness and her meticulous attention to detail. I particularly admired her utter recall of the day's, week's, even month's business.

"I haven't seen Mr. Gorton, ma'am." Miss Dowling widened her watery blue eyes into an expression of keen alertness, as if she hadn't been gossiping in an undertone with Miss Green for the last twenty minutes. "He hasn't been on the floor today."

Mrs. Crowford tutted. "I suppose I'd better take this up to his office." She put the accordion folder she carried on the counter and steadied it with her right hand while she flipped up the watch pinned to her bodice with the other.

"I could go," I offered. "I'm due to take my twenty minutes." I had made quite a specialty of offering to fetch and carry. Such tasks gave me opportunities to walk around the store and keep my eyes and ears open—so far, with little result.

"Yes, very well." Mrs. Crowford put the folder—which turned out to be remarkably heavy—into my arms. "Tell him it's the orders he was asking about, only he'll have to get one of his clerks to make the précis. I haven't had the time."

"Will it be all right if I wait five minutes until Miss Sweeny gets back?" I asked and received a nod in return as Mrs. Crowford departed in the direction of the glove counter.

"She did that on purpose," Miss Dowling said as soon as Mrs. Crowford was out of earshot. "She knew you'd offer, so *you* can get into hot water with Mr. Gorton instead of *her*. He won't be too pleased to hear there's no précis."

I shrugged. "I'll manage. Will he shout at me?" I grinned at her.

"Not him. Freeze you, more like. Finish your ribbons, quick. You can take an extra ten minutes since you're running an errand."

Five minutes later, I made my way up the staff staircase to the offices on the building's fifth floor. By the time I reached the top, I was panting. Shopgirls were not permitted to use the elevators, and the folder grew heavier with every flight of steps I climbed.

I knew vaguely where the managers' offices were, but it took me a few moments to find the door with "F. Gorton" painted on it. I knocked.

"Yes." The voice sounded impatient.

Balancing the folder on one arm, I opened the door.

"I'm sorry to disturb you, Mr. Gorton." Then, realizing he wasn't alone, I affected dismay. "I'm terribly sorry, sir. I would have waited if I'd known you had a visitor."

My heart began to beat more rapidly. The visitor was the man called Christopher Columbus Crabb, and the light of recognition was in his eyes. I had at last stumbled upon something, but I had a part to play.

"Are you sure you don't want me to come back later?" I sincerely hoped not, but I didn't want to seem eager. I gave Mr. Crabb a smile that I hoped walked the line between flirtatiousness and the professional friendliness of a saleswoman and said, "It's good to see you again, sir."

Gorton waved me into the room with a brusque gesture. "We are nearly finished, and I go out soon. Tell me what it is."

I proffered the folder I was carrying. "Mrs. Crowford asked me to bring you this. She sends her compliments and says she hasn't had time to make a précis."

A frown of annoyance marred Gorton's handsome face. Seen up close, his head, with its mass of black hair, looked a little large for his slender, elegant body. He wore a morning coat of the finest cut. His silk cravat sported a large diamond pin that reflected sparks from the gaslight.

"No précis." He began pulling papers out of the folder and replacing them after a brief examination, muttering in French under his breath in a way that boded ill for Mrs. Crowford. All I could do was stand and watch. He seemed to have completely forgotten my presence.

Crabb hadn't. He lounged back in his chair, stretched his legs out in front of him, tipped his curly brimmed bowler hat forward, and looked at me from under it in an impertinent manner.

"Are you really a shopgirl?" he asked after a few minutes' perusal. "You don't look like the kind of girl who'd be desperate to work at Gambarelli's." He brushed his mustache with one gloved hand in a manner that was some-how suggestive. "You look like you're destined for better things than that."

I tried to sound a little put out. "I'm a dressmaker by profession, but it's not easy to find a job when you're new to a town and don't know anyone."

"I could introduce you to people." One side of Crabb's beautifully shaped mouth curled up under the fringe of his mustache. I realized he reminded me of my cousin Jack. "There are far better ways to make a living in Chicago than standing behind a counter."

"Don't tease the girl, Crabb." Mr. Gorton was making rapid notes on a sheet of paper.

"Does he mean something that's not respectable?" I asked, appealing to the Frenchman. "I hope you won't think I'd listen to him, sir."

"He is a young ass," said Mr. Gorton distinctly, making the sibilants hiss. He looked directly at Crabb, his eyes shaded by their thick lashes. "I don't know how things are at Field and Leiter's, Crabb, but in this store, the young women are not to be insulted by such insinuations."

"No insult intended," Crabb said smoothly.

Mr. Gorton had finished extracting what he wanted from the folder and handed it back to me. "Please return this to Mrs. Crowford, with my compliments. And kindly remind her, from me, that I require a précis next time, or we will have words."

"Yes, sir," I said meekly, all the while trying to reformulate Mr. Gorton's words into something less likely to make Mrs. Crowford lose her temper with me.

"Thank you, Miss——"

"Harvey."

"'Arvey. You may go. Crabb, you too must leave——I have to see Mr. Alessandro."

Mr. Crabb rose promptly and gracefully to his feet and held the door open for me with an ironic bow. I heard him shut it behind me as I headed for the staircase. Then my progress was arrested by a strong hand grasping the back of my arm.

"There's much more money to be had than in working in a place like this," said Crabb softly in my ear. "The name's Christopher Columbus Crabb. You can wait for me outside the employee entrance at Field's, any evening at seven. Don't make it too obvious."

His grip loosened a little, and I pulled away. "I'm not what you take me for."

"They never are until they're short of cash."

My retreat toward the stairs was followed by a low chuckle, barely audible under the sound of my hastening footsteps.

"You'd be a complete fool to get mixed up with Crabb," I muttered to myself later that day as I headed north on State Street. I had been assigned to the early dinner shift this week and had eaten fast, obtaining leave to absent myself for an extra forty-five minutes. I intended to purchase bonbons, to ingratiate myself with the gossipy sales clerks——both men and women——from the dress goods department. I was glad enough of the small taste of freedom this errand gave me and had even found time to change my work dress for one I'd made myself.

I was fairly sure that Crabb meant absolutely what I thought he meant. He had inferred that the way to make money in Chicago was by engaging in the sort of life that Lizzie Allen led, or worse. I'd been at Gambarelli's long enough to realize that some of the girls managed to get around the limitations of what could be earned by selling goods in the store by ensuring that they had at least one man on the string.

These men did not usually work at Gambarelli's. The hours at the store were too long and the pace of work too intense for male and female sales clerks to form romantic attachments. Besides, most of the girls affected to despise the idea of marrying a sales clerk. There were flirtations, to be sure, and I knew one or two young women who seemed genuinely stricken with romantic love. They would blush when a certain young man from umbrellas or shoes strolled by their counter—Miss Green was one. But most of them were being courted, if that were the word, by men outside the store.

So I wasn't the only shopgirl at Gambarelli's who shot away from the store like an arrow from the bow as soon as the Sunday service was over. In fact, my rapid exit—in the direction of the quiet street where Arthur Nutt sat waiting for me atop the rockaway—was clearly taken to mean that I had a lover. I realized after a while that even had I been seen climbing into the carriage, many of the girls wouldn't have batted an eyelid. Miss Sweeny sympathized when Miss Dowling sighed after a life of wedded bliss with a respectable husband and eyed every prosperous-looking male customer with an avid eye, but the gentleman who waited for her outside the employee entrance every week had the aura of being married—to someone else. I also suspected some of the girls of working at a certain establishment any evening they could sneak out of the store.

So Crabb's hints were rather less of a surprise than I'd pretended. And if he were indeed engaging in espionage of some sort, he might be a useful acquaintance to cultivate. Yet to do so could lead me down a path I definitely didn't want to take.

The confectioner's shop I sought was just north of Madison Street, not far from Field and Leiter's. I had already crossed to the eastern side of the street, but as I drew opposite Rutherford's, my footsteps faltered, as they always did.

I instinctively hesitated to venture into Martin's store as Amelia Harvey. Despite his release, a small but persistent group of journalists haunted the corner of State and Madison, watching for any sign of Martin's comings and goings or any hint of something new. And I knew intuitively that Martin would avoid being seen openly with me until the real killer had been found—and possibly even beyond that.

As I watched from across the street, there was a general movement of the newspaper men toward a dappled gray horse, riderless, that had been led to a convenient spot on State Street near the Rutherford's entrance. My eyesight was keen enough at a distance that I could see the journalists had an unhurried air, but it was an expectant one.

And then Martin emerged. I couldn't mistake him—his hair always gave him away. Besides, I would have known him anywhere. He wore a frock coat and tall silk hat, the very picture of a prosperous gentleman. I wasn't surprised to see him head straight toward the gray horse. Passing carriages occasionally impeded my view, but I could see that a gaggle of passersby had joined the journalists who gathered around him. I could hear nothing above the din of the street, but I realized I was witnessing an ordeal that Martin went through more than once a day.

I saw him urge the horse into a fast trot as he headed along Madison Street away from me. He was no doubt returning to the Grand Pacific, with his day at the store ended. Or perhaps he had planned a longer ride to exercise his muscles and remove him, for a while, from the attention of the curious. Perhaps he even had a social engagement, a dinner with a friend to look forward to.

I stood watching until I could no longer see him amid the carriages and horse cars. A feeling of utter blackness descended upon me.

Whatever he was doing, I wasn't part of it. I might never be part of it. This was Martin's normal life, or as close to it as he could get, and I was as removed from it as if I'd still been in Kansas. I didn't even know if our remoteness from one another mattered as much to Martin as it did to me. I was an onlooker from afar, more so now than when we'd been hundreds of miles apart but connected by our letters.

Suddenly, my scruples about talking with Crabb fell to the wayside. What did any kind of risk to myself matter if it would lead to the discovery of Lucetta's killer? I was sure I could talk myself out of any situation that would involve sacrificing my virtue or putting myself into direct physical harm. If I could help Martin in any way, I should.

It was time to act. I unbuttoned the top of my paletot and fumbled for the timepiece pinned to the bodice of my dress. Twenty minutes to seven. Crabb had told me I could wait for him outside Field and Leiter's at seven. I would still have just enough time to buy the bonbons that were the ostensible reason for my outing on my way there.

I turned away from the street corner and plunged back into the stream of pedestrians. The street was quieter now that the dinner hour had come and gone, but it was still crowded, and I would have to hurry if I wanted to be absolutely sure of Crabb.

"Yes, I'd be a fool to get mixed up with that man," I said under my breath, lengthening my stride as much as my skirts would allow. "But I'd be more of a fool to let this opportunity slip by. After all, it's the first one I've had."

ৼ

Five minutes to seven found me waiting outside Field and Leiter's, my eyes on the side entrance from which employees were emerging. The store was a huge, imposing block, more massive than either Gambarelli's, with its disjointed facade made out of several buildings, or Rutherford's neat, contained exterior. It had row after row of arched windows separated by cornices of a darker color. The light of the setting sun made the pale stone at the top of the building gleam. At street level, it was already almost dark, the passersby illuminated by pools and splashes of light from windows and streetlamps.

It seemed like an age before I saw Crabb emerge. I recognized him easily by his tall, broad-shouldered form and the curly brimmed hat of the sort affected by mashers and vain young men. I was glad to see he was heading in my direction so I wouldn't have to run after him.

"Mr. Crabb." I stepped into his path.

Even in the gathering gloom, I could see the amusement in his eyes and mouth, but all he said was, "Well, then." He doffed his hat to me and offered me his arm. I took it. It was hard with muscle, the forearm broad and strong, and this close to me, he seemed even more imposing. He smelt of cologne.

"Come and have a drink."

I pulled my arm back a little. "No—I don't—I mean, I have to be back at Gambarelli's soon, or I'll be marked absent. But what you said—"

"About earning some extra money?"

"Yes, but not—I mean, I think you were referring to a certain profession, and I don't want to do that. I wanted to see if there were other ways." I looked down at my feet. "I don't need much more than I earn now. I have a—a child, and I have to pay for her keep."

"I had a feeling about you," he said, smiling. "Still, I've got a weakness for hoity-toity girls, so I'll listen to whatever you're going to ask me. I'll walk you to Gambarelli's while we're talking. But why not make some money the easy way?"

"I'm afraid of getting sick or—in a situation again." I looked up at him. "I've learned my lesson about that." I was able to say it with perfect sincerity.

"So what are you proposing?"

I swallowed, my throat dry. "I heard you need other things. Information."

"I've got all the information about Gambarelli's I need."

I thought furiously. "I could get a position at Rutherford's, I'm sure I can. As a dressmaker."

He snorted in derision. "You think. They only employ the good ones there, Miss Harvey."

"I'm good. I'm very good."

"Then why are you working at Gambarelli's?"

"I only came here from Kansas in March, and I had to find a situation. It's hard when you're new. But I've got a friend now who can get me considered at Rutherford's."

We walked on in silence until Gambarelli's was in view. Crabb let go of my arm and turned to face me.

"I'll admit it's not such a bad idea. It's hard to get new people into Rutherford's. Those that get in, stay in, and they all earn enough to make them loyal." His eyes narrowed as he scrutinized my face under the light of a lamp. "If—and, mark you, *if*, because I doubt you're good enough—you can get into Rutherford's, you can come back to me and I'll see what I can do. If you can't get in and you're not willing to work on *my* terms, don't bother me again."

TWENTY-FIVE

Working at Gambarelli's naturally meant that I hadn't seen Elizabeth Parnell. I had written to her, of course, letting her know we were well settled in at Aldine Square, and had received several letters from her in return. When I was at home on Sunday afternoons, I tried to find time to write back, claiming to be busy settling in to our new life. I hadn't always succeeded, and some of her letters had gone unanswered. Since our friendship was of recent date, I wondered if she would interpret my sporadic responses as a sign that my interest in her was cooling. There was little I could do about that, and perhaps our friendship would be one of the sacrifices I'd have to make for Martin's sake.

I knew she didn't like Gambarelli's all that much and felt safe from discovery. So my dismay was all the greater when, a couple of days after my meeting with Crabb, I heard her voice behind me.

"I'd like to try this on, Miss."

I turned to find my friend pointing at a light blue hat with the peaked brim I'd suggested to Mr. Gorton. It was trimmed with white feathers and sprays of cornflowers. Although not of the best quality, it was an attractive enough article. Elizabeth was staring at me, indeed *through* me, as if she didn't know me at all.

"Of course, Madam." I smiled brightly and removed the hat from its wire support, waiting until Elizabeth had unpinned her own hat. "It's a perfect match for your eyes, if you don't mind me saying so."

I positioned the blue hat atop Elizabeth's abundant hair and fetched a mirror so she could see it. Out of the corner of my eye, I could see that Miss Sweeny and Miss Green were busy with other customers.

"Just how angry are you?" I said in an undertone while smoothing the large, curly white feathers so that they hung at the correct angle.

Elizabeth's eyes widened. "My dear," she said just as quietly, "I'm not angry at all. I was a little annoyed that you seemed to be putting me off in your letters, especially after you'd been at Aldine Square for three weeks. It's a pretty little place, isn't it?"

"You've been there?"

"Of course. I really need to talk to you, otherwise I wouldn't have intruded."

"Perhaps you'd like to try this one as well," I said in a louder tone. I took down a similar model, of a darker blue trimmed with white silk roses and pheasant's feathers. "If you don't like the feathers, we can alter it for you."

"Clearly, this is no time for a conversation," Elizabeth said. "Do they let you out of this cage occasionally?"

"I could get outside at six," I said. "Say ten minutes past. Are you at the hotel?"

Elizabeth's pretty pink lips tightened into a straight line. "I am, for the moment," she said. "But I'll tell you more later. I'll be waiting for you."

At ten minutes past six, I walked into the Palmer House, feeling oddly out of place. I had changed my dress, but I could still feel the Gambarelli's uniform on my back, so much had it become second nature to be employed.

Elizabeth thought differently. "Thank goodness you're out of that dreadful rag." She hugged me hard and kissed me on both cheeks. "It's good to see you looking like yourself."

"It's not all that bad," I said. "Especially after I made some alterations so that it would fit better. I presume you talked with Tess?"

"It took me a little while to convince her to give away your secret." Elizabeth grinned as she led me to the far corner of the huge parlor, seating me in a winged chair that would hide me from casual observers. "You see, I can be discreet too. And persistent. Tess was marvelous—she didn't crumble under my expert interrogation, and I'm my mother's daughter and can usually winkle information out of anyone. She only spilled the beans, as the saying goes, when I told her how desperate I was to talk to you. Imagine my astonishment when I found you'd been working as a Gambarelli's shopgirl all this time." Her smile vanished, and she took my hand and squeezed it. "You must truly love Mr. Rutherford."

"I do, rather. I'm not sure how he feels about me at the moment though."

Elizabeth tilted her head to one side, looking remarkably like her mother in that gesture. "Do tell."

"There's not much to tell." I had removed my gloves and now laced my fingers together, looking down at the bare spot where my wedding ring usually resided. "I barely see him, and when I do, we seem to argue all the time. Or he looks at me in that dreadful blank way he uses with strangers when he's hiding his feelings." I swallowed. "He needs time, I know. He's numb, I think, and terribly angry inside. I'm too impatient."

"And you need reassurance too. It's only human." Elizabeth curled her hand into a fist and gently rapped her knuckles on the back of my hand. "Poor Nell. I wish I could help you." She was silent for a long moment and then spoke again. "Mother's sending me back to Lake Forest tomorrow."

"You make it sound like an exile." I was amused.

"It is." The words came out so vehemently that I was surprised. "It's a punishment."

I raised my eyebrows. "Punishment for what?"

Elizabeth stared hard at the blue cuff on her day dress, picking at a tiny flaw in the silk. "For making a fool of myself over David—Mr. Fletcher. For writing to him, setting up assignations with him, and inviting him to dine at the hotel. Without a chaperone." Her rounded cheeks were aflame.

"Oho," I said. "I take it that nothing drastic has come of your efforts. Or should I say nothing worthwhile?"

"Nothing but Mother's edict that I shall no longer correspond with David or try to meet with him. Honestly, Nell, she treats me like a child."

I rested my forehead on my hand, thinking, and then looked hard at Elizabeth. "And how has Mr. Fletcher taken your attempts to seduce him?"

"With damnable insouciance." Elizabeth drove the heel of one neatly buttoned boot into the carpet. "That's the worst of it. I think he likes me—*really* likes me—but how am I going to find out if I can't spend five minutes alone with him?" The last words came out in a wail. I waggled my hand to indicate she should lower her voice.

"Is that what you want from me?" I asked. "To find out if he really, *really* likes you?"

Elizabeth's lower lip protruded a little. "I need you to talk to him. Work out a way I can speak with him and he can speak with me."

"A correspondence that would be expressly against your mother's wishes."

"So *what?*" This time Elizabeth's voice was decidedly too loud, and I wondered if we were attracting attention. "Nell, in the name of friendship—"

I held up a hand to stem the flow of words. "I can't be a party to your schemes of seduction. But"—I put up the other hand as her mouth opened in protest—"I should talk to Mr. Fletcher anyway. I've let financial matters at Aldine Square slip. I could use the opportunity to see where the land lies, as far as he's concerned. If he's set on courting you, he'll find a way—if you're patient. If not, there's nothing much you can do. I'm learning that myself," I added ruefully.

"Oh, do talk to him. And—oh, I don't know. Convey to him that my interest in him is more than passing. Or something. Oh, this is useless." Elizabeth flung herself back into her chair, heedless of her dress.

"It's all the worse because now Frances is in town," she continued. "My sister. I have so much to tell her and so much to ask her. Now Mother's making sure I'll only see her in Lake Forest when she and Father accompany them from town. It's mean of her. Oh!" Elizabeth sat up straighter.

"What? Don't try to give me suggestions about how to proceed with Mr. Fletcher."

She waved her hands expressively. "No, not that. Change of subject. At least, it's to do with Frances, or rather with that friend of hers, Grace Fairgrieve. That's whom Frances is visiting." She looked at my face and sighed. "You've forgotten. Lucetta Rutherford's friend? Who has the maid who used to be Mrs. Rutherford's."

"The Irish girl? I remember her from Kansas." This was interesting news in that the Irish maid could provide a clue as to Lucetta's behavior, but not terribly exciting.

"No, not that one. The Italian girl she had after—who stayed on in New York after Mrs. Rutherford went there. Before she returned and was murdered."

"Wait. The *Italian* girl? The maid Lucetta had at the time of her murder?"

"Only she didn't. The girl stayed with Mrs. Fairgrieve. What does the maid matter, anyway? The point is that Mrs. Fairgrieve is here, and I could arrange an introduction to her. Perhaps you could find out something about Mrs. Rutherford's state of mind when she returned to Chicago."

"Perhaps. But an introduction to the maid would be even more useful." My palms were sweaty. Obviously, Elizabeth hadn't heard that the Italian maid was supposed to have gone missing after Lucetta's murder. Thinking back, it wasn't an element of the murder that was frequently mentioned in the papers.

Elizabeth grinned. "One doesn't arrange introductions to maids unless you're proposing to hire one. But if you want to meet Grace Fairgrieve, I'll write a note. And I have one more favor to ask of you."

"What?"

"Let me invite Tess and Sarah to Lake Forest for a while. Chicago gets so dreadfully odorous and disease ridden in the summer. Removing them from the city will give you peace of mind—and, more to the point, I won't be nearly so bored with some company around me. Do you think Sarah's governess would like to come too?"

"I have no idea—you'll have to ask her. Why? Do you think Sarah will get behind with her schoolwork, or are you nervous of looking after a small child?"

"Neither." Elizabeth's eyes gleamed. "I had a few words with your Miss Baker when I visited your house. I detect a kindred spirit as far as the rights of women are concerned. I'd enjoy getting to know her better."

※

"Thank you for making yourself available on a Sunday, Mr. Fletcher." I waved the banker to a chair. "I've been quite busy, you see, and finding time to meet with you during the week has proven difficult."

"That's perfectly all right." Many men in the banker's position would have made some ingratiating remark about being at my entire disposal. Mr. Fletcher merely took the proffered seat and opened his notebook, raising his intelligent eyes to me once he'd found the first blank page.

"I can be brief, as far as the business portion of our conversation is concerned." I handed Mr. Fletcher a half sheet of paper. "I find that I overestimated our expenditure and that we have a surplus. Here are the correct figures, and there's a summary of the excess funds I have on hand. I'd like you to adjust what the bank is sending to us accordingly."

He took the paper, perused it, made an entry in his notebook, and looked up at me again. "That's an easy task. What else do you need, Mrs. Lillington?"

"Nothing for myself. I've been charged with a message—"

Mr. Fletcher rose rapidly to his feet and loomed over me with all of his broad-shouldered height. "Miss Parnell put you up to this, didn't she?" He sounded annoyed. There was even a note of anger, although it was quickly subsumed as his professional instincts rose to the fore. He sat down again and cleared his throat.

"Mrs. Lillington," he began. "Would it be possible for me to ask you—*beg* you—to leave matters as they stand as far as Miss Parnell is concerned?"

"You don't love her, then? I'm sorry—it's not my wish to interfere, believe me. But I don't think Miss Parnell is going to leave matters where they stand, even from Lake Forest."

"Lake Forest?" He sounded perplexed.

"She's been sent back there by her mother—you didn't know? Elizabeth wanted me to help her find a way of corresponding with you—if that's what *you* want. But if, as I suspect, the idea is repugnant to you, let me know, and I'll find some way of letting her down gently. I don't think you wish to trifle with her feelings."

"Of course I don't." A slight flush overspread his cheeks. "And nothing about Miss Parnell is repugnant to me. I hope I never gave her that impression."

"Perhaps my words were too strong. Let's say this: If you are not in love with her, please tell me, and I'll do what I can to deflect her interest from you. She's headstrong, but I'm sure her self-respect will conquer her emotions in time."

Mr. Fletcher sank his head into his hands and stayed that way for a full minute. When he looked up again, his face was a battlefield of conflicting emotions, his eyes bright. He took a deep breath.

"I can't tell you that I'm not in love with Miss Parnell."

"Ah."

"But for heaven's sake—can't she leave me to do my own wooing? This is—just—preposterous."

"I think she'd call it modern." I was beginning to feel amused.

"But I'm *not* modern. I wish to put my finances on a sound footing before I approach her father for her hand. I'm waiting for a promotion that should make marriage possible. Not until then will I court Miss Parnell—or any woman."

"So you *do* love her?" I couldn't help it—a grin had broken out across my face.

"Since you're clearly not going to desist, I have to confess to tender feelings for Miss Parnell." The young man had regained control of himself, and his gaze was steady. "I admire her spirit, her intelligence, and yes, even her persistence. But I am not prepared to do anything improper, even for the sake of the principles she holds dear." He looked up at the ceiling and then at me again. "My father is a Presbyterian minister, and not for all the world would I do anything to disgrace him. Tell me the truth. Do you think Miss Parnell likes me for myself? Or do I merely represent an experiment she can essay to prove how much more advanced she is than her parents?"

I was silent for a few moments, considering his question—which was eminently fair. "I think," I said slowly, "that Miss Parnell's not entirely clear on what she thinks. She's impulsive and headstrong, and—quite possibly—in love for the first time. I don't think she's toying with your affections. I don't believe that she would be any less loyal to you if you entered into what you call an improper arrangement than if you married her in a church. She sincerely believes, I think, that a relationship based on Free Love would be a freer and happier state of affairs than if you entered into a marriage that, to her, is founded in a sort of principle of ownership—by the man of the woman."

"Do you believe that?" For a moment, Mr. Fletcher looked much younger. He really did love her.

"No." I shook my head. "At least, I believe such an arrangement would be a free and beautiful thing indeed, if it didn't automatically place the woman outside the pale of respectable society. I suspect that respectable society may be wrong—but it's what we have to live with. One day, perhaps, we'll arrive in a world where women and men can love each other freely. To believe that utopia is achievable in our time is perhaps a little too optimistic."

"Well said." Mr. Fletcher smiled. "Mrs. Lillington, since you've been drawn into this mess, could you try to convince Miss Parnell that I would welcome the chance to be a perfectly boring, conventional admirer of hers? If she can be patient, I could certainly be brave enough to beard Mr. Parnell—who has the reputation of being a fair man—in his den, so to speak, and beg for the chance to start afresh. Sometimes a man simply feels the need to wait until the timing is right for him. Tell her I won't countenance a meeting between us for the time being—and that I don't wish to correspond with her either—but I will look forward with fervent hope to a day when such meetings and correspondence are possible."

I nodded, and, shaking my hand cordially, Mr. Fletcher made his goodbyes and left. I watched him from the parlor window as he ran down the steps and set out in the direction of the street, making a good pace with a lively, athletic stride.

Sometimes a man simply needed to wait until the timing was right. Was that the case with Martin? He too had a keen sense of the proper way in which to act. In the last few weeks, I had often wondered if his invitation to me to come to Chicago was a rare instance of rashness on his part. Yet my instincts told me that when he'd made that invitation, my well-being had been uppermost in his mind. He'd wanted to assure himself that I had all I needed to put whatever new life I chose onto a sound footing. He would have helped me, and then, at whatever cost to himself, he would have let me go.

And was what I now interpreted as coldness part of the same sense of fairness and balance? He'd made it clear to me that he'd mourn Lucetta for the proper duration of time. Perhaps he was resolved that we should be apart until that time had come to its conclusion. The knife that had severed Lucetta's throat had just as suddenly cut away the dilemma we'd been in, with no honorable solution to our passion for each other in sight. Yet it had somehow thrown us back into our former roles of old friends.

And it was strange, I mused, watching the flame of Sarah's hair as she ran back home from her outing to the garden with Tess. Now it was I who felt protective of Martin. Thanks to him, I was a wealthy woman with the freedom to do as I chose. *His* freedom was constrained by the newspapermen and those who thought him a murderer. Circumstances that nobody seemed able to unravel had trapped him.

Was it selfish to think of Martin and me when Lucetta's very life had been taken from her? Yes, perhaps. But Lucetta was, I hoped, at peace, and in my human frailty, I couldn't help thinking of the future—the uncertain future. With one stroke of the knife, the relationship between me and Martin had shifted on its axis, teetering gently on the brink of an irreversible change.

č

"Has the tall gentleman gone?" Sarah peeped cautiously around the door.

I held out an arm to her. "He has. Did you have a nice time in the garden?"

"We floated my boat, and we saw a fat white duck who said 'quack' to me." Sarah ran to me and climbed onto my lap. "You feel nice and warm."

I folded my arms around her and buried my nose in her springy hair, which smelt of damp earth and salt. She shifted so that her head lay more comfortably against my bosom, and a sigh escaped her.

"Momma, is it the tall man who's going to be my Poppa?"

I ducked my head, encountering two jade-green eyes peering anxiously up at me. "What?" I asked in astonishment. "Didn't Tess tell you it was the gentleman from the bank?"

"Yes, but she said you liked him. When ladies and gentleman like each other, don't they get married?"

"We-e-e-ll, yes, sometimes. But sometimes they just like each other as friends do. And Mr. Fletcher's not even a friend, really. He's a gentleman who helps with money."

"Oh." Sarah was quiet for a moment and then spoke again. "Then is it the gentleman with the nice carriage who's going to be my Poppa?"

"Which gentleman?"

"He has a nice shiny carriage, and he wears a tall hat. His horses are pretty brown ones with black manes and tails."

"Mr. Salazar?" I smiled. "No, not in the least. Mr. Salazar is a Poppa already, to three children. I don't think Mrs. Salazar would like it if I took him away." I put my hand gently under Sarah's chin, lifting it so I could see into her eyes. "What on earth makes you think I'm going to present you with a father all of a sudden?"

To my surprise and dismay, Sarah's eyes filled with tears. "You're gone all the time, and nearly every day I don't see you, and nobody will tell me why. And Zofia told me courting couples like to spend time together. I was watching a lady and gentleman walk around the garden, and I asked her why they just kept walking round and round. And she said that when people are going to get married, they aren't interested in anybody else."

"Oh, Sarah, darling." I dabbed at her tears with my handkerchief and kissed her several times on her cheeks and forehead. "I'm not off spending time with a gentleman, I assure you." I hesitated then plunged on. "You remember Mr. Rutherford?"

"Martin?" Sarah had caught the habit of referring to Martin by his given name from me and Tess. "He's nice. Where is he?"

"In Chicago. But he's been in trouble—grown-up sort of trouble. People are saying he did something he didn't do. And he's the best friend I have in the world, and I'm trying to find out who did those things so that Martin can be happy again." I felt tears prick behind my eyes.

"Is the pretty lady with the dresses in trouble too?"

"Mrs. Rutherford? She's in heaven, sweetheart." I swallowed hard.

Sarah's eyes were as round as marbles. "In heaven? Did she get sick?"

"Yes." Because I wasn't going to breathe a word about murder anywhere near my daughter. Perhaps, one day, when she was a lot bigger and Martin was happy again, I could tell her.

Sarah threaded her dainty, slim-fingered little hands into the fringe that decorated the bodice of my dress and hummed tunelessly, watching the fringe slide over her fingers. She did this for at least five minutes, giving me a chance to wage battle against the emotions that threatened to overwhelm me. I was tired, no doubt. I was anxious about the prospect of exchanging the known rigors of Gambarelli's for the new challenges of Rutherford's. I was fearful that Martin would simply refuse to have me work in his store and destroy the opportunity I had so painstakingly built up.

"Is Martin going to be my Poppa?" Sarah stopped her fidgeting and became still, resting her head once more on my bosom.

"I don't know." I had to grit my teeth hard so that Sarah wouldn't feel my chest move and know that I was crying.

TWENTY-SIX

"I'd like to see the General Manager, please."

"On what business?" The clerk who'd opened the side door of Rutherford's in response to my persistent rapping eyed my Gambarelli uniform with well-trained indifference.

The narrow alley in which the door was located was almost completely filled by three large drays. A host of men were unloading packages and placing them on metal ramps that led down into the basement of the store, great mouths that swallowed the merchandise whole. Their shouts and laughter rang out and bounced against the alley walls, windowless for twenty feet up and then studded on both sides with rows of utilitarian rectangles of glass.

"To ask for a job. Please." I didn't quite put my foot in the door, but I thought he could see by the look on my face that I was considering it. "I'm a friend of Mr. Salazar's wife—he'll be pleased to see me, I assure you." I smiled at the clerk, a bald-headed, middle-aged man whose expression was now shading toward the paternal. "I'd come during store hours, but—" I looked down at my uniform.

"You'd better not be wasting my time." The clerk opened the door wider and jerked his head to indicate I should step in. "I'll take you up. I suppose I can give you the benefit of the doubt about your claim to be a friend."

He led me through the store, which at this early hour was bustling with employees working on the displays. Some were arriving with new merchandise to add to what was already there; others were ensuring that their area was spotlessly clean. Men on tall, stout ladders with hooks on the top worked on the walls of the central area. Their task was to refresh displays that consisted of a bolt of fine fabric hung high on the walls, cascading downward to end in a glorious artlessness of shimmering folds. Several other men, impeccably dressed, strolled around the floor with their hands behind their backs. They seemed to be checking every detail of the displays and frequently tapped a subordinate on the shoulder to offer advice or reproof.

Ignoring the elevators, the clerk led me to a side staircase, and we climbed to the third floor, emerging onto a corridor buzzing with a different sort of energy. A purposeful hush would perhaps be the best way to describe it. Or perhaps the muted hum of a hive too busy with producing honey to pay much attention to anything else. As we passed the doors, I could see clerks at desks, muttering to themselves as they counted slips of paper and noted down totals. A huge cash office dominated a large portion of one wall. Its counters were empty except for one or two older men talking to younger people—clearly sales clerks—who were listening respectfully, nodding their heads at intervals.

We arrived at the middle of the corridor, where a series of large, imposing mahogany doors with brass name plaques were partly open, but not enough that the activity inside was visible. The middle-aged clerk halted in front of one of those doors, the plaque reading "Mr. Jos. Salazar, General Manager," and looked round at me.

"What name?"

"Mrs. Amelia Harvey."

I waited outside the door while the clerk insinuated himself around the side of it in a manner that barely opened it any more than it had been. He returned in a moment, a broad smile on his face.

"He'll see you, and welcome." He nodded approvingly. "When you're done, just go down to the sales floor and ask any of the floor managers to let you out." He opened the door in an inviting manner, and I walked in.

Joe Salazar rose to his feet as I entered. Beside him, Martin straightened his tall frame from a stooping position, where he had been inspecting two or three piles of paper on Joe's desk. My heart engaged in a small frolicking jump as he smiled.

"How are you, Nellie?" He left the papers he'd been studying and pulled out a chair for me. When I was seated, he retreated to the wall behind Joe's desk, leaning against it with his arms folded.

"Amelia Harvey," he said with a grin. "I wonder what your mother would have said to see you using her maiden name to engage in subterfuge?"

"She probably would have encouraged me." I grinned back. "Mama was far braver and more daring than most people gave her credit for. If it weren't for her illness, I'm sure she'd have had adventures of her own."

Martin nodded. "I gather it's Joe you've come to see, not me. Is this to be a private talk?"

"It concerns you, so no." But I addressed myself to Joe. "I'd like to apply for a job in dressmaking."

Joe pushed aside the papers in front of him and leaned his forearms on the desk, hands clasped, his eyes on my face. "You wouldn't ask such a thing without good reason. What have you found out?"

"Nothing you probably don't already know. Such as, for instance, that Mr. Gorton is as thick as thieves with a certain Christopher Columbus Crabb."

Joe's face darkened. "I'm always surprised Gorton tolerates that conceited puppy. But, of course, what Crabb sells is information. He began some time ago by passing along information to Alex Gambarelli about Field and Leiter's—some of it quite valuable. Since then, he's extended his reach so that he employs some fifteen or so spies, all clerks in other stores. Not in ours though, I'd stake my life on it."

"Not until now." I tried not to look at Martin's face. "If you'll give me a position, I can become the sixteenth or so spy in Mr. Crabb's employ."

Martin drew in his breath with a sharp hiss. "No. Don't you realize the company that man keeps? Thugs. Brothel keepers. Women of ill repute—"

"Such as Lizzie Allen," I interrupted. "I've met her." Gratified at the expression on Martin's face, I didn't give him the chance to speak. "At Gambarelli's, of course, although I understand that she and—what was her name?—Carrie Watson shop at Rutherford's." I tilted my head to stare straight into Martin's eyes.

A faint flush tinged his cheekbones, and I rejoiced. Anything was better than the flat, pale, dead look I'd seen of late. "I don't turn them away. I don't turn any woman away," he said with a certain stiffness of demeanor. "But that's not the same as actually consorting with them, which is what you're proposing to do."

I lifted my chin. "If you must know, I explicitly refused any role that would lead me into consorting with such women. What do you take me for? I offered to provide information instead. Crabb seems quite keen on the prospect—if I can get into Rutherford's."

Joe had been watching us, turning his head from one to the other as we bickered, a light in his eyes. "You'd have to be good enough," he said to me. "I can't engage anyone who doesn't come up to Madame Belvoix's standards."

"She's good enough," Martin said shortly. "But I don't agree—"

"What you agree to is neither here nor there," I said in my best imitation of Mama. "You can't claim you've given me my independence one moment and try to restrict my actions the next." Then, dropping my hauteur, I added: "For heaven's sake, Martin, I'm not proposing to put myself in any kind of danger. Crabb's provided me with a means to meet him openly, on the street, and I've already refused to go elsewhere with him."

I saw Martin's eyes darken at that, but he said nothing. "You can give me just what information you think might be useful to Crabb," I continued. "All you have to do is make it convincing enough." I turned to Joe. "Who is Madame Belvoix?"

"The terror of the dressmaking staff." Joe's mouth twitched as if he were trying to suppress laughter. "She's in command of the workshops—and when I say 'command,' I choose my words carefully. She really is French—or at least Alsatian, which is close enough. Came here as a result of the Prussian occupation. She knows her fabrics and her techniques backward, can spot a badly cut dress from twenty yards away, and has been known to reduce a seasoned couturière to tears with a single word."

"She sounds delightful," I said. "When do I meet her?"

Joe coughed. "On Mr. Rutherford's recommendation—since he has been kind enough to vouch for you—I could arrange a meeting for tomorrow evening at seven. You'll have to wear one of your own gowns. But I warn you, she may start you off in a lower position than you think you deserve. Are you tolerant of humiliation?"

I couldn't help smiling. Much as I liked Joe, I wasn't about to tell him about the Poor Farm. Somehow I doubted Martin had regaled him with that story. I turned so that I faced both men and confronted Martin's exasperated expression with a challenging look.

"I can work under any number of French tartars if it will advance our case." I caught the look in Martin's eyes at the word "our" and swallowed back the lump in my throat. "Besides, it'll make a nice change from hats. I hope Madame Belvoix approves of me."

From Joe's description of Madame Belvoix, I had pictured a tall, imposing Valkyrie of a woman with a commanding air and fearsome eye. What I found was a small, plump, soft-looking, grandmotherly lady who spoke in the mildest of tones. Only her eyes gave her away, steel-gray balls that remained fixed on me as I spoke. I had the impression that every inch of my person was under her scrutiny, particularly the dress I wore.

"You are in millinery at Gambarelli's." It wasn't a question. If anything, it was a criticism.

"Only temporarily." I knew I sounded apologetic. "I came from Kansas with my daughter in March, and I had to find a situation quickly." I twisted Hiram's wedding ring, now returned to my finger. Joe had told me that couturières with children were not unheard of, and however keen I was to get into Rutherford's, seeing Sarah and Tess only once a week was becoming unbearable.

"You wish to leave the store at four o'clock." Again, it sounded like an accusation—and again, Joe had told me it was possible.

"I'll come in as early as you wish and work without a break if you want me to." I looked hard at the little Alsatian woman, trying to impress her with my earnestness. "I'd just like to see my little girl before she goes to bed. She's only five."

"Who looks after her?"

"A spinster friend."

"She does not work, your friend?"

"She's a housekeeper. The lady of the house doesn't mind having the child there." It worried me, sometimes, how I'd learned to twist the truth.

"And you live where?"

"Near the stockyards."

"If she is sick, you will disappear for days on end."

"She's not a sickly child."

"Hmph. You have only been at Gambarelli's since March."

"That's right."

It was dawning on me that my eagerness for the position, which had at first been due to the possibility of helping Martin, was transmuting itself into a genuine thirst. Before this interrogation, Madame Belvoix had taken me through the dress goods department and thoroughly ransacked my mind for everything I knew about fabric. I'd been dismayed to realize I didn't know as much as I thought. Certainly not as much as this little woman. Her ability to rattle off the exact origin, designation, and qualities of bolts that had come from faraway China and Japan, India, France, Germany, or England, was encyclopedic. I longed to work with this phenomenon.

"Well, Gambarelli's." Madame Belvoix dismissed her rival with a wave of her fat little hand and a genteel sniff. "You cut your dress?"

"I cut and sewed this and many more when I had my dressmaking business in Kansas." My two-piece was of an extremely lightweight wool, a difficult fabric to cut. It had a subtle check woven into it so that the gray was shot through with purple, and I had experimented with the effect of the checks. I had cut it so that the bias met interestingly in the middle and fell away to drape the sides of the narrow skirt before being gathered up in a series of pintucks at the rear. The bodice also used the art of the bias to make the faint purple seem to shift with my own movements.

"Hmph." Madame Belvoix began pinching and pulling at my clothing, looking for aberrant creases or carelessly sewn seams. She would find none.

"Do you embroider or bead? Many of our articles are quite elaborate." As intimate as a lady's maid, she put her hand under my arm to indicate I should lift it and ran her finger along the seam of the armscye.

I shook my head. "I can do both and enjoy it sometimes, but I'd hesitate to claim my work is of the quality you'd require."

"What you have done in the front is good." She bent to inspect the extra insert I'd made in the front of the skirt in the shape of an inverted *V*, turning back the flaps thus created and fastening them with gray pearl buttons. Inside the *V*, I had created tiers of pintucks that flowed into the pintucked hem of the underskirt.

"It allows me to cut the skirt narrower and still walk fast." I put out one foot in illustration. "The fashion plates are showing quite an elongated form. Since my own figure is somewhat elongated, I can exaggerate the effect a little. This idea could be adapted for a train, don't you think?" I twisted to one side to see my work.

"Do you draw?" The gimlet eyes gleamed.

"Yes."

"Then show me your idea." The little woman turned to her neat desk and handed me a sheet of paper and a charcoal pencil.

I almost forgot her as I worked. It was always absorbing to figure out my ideas on paper. I sketched my concept quickly, adding a separate bodice with pintucking down the sides.

"The panels could be in a contrast fabric, and you could use a double row of pearl or abalone buttons here." I added a note to the drawing.

"Hmmm." This time the noise that came from Madame Belvoix's throat had a faintly approving sound. "You come with a strong recommendation from Mr. Salazar."

"I hope I've justified his confidence in me."

She gave a regal half nod. "You evidently have some sense. You may start as an assistant in cutting and piecing, and we will also have you sit in on some of the other stations. You will be allotted an hour each day to study the journals in the reading room for the first month. After that, you must find your own time, and it is imperative that you see every new journal that comes in." She touched my skirt with a fingernail. "This dress will do, and any other day dress you have of gray, black, or dark blue—but only if the cut is recent and the trimmings restrained. You must have at least three, and do not wear the same one all week. You may have an advance on your wages to purchase the fabric at cost if you don't have enough, and we will fabricate it at no charge."

I nodded, trying not to show the excitement I felt. "Thank you, Madame."

"Your hours can be eight till four, with twenty minutes at ten and thirty minutes at two. You must eat, as I do not employ girls who fall down with the hunger when they're working. You will wash your hands most carefully at the start of each working session."

"I always do."

"Yes, they are clean and well kept. Your appearance and speech are good, so you may also be present on the sales floor every Thursday to help Mrs. Nippes with advising the clients."

"Thank you." That prospect thrilled me, and I saw my delight reflected for a moment in the little woman's face. "What kind of notice should I give Gambarelli's?"

"One week." She shrugged. "They are always losing girls. Your wages—" and she named a sum that would have delighted a Mrs. Amelia Harvey who had been working in millinery, so I smiled broadly.

"Thank you *most* kindly, Madame."

"Do not thank me. Mr. Rutherford expects the utmost hard work from his employees and pays them well enough that they do not leave us once well trained. It is good business. If your work is of bad quality or your habits slipshod, you will receive a week's notice. Are we agreed?"

"We are."

"Very well, I expect to see you in my office at eight in the morning, one week from now."

I arrived at Madame Belvoix's door ten minutes ahead of the appointed time. I was dressed in a light gray dress I liked very much but hadn't had many chances to wear. It boasted little trim except a row of shining gray pearl buttons on the bodice and a deep, shimmering fringe of silver hue.

"Hmmm." Madame's sharp little eyes became sharper as she took me in. "I could swear I've seen those trimmings before. About a year ago, among our samples. We could not get a sufficient quantity of them for the store, and Mr. Rutherford was sorry because he'd liked them. Where did you get them?"

I felt the heat rise to my face. Of course, the trimmings had come from Martin. He understood as well as I did that such subdued colors brought out the best in my pale skin and unfortunate shade of reddish-bronze hair.

"I got them in Kansas," I said, slightly bending the truth. I had certainly opened the parcel in Kansas. "You don't think the fringe is too showy, do you, Madame?"

"It looks well on you. Though it's strange that you happened across just such a combination of trims, all those hundreds of miles away."

There was nothing I could say to that without lying, so I merely dipped my head. I followed the plump woman, who was dressed in a striking combination of black and white, to the top of the building. I felt an odd sense of pleasure at the notion that I was, at last, part of Martin's business. The more I saw of Rutherford's, the more proud of him I was.

We entered a huge room lit by a wall of windows. I could see straightaway that they faced north—good. Even better was the enormous structure that ran down the center of the room. It was a massive table with rounded ends, divided up into bays of differing sizes separated by low ridges of polished wood. Each bay had compartments built in underneath the tabletop, holding spools of thread, scissors, tape measures, and pincushions. Similar tables ran along the wall under the windows. Every one of them was occupied by a woman doing some kind of close work, such as embroidering or working on the details of a sleeve or panel, helped by the bright morning light. Sewing machines were lined up on the opposite wall, and dress forms clustered at the ends of the room. It was wonderful.

"You will not be assigned to a table yet," Madame said. "You may move around and work on such auxiliary tasks as the other ladies agree to. They will explain our ways. Each set of compartments holds exactly the same equipment. All must be left precisely as it is at the end of the day, replacing what has been used up. You will see that many of our ladies keep a *trousse* on their person with needles, scissors, and the like that they bring from their own homes. We all have our favorite tools of the trade."

A few glances were directed at me from time to time, but for the moment I was being quietly ignored. There were old and young women of all shapes and sizes, some in beautifully cut dresses, others in plainer garb covered by a simple apron.

"*Mesdames.*" Madame Belvoix clapped her hands, and every woman immediately stopped what she was doing. "This is Mrs. Harvey—cutting and piecing, and with Mrs. Nippes on Thursdays. Her hours are eight till four. You will kindly assist her in learning our methods."

Several of the woman said, "Yes, Madame," while others murmured a greeting to me. I smiled and nodded at those closest to me.

"I leave you to observe a little and ask questions. We will see how things go." And with a sharp, all-seeing glance around the room, Madame swept out, looking a little like a gray-haired penguin.

"Sink or swim." A woman about ten years older than me grinned at me. "What experience do you have?"

"I had my own dressmaking business in Kansas." The pieces of outfits scattered around the huge room were starting to resolve themselves into whole costumes in my mind. A reception dress with a long embroidered train. A frothy white confection, probably for a girl of around fifteen or sixteen. Day dresses of varying degrees of ornamentation. Light colors abounded, it being summer, but I could also see an autumn walking dress in a deep shade of rust. Its skirt was being separately assembled with layers of ruffles and shirring while its bodice was being fitted to a dress form. One of the embroiderers, a Chinese girl, was working on a wrapper covered in a field of silk ribbon flowers, lilies of the valley and daisies.

More questions followed, although the women all quickly resumed work, and our conversations proceeded in fits and starts. I asked questions and learned much about the work in progress. By the end of the day, I was able to connect each woman with her current task, even if I didn't know her name. Most of the embroiderers spoke little English but were clearly proud of their work, which was exceptionally fine.

I enjoyed myself so much over the next three days that I almost forgot my reason for being at Rutherford's in the first place. I rarely saw Martin. He had seen me in the fitting rooms on Thursday afternoon and inquired, as conventionally as if he hadn't known me, how I liked my job. I had replied in the same vein, and Martin had walked on without looking back. Yet I hadn't minded nearly as much as I would have thought. It was enough, for now, to know that we were only separated by a few walls and floors.

It was that encounter, however, that shook me out of the bedazzlement of having a new, and most congenial, occupation. So on Thursday at four thirty, I entered Field and Leiter's in search of Christopher Columbus Crabb.

He didn't look quite so imposing behind a counter with a sheaf of papers from which he was copying entries into a large book. He worked in the department that sold rugs and carpets. The vast room was empty of customers except for two pairs of ladies and two couples engaged in scrutinizing the merchandise that was hung, rolled, or simply piled waist-high.

"Good afternoon, Madam." Crabb looked up briefly, then down again to finish the entry he was writing. With a final flourish of his pen, he drew himself up to his impressive full height—and then recognized me.

"Oh, it's you." He looked annoyed. "I'm not likely to forget that hair, Miss Hoity-Toity. Did Gambarelli's throw you out, or did you leave?"

"I left." I made myself sound a little indignant. "It was just like I told you—I got a position at Rutherford's. Like I said, I'm a good dressmaker, and they were happy to take me on."

He narrowed his eyes. "You're a bundle of contradictions, you are. You arrive fresh from Kansas and go from selling hats at Gambarelli's to a plum job any Field's employee would give their eyeteeth for. And look at that dress, and there you are saying you're behind with your rent. You could pop it for two weeks' wages."

"I'd be insane to pawn my clothes." I sniffed loudly to illustrate how ridiculous his idea was. "They're my shop front—how do you think I got the job at Rutherford's?" I smiled up at him, giving him the full effect of my large blue eyes. He didn't seem to admire my personal charms, but there was no harm in trying. "I earn more now, but I could still use a little extra, just to catch up and buy myself a few things."

Crabb's eyes were on a couple walking toward us, and he spoke rapidly under his breath. "Very well, let me give you a little assignment. The names of suppliers of silk out of San Francisco, do you understand? And never come here again. The door, at seven."

I nodded, although that meant I'd have to wait three hours. "I understand."

He raised his voice, speaking to me as the couple came within earshot. "I'm sorry we don't have quite the article you desire, Madam. I'll consult with Mr. Field himself to see if we might expedite the matter."

I dipped my chin in a regal nod, as befitted a difficult customer. "Good day." I turned my back on Crabb.

But he was already addressing the couple, ignoring me. Still, I'd put my foot in the door, so to speak, and my first task was an easy one. My career as a spy had begun.

TWENTY-SEVEN

Even with shorter working hours, I would not always be able to see Sarah into bed. After all, I had an investigation to conduct. Elizabeth having written the appropriate letters of introduction, I paid a call on her sister's friend, Grace Fairgrieve. She was a woman of about Lucetta's age and had clearly been a beauty. Now her looks were fading, marred by two deep lines between her eyebrows and a mean, pinched look to her mouth.

"So you knew Lucetta?" she inquired after we'd spent twenty minutes on the social preliminaries and were sitting in Mrs. Fairgrieve's suite of rooms at the Tremont Hotel. "Poor darling, she was so badly used by that husband of hers. And I used to think he was such a nice man."

"But you don't think he killed her, do you?" I asked. "The newspapers said he was freed for insufficient evidence."

"Which is not the same as being found innocent." Mrs. Fairgrieve spoke in a quick, arch tone, as if she were used to getting her own way and didn't like people disagreeing with her. "I suppose if they do find him innocent, I will have to receive him. I rather hope he won't come to New York, or that at least he will stay away from society." She shuddered. "I will never reconcile myself to him being free while poor, dear Lucetta lies in her grave."

Personally, I thought Martin would be delighted to stay away from Mrs. Fairgrieve's society. At least Mrs. Fairgrieve's feelings about Martin might prevent her from running into me at Rutherford's.

"Did you know Lucetta well?" I wondered if there was anyone who knew Lucetta well enough to have heard from her lips about a certain redheaded woman in Kansas whom Lucetta suspected of stealing her husband's heart.

"We were school friends." Mrs. Fairgrieve's bony fingers fiddled with the lace on her sleeve. "Great friends in our young days, to be sure—we told each other everything." She sighed. "Since I married and moved to New York, we've seen very little of each other. I was quite surprised when she wrote me asking to stay."

This was news to me, but I tried to pretend I knew all about it and hoped I wouldn't get caught out in a lie. "I think Lucetta needed someone to talk to," I said. "I hadn't known her for nearly so long. She didn't confide much in me. I felt in my heart that there was something weighing on her when I last saw her." I extracted my handkerchief from my reticule and held it as if I felt that tears were imminent.

"I had that impression too. That's why I feel her husband is at the bottom of it all. Lucetta seemed almost ill—and then that silly maid of hers became infatuated with my groom, John, and refused to return to Chicago. The poor dear—deserted by her husband *and* lady's maid, and returning to an empty house with only half a dozen servants for company. No wonder she was thinking of going to Europe."

"She was?"

"Indeed—she was talking about visiting Paris. Such an amusing city, but Lucetta didn't seem to be looking forward to it all that much. I thought—but no, it's impossible. Did you think she looked ill when you last saw her?"

"Not at all." Of course, the last time I'd seen Lucetta was in Kansas, some six months before her death, and she'd looked quite beautiful. "I heard she went to Domenico Gambarelli's Christmas feast—which I wasn't able to attend this year—and was in splendid looks then."

"Oh, she probably looked well *then*," said Mrs. Fairgrieve. "You haven't seen her since?"

"We had plans to meet when she returned." I sighed in a dramatic fashion. "What did you think was wrong with her?"

"I probably imagined things." Mrs. Fairgrieve's mouth pursed in a way that showed lines above her lips. "That silly Nicolina would know, but she's long gone. Decamped with John, and I'm almost certain one of my solid gold saltcellars went with them. I don't suppose I'll ever know for certain. I should have dismissed my butler for leaving the silver safe open, but he's worth far more than a gold cruet. It's just impossible to get loyal servants these days, isn't it?"

I agreed heartily, and the conversation turned away from Lucetta with no apparent way to turn it back again. Mrs. Fairgrieve was on far more solid ground complaining about servants and the weather than talking about Lucetta. I had the feeling that her friend's death had made little impression on her other than leaving her with an ineradicable prejudice toward Martin.

I almost felt I had wasted my time. Yet I was sure nobody else concerned with the Rutherford murder knew that Lucetta was planning to go to Paris, nor that she had seemed ill when she was in New York. Both facts suggested something that I too thought was impossible. I wasn't going to reveal either of them to Martin until I had made quite sure. And the only person who might know, other than the maid, was, in my estimation, Frank Gorton.

My duties as a mother, so joyously resumed when I quit my job at Gambarelli's, were about to be interrupted again. Elizabeth had easily convinced Tess and Sarah—and Miss Baker—that a few weeks in Lake Forest would be just the thing. I didn't blame them. The smell of the stockyards for which Chicago was notorious had settled on us with summer. It was a smell that combined sweet with fetid, rancid with musk, in a way that could not be ignored. It even came as far north as Rutherford's at times, competing with the river's stink of sulfur and rotting vegetables. As the breezes of spring gave way to the humid heat of summer, the hot, odorous air seemed to settle on us like a smothering blanket. All Chicagoans longed for days when the breeze would bring the smell of lake water and smoke from the railroads across us, for a nice change.

It was very early when we reached the station at Wells Street, but already unpleasantly warm and sticky. The racks of newspapers cried news of an outbreak of cholera. Sarah, unusually for her, clung to me like a red-haired limpet.

"I don't like this place, Momma. It's dirty."

I hugged her to me, catching a sympathetic look from Miss Baker. The governess had a skill I particularly appreciated, that of receding gently into the background whenever we were both with Sarah. I blessed her for not interjecting her own rules and opinions, but leaving us to find our own way through our changing lives. I found I looked forward to seeing her unremarkable—even plain—face and boyish figure at the end of my working day. Goodness only knew what she thought I was doing during my absences. I never informed her, and she never asked.

"It certainly is. A dirty, nasty hole," said Aileen, who, along with Mary, had come to see their sister off. The two sisters flanked Tess like tall bedposts and insisted on carrying her bag rather than giving it to the porter who'd stacked up the trunks on a small wagon. "All this traveling will make you ill, Tessie."

"I'm all right." Tess was too excited to complain. "I like trains. Elizabeth has been telling me all about the house in Lake Forest. We can picnic in a pavilion in their garden, and the breeze comes off the bluff to keep us cool."

"Living on the charity of others," said Mary under her breath.

"It's not charity," I said rather tartly—I didn't think Mary intended me to hear her remark. "It's a visit. It's the way things are done."

Mary sniffed loudly. The two sisters had raised a great many objections to Tess's accompanying Sarah to Lake Forest.

I sighed. "You don't have to go if you don't want to, darling," I said softly to Sarah, who had buried her face in my neck.

"But there's a pony." Sarah straightened up and looked me in the face. "And prairie like in Kansas. Will you be all right here on your own, Momma?"

"I'll be fine. After all, I have Mrs. Power and Mr. Nutt and Zofia and Alice to look after me. And I'm going to visit you very soon."

Elizabeth had been talking to the porter but now returned to us, picking her way over the tobacco quids that liberally decorated the floor of the wooden building we were in. It was little more than a large shack and quite disreputable looking. I understood it had been erected as a temporary measure after Chicago's Great Fire, but no replacement was in sight.

"Won't you let Elizabeth carry you for a while and give your mother's arms a rest?" Elizabeth asked Sarah. "I'll tell you all about our horses."

Sarah transferred herself easily into Elizabeth's open arms, and I shook out my shoulders in relief. I saw Elizabeth and Miss Baker exchange a smile. They seemed to get on remarkably well. I'd heard Miss Baker speaking passionately to Elizabeth about the plight of the poor in England's cities.

Behind me, Aileen expelled a short breath from her nostrils. "If this train would only come," she said in the irritating, nasal way she often affected. "I don't hold with all this traveling, Tess. It's a lot to ask of a body, and who knows what at the end of it."

Elizabeth hoisted Sarah up a little more firmly and gave Aileen a look reminiscent of her mother. "At the end of it is a very pleasant visit," she said. She had received my news about David Fletcher thoughtfully and had since made few allusions to the young man. It was as if she were giving some considerable thought to his request to be left to do his own wooing. Indeed, there was a quietness and stillness about her demeanor that I hadn't seen before, and I wondered what that meant.

"Tess deserves a rest," I said to Mary and Aileen. "She's under no obligation to work for me." I smiled at Tess. "Alice will keep your ledgers in order."

"And you can make your social calls at your leisure," said Aileen with a pointed look at both of her sisters. "Without encumbrance."

"I don't make social calls," I said, exasperated. "And if I did, Tess would come with me." What I wanted to ask was just how much leisure or society Tess would have in the Back of the Yards, in Mary's house, with four boys to care for. But politeness and consideration for Tess prevented me from replying to the barbs sent constantly in my direction by her sisters. I didn't want to make Tess feel like a rag doll being fought over by two children, but the net result was that her sisters' opinions were drowning out my own.

"Here's the locomotive," said Elizabeth. "Sarah, say good-bye to your mother." She put Sarah down, avoiding the worst of the deposits on the ground. I bent to take my daughter in my arms for one last hug, breathing in the scent of her. This separation would be far harder on me than on her.

"May I please ride the pony today?" Sarah asked as the train drew closer, expelling steam and smoke as its brakes squealed on the rails.

"You may do anything Miss Elizabeth allows you to do." I rained kisses on Sarah's forehead, which was damp and salty with perspiration, then placed her hand in Elizabeth's and turned to Tess. Behind us, Miss Baker was tucking a serious-looking journal into her valise.

"I miss you already." I bent to hug Tess, who was positively staggering under the burden of the last-minute advice being fired at her by her two sisters. She gave me a look I couldn't interpret. Did she think I was sending her away because she was an inconvenience? But she had readily agreed to the idea, which had come from Elizabeth and not from me.

Ten minutes later, I stood waving my handkerchief at the departing train. Mary and Aileen stood a little way apart from me with dour faces, making predictions about train crashes, the sudden epidemics that might sweep through a small town, and the dangers of walking too near the edge of a bluff. When the train was out of sight, we parted, and I set out briskly in the direction of the LaSalle Street Tunnel.

My feelings were that odd mixture of liberty and heaviness that comes when a burden you shoulder cheerfully is lifted from you for a while. Tess, Sarah, and I had barely been parted since Sarah's birth. Although my time at Gambarelli's had obliged me to be away from home, I had still felt responsible for their well-being. I knew they would be happy at the Parnells', and I no longer had to feel guilty about the time I spent away from home. I would be free to do all I could to help Martin, and that meant the world to me. And yet the knowledge that I was not, after all, indispensable to the happiness of two of the people I loved most in the world was a little depressing.

I walked fast, dodging around benches, drinking fountains, and people. I was careful not to catch the eye of the numerous peddlers or the loafing men who would whistle, make rude comments, or even grab at any woman unwary enough to pass near them. I was becoming quite the Chicagoan and increasingly ready to venture onto the streets despite Mrs. Parnell's dire warnings. I had told Mr. Nutt to take the carriage home rather than try to wait amid the chaos of Wells Street on a Monday morning. As I walked, my mind began running over the day's tasks, even though a large piece of my heart was on a northbound train.

TWENTY-EIGHT

I arrived at Rutherford's early enough to encounter Joe Salazar climbing down from his landau. He greeted me cheerfully and asked after Tess and Sarah—he knew I was seeing them off at the station that morning. The store was not yet open, but an employee had been looking out for his arrival, and we entered by the main door rather than the one in the alley.

"I need to talk to you about—something," I said, my eye on the other employees. "Sir."

Joe nodded and gestured for me to follow him up one of the staff staircases located at each end of the building.

"I have instructions from Crabb," I said softly as we climbed, once we were out of the hearing of anyone else. "It's straightforward—I should only take a minute of your time."

Joe looked at me a little oddly but then seemed to make up his mind to speak. "Martin swore at me for letting you get mixed up with that character."

"Did he now?" I felt my eyebrows—and my hackles—rise. "Why should *you* get the blame? Why should I, for that matter? It's none of Martin's business if I want to help him."

Joe, in the act of pulling open the door that led to the offices, gave me a look of such outraged astonishment that I burst into laughter.

"I mean—Joe, you know what I mean. In any case, Martin certainly shouldn't swear at you. What did he say?" For some reason, I found the idea of Martin swearing humorous. He was generally very proper in his speech.

"I'm glad you find me funny."

My laughter evaporated at the sight of Martin, standing in the doorway to his outer office with a decidedly sulky expression on his face. He turned on his heel and stalked into his inner office, making a peremptory motion with his hand that indicated we should follow him. I rolled my eyes at Joe and complied, feeling as if I were a small child again and Martin the ruler of my days—which he'd never been. If anything, I was the one who had bossed *him* about.

Martin shut the door with a bang, not looking at me. "May I remind you that you're working for me?" he said, his tone laden with frost.

"Working for you?" I took a seat, although he hadn't offered me one. "Yes, I am. I also happen to be a shareholder in your business, in case you've forgotten. I'm *working* for you because, while you're wallowing in self-pity, there are things I can do to help you."

"*Self-pity?*" Martin bellowed out the words as if I'd been two streets away and not sitting across the desk from him. One large hand closed on the papers under it, crushing them in his fist. Behind me, I could sense Joe, carefully immobile.

"Oh good, at least you're looking me in the face now. Since I've got your attention, Crabb wants to know the suppliers of silk out of San Francisco. Can you give me that information without too much damage to your business? It seems innocuous enough to me."

Martin glared at me for at least thirty seconds, as if he were about to start shouting again but didn't know which point to tackle first. I returned the glare with interest, determined not to let him intimidate me. Something changed in his eyes, and his shoulders slumped just a fraction of an inch.

"All right, you win." He ran a hand through his hair, which was now about an inch long all round. It stuck up a bit where he'd mussed it, leaving him looking a little disheveled and wholly appealing. I swallowed.

"How do I win?"

"You have my full cooperation, and I apologize for not treating you like the lady you are. And a shareholder. And for being a boor, and being angry at you when you're doing all you can to help. And for not trusting you to take care of yourself. Will that do?"

"For now. Can you give me that information?"

Martin sighed and looked up over my head. "Joe, can you take care of it?" He looked down at the piles of paper on his desk.

"You seem rather busy," I observed. "Are these all matters your staff can't take care of?"

Martin stared dumbly at the stacks of documents, which had been neatly arranged, and then smiled at last. "Only about one-fifth of these are for the store. Joe, for heaven's sake sit down. I'm sorry I lost my temper last night."

Joe seated himself beside me. "Most of that's nothing to do with Rutherford's," he said, nodding at the papers. "I can certainly give you the information you need, Nell. It could be damaging in the hands into which Crabb will place it, but that's a risk we have to take. We're forewarned of the danger, after all."

Martin rested his hand on a pile of charts neatly drawn in red, blue, and black ink. "I suppose—since you are a financial participant in my affairs—I owe you a little explanation." He pulled his watch out of his vest pocket to check the time and settled more comfortably in his seat.

"Joe takes care of most of the paperwork for the store," he said. "I sign the papers he lays before me, insinuate myself among the customers as much as I can, and decide what the fashion will be next season."

"Decide?" I grinned.

"You'd be surprised. Even Madame Belvoix listens to me." There was a faint look of pride on his face as he said that. "If she ever trusts you enough to let you loose on the really important customers—the ones who set the style—you'll understand that a store like ours doesn't just follow fashion, it mandates it. Of course, the store is always a preoccupation of mine, but it's more necessary to me than I am to it, if you see what I mean."

"I'm surprised. So what is all this?" I indicated the papers.

"It's odd." Martin's expression had taken on a faraway look. "I always thought I'd bring my income up to fifty or a hundred thousand a year and be content. But business has a way of breeding business, like mice breed mice. You end up constantly looking for ways to use money. I could build vast stores or an empire of traveling salesmen, like Field, or print up catalogs, like Montgomery Ward, but I prefer smaller, more intimate stores. Of course, some of this is purely personal financial business—stocks, bonds, and similar bread-and-butter work—although I don't do much of it during business hours."

"Of course," I said faintly. Fifty or a hundred thousand a year! I hadn't even realized such an income was possible.

"A good piece of my money is now in the venture with Fassbinder," Martin continued. "That's a great deal more interesting—and that, you should know, is where I feel there's something wrong. A rattle in the machine, if you like. Before Lucetta's . . . passing, I was away on precisely that errand. That's why I never got your letters. I should have had them sent on, but I didn't know where I was going to be."

"Where did you go?"

"Saint Louis, at first. Fassbinder showed me a letter he'd received from an old friend in Jefferson City, Missouri. There's a state penitentiary there. His friend, a German who works in the penitentiary, knew of Fassbinder's association with me. He wanted to warn me that one of the prisoners was telling everyone I was responsible for the crime he'd committed."

"Good grief." I frowned. "How did he come to that conclusion?"

"It's probably just a mania or delusion. He picked my name out of the papers, something like that. He was imprisoned for beating a prostitute to death. Claimed he was innocent, that the brothel where she worked was financed by me, and that I'd framed him. I thought at least I'd better go to Jefferson City to reassure its prominent citizens we're on the level, as the new slang goes. We've been building a store there and don't need bad publicity. I explained to them I was in Kansas on business in early December when the crime took place and could call on a respectable pastor for confirmation if need be."

His smile this time was warm and intimate, and for a moment I just wanted to bask in it and forget that the last three months had ever happened. But I reminded myself sternly that Martin needed a friend more than he needed me making calf's eyes at him.

"I suppose you can prove that you're not setting up brothels," I said. "If need be."

"If absolutely necessary." Martin shrugged. "It's true that as the small towns we build our stores in become more prosperous, parlor houses seem to be springing up. We've had a problem with more basic houses of, er, entertainment appearing in the vicinity of our construction crews. Fassbinder's had to speak with John Powell on more than one occasion about the men's conduct. But parlor houses only exist where so-called respectable men allow them to exist."

"John Powell—Lucetta's cousin," I said. "Joe told me you still employ him. Why?"

"I wasn't in a position to make changes in the second quarter of this year," Martin said drily. "Now that I am, I'm thinking of dismissing Powell. I've had reports he's drinking heavily. That doesn't surprise me since he was overly fond of Lucetta, as they all were." The hand on his desk curled briefly into a fist, then relaxed. "But if I'm going to fire him, I'll do it to his face. That means either traveling to meet with him or waiting until he returns to Chicago. I hired him for Lucetta's sake, but I don't feel justified in just throwing him off without stating my reasons to him in person."

"That's eminently fair of you. More than fair." I dismissed the small, mean voice inside me that pointed out another sign of attachment to Lucetta's memory, and nodded in approval.

"He's been a better manager than I anticipated, and extremely effective at finding towns that will welcome us with open arms. I can't blame him for being grief-stricken." A faint expression of something like guilt crossed Martin's face. "Besides, I still employ Lucetta's brother Sam, and have no intention of dismissing him. He's an excellent buyer for the frontier stores."

He looked at his watch again, and I mirrored the action with my small timepiece. "I'll have to start work," I said, rising from my chair. The two men rose to their feet also, and Joe stepped back so that I could pass.

"I'll give that information to you at four if you drop by my office when you finish work," he said. "Don't take it to Crabb too fast though, or he'll wonder why it was so easy. Wait a few days. And Martin, why don't you set the Pinkerton Agency onto looking into Crabb's business dealings? It'll make you feel better and may turn up some useful information."

℃

My work at Rutherford's proceeded slowly from the status more or less of an apprentice to more important tasks as I was gradually given opportunities to show my skills. I found I was among women of great talent and expertise. I enjoyed learning from them and didn't resent my lowly position. For the first time since I'd learned dressmaking from my grandmother, I was no longer the most knowledgeable woman in the workshop. Every day brought me some new gift as I sat with embroiderers and beaders, cutters, piece workers, and those most exalted beings of all, the true couturières. Each of those women had their own loyal clients. As the newcomer, when I worked with Mrs. Nippes on Thursdays, I dealt with customers of lesser means. Many had ventured into Rutherford's for the first time, seeking a dress for a special occasion that to them was perhaps the fruit of a year's careful economies.

With Sarah and Tess away from home, I often worked well past the official end of my day. One of the benefits of my later hours was that I was able to work right up till seven o'clock, my appointed time for waiting for Crabb outside Field and Leiter's. Joe fed small pieces of information to me that might be of interest to rival stores, and I duly reported them to Crabb. He paid me well, especially for tidbits about forthcoming purchases. Rutherford's was prevented from scoring a coup with an exclusive new Paris silk because of me. My ears burned when I heard Madame Belvoix lamenting that Field and Leiter's had bought up the entire stock of the manufacturer in question.

And yet, as Joe told me, the fact that he knew which information I was passing on allowed him to understand Crabb's network better, and that would be useful in the future. So the loss to Rutherford's was, in some way, mitigated.

I tried to bear that in mind as I waited for Crabb one August evening when the heat was rising from the flagstones as if from the base of an oven. He was late. I could feel my face reddening as the perspiration trickled uncomfortably down my back and limbs. When Crabb arrived, his broad grin told me he'd noticed my color.

"We'll have some ice cream." Crabb steered me toward an Italian peddler who stood sweating beside a large box on wheels. "Two," he said to the man, handing him some coins.

"I don't want—"

"You'll eat it up like a good little girl." Crabb grinned in a way that wasn't quite friendly.

The ice cream came on two pieces of waxed paper, each with a wooden spoon, and began to liquefy the moment it emerged from the icebox. Crabb and I retreated to the shade of a building and spooned the creamy stuff into our mouths. It was better than I'd expected. Despite Mama's injunctions that a lady never ate in the street, I had noticed that it was a common practice in Chicago. Unaccompanied women of the more genteel sort didn't venture into eating establishments, and such restaurants as did welcome them—hotels, store tearooms, and the Mrs. Clark Co. Lunch Room on Wabash—were expensive.

"That's better. I like a little something sweet after I eat." Crabb belched, sending a wave of beer and sausage odors over me. "Beg pardon." He thumped his chest with a closed fist.

"You made me wait because you were eating?" I asked. "You've got a nerve."

"A man needs to eat, and I've got a long night ahead of me. What have you got for me today?"

I outlined the details of a consignment of slink calfskin gloves currently being assembled in England. Crabb listened attentively and made me repeat some of the figures more than once. I'd discovered he had an excellent memory and never wrote anything down.

"Good. Payment terms as usual." Our arrangement was that I'd happen to visit a certain vendor of paste jewelry on Fridays and linger in that store until any other customer had left. Then I would state my name, and the merchant would hand me an envelope. I was glad enough not to be seen receiving money from a man on the street.

"And Mr. Fassbinder's in town," I added. "Is that useful to you?"

"We know *that*," said Crabb scornfully. "In fact, I was going to ask you to do something a little more difficult for me."

I frowned. "What?"

"Fassbinder brought a document with him." Crabb dabbed impatiently at the sweat that ran down the sides of his face. "I heard that from—someone else." He grinned. "It lists a number of locations I'd very much like to know. Get a copy for me."

The genuine alarm I felt must have showed on my face. "But that'll be well-nigh impossible," I protested. "Mr. Fassbinder's incorruptible. I doubt anybody high up enough at Rutherford's to have received such a document would leave it lying around. They're pretty sharp about locking things up in the big safe, and that's kept in a locked room in the back of Mr. Rutherford's inner office. I saw it once when I carried up some account books."

"Nothing's impossible." Crabb took off his hat and scrubbed at his face with a red handkerchief. "That one's worth at least five dollars, possibly a lot more. And anything you might hear about Rutherford's frontier business with Fassbinder."

"His what? I've never heard anything about that." As Amelia Harvey, I wouldn't have. "I can't possibly—"

"Ten dollars, then," Crabb said smoothly. "Perhaps even twenty if it's good information. It's important to me, Miss—or is it Mrs.?—Harvey." This time his grin was decidedly nasty.

"It could take me quite a while." I was as worried as I knew I looked. This wasn't just one more small act of espionage. I could tell by Crabb's demeanor as much as by the high price he offered that this was something different.

"I'll wait." Crabb patted me on my arm, which was his way of dismissing me. We had been walking side by side, conversing in low tones. Crabb always led the way, using circuitous routes that avoided too many people but invariably ended back near State Street. I often wondered if I'd been seen by people from Rutherford's or Gambarelli's who knew me, and what conclusions they'd drawn. Still, it couldn't be helped.

I quickened my pace despite the heat, heading south to where I knew Mr. Nutt would be waiting with the carriage. The fast walking helped soothe my agitation a little, but I could predict a sleepless night ahead. I had become far too comfortable with the small role Crabb had assigned to me and had dismissed Martin's predictions of danger as nonsense. Now I began to wonder if he was right.

TWENTY-NINE

I was undoubtedly hollow-eyed when I knocked on Joe Salazar's door early the next morning. I'd been awake since three, up at four, and was now at Rutherford's well before opening hours. It was a Friday, the day when the displays were usually changed. I'd encountered the curious stares of a whole bevy of men carrying the long, hooked ladders stored along the walls of the fourth floor.

I supposed I shouldn't be surprised to find Martin there. He was an early riser, like me, and like me, he looked as if he'd had a bad night. He didn't look pleased to see me.

"Have I come at a bad time?" I asked. "I've got something to tell you that can't wait."

Having pulled out a chair for me, Martin resumed his perch on the edge of Joe's desk. There was something edgy and fidgety about him that worried me. It was a mood that had been growing in him as the summer advanced and nothing more surfaced that would lead to the identification of Lucetta's killer. The possibility I had deduced from my meeting with Mrs. Fairgrieve gnawed at my mind, but I wasn't going to mention it to Martin until I was certain, out of consideration for his feelings.

Frank Gorton, blast him, had not been at Gambarelli's for weeks. I had at last resorted to asking Miss Green, the most discreet of my former colleagues, to send me a note when he returned. No matter that I'd had to endure her simpering assumption that I was in love with the man.

I looked at Joe, sitting across the desk from me, rather than at Martin, who loomed above me, fiddling uncharacteristically with his tiepin. The look Joe returned was of mingled sympathy and concern. I was sure that he too worried about Martin.

"Crabb's given me a difficult assignment," I said. "I think it's a great deal more serious than anything I've done for him up till now." I briefly outlined Crabb's request for the list brought to Chicago by Mr. Fassbinder.

Martin twisted round, and the two men exchanged a long look. Joe let out a low whistle.

"You were right," he said to Martin. "There's a connection."

"What connection?" I asked.

Martin was still sitting on Joe's desk, which fortunately was quite clean of papers. His long legs, clad in immaculate gray pantaloons, shiny pumps, and spats, dangled before me. He was still wearing his frock coat as if he'd come straight to Joe's office upon arrival, and had gathered its tails over his knees. Now he crossed one leg over the other and grasped his knee. I could see the tension in his body by the whiteness of his knuckles.

"I had a feeling someone else was mixed up with our problems in the frontier stores. I'm beginning to suspect it's Crabb," he said. "I've had the Pinkerton Agency looking into him—out of concern for you. They're pretty sure that money is coming from the frontier to Crabb, from the bawdy houses that open up in about three out of five towns where we build our stores."

"As far as we can see, it goes like this," Joe said. "And it's another reason to dismiss John Powell, when we can find him. Powell lets Crabb know which towns are to receive an FR Emporium—that's the name of the stores. Crabb uses his contacts in Chicago to provide girls for a parlor house. He either buys or constructs the building himself or receives money for arranging matters with a third party."

"We suspect John Powell has some prominent citizens in each of the towns in his back pocket. Blackmail, perhaps, although I don't really think he's intelligent enough for that game," said Martin. "It could simply be that this is

Powell's compensation for choosing one town over another. It's the game the railroads were playing before the crash. You find two growing towns a few miles apart and set them one against the other. The one that's willing to pay, or pay the most, gets the railroad and prospers. The other sees its trade dry up. Fassbinder's name makes the prospect of one of our stores most attractive, especially among the German frontiersmen."

"Which would explain the bonus payments Powell was able to get out of the towns." Joe took up the tale as Martin drew breath. "He probably takes his own cut, but what he passes along to us makes him look good."

"So why is this list of Mr. Fassbinder's important?" I asked.

"It's the towns he's proposing to prospect by himself," Martin said. "Since we no longer trust Powell. Fassbinder intends to warn the townspeople to look out for any signs of an increase in vice. This is not something we want our names connected with. By keeping his plans close, and getting rid of Powell, we're hoping to make life a lot more difficult for Crabb—if it *is* Crabb. He's known, according to the Pinkertons, for having ambitions as a property speculator. It's rumored that Lizzie Allen has promised to make him her solid man if he can become wealthy enough. So he is, as you might say, motivated, and therefore the most likely suspect."

I was silent for a moment, thinking through all that Martin and Joe had told me. "Do you think any of this has anything to do with Lucetta's death?" I asked at last.

"Why would it?" Martin said, lines of strain creeping into his face at the mention of Lucetta. "She wasn't particularly fond of Powell. None of the Gambarellis are, although they tolerate him since he's family. Neither can we find any connection between her and Crabb."

"She had a connection with Frank Gorton, and he's friendly enough with Crabb," I reminded him.

"That's true—but as far as we can see, Gorton's role is confined to receiving information from Crabb about his rivals. It had occurred to us that Crabb might have killed her because she found out about their business relationship—but what sense does that make?"

"Gorton could have killed her because she was flirting with Crabb." I hated to raise the topic of Lucetta's unfaithfulness, but I had to make the suggestion.

Martin shook his head, looking down at his hands. He had been running a finger repeatedly over the satin lining of his coattails, an action I was beginning to find irritating. "And cheerfully continue his business relationship with Crabb after having murdered her?" There was a strained note to his voice that was odd. "Gorton has never seemed to care much about her . . . side interests."

Becoming aware of the unconscious movements of his hand, he stopped fidgeting and laced both hands tightly together again. "Since we're on the subject of Lucetta, there's a favor I need to ask you."

"What?"

Martin still wasn't looking at me. "I'm sending in some Pinkerton agents, four men and a woman, to search my house again. I want you to accompany them—as Mrs. Harvey, of course, and we'll find some excuse—and I want you to search Lucetta's clothing. Thoroughly." He looked up at last, and there was a beseeching look in his eyes. "You know how a gown is made. You know where a dressmaker might sew in a discreet pocket better than anyone else I can trust."

I was so shocked that I stared at him for a full minute before replying. "You couldn't have thought of a more distasteful task for me to do if you'd written it out with both hands," I said at last, craning my neck back so that I could glare at him more thoroughly. "Why can't you do it yourself?"

Martin slid off the desk and seated himself on the chair beside me. He looked as if he were about to take my hands in his, but then he thought better of it.

"Nellie, please." His voice was raw. "I can't go there—I'm never going inside that place again. As soon as I can, I'm selling it lock, stock, and barrel. But it's never been searched as thoroughly as it should be, and I want it turned inside out. I'm desperate for even the smallest clue."

Joe cleared his throat. "If it's any comfort to you, Nell, I'll be there too."

I looked Martin in the face, my anger dissipating as I saw his expression. He looked like a man whose nerves had been strained to the limit. Of course, he had gone from jail back to work with no rest in between, and had, as far as I could see, taken little time for himself ever since.

"I'll do it," I said shortly.

"Bless you." Martin looked down at his hands again, then up at me. "I'm anxious to clear my name before I spend the winter in Europe."

I was struck dumb. I looked across at Joe and saw by his expression that he already knew.

"You're *leaving?*" I closed my eyes, calculating. "You'll have to sail before November, and the shipping lanes may not be open again till—April. You're going to abandon your business for almost half a *year?*" And me, I thought. You're going to abandon me.

"Joe can run the store," Martin said. "And—you're a shareholder. You'll have my power of attorney in case any major decisions have to be made, and you can consult with Fassbinder at any time by telegraph." He swallowed. "I can't stay, Nellie. I can't bear it here right now. I'm sorry."

"Martin will use some of his time in Europe for the benefit of the store." Joe broke into the strained silence that followed Martin's last words, spoken in a near whisper. "And for the rest of the time, I've recommended the Swiss Alps—a wonderful place to recuperate, I hear." He rose to his feet. "To be honest, Nell, it's I who've been pushing Martin to go." He leaned over the desk and placed a hand on my arm. "I'd tell any employee who'd suffered a bereavement to take time off. And when the principal of a firm is constantly irritable and nervy, the whole company suffers. If he's stranded in Europe for the winter, he'll appreciate us all the more when he returns."

Joe's tone was light and cheerful, but the hand on my arm was exerting a definite pressure. I nodded at Martin, wishing I could hug him. Or slap him, for leaving me. If only I didn't love him so much.

"I'll search Lucetta's dresses," I said. "If that's what you want."

And I would hunt, very hard indeed, for any clue that might prove or disprove the terrible theory that was growing in my mind.

The foyer of Martin and Lucetta's house was palatial. Pink-veined, dark gray marble columns rose out of a black-and-white marble floor. On the ceiling, gilding enhanced the elaborate plaster molding, featuring a repeating motif of cornucopias spilling their fruit in eternally frozen bounty.

Heavy, ornately carved doors led off the foyer, presumably leading to reception rooms; they were all shut. On the walls between the doors, paintings were vibrant gleams of color, like flowers in a dusk-filled wood. Heavy velvet drapes adorned the windows, dimming the light from the street outside. Both the noise of carriages and the sullen Chicago heat diminished as the housekeeper shut the door behind me, Joe, and the Pinkerton agents.

Joe spent a few minutes in consultation with Martin's housekeeper, a sturdy woman with a broad, flat face that creased in puzzlement as she read Martin's note.

"You won't find anything I wouldn't already have found, sir," I heard her say to Joe. "Almost every nook and cranny of this house has been cleaned and dusted and turned over and brushed time and time again." Her expressionless gaze swept the Pinkerton agents, who were standing around Joe in a semicircle while I hung back a little. "I got out all the private papers and things for the police detectives back in March. But since it's Mr. Rutherford's direct orders . . ." She tailed off.

"It's what he wants." Joe's smile at her was kindly. "We're sorry to put you to any trouble." He motioned to me to come forward. "This is Mrs. Harvey, from the store. She will look at Mrs. Rutherford's dresses."

The housekeeper's gaze took me in for a moment. "Very well," she said. "Perhaps you'd like to wait in the parlor for a few minutes, Madam, while I open the mistress's rooms up for you." She looked doubtfully at Joe. "You too, sir."

Joe shook his head. "No need. We know where to go and have plenty to do, so we'll make a start straightaway while you take care of Mrs. Harvey." He motioned to the Pinkerton agents, who followed him into one of the rooms, their footsteps echoing faintly as they crossed the foyer floor.

The housekeeper watched Joe shut the door before turning back to me. "Despite what I said to Mr. Salazar, I'll admit I haven't had the heart to turn out Mrs. Rutherford's clothes as thoroughly as I'd like, not without consulting the master," she said. "You'll understand when you see them. And that Nicolina, who was good with clothes, I'll concede, going off like that—well, I put away the things from Mrs. Rutherford's trunks the day it happened, but please tell Mr. Rutherford I'm awaiting his instructions as to what to do with all of those dresses."

"I will," I said and dropped my voice to a confidential level. "I feel sorry for the poor man—he's been through so much. I don't for a moment think he's guilty."

The housekeeper's expression didn't change, but a little animation crept into her eyes. She moved toward one of the doors, motioning for me to follow. "Mr. Rutherford's a kind man," she said to me as she turned the knob and swung the heavy, highly polished door inward. "It's a shame he can't bear the house now, but I understand his feelings."

"Did you like Mrs. Rutherford?" I paused on the threshold of the parlor, the question coming unbidden to my lips.

The woman's face moved upward as she frowned in consternation. "Not like, exactly. It isn't my place to like the mistress of the house. But she knew how to be the mistress, I'll say that. Brought up accustomed to servants and to getting her own way. But very beautiful, very elegant."

"She was." I strained to see in the gloom as the housekeeper crossed to the window. I could see furniture shrouded in dust cloths, looking ghostly and somehow menacing. The air smelled sweet, like potpourri, but not fresh. The windows hadn't been opened for a while.

The housekeeper tugged at the thick, heavy drapes, and a wide band of sunlight cut the room in two. My heart leaped into my throat, and I almost cried out.

I hadn't known what to expect from my first encounter with the private side of Martin's married life. I knew I hadn't expected the life-size paintings that hung on either side of an enormous chimneypiece of carved white marble. I moved into the center of the room as the housekeeper opened the rest of the curtains, letting light and the faint sounds of the street into the room.

To the left of the fireplace hung Lucetta's image, almost as vibrant as in life, dressed in a silk brocade ball gown in shimmering antique crimson and gold. Her glossy black ringlets poured over one shoulder, and the artist had caught well the glitter of rubies at her ears and throat. Rubies were also set into a heavy gold bracelet encircling the slender wrist that held a folded fan. The eyes were as I'd known them, huge, black, and thickly lashed. The smile that curved her lips was the smile of a woman who concealed an amusing secret.

The door bumped shut behind me, and I realized the housekeeper had left. I closed my mouth, which had been hanging open, and swallowed to moisten my throat. Lucetta's neck was a column of alabaster, pure in line and hue, set off to perfection by the magnificent necklace of ornately wrought gold spangled with rubies and diamonds. The deep neckline of her dress showed a smooth, white, perfect bosom, glowing with an almost unearthly light. I had the odd impression that the painting was more alive than I was.

And Martin—dear God, could that possibly be my Martin? He was in three-quarter face, his dark clothing contrasting abruptly with the pale hair, against an inky background that held fugitive gleams of gold and the same antique crimson color as Lucetta's dress. The portraits had clearly been painted as a pair, the soberness of Martin's appearance a necessary foil to Lucetta's magnificence. Martin wore a frock coat over a dark gray vest, darkness against darkness, absorbed into the background and yet standing out against it. The gleam of a watch chain under his heart was repeated in the gold of a tiepin, set with a ruby, in his gray cravat. He stared out of the canvas with what I would swear was the weight of the world on his shoulders.

"I make the money, and she spends it," I murmured. The paintings suggested a transformation to me. They said that the wealth Martin had the ability to create was intended by fate to adorn the only woman who was a suitable stage on which to display it. In contrast to Lucetta's serene, amused confidence, Martin's portrait spoke of power, of responsibility, and of a kind of fierce determination to play the role assigned to him.

I felt suddenly uncomfortable in the large, luxurious room with its hidden furnishings, an intruder in this world of power and wealth. Of course I was a rich woman, thanks to Martin, but would I ever be part of the society that built this kind of house and commissioned this kind of portrait? After Martin's arrest, I had sidestepped society, removing myself to its fringes to play the role of an ordinary dressmaker. Was I doing that for Martin . . . or myself?

Martin's portrait told me, as his words never could, how much he had grown away from the Martin Rutherford of Victory. I had thought so when I'd first seen him in Kansas after a gap of more than three years. And then I'd fallen in love with him, and the acknowledgement of that love between us had seemed to bring me close to him again. His touch, his kiss, his concern for me had bridged the gulf between the Martin of then and the Martin of long ago. I had thought of little more than the practical matters that held us separate, his marriage as the barrier that kept us apart by law.

"But there's more to it than that, isn't there?" I spoke the words out loud in the parlor, and they were absorbed and dampened by the plush surfaces around me. No wonder I was having trouble reaching Martin now—I had never had what he had lost, the riches and the position in society. Until Lucetta's murder, he had led a life of which I had never even dreamed.

"How am I supposed to fit into all of this, Martin?" I gestured at the room, speaking to the painting, tears pricking at the back of my eyes. "Look at you—you and she together, fitting into society, belonging to it. I am Nell Lillington of Victory, the daughter of a feed merchant and the mother of an illegitimate child. Whatever my antecedents and my good manners and my—my—*deportment*," I spat out the word, "you've left the sort of person I am behind you. Is that why you no longer look at me as a man looks at a woman he loves? You know I'm not right for you. *She* was, but I'm not. You've been trying to send me away, and I've been too stupid to see it."

I clenched my fists, trying to get a grip on the trembling in my arms, and turned away from the portraits. I had just begun to recover myself when the housekeeper entered.

"Are you ready, Madam? I've opened all the cupboards and cabinets for you. Would you like me to help you remove the dresses? Some of them are heavy."

"No, I'll be fine." I forced a smile to my face. "Thank you."

She turned, and I followed her. Well, I thought, I could at least finish the job Martin had sent me to do. A menial, degrading job—sending in the potential mistress to search the most intimate possessions of the wife. The rival who would always have defeated me, if she'd lived. Perhaps even now, in death, she had the upper hand.

THIRTY

I had been searching for two hours, and I was weary. Lucetta had a great deal of clothing. Too much, in my opinion. It was crammed into every available space. Every drawer was so full it barely shut, every closet overloaded with dresses crushed against each other. I wondered at it and asked the housekeeper when she arrived with a cooling drink.

"Why didn't Mrs. Rutherford's maid go through her dresses regularly?" I gestured at the pile on the bed. "Some of these are out of date. I can't imagine why Mrs. Rutherford would want to keep a dress cut for two seasons ago instead of giving it to her maid or a less wealthy relative."

"Don't blame her maids, Mrs. Lillington." The housekeeper shook her head solemnly. "Trudy, the one she had before, was always asking to clean out her closets. Even that Nicolina, although an impertinent, headstrong girl in my opinion, knew her job. Mrs. Rutherford had a real aversion to giving her things away. Once she owned something, she hated to part with it."

I sighed. "She could at least have given them to her dressmaker to remake. I can't see how she'd have worn them once they were out of fashion."

"No more she did, Madam." The housekeeper smoothed a hand over a paletot cut for the larger bustle of two years ago, in blue velvet trimmed in silver fox fur. "I don't suppose it ever occurred to her to reuse things. She'd complain sometimes that she didn't have enough space."

Lucetta's bedroom, boudoir, and dressing room were almost the size of my house. I gritted my teeth.

"And everything mixed up so," I said. "The old dresses among the new—I find that so odd. I thought at first that I could start with the newer dresses, as that would make sense, but see? I'm sure this is from this year, and it was right at the bottom of the pile."

"Sometimes she would have the maid get things out and then put them back in any order, Madam. She'd spend hours looking at her gowns, even the old ones."

"Well, I've searched through everything on the bed," I said. "Perhaps you'd be better off not trying to return them to the closets, but packing them up." I looked up at her from where I was stooping to get at the boots thickly crowding the bottom of the closet and spoke tentatively. "I don't suppose Mr. Rutherford will care to see them again."

She gave me a long look. "I don't suppose he will," she said. "The poor man."

Her words were ambiguous. Was Martin a poor man because he had been widowed, or because he had been married to Lucetta? It was hard to discern where her loyalties lay. But she hefted a pile of walking dresses into her thick, muscular arms and carried them out of the room.

I had found precisely two pieces of paper. One was torn from a newspaper advertisement for hats. The other was a folded visiting card of Martin's, his name looking oddly sharp and clear against the white stock. And I'd found two nickels and a dime, a lace handkerchief, and a broken toothpick.

I didn't blame her maids for not emptying every pocket. Dressmakers, as I well knew, tended to sew pockets where they could hide them among the trimmings rather than putting them in an obvious place as they did with men's clothing. Many women, myself included, preferred hidden pockets to the decorative ones you could buy to pin or tie to your skirts. Their existence was something of a hallmark of good dressmaking.

At least my discoveries proved that, as the housekeeper had suggested, nobody had yet searched through the clothing with the thoroughness that was needed.

I finished looking at the boots, leaving them on the floor by the bed, and turned to the next closet. It overflowed with silks, fine wools, gauzes, and rich brocade. Everywhere I saw ruffles, embroidery, fringes, and buttons. Lucetta's dresses were fashionably overloaded with detail. With all the doors open, I was surrounded by the scents of lavender and cedar from the bags of dried flowers and shavings that guarded against moths. Above those earthier notes, I could detect wisps of Lucetta's own gardenia scent, a powerful sweetness that yet contained something sharper and more feral, a musk that clung tenaciously to some of her dresses. It was stronger here than in the last closet, I thought. I surveyed the dresses, wondering where to start.

A gleam of gold caught my eye, startlingly clear against the dark brown of the closet's cedar lining. Martin had said Lucetta had worn gold the last time he'd seen her, at the Santo Stefano dinner given by her father. I shoved hard at the surrounding dresses and extracted the golden gown from a mass of gauze that belonged to another ball gown. It was remarkably heavy, a fact explained by the long train at the back and the richness of the brocade.

I shook it out a little to loosen the creases and held it up, turning it so that I could see it from all sides. It was possibly the most spectacular creation I had ever seen. The more I looked at it, the more my dressmaker's heart wept that such a glorious work of art had not been more cherished. Particularly since, if I was any judge, it had only been worn once. It was of a cut that not only followed the latest fashion, but anticipated it.

The gold brocade was figured in a pattern of roses and rosebuds on a pale gold silk, the flowers showing a brighter gold so that the dress would catch and throw back any source of light. The lining and underskirt were of the subtlest pale amethyst. There was gold lace at the neck and cuffs to match the tiers of lace that outlined the overskirt. The train was so wide and heavy that as Lucetta walked, it would have spread out behind her like a peacock's fan. It was an evening dress of the grandest kind, and only a court dress could have outshone it.

I laid it lovingly on the bed and inspected the lining of the bodice. With a pang of strange, poignant avarice, I found the proof I'd been half expecting—a gold silk label embroidered with the words "Worth – 7. Rue de la Paix. Paris." So Mr. Worth really did put his name inside his creations. The peculiar notion brought a smile to my face, imagining "Lillington – Chicago" in its place.

I turned back toward the closet, wondering whether Lucetta had more than one gold dress or whether this was really the one she'd worn the day after Christmas. But the recent cut of the dress tempted me to believe it had to be the one. I shoved the other dresses to one side and spread the gown out as much as I could on Lucetta's high four-poster bed.

Yes, it had been worn. I could see where the hem had been brushed free of dirt, and a small spot of grease on the bodice had been almost entirely removed, probably by using a paste of saleratus. It wouldn't show unless you were looking for it.

Now that I saw the dress laid out flat on its back, there was something odd about the way the bodice met the overskirt. I unbuttoned the bottom of the bodice and turned back the panels, frowning.

Yes, somebody, presumably Lucetta's maid, had altered the dress by letting out the sides of the bodice a little and easing the fit of the skirt. The lining hid the seams, but I could feel that they were too slender. Some seams could even give way if the dress was worn too often. I could see that the lining had been unpicked and resewn to give access to the seams.

For a few minutes, I was frozen in place by my swirling thoughts. Mrs. Fairgrieve had suggested something impossible, and this dress confirmed it. For who would alter a Worth dress, presumably made at the start of the season? A dress made to fit the wearer exactly. Unless that wearer needed more room for a belly that had grown since the dress was made.

I could be wrong, of course. A woman's figure did change, especially as she grew older. I suspected that Lucetta might even be a little older than the age the newspapers had given. At least four years older than Martin, at any rate. But to change so much between the confection of a new dress and the wearing of it . . .

I rarely swore, but I did now. It was the thought of telling Martin that tormented me.

I ran my fingers around the top of the skirt, noting that the train was not detachable, as they often were, but securely sewn. This was not the dress of an economical woman, but of one who liked to look perfect. There would probably be considerable reinforcement on the underneath of the amethyst silk that lined the train and the swag that both hid and drew attention to the most salient portion of the wearer's rear anatomy. All investigations aside, I owed it to myself as a dressmaker to find out how Worth did it. Five minutes of enjoyment would be a reasonable return for these hours of unpleasantness.

I slid my arms underneath the dress and turned it over, then gathered the heavy train up and turned it inside out. The reinforcing was cleverly done and must have taken hours, even days. I smiled as I ran my hand over the back of the skirt—and then frowned. My fingers had encountered a small, hard lump inside the skirt, about the size of a coin purse.

I turned the dress over again and rummaged inside, then yelped and withdrew my hand, sucking at the tiny blossom of blood that was welling up on my middle finger. Surely, Worth hadn't left a pin inside the skirt.

I sucked my finger until the bleeding stopped, then returned to my investigation—a little more cautiously. A few moments' work revealed that the pin had been used to secure the chain of a tiny object. It was not exactly a coin purse, but one of those very small compartment purses a lady would take to a dance, designed to loop over the wrist with a chain while dancing. It was probably solid gold, and set with amethysts—almost certainly purchased to match the dress, which was why it was pinned inside. I couldn't imagine who'd want to pin a purse inside the skirt when the dress was put away, rather than in the more sensible location at the back of the neck if it were desired to keep the two items together. Still, it would have been Lucetta's maid who did it rather than Lucetta herself.

I sat down in a fragile-looking chair and fiddled with the purse. It had the usual fittings—slots for nickels and dimes, a hinged clip for holding a dance card, and a mirror. The mirror was set in its own frame and could be raised to reveal a not-so-secret compartment, useful for secreting *billets-doux*. Which was exactly what the compartment held.

The writing was bold and slanting, almost as if the writer were overconfident of himself. It said, simply, "You look very beautiful tonight. G."

"What's wrong?" Martin asked practically the moment I walked through the door of his hotel suite.

"Why should something be wrong?" I replied tartly. I was thoroughly out of sorts by the time I had taken my leave of Martin's housekeeper, his house, and the ghost of his wife. Still, I doubted Martin would understand. I'd asked the housekeeper to make my excuses to Joe, walked west at a fast clip until I encountered the Clark Street horse car, and ridden north unaccompanied. I had arrived at the Grand Pacific overheated and in a superbly bad temper. Fortunately, I'd happened upon the friendly concierge so was spared a public declaration that I intended to proceed to Mr. Rutherford's rooms alone.

Martin opened the inner door to admit me into his parlor, stepping back a pace and folding his arms to look at me. It was six in the evening, and the gaslights were already lit to allow him to continue working. The harsh yellow light threw the shadow of his beaky nose across his face and struck gleams from his pale hair.

"Something's definitely wrong," he said. "Where's Joe?" He looked around as if he expected Joe Salazar to appear from the floor, like a stage demon. "Didn't he bring you?"

"He didn't know I was leaving. As far as I know, he's still busy with the Pinkerton people."

"You came up here by yourself? How?" Martin looked more closely at my face. "Never mind how. You clearly managed just fine on your own, you're in a very bad mood, and you're hungry."

"I'm not hungry."

My stomach interjected its own opinion on a bass note that could be all too clearly heard. Martin walked to the wall and pushed the service button.

"We'll have some supper."

"It's probably highly improper," I said sullenly.

"To blazes with the proprieties." Martin smiled suddenly. "To be quite honest, the thought of being able to eat a quiet supper with you is a pleasure made all the sweeter for being totally unexpected."

I turned away, annoyed at the blush I felt rising to my cheeks—particularly in view of what I'd been thinking when I looked at those paintings. I stalked to a plushly upholstered settee and seated myself, resisting the temptation to scratch under the top edge of my corset where the damp heat of my clothing was the most irritating. It infuriated me suddenly that Martin should assume I wanted nothing more than to be with him—all the more because it was true.

"Are you going to tell me what's wrong?" Martin sat down in a chair opposite me. "You're tired and hungry, that's clear, but it's something more than that. Something's shaken you. What is it?"

Did Martin really have to walk around inside my thoughts and feelings as if I were some sort of glasshouse, and make himself so thoroughly at home? I breathed hard through my nose for a moment. Then I plunged my hand inside my reticule and brought out the small gold-and-amethyst purse.

"Do you recognize this?"

Martin shrugged. "No."

For a moment, relief overcame me. Perhaps it wasn't Lucetta's. But then I remembered that the note was only one of the things I needed to tell him.

We were interrupted by the arrival of a hotel employee. He took Martin's order of white fish and fried chicken with a perfectly impassive face, not looking at me. Martin, perhaps a little distracted himself, had forgotten to consult me but had automatically ordered my favorite dishes. Somehow that made me angrier.

"Isn't this Lucetta's?" I asked when the servant had gone, holding out the purse again. Martin took it, turning it around in his fingers.

"It looks like it could be. It's the sort of thing she'd own." He looked up at me. "It's been some time since I paid any attention to what Lucetta wears—wore."

"You did remember that she wore gold to the Santo Stefano dinner," I reminded him, not without a hint of acid. "You said she shone under the lights like treasure."

Martin looked blankly at me and then at the purse again.

"A gold Worth brocade dress with gold lace and an amethyst lining." My voice reflected my growing irritation. "Don't tell me I spent all that time on the wrong dress. This was pinned inside it."

"I *do* remember." Martin sounded almost surprised. "She put this in my pocket for a few minutes while she went to the retiring room."

There could have been no better way to put the finishing touch on my vexation than by recounting this little piece of marital intimacy. I leaned forward and snatched the purse out of Martin's hands, opening it and extracting the note.

"This was inside."

Martin unfolded the paper and read it. "'You look very beautiful tonight. G.'" He looked at me, puzzled. "It's fairly anodyne. Given Lucetta's . . . nature, it's reasonable to assume that men paid her many compliments." He frowned. "I do seem to recognize the writing though."

"Do you suppose it could be Frank Gorton's?" Treacherously, my body chose that moment to recall that Martin's fingers had brushed against mine when I'd taken the purse, and how that had felt. I clenched my fist around the tiny purse, closing it with a snap.

"If you'd wanted to check if it was Gorton's writing, the correct person to have asked would be Joe," Martin said mildly. "After all, he worked with the man."

He was right, of course. But that didn't help. I stood up.

"I'm leaving," I said.

Martin stood too, bending down to look at me again so his hair, grown longer now, flopped forward over his forehead. "I thought you were having supper with me?"

"I'd rather not, thank you." I had to get away—now.

Martin's large hand curled gently around my upper arm. "Could you please tell me what's wrong?"

That did it. "*Wrong?*" I spat. "What *isn't* wrong? You're being singularly unhelpful after I spent hours going through your dead wife's clothing because *you* couldn't bear to. In point of fact, you're being about as useful to the furtherance of this investigation as an umbrella in a hurricane. You hate yourself because circumstances have robbed you of the life you built—well, fine. Go to Europe and mope around there—you're free to do it, after all. Weep for Lucetta all you like. Her death has made you see what she really meant to you, hasn't it? She introduced you to an entirely new world, and you had some juvenile dream that you could somehow cling to that world and have me too. 'Come to Chicago,' you said, and like an idiot, I obeyed. And now all I'm fit for is to do your dirty work—"

I stopped to draw breath. Martin's eyes were two dark pits, his mouth set in an ominous line.

"You're lucky I'd never hit a woman," he said.

I drew myself up and faced him squarely. "Go ahead."

"Don't be ridiculous."

"Don't call *me* ridiculous."

"Then stop acting like a child."

"*Me?*" I inquired ungrammatically. "*I'm* not the one sulking in the corner while everyone else runs around after him."

"Is that really what this is about?" Martin took three or four rapid steps backward, putting the chair between us. "Because I asked you to do something for me? I thought you'd understand why I couldn't do it. I thought you wanted to help me."

"Of *course* I want to help you," I wailed. "But I want you to help *yourself*. To behave as if you cared."

"What do you think I do all day?" Martin waved a hand wildly in the direction of his desk. "I spend hours every day talking to the Pinkerton men, writing to every politically connected man I know to get the damned journalists off my back. I pass all my free time talking with Joe, thinking, thinking, pacing these rooms when I'm alone in an attempt to wear myself out so I can sleep. Then I close my eyes and see that room full of blood and Lucetta lying on the floor, split open at the throat." He swallowed. "I liked it better when I was sleeping all the time."

I frowned. "When was that?" Having spent the main force of my anger, I was subsiding into exhaustion and unhappiness. Naturally, I wished I'd never lost my temper in the first place. I crossed my arms, almost tangling them together, and hunched my back defensively.

"Just after I was released—when you were at Gambarelli's." Martin retreated to his desk, where he perched on its edge in a similar attitude to my own. "There were days when I didn't seem able to get out of bed, when sleep was my only refuge. And then, somehow, one morning I decided I would get up early, shave, and dress. The next morning I did the same—and the next. It was you who inspired me, I think. Knowing you were working for me." His own brief surge of rage seemed to have spent itself like a wave crashing on the shore, and his voice was gentle.

We stared at each other for a long moment, huddled in our defensive positions either side of the room. Then Martin slowly, tentatively, crossed the room and seated himself at my side.

"I feel as if I'm digging myself out of a deep hole, Nellie." He looked down at his knees, which stuck up rather—the settee was a low one. "There are days when I still wake up and wonder if the police will walk into these rooms and tell me that they're not convinced of my innocence after all and have come to take me back. I'm not sure what I'd do if I had to go back again."

"Does that have something to do with going to Europe?"

"Yes," Martin replied, still looking down. "I need to know that I can leave Chicago as much as anything else. I need to know that I'm truly a free man. And, believe me, despite the impression you've received, I'm quite as anxious as you that we should find the killer before the day I step on board ship."

It was on the tip of my tongue to tell him what else I'd learned, what I suspected, but his next action forestalled my words. He put the back of his hand to my cheek, gently, and I tensed against the urge to turn my head and kiss his fingers. I too was in a deep pit. I had fallen in love with Martin completely and irrevocably, with no way of ever getting out again.

"Please stop," I whispered. The mood between us had shifted again, but I didn't know in which quarter it now lay.

He withdrew his hand. "Look at me."

I looked up into a face that was stern and remote, and yet his eyes said something different. I knew what it meant when people said their hearts were full. Mine seemed to be taking up far too much room in my chest.

"My dear," Martin said, his voice hoarse and strained. "Do I really need to point out to you, yet again, that you're the light of my life and the center of my world? That hasn't changed one whit. But I've changed, as a man—my place in the world has changed."

He was silent for a moment, seeming to ponder what he would say next. "And yes, I do mourn Lucetta," he said finally. "Not as a wife I loved—I have the unfortunate trait of only being able to love one woman at a time—but as a wife, nonetheless, whose death deserves pity and some measure of dignified respect. I don't think, if you search your heart, that you'd want me to turn from her graveside into your arms as easily as if I were changing my coat."

I hung my head. He was right, of course.

"And because of the circumstances, I wasn't even able to stand at her graveside. I can't go there now for fear of the journalists hounding me and drawing unwonted assumptions. I have to find a way to say good-bye to her in some human, ordinary fashion without seeing that horror of blood every time I think of her. And I know for certain I can't do it in that house. It holds the failure of our marriage, everything that was sour and mean about our last few months together. I think I'm selling it complete with its contents to the first buyer I can find once all this is over."

"Not the portraits." My response came so swiftly it surprised even me.

"You saw those, did you?" Martin's eyebrows lifted.

"Yes, and they're much of what made me feel so—well, I didn't feel I could ever be part of the world they represented. They—that house—" I could feel a treacherous, hot tear gathering at the corner of my eye. "I can—maybe—understand why you can't—love me right now. But I don't see how you ever can, once you've gone to Europe and left me behind here." The tear broke free and slid down my cheek to my jawline. It lingered there, leaving a wet, slightly itchy trail behind it.

A knock at the suite door made us both jump. Martin rose swiftly to his feet. I dragged the back of my hand across my face as he crossed to the parlor door, stepping into the tiny hallway.

It was the food, of course. We were obliged to stand by while the two men set up a folding table, draped it with snowy linen, and laid it with sparkling silver and crystal. One of them handed me into a chair with a solemn air of accomplishment that might have made me laugh in other circumstances.

I saw a generous tip exchange hands, which probably ensured the men's discretion. Martin poured out water for both of us and served the fish in silence while I stared at my plate, wondering how I was going to eat. Emotion always robbed me of my appetite.

"Now then, Nellie Lillington, none of your tricks." Martin seated himself and nodded at my plate. "Eat your food. You were very hungry when you arrived, and you'll faint from inanition before you get home if you don't put something inside yourself. Try a little fish, to encourage your appetite."

How well he knew me. After the first, difficult act of swallowing, my hunger revived. Martin talked about impersonal topics—the endlessly

rehashed opinions on the forthcoming presidential election figuring prominently—until I'd eaten most of my portion of fish and a drumstick of very
fine fried chicken. I began to feel not exactly calmer, but definitely less likely
to explode.

"That's better—a real smile at last." Martin, who had managed to eat well
while talking, wiped his mouth on the beautiful damask napkin. "Now let me
say the rest of what I wanted to say to you. I've been turning it around in my
mind for some time."

He stood up and crossed to his desk, donning the sack coat that hung
over his chair. He straightened his cravat, pulled down his vest, and generally
made himself tidy. The black armband he wore on his sleeve had slipped out
of place, and I saw the swift look he gave me before he adjusted it carefully.
He was donning his armor again, I realized, but not as a protection *against* me.
In some odd, masculine way, he was making himself presentable *for* me. I felt
the tension in my shoulders ease.

He returned to the table and held out his hand, leading me back to the
settee, but this time seating himself in the chair opposite me.

"The world I lived in with Lucetta has gone," he said without preamble as
soon as he saw I was comfortable. "It wasn't really my world, anyway. Those
were her friends, her family, and her music. Even when we entertained my
business acquaintances, it was at her insistence, not mine. You and I will start
the world anew, when the time is right."

"And you'll still carry it on your shoulders," I murmured.

"What?" Martin gave me a quizzical look.

"Your portrait. You look like you're bearing the weight of the world."

"Do I?" Martin looked interested. "He's a clever fellow, that Sargent boy.
An American lad, very young, who was introduced to us in Paris. He doesn't
really like doing portraits, but he's studying under a society painter who
thinks Sargent needs to learn some bread-and-butter work before he indulges
his own tastes. He's got talent, hasn't he? That portrait of Lucetta is quite
magnificent. I can't say I care for mine all that terribly though. Perhaps he
saw into me too much."

"I have my qualms about living with it as well," I admitted. "But if we do
start the world anew, Martin, well—that portrait is *you*. I wouldn't want to
let it go. And it would seem wrong to split the paintings up, don't you think?

They're so obviously a pair, and would be a pair even if they were continents apart."

"It would be a crime against art," Martin agreed. "Some people don't think portraits are real art—but whatever I might feel about those particular paintings on a personal level, I think they *are* art, and astonishing at that. I suppose we could shut them in a room somewhere."

I shuddered. "I don't like that idea. I feel like they'd change behind our backs if we didn't look at them. Grow older, perhaps."

Martin stared at me. "That's possibly the most horrible feat of imagination you've ever achieved, Eleanor Lillington. And you a woman of such great practical sense." He winced. "It'll give me the horrors to look at them now."

"But don't you think they're your responsibility?" The thought rose to my consciousness like a bubble in a glass of champagne, popping into bright clarity so that I sat upright, suddenly alert. "I mean—what you said earlier about your lost world with Lucetta—it's not really lost. The past is something you and I will have to carry with us, always. We shouldn't have to fear that burden."

Martin smiled, shaking his head. "That 'we' makes up for everything. For giving me horrible thoughts about the paintings, and for practically calling me a coward and a cad. Thank you for that."

He rose to his feet and went to press the service button. "I'll get them to find a hired carriage to take you home. Listen—I don't even know what the world will be like for me once I'm free of this mess. I still intend to go to Europe, for a hundred good reasons. But I desperately want you to understand that I'm resolved to spend the rest of my time in this world with you, if you'll only have the patience to wait for me to straighten out the warp and the weft of my life."

"As long as you love me." That, when it came down to it, was all I needed to know.

"With every fiber of my being."

He raised my hand to his lips and kissed the tips of my fingers gently. I wanted more from him—I had been waiting for an eternity for more. But I would have patience, as he asked.

So I nodded. "That'll do."

And it wasn't until I was following the concierge back through the maze of tunnels that I realized I'd never told Martin about my suspicions.

THIRTY-ONE

The concierge led me to a side door, well away from the main lobby. There were just two armchairs there, set discreetly behind some columns. I was about to seat myself when a familiar voice assailed me.

"Mrs. Lillington! Nell!"

It was Joe.

"I'm so sorry to be lying in wait for you." He waited until I was seated in one of the armchairs before taking the other. "But I knew, as soon as the housekeeper told me you'd gone, that I'd find you here. Why didn't you ask me for the carriage?"

"I was in a bad mood," I admitted, smiling ruefully. "It was those portraits."

Joe grinned. "They do rather blot out every other thought, don't they? I've never been sure if I like them or not. They're quite the cleverest thing I've ever seen though." His dark, intelligent eyes were fixed on my face. "I expect they made you feel rather excluded."

"They did." I smiled. "But I'm starting to see them as two people living in their own worlds. They're linked by the past and the artist, but they are, after all, bound by their own frames."

Joe laughed. "You're turning into a philosopher. Besides, you're doing more than Lucetta ever did. You're becoming part of the one thing that's uniquely Martin's. The store."

The thought made me glow inside. "Thank you, Joe. You have a great knack for saying the right thing."

"That's why I'm good at my job. And by the way, I've sent away the hired carriage. I'll take you home. Now that you're here, let me go find my driver and tell him to get ready. He should be somewhere around the front. It'll only take five minutes."

He rose and disappeared in the direction of the main lobby, leaving me alone with my thoughts. I wondered briefly if Joe and the Pinkerton agents had found anything. I decided they probably hadn't, or Joe would have come up to Martin's rooms. I would have to tell him about the paper, which Martin had tucked away in his vest pocket. Joe could certainly rule out Gorton's handwriting.

"Mrs. *Lillington*." A voice spoke softly in my ear, and I jumped. "Or is it Mrs. Harvey? What an interesting woman you are."

My insides turned to ice as Christopher Columbus Crabb lifted his hat with a smile, looking down at me.

"I'll be quick—I don't want Salazar to spot me. And, if you please, don't tell him I was here. I've been following you all day. Very interesting. I knew there was something about you that just didn't fit."

"What are you going to do with the information?" I tried to keep the fear out of my voice, but I didn't think I was succeeding.

"The information that you're Martin Rutherford's mistress, perhaps?" His tone was teasing.

"I'm not." I felt my cheeks flame. "I'm most certainly not."

"Is that so?" He raised an eyebrow. "Going to his rooms alone in the evening definitely looked like it. Most compromising."

"So you're going to blackmail me. Or ruin me? Go ahead and try." I stuck my chin out.

Crabb held up his hands. "I promise you I'll do nothing hasty. I have to give all of this a good thinking-through. You'll be hearing from me—and in the meantime, be a good girl and keep your mouth shut. It'll be better for all concerned if you do."

He tipped his hat again and was gone, sliding behind the columns and heading in a different direction from Joe.

"You're an idiot. The worst kind of idiot," I said to myself. I could see I might have made things a great deal worse for Martin. But I had little time to fret. There was Joe, walking toward me, a smile on his face.

"All ready," he said cheerfully—but his face fell as he saw mine.

"Is something wrong?"

"Nothing." I forced a smile, remembering Crabb's injunction to keep my mouth shut. "Did your investigation turn up anything, by the way?"

He shook his head. "A complete waste of time. What about you?"

"A piece of paper—which Martin thinks is probably of little significance. I'll tell you about it in the carriage."

We exited into the street, which had just been sprinkled with water to lay the dust and had the odd, metallic smell of dampness on a hot day. Even this quieter street was full of passersby, mostly well-to-do couples in evening dress. The life of Chicago flowed around me, ignoring me, ignorant of me.

Crabb could change all that.

THIRTY-TWO

Even amid the joys of absorbing employment, the tumultuous affairs of the heart, and the frustrations of an investigation that was going nowhere, I still had to find time to visit Tess and Sarah in Lake Forest. So the next Sunday afternoon found me sitting against a tree on a picnic blanket on the Parnells' beautifully kept lawn, watching Sarah and Tess play a game Elizabeth called battledore and shuttlecock. I had spent a good forty minutes trying to hit the feathered birdie toward Sarah. I had at last handed the job over to Tess, who was far closer to Sarah's size and made a much better partner.

"Have some more lemonade," said Elizabeth, motioning to the very young, dark-skinned maid who hovered shyly at my elbow. "I wish it were chilled white wine, but Mother doesn't approve of alcoholic beverages on a Sunday."

"I certainly do not," said Mrs. Parnell, looking over the spectacles she had donned to read a respectable-looking volume of sermons. She didn't seem to be getting on fast with them—she hadn't turned a page in an hour. "And you know very well Mrs. Lillington doesn't drink—most commendable." She nodded at me in a friendly way.

Mrs. Parnell appeared to have decided that I was a repentant sinner and thus quite fit for society. She had cheerfully introduced me to several women at her church that morning. They seemed to regard Mrs. Parnell as an authority as to who was socially acceptable. They had immediately pressed me to let them know when I, my delightful little girl, and my companion could join them in such summer pursuits as bathing in the lake and indulging in the exciting new game of lawn tennis, which was threatening to become all the rage in Lake Forest. I put them off as best I could, promising to write to all of them when my other social engagements allowed. I left suspecting that Mrs. Parnell had informed them of my wealth and that this was to be the social glue that bound them to my side.

Elizabeth stretched and yawned in a way guaranteed to make her mother wince—which it did. "Well, I like to take a drink of wine," she said. "And *she* does, given the chance." She winked at me.

"*She* is the cat's mother." Mrs. Parnell's tone was reproving but her blue eyes twinkled.

"I beg your pardon, Mother. Nell, can you see how in favor I am now that I've promised to play the part of the passive little woman and wait for Mr. Fletcher to woo me? Mother pretends to be cross with me, but she's secretly delighted I've landed a potential husband. If he asks me, that is."

"Impudence," Mrs. Parnell said, but the corners of her mouth twitched upward. "Who wouldn't want to ask for your hand, my pretty Elizabeth? And yet I admire the young man's scruples about waiting for his promotion before he approaches your father."

"Scruples," groaned Elizabeth. "It sounds so very boring."

"You think Mr. Fletcher's boring?" I teased her.

"I think he's—" She rolled her eyes dramatically and laid a hand on her heart. "But I'm still a Feminist. Which reminds me—" She reached for the bag beside her, withdrawing a sheaf of papers.

Mrs. Parnell gave up the pretense of reading and removed her spectacles. "I suppose we must get the latest lecture over while little Sarah is out of earshot. I don't want you to corrupt her."

"Perhaps you should send Betsey away too." Elizabeth motioned with her head at the little maid. "Although, Betsey, you should listen hard. You're a free woman, after all, and the future is as much yours as Sarah's."

"Yes'm." Betsey looked as if she'd rather be playing with Sarah, but her training held and she hastened to refill Mrs. Parnell's glass. Twenty feet away from us sat Miss Baker and my lady's maid, Alice. Miss Baker was talking fast, and I wondered if Alice was also getting a lecture on women's rights. Elizabeth thought Miss Baker was a wonderfully progressive woman.

"So what's the latest startling notion about the iniquities done to our sex?" Mrs. Parnell asked. "I suspect this is about the women's franchise again."

"And much more." Elizabeth grinned at me. "A pink dress and a highly conventional suitor do not a submissive little wife make." She looked complacently down at her dress, a light but graceful confection of pink cotton covered with white gauze.

"Don't come crying to me when Mr. Fletcher casts you off as an unrepentant virago," said her mother. "Well, out with it."

Elizabeth straightened up and gathered her audience's attention with a regal sweep of her head. "The Declaration of the Rights of Women of the United States," she intoned. "Presented by Mrs. Susan B. Anthony herself at the Philadelphia Centennial Exhibition, on the occasion of our nation's birthday last month. I wish I'd been there."

"God forbid," murmured Mrs. Parnell. Elizabeth ignored her.

"Listen to this, Mother," she said. "'The history of our country the past hundred years has been a series of assumptions and usurpations of power over a woman, in direct opposition to the principles of just government acknowledged by the United States at its foundation.' And it goes on to give examples." She flapped the papers she held at me. "Do you know, Nell, that we have fewer rights now under the Constitution than we had when our nation was founded one hundred years ago?"

Mrs. Parnell sniffed. "Rights. There's a difference between the rights we may or may not hold and the reality. Your dear father is the titular head of the household, of course. But the powers he *thinks* he has are illusory."

I stifled a snort of laughter. I had met Mr. Parnell that morning. He was both tall and large, dwarfing his wife and even making Elizabeth look petite. Yet there had been no doubt that he deferred to his wife's opinion in all things except his business. Not that he seemed at all henpecked or even faintly bothered by Mrs. Parnell's assumption of authority. He had listened to her opinions with perfect equanimity, and after luncheon had simply said, "Well, my dears, you'll see me at the usual time," before disappearing from view.

"*Mother*," Elizabeth said impatiently. "Listen, Nell. 'The marital rights of the husband being in all cases primary, and the rights of the woman secondary.' That's in a clause explaining that a husband can keep his wife unjustly imprisoned with impunity. Imagine it. And yet so many young women run into marriage as lightly as they would go to a party. And see here." She waved the papers under my nose. "Mrs. Anthony condemns the absence of women from juries—even when it's a woman on trial."

I frowned. "So long as the jurors are just and true to their task, does it matter if they're male or female?"

"How can a man fairly judge a woman?" Elizabeth snorted in derision.

Mrs. Parnell's eyes gleamed. "If you are at all susceptible to the wooing of Mr. Fletcher, my dear, you had better accept that some men possess an iota of intelligence. If you do not, perhaps you are better off a spinster."

Elizabeth's round cheeks, already reddened by the heat, flushed a deeper hue. "I'm talking about men in the generality."

"The problem is, my precious, we only marry one of them at a time."

"Honestly, Mother, you're quite impossible. Don't you want women to have an equal status with men?"

Mrs. Parnell's intelligent face assumed a thoughtful expression. "I'll admit we seem to have steered into a most backward course, legislatively speaking. Those who do not have a good, provident, kind husband like your father have few options for freeing themselves. But then a man with a faithless and dissolute wife has little recourse either." She glanced briefly at me as she spoke, and I wondered just how much she knew—or surmised—about Martin.

"I could never countenance any man—or woman—acting outside their legal means of freeing themselves," I said, more in answer to her implication than to her statement.

"No, I don't think you could," said Mrs. Parnell softly, and it was as if some kind of understanding passed between us.

"'Universal Manhood Suffrage,'" read Elizabeth, "'by establishing an aristocracy of sex, imposes upon the women of this nation a more absolute and cruel despotism than monarchy; in that woman finds a political master in her father, husband, brother, son. The aristocracies of the old world are based upon birth, wealth, refinement, education, nobility, brave deeds of chivalry; in this nation, on sex alone; exalting brute force above moral power, vice above virtue, ignorance above education, and the son above the mother who bore him.'"

The arrival of Sarah and Tess prevented Elizabeth from reading more. I jumped up and began arranging cushions against the nearest tree, fussing over Tess, whose color wasn't good. The Parnells had a house on a long, narrow lot that gave onto a park bordering the bluff, and the breeze was pleasant. Beyond the park, the lake looked blue and smiling in a way it rarely did in Chicago.

The change in activity gave me time to think, and I needed it. The words Elizabeth had read out reminded me sharply of the absolute helplessness I had found myself prey to when I was a disgraced girl. My stand against marriage had put me more firmly into the power of my stepfather, Hiram.

Cruel despotism indeed—and it had almost cost Sarah and me our lives. Yet wasn't I contemplating making Martin my despot? Because if—when— he asked me, I didn't see how I could possibly refuse him. It shocked me, at times, to realize how much I ached for the very thing I'd sought to avoid when I was young. I was morally certain that Elizabeth, despite her progressive views, would accept David's offer of marriage. Did she feel the same visceral pull as I did, the yearning for a mate—the thing that the world called Love, and which seemed to override all other considerations?

"Walk with me, Nell." Elizabeth had also risen and looped her arm through mine. "I haven't had nearly enough exercise." And she tugged me in the direction of the park, leaving no opportunity for anyone else to accompany us.

"Stop looking so worried," she said as soon as we were far enough away from the house. "Mr. Rutherford will come back."

We had spent some time the previous evening discussing the fact that Martin was absent from the store and had been for about four days. Worse, Joe was gone too, leaving me to conjure up frightening reasons why the two of them should need to leave the store at the same time. The staff had remarked upon such an unusual practice. I'd received no word from either of them, and yes, I was worried. Furthermore, I had deliberately kept information from them—an omission that might, I didn't know how, put them in danger.

"Love is a highly complicated business." I looked to where Tess and Sarah sat together under the tree, now reading a book. "Especially where marriage is concerned. Marriage affects more than just two people—it affects society."

"Exactly, O wise one." Elizabeth raised her hands in ironic mockery. "Which is why Free Love is such a good idea. But I suppose if David won't hear of it, I'll have to give up on the notion." She paused for a moment and looked at me from under her lashes. "Though I'm sorry to delay the opportunity to find out about—you know—*it*."

"I hope you're not expecting expert advice from *me*," I said.

"I asked Frances." Elizabeth's tone was thoughtful. "She said it was utterly enjoyable—except, of course, for the constant worry about starting a baby. She gave me the most interesting description." She looked into my face. "What was it like for you?"

"Brief and unsatisfactory," I said in a discouraging tone. I had no intention of discussing Jack. I wished I'd heard Elizabeth's sister's interesting description.

"And yet you wish to—well, you would again, wouldn't you? With Mr. Rutherford."

"Yes. Can we change the subject?" I was warm enough already and didn't need to think about Martin that way.

We were about ten feet from the edge of the bluff, and Elizabeth flung her arms out to receive the full effect of the breeze.

"Blast courtship," she cried out, her words swept back from the lake by the wind. "I feel as if I'm going to have to wait forever."

You, I thought, are not the one whose putative mate is proposing to abandon you for the entire winter.

THIRTY-THREE

The Parnells' driver took me to the station at Highland Park in time for the first train at six in the morning, so I was at the store by more or less my usual time. Naturally, the first thing I did was to go to the third floor. The relief that coursed through me when I heard Martin's and Joe's voices coming from Joe's office made me quite weak at the knees.

"Where were you?" I barely gave Joe time to respond to my knock. "Have you any idea how worried I've been?"

Martin was seated in the chair that would normally have been Joe's so that he could look over the ledger in front of him. Joe sat beside him, although both men stood when I entered the room. A look passed between them.

"I'm sorry," Martin said. "I've become so accustomed to not contacting you, for your own protection from the press, that I couldn't bring myself to risk it. Especially after you came to my rooms. You've been taking a lot of chances."

"I'm rather tired of avoiding risks." I sat down and waited till both men had reseated themselves. Despite Crabb's instructions, and despite—or perhaps because of—Martin's discretion, I had resolved to act openly myself.

My worry over Martin's absence had brought me to a decision. The time for secrecy was past, and I had things to tell.

"Crabb knows my real name," I said. "He followed me to the Grand Pacific, saw me with Joe, and put two and two together. So there may not be any point in trying to protect my good name anymore."

"Has he contacted you since that day?" Martin looked concerned, but not overly so.

"No."

"I've been through my private mail already, and there was nothing from him in there either," Martin said to both Joe and me. "It could be that he's decided not to act, for reasons of his own."

"Or he's waiting for the right opportunity."

"He followed you?" Joe asked. At my nod, he looked at Martin. "You were right—we need to arrange for some protection for Nell. Not that we think Crabb's a particular danger," he added hurriedly, seeing my face. "From everything we've found out about him, his main interest appears to be to make himself money. But still—I can't countenance the thought of someone following you. I'll speak to Pinkerton's." He pulled out his notebook and jotted down a few words.

"Are you going to tell me what you were doing, or leave the matter to my imagination?" I asked Martin. "Because, believe me, I have been imagining things. All sorts of things."

For some reason, that made Martin smile—which made me feel embarrassed. But he spoke steadily.

"We went in search of John Powell," he said. "I told you I recognized the writing—I ought to. I realized whose it was when you had gone."

"So he was G?" I asked.

"His Italian name is Giancarlo," Martin said. "I wanted to ask him about it. It's the only clue to anything out of the ordinary with Lucetta in the last few months."

No, it wasn't. But I needed to hear what Martin had to say.

"You don't think he's the murderer, do you?" I asked.

Martin shrugged, but he looked uneasy. "It seems unlikely."

"He adored her, of course." I sighed. "All the Gambarelli men adored her."

"And a little note with a compliment doesn't make a man a murderer. It could just as easily have been that Powell flirted with Lucetta, and Gorton killed her in a rage. But that doesn't seem likely either."

"Did the police ever interrogate Gorton?"

"Why would they? He wasn't a suspect. The people who knew he was Lucetta's long-established lover are mostly in this room." Joe's tone was dry. "Don't think we haven't had the Pinkerton agents following him all around the city and inquiring into his bank account. He works hard, lives modestly for the most part, and sends money to his brother in Bordeaux. He meets with Crabb as regularly as clockwork, always at Gambarelli's. He never sets foot inside a shady establishment, is never seen with a woman, and, in short, leads the most boring and regular life possible."

"John Powell, on the other hand—" Martin began.

"Wait," I interrupted. "Why don't you simply ask Gorton for his version of events? Or tell the police about him so that he *does* become a suspect?"

Martin and Joe looked at each other again. I rested my forehead on my hand.

"Because your pride won't allow you to admit publicly that you knew he was Lucetta's lover and did nothing about it." I groaned. "Men."

A flush tinged Martin's cheekbones. "Not until we have some kind of evidence," he said shortly. "And I don't see what pride has to do with it."

"Don't you?" I shook my head. "What were you saying about John Powell? Did you find him?"

"No," Joe said. "He was supposed to be in Salina, Kansas, working on clearing the land and getting the foundations dug for a new store. He wasn't, and nobody knows where he is."

"We spoke to the foreman. He confirmed that Powell has been drinking himself into insensibility by the end of every day," Martin added. "I know he's mourning Lucetta, but this seems excessive, even for him."

We were all silent for a moment while I studied the two men. Finally, I said, "You *do* think he might be the murderer, don't you?"

"I think he may be *a* murderer, if not Lucetta's," said Martin, his face grave. "Do you remember I told you about a murder that took place in Jefferson City, a prostitute who was beaten to death? The man who was hanged for the crime went to the gallows protesting his innocence and specifically named me as the guilty party. If I hadn't been able to prove I was in Kansas at the time, I might have had another murder charge hanging over my head. But I began to wonder if he didn't mean me, the man—if, perhaps, he meant me, the corporation. The frontier stores are named FR Emporium, but their connection with me is well known. Everyone who deals with them tends to refer to them informally as Rutherford's."

Martin delivered the latter part of this speech to his feet, in which he seemed to have taken a sudden violent interest. I could see from the set of his shoulders that the anger he sometimes had to fight to control was stealing over him. My heart plummeted to the level of my boots. But it was no good—the time to speak was now, and speak I must.

My voice sounded small. "I've worked out a possible motive for the murder," I said. "Something that might have made Powell—or even, perhaps, Gorton—sufficiently angry to kill Lucetta."

"What?"

Martin let the word drop into the waiting silence. He had leaned forward, no longer looking at his feet, his forearms and clasped hands resting on the desk, his head hanging. He looked like a man waiting for a blow.

I had to work to get enough saliva into my mouth to speak. When I managed it, my voice didn't sound like mine.

"I think Lucetta was with child."

I didn't know how much time passed—seconds, minutes?—as I watched all color drain from Martin's face until he was white to the lips. I could hear the sounds of the store, the bustle of clerks in Martin's outer office, next to Joe's, laughter from the cash room and accounting offices that lined the corridor as arriving employees greeted those who were already there. I knew that my appointed time for appearing in the workshop was probably past. But I couldn't, for all the world, perform such a mundane act as looking at the watch on my bodice or twisting round to view the clock on the wall behind me.

The tick of that clock was, perhaps, the only thing that kept me grounded in reality. I felt as if the floor had disappeared and I was floating in the air, hovering around Martin as if I could catch him when he fell.

It was Joe who brought some sense of the real back. "What makes you think that?" he asked, his voice neutral.

I explained, in detail, the suspicion that had first entered my mind when I talked with Mrs. Fairgrieve. I went through every moment of my examination of the gold dress. At least I was in the presence of gentlemen who understood the construction of a dress and would not scoff at the experience I brought to bear.

"I stopped searching at that point, or just after." I felt myself redden, conscious that I had not, after all, done the thorough job that Martin wanted. "I found the piece of paper, and—well, I behaved childishly. I let it all—the house, the room—upset me. I'd be happy to go back there and look through the rest of the dresses to see if they've been altered, if you wish."

Martin blinked, the movement oddly slow, and moved his lips as if trying to speak. He finally succeeded.

"It's not possible."

"I do understand that," I said. "And that was what Mrs. Fairgrieve thought too. But—Martin, I remember Joe telling me he was surprised that the Gambarellis buried Lucetta so quickly. Before her brother Sam was able to travel to Chicago, for one thing. What if they knew? Do you think it's possible that the employees at the Cook County morgue were bribed to falsify their report? It might also explain why the Gambarelli family was so determined to keep you in jail. I can think of reasons why that might be, none of them pleasant."

"Such as?" Martin looked directly at me, and I quailed at the look in his eyes, although a little color had returned to his face.

"They might have thought it was yours—"

"It *wasn't*." Martin broke into my words, his voice a howl of anguish. "It couldn't have been—I didn't—"

"I *know*," I said gently. "But the Gambarellis undoubtedly *didn't* know. If they thought it was your baby, they could be furious at you for living apart from her when she was with child—for failing to protect her. If they suspected it wasn't yours, they might easily think you killed her—or had her killed—to satisfy your honor. They might even have understood that—didn't one of you tell me that the family honor means a great deal to them? But they would want to make you suffer all the same." I paused, but I knew I had to continue.

"It would also explain why Lucetta was willing to wait for you for so long that day, and in such an isolated location. She was going to tell you, wasn't she? She was going to throw herself on your mercy and ask you to take her back."

My voice broke on those last words. Martin, who had visibly flinched at the word "baby," let his head drop onto the heels of his palms. He drove his long fingers into his hair as if he was ready to tear it out. I knew he was thinking the same thing as I was. If he had returned to the store only an hour earlier—if Lucetta had spoken with him—he would have taken her back and reared the child as his own. He would have turned his back on me and cleaved to his faithless wife for the sake of the child—perhaps the son—he so desperately wanted. And I knew I would have accepted his decision and moved away, for what else could I do? Lucetta's killer, whoever he was, had spared us that. But it was a bitter, horribly bitter, reprieve.

"And she—Lucetta—tried to seduce you, didn't she?" I could barely stand to look at Martin. Beside him, Joe sat listening with a drawn face, the lines bracketing his mouth deep furrows. "You told me so. Soon after you returned from Kansas in December. I've thought such a lot about that dress, Martin—and about what I know from bearing a child of my own, and from making dresses for women who are with child or who have borne children before. I think Lucetta conceived the child in November, after you returned from Kansas. Time enough for her to have become aware of the fact, and in good time to convince you that the child was yours had she succeeded in seducing you."

I knew I had to finish, to lay everything that was in my mind before Martin, but it was so hard. I felt as if, with every word, I were driving a knife deeper into his heart. But I had made my resolution and plowed on. "In good time, also, to convince another man—perhaps *not* the father of the child—that he *was* the father. That man could be John Powell."

Joe moved in his seat. "He was always in love with her, I think," he said softly. "And a fool. I remember from my days at the Gambarelli store how he would trail around after them all, and how they'd laugh at him behind his back. I remember thinking, when Lucetta convinced you to give him a job, that she did so purely to get rid of him." He looked at me. "It's a neat theory, Nell. You could be entirely wide of the mark, but . . ."

"But your instincts are telling you I'm right, aren't they?" I could see it on both men's faces. "We can confirm it in more than one way. We can talk with Frank Gorton because he seems—to me, at least—the most likely candidate for fathering the child. We can find the morgue assistants who dealt with Lucetta's body and find a way to make them talk, although I'll admit that might be tricky. Or—"

But Martin had risen from his seat behind Joe's desk, moving around the chair that held Joe and heading for the coat stand to grab his hat and frock coat. The look on his face was one of pure fury.

"—or go to Gambarelli's and ask Lucetta's brothers," I finished lamely. "Martin, you won't hit anyone. Please. Don't give them reasons—"

"I strongly advise against this." Joe's face was almost as white as Martin's had been a few minutes before. "Or at least let me go with you."

Martin turned in the doorway and shook his head.

"This is between me and the family, I think. I'm sorry, Joe." I was relieved to see that as he spoke his expression became more normal, even if "family" was another arrow through my heart. "I've been avoiding going to see them—I knew I would have to do so eventually, but I've been a coward about it." He looked at me. "I won't hit anyone, I promise. But I need to know—*now*—what they know. And I need to tell them it wasn't my child if they confirm what you suspect. I can't let them think that, don't you see? I can't let them imagine that I would have done anything other than—cherish a child of Lucetta's." His expression altered. "I know those words must hurt you, Nellie. But I owe you the truth—and I'll make it up to you somehow."

I nodded. "I know you will."

"Can you at least take one piece of advice from me?" Joe sounded exasperated. "Don't run down State Street. The press is going to have a field day with your visit to Gambarelli's as it is. Don't turn it into a headline. Take a carriage or get your horse—don't make it easy for them."

The ghost of a smile stretched Martin's lips. "That advice I can take," he said, and then he was gone, leaving Joe and me staring at each other.

"In case you're about to ask me," I said eventually, "I am aware of the implications of the fact that Martin and Lucetta lived as man and wife for—what? two years or so?—and that she didn't conceive a child with him. I do realize it was a true marriage at first. I've had a lot of time to think about this, Joe."

Joe came to me and put a hand on my arm. "The more time I spend with you, the more I can understand what Martin sees in you." He frowned. "That wasn't a very well-shaped compliment, was it? But it was meant to be. If anyone can pick up the pieces of Martin's life once this is all over, you can."

I smiled, but another thought had begun to take up space in my mind. I turned to look at the clock, which showed a quarter past nine. "I'm dreadfully late for work."

"I'll walk you up to the fifth floor and tell Madame Belvoix I detained you."

"No—make my excuses to her. Tell her it was unavoidable."

"What was?"

"That I left the store. I'm walking down to Gambarelli's too. To see Frank Gorton."

THIRTY-FOUR

Thirty minutes later, I was sitting on a particularly hard chair outside Frank Gorton's office, listening to the muffled voices of men within. They were jovial, which meant that Martin hadn't come to Gorton's office—yet. A part of my mind wondered where Martin was. I longed to know if he had found any Gambarellis to speak to, and I ached to go stand beside him and protect him, if necessary. But he was right—this particular matter was between him and the Gambarelli family. To attempt to protect him would imply that I thought he needed protecting, and he didn't.

I also wondered whether there were Pinkerton men on Martin's tail—or mine. If either of us were attacked, would they suddenly appear to save us, like the rescuers in a sensational novel? Twice in my life, I'd been in mortal peril. I'd been rescued on the first occasion by what could only be an act of sheer Providence, the second time by Martin. As the minutes ticked by and the chair's seat dug into my posterior, I amused myself by imagining how both episodes could be worked up into an exciting chapter or two. Yet the actual experiences hadn't been in any way exciting. Besides, I had no talent for writing.

Eventually, a number of men emerged in a cloud of cigar smoke. The clerk in the adjoining office—he who had told me to wait—stuck his head out and gave me permission to importune Mr. Gorton.

I entered that gentleman's office to find him fastidiously opening windows, cleaning up cigar bands, and generally ridding himself of any sign of his erstwhile visitors. He greeted me briefly without any sign of recognition.

"Don't you remember me?" I asked. "I worked for Gambarelli's for a while. In the hat department."

He frowned, and then his face cleared. "That hair, of course. Quite the wrong color for millinery. Your name again, Mademoiselle?"

"You knew me as Miss Harvey. But that's not my name."

He paused in the act of whisking a little cigar ash from his desk into his cupped hand and looked more closely at me. "Ah. You are one of Crabb's, are you not? So you are a professional spy? I thought you were merely some *ingénue* he had recruited. There are so many who cannot live within their income and are grateful for the extra money." He jerked his chin, his mouth turning down in derision. "I remember now. You didn't like his implication that you must make your way in the world by finding yourself a lover. How impractical you Americans are."

He emptied the ash into a papier maché receptacle, brushed all traces of it from his palms, and sat back in his chair. "If you are looking for work from me, quite impossible."

"I'm not looking for work. And I'm not a spy. I'm here for our mutual benefit."

His expression changed. "My dear young woman, I am quite lacking in susceptibility in that respect also. At least, I prefer to do my own choosing."

"And I'm not here to offer you—myself." I was getting annoyed at him, especially at the grin that was spreading over his handsome face. "I want information from you, and in return I'll give you something valuable. Believe me, I'm in earnest."

The grin widened, and he spread his hands in a gesture of invitation. "Very well. Impress me."

"Lucetta Rutherford was with child, and I believe you may be the father. Was that true?"

I was gratified to see the color withdraw from his face, leaving it pale underneath faintly tanned cheeks. "A journalist, *sacré nom de Dieu*," he muttered. "Mademoiselle, I have nothing to say to you."

"I'm not a journalist either. *Will* you listen to me? I'm a close friend of Martin Rutherford's—"

He sat up straight. "Kansas. You are the little redhead from Kansas." He looked me up and down in a rather insolent fashion. "You are hardly little. But I suppose she meant young."

"Being rude to me might just cause me to walk out of the door," I said. "And trust me, you want to know what I'm going to tell you. But first you're going to tell *me* if Lucetta was going to have a baby. You're well versed in the information game, Mr. Gorton. You should know by now when someone's got something truly valuable to tell you."

We sat like statues for thirty or forty seconds, staring at each other across the desk while I watched a range of emotions playing over Gorton's face. Finally, he spoke.

"You give me your word you will not use anything I tell you against me?"

"I have no reason to—unless it was you who killed Lucetta."

He shuddered. "I would never have done such a thing. And besides—"

"You were here, in this store. I know that. But you could have had her killed."

"Never." This time it was a whisper.

"Good. But did you know she was going to have a baby?"

He nodded, just once.

"And was it yours?"

His expression changed again to something almost like relief, and I felt some cynical satisfaction in knowing just how short-lived that relief would be.

"It was my child." He looked down at his neatly manicured fingernails. "Quite some surprise."

I could feel a hard lump of anger growing inside me. "You knew it was yours, but you weren't going to acknowledge it, were you?"

His thick black eyebrows almost met his abundant hair. "Of course not. That would be, as you say, the death of me. Lucetta understood that."

"You were ready to allow your child to be raised by another man?"

He shrugged. "That would have been an elegant solution."

I could feel the anger rising like heat in my belly. "Did you particularly care which man would stand as father to your offspring?"

He tilted his head to one side, regarding me cautiously. "I am wondering if you know what you think I know. And if you know that I know it." He said "know" each time with a sort of mocking emphasis. Did he despise me in particular or women in general?

"Speak plainly. Remember, I have something valuable for you. Name the name."

After a few moments' silence, he did.

"John Powell." The last name came out as "Pow-ell."

"Do you think he killed Lucetta?"

An expressive shrug was the only answer I got. Gorton, I realized, neither knew nor cared.

"How can you even remain in Chicago?" I asked. "Aren't you afraid?"

He shrugged again. "Of Alex and Jacky—and Domenico—*bien sûr.* They are dangerous men. But if Frank Gorton disappears all of a sudden, he becomes an object of suspicion. Alex begins to ask himself questions—and his reach is long." He folded his arms. "I stay here, there are no questions, and why should there be? I am always so very discreet. Thanks to Alex, the police do not know about the child. Alex thinks it was Rutherford's. So I bide my time." He smiled and patted his breast pocket. "But not for so much longer. My notice is given, and I go to join my brother in Bordeaux in a few weeks. And, as Lucetta, *la pauvre,* once told me, one day I marry an obedient little French girl."

"You are the most despicable man I've ever met," I said. "And believe me, I've met some despicable men."

He grinned at that. "You mistake me," he said. "I offered to have the child brought up by a cousin in Paris. I thought, in fact, that Lucetta had decided to follow my advice—that she would sail for Paris straight from New York. I was as surprised as anyone else to hear she'd returned. But, well, she did not get in touch with me, and I assumed, correctly, I think, that she had come to tell Rutherford about the child and throw herself on his mercy." His grin turned malicious. "She would not have lost him to *you.*"

I grinned back, refusing to be upset. I'd thought that possibility over enough times by now that I was quite inured to it. "Thank you for the information I wanted. Now would you like to hear mine? I'm surprised you haven't worked it out for yourself. Remember, I told you I'm a friend of Martin Rutherford's. And that I know Lucetta was *enceinte*." I raised my eyebrows at him. "You don't understand yet? I'll make it plain. Mr. Rutherford is, even now, telling Alex Gambarelli that the child was not his. He may even be mentioning your name."

He wouldn't be, but I was angry enough at Gorton to enjoy the lie. I watched him as the news sank in.

"I didn't think people really went green with fear," I said pleasantly. "Now I know it's true."

And when his office door opened suddenly, I thought he was going to faint.

Christopher Columbus Crabb slid into Gorton's office with the speed of a coyote returning to its den. He shut the door smartly and then appeared to see me for the first time.

"Oh, it's you." At first, he seemed ready to dismiss me from his thoughts, but then his gaze sharpened. He took a second look at Gorton, sitting somewhat stiffly across the desk from me.

"What's *she* doing here?" he asked. "Martin Rutherford's—"

"He already knows that Mr. Rutherford is with the Gambarellis, if that's what you came to tell him." In other circumstances, I might have enjoyed myself. "Mr. Rutherford is making it clear that he was not the father of the child his wife was carrying when she was murdered."

Crabb stared at me open-mouthed for a moment and then swore long and fluently. "So *that's* what he was talking about," he said at last.

"Who?" I could see Crabb was agitated.

He ignored me and spoke to Gorton. "Can you get her out of here?" he asked. "I've got something to say to you."

"Oh no." I shook my head. "If I leave this room before I'm quite done, I'll go straight to Alex Gambarelli's office and tell him everything. Whatever it is, you can say it in front of me."

Crabb looked decidedly deflated. "There's a chap in the hallway who shouldn't be there," he informed Gorton.

"That would be the Pinkerton agent assigned to keep an eye on me—to make sure you wouldn't follow me again." So I *did* have a rescuer at hand if I screamed. How thrilling.

Gorton cast his eyes up to the ceiling and rose to his feet. "I leave. Now. It is opportune that you've come, Crabb. I will pay you well to assist me to leave Chicago in one piece."

"But what about Powell?" Crabb was almost shouting.

"What about him?" Gorton was pulling out the drawers of his desk and stuffing various small articles into his pockets. "He may hang for all I care."

"I think that would be his preference," Crabb said. "That's why I came over. He's holed up at Lizzie's, and she wants him off her hands today. And I'm done with the information game, and with the Gambarellis. Lizzie won't have it anymore. I've made enough to get by just fine with investing, and she won't have me as her solid man till I'm out of this messy business. You have to take Powell."

"I will not."

"I will," I said. "I can probably even offer him a measure of protection. The gentleman from Pinkerton's can help me with that."

Crabb fingered his mustache, appearing to assess my offer. "I should sell him to the highest bidder," he mused. "Which would be Alex. But I don't like the thought of what Alex might do to him after what I've heard." He shuddered.

"Then deliver him to Mr. Rutherford's office by two o'clock, and I'll do the best I can for him," I said.

"Crabb, time is of the essence." Gorton had moved toward the door, grabbing Crabb's elbow as he did so. "I hope very much that Alex's attention is, as you say, diverted for a little longer. You must find me a route out of this country."

I followed the two men out of the door. In the corridor, a man sat on the hard chair, reading a newspaper, but the alert look in his eyes as he saw me indicated he was no ordinary visitor. I made a gesture to him to show I was in no danger.

"Two o'clock," I said to Crabb as he passed. Gorton was striding ahead of him, jamming his silk hat onto his overly large head.

"It's a deal."

I turned to the Pinkerton agent and smiled. "We're going to need a few more of you, and perhaps the police. Could you please escort me back to Rutherford's? I'll explain on the way."

THIRTY-FIVE

By half past one, we were all assembled in Martin's outer office, the inner one having been deemed too small for the gathering. The usual traffic of clerks and employees visiting the accounting offices and cash room on the third floor had been halted by Joe's orders. A man was placed on each staircase and by the elevators to prevent anyone entering the floor. Four Pinkerton agents and a brace of police detectives stood along the wall, having refused Martin's offer of chairs. Two uniformed policemen stood guard at the office door.

"Should the lady stay, sir?" one of the detectives asked as Martin arranged a chair for me, well away from the seat assigned to John Powell. "It doesn't seem right for her to witness this."

Martin had returned from Gambarelli's as pale as parchment, and I wondered if I'd ever know what he'd learned there. He was still somewhat white in the face, but a mood of resolution seemed to have settled over him, and he had greeted my news with little emotion. I dreaded seeing him come face-to-face with Lucetta's murderer—but the detective's words sent a pang of shock through me. I wanted to stay. I looked at Martin anxiously.

"The lady stays right here," he said evenly. "She has been a valuable part of the investigation—in fact, I don't know what I'd have done without her." He turned to me. "You could say we're even now. A life for a life. Thank you for giving mine back to me."

I didn't know what to say to that, especially in public, so I said nothing. But a warm glow spread through me all the same.

We waited in growing tension until twenty minutes past two. I had no reason to trust Crabb. Would he simply run, as Gorton was doing? But at length, we heard voices in the corridor—two men, speaking in cajoling tones, as if they were trying to get a reluctant child to go for a walk.

"You'll need coffee." Crabb had a tight hold of John Powell's arm. Another man—a thin, weaselly looking man with scant black hair—supported him on the other side. I looked at Powell with curiosity as they seated him in the chair. After all, I'd never seen him.

In other circumstances, he might have been a pleasant-looking man. His forehead was broad and smooth beneath thick chestnut hair, which ran down into whiskers that looked as if they had once been neatly trimmed. His chin was a little weak, to be sure, but his mouth was wide and pleasantly shaped, curving up naturally at the corners. The irises that stared in terror at Martin out of bloodshot whites were an unusual color, a sort of light amber. He looked to be a strong man with broad shoulders and legs. The overall effect of him must once have been a kind of boyish athleticism.

Crabb looked at Martin, then at me, and held up his hands. "I've done my bit. I'm leaving now, all right? I give you my word you won't be hearing from me again."

"Some word," one of the detectives said, and the other sniggered.

"I'm not mixed up with any of this," said Crabb defensively. "I'd take a drink with him when we happened to be in the same establishment, was all. All I knew was that he—well—he and Mrs. Rutherford—" He looked furtively at Martin. "But only once. He spent a lot of time crying on my shoulder about that. The great love of his life and all."

He looked at Powell, whose head had dropped forward. They'd evidently spent some time cleaning him up but hadn't changed his clothes, which were blotched with damp spots where something had been scrubbed from them.

Vomit, from the faint residual odor. And probably worse. I had the impression he'd soiled himself.

"Should we cuff him to the chair?" one of the Pinkerton men asked quietly.

"He won't run," said Martin.

Joe, who had left the room for a moment, returned. "I'm having a pot of coffee sent up," he informed us.

"Can we go?" Crabb asked. "I'm rather busy today." He shot me a look, which I returned with a candid stare. No, I wasn't going to set the police on Gorton. I suspected that gentleman might find it more difficult than he realized to live safely in France now that the Gambarellis knew the truth. I was inclined to leave him to his fate. Lucetta deserved that justice, at least.

One of the detectives jerked his head at the other, and they left the room for a moment. When they came back, the detective who appeared to be in charge spoke to Crabb.

"Hop it, then. But stay in Chicago, and behave yourself. If we need you, you'll be hearing from us."

Crabb tipped his hat at me on the way out.

The coffee arrived, and a fair quantity of it was gradually coaxed down Powell's throat. He vomited once, but fortunately one of the Pinkerton men was quick at shoving a metal paper bin under his nose. The nasty mess was quickly removed from the room and the windows in both of Martin's offices opened. After some forty minutes' work, Powell was more or less restored to some semblance of humanity and sat staring fearfully at Martin. Who, I was glad to notice, did not look particularly angry.

"Now then." The detective in charge hunkered down on his knees beside Powell's chair. "All we need is enough of a confession from you to make an arrest, and then we'll put you in a nice, safe cell to sleep it off. Did you kill Lucetta Rutherford on Tuesday the twenty-eighth of March last, in this building?"

"Yes." Powell whispered the word and then looked up at Martin. "Hang me. Have mercy."

His face crumpled, and he began to sob while the assembled men looked at each other in disgust.

"How did you kill her?" the detective said, his tone remarkably gentle.

"With my knife. I cut—I cut—" He began to sob again. "*Mia cara* Lucetta. I would give the whole world not to have done it, I swear to you." He looked at Martin again, his face red and tearstained, clear trails of mucus running from his nose down to his chin. "I was angry—I get so angry—like a demon inside me."

"We all have our demons." Martin's face had assumed the blank look that hid his emotions so well. "But a man learns to control them."

"She said I wasn't a man," Powell groaned.

"Mrs. Rutherford?" asked the detective.

"No." Powell's voice was thick, and he cleared his nose with a great snort before continuing. "There was another."

"You're confessing to *another* murder?" The detective looked up at his colleague and shook his head in seeming amazement, a half smile on his face. "In Chicago?"

"Jefferson City." Powell's voice strengthened. "I didn't mean to kill her. I hit her a bit too hard."

"And you let another man hang for it," Joe said. He seemed to be suffering more than the others from the varied smells in the room. I'd seen him put his hand to his nose several times.

"Let's stick to *this* murder," the detective said a little impatiently. "So you're telling us you cut Mrs. Rutherford? With what?"

"My hunting knife. I carry it for protection—I'm on the frontier a lot." He squeezed the palms of his hands together as if to calm their trembling. "I didn't mean to kill Lucetta either. I was so happy when I saw her. I was on the way to the store to talk to Rutherford, and I saw her go in. I didn't understand why she was on the fourth floor, waiting in some storeroom. I thought Rutherford would be coming up any minute, so I waited in the room opposite. The one with the hats." I saw Joe nod at this.

"After a while, she went to use the washroom, and I thought she'd go downstairs. But she came back." Powell was more alert now, his body rigid. The look on his face was earnest, almost as if he would try to convince us of his innocence. "I had to go and talk to her. All I could think of while she was away was her. I thought maybe she felt the same. Maybe she'd seen me follow her and found a place we could talk alone—was just waiting for me to realize it."

I saw one of the Pinkerton men roll his eyes at another, but the second man shook his head sternly.

Powell had started to shake. The detective in charge straightened up for a moment to ease his knees, wincing, and then hunkered back down, still speaking in the same calm voice, as if to gentle a frightened horse.

"Why did you kill her?"

"She had a child in her belly." The shaking was getting worse. "She tried to hide it—didn't want me to know. I asked her if it was Rutherford's, and she—she—" He began to cry again. "The way she said it made me realize she wasn't sure. But it wasn't mine—I could see it in her eyes. I've watched her face all my life—her beautiful face—and I knew it, right then. My Lucetta was a *puttana*. A whore. A shame to her family. And she wouldn't even admit it to me."

"You killed her for the family's honor?" one of the Pinkerton men asked, and the detective looked up in annoyance.

"Yes—no—she said I wasn't a Gambarelli man. That I had no right to punish her. No *right*."

His voice rose to a scream on the last word, and he tried to rise to his feet, but fell. The two detectives and the Pinkerton men sprang forward in unison, dragging him upright. The detective must have spoken formal words of arrest. Yet all I could concentrate on was Martin's face as he watched the thick manacles, in the shape of the figure eight, being placed on Powell's wrists. Was he remembering his own arrest?

One of the uniformed men had entered the room when Powell screamed. "Do you want the Black Maria at the side entrance?" he asked the detectives.

"No." Martin's voice was harsh. "You owe me that much. Make sure he goes out the front way—through the store—for everyone to see."

There was a pause of a few minutes while the detectives debated the merits of clearing the store, which gave Powell time to leave a disgusting puddle on the linoleum of the office floor. His moment of clarity seemed to have passed, and he had retreated back into some state that was neither drunk nor sober, muttering to himself in Italian and occasionally opening his eyes and mouth wide, like a fish. In the end, a small procession formed with the two uniformed men holding onto Powell, and the detectives and Pinkerton men flanking him. The elevators were cleared of customers, and the procession proceeded into one of them. The last view any of us had of Powell was of his amber eyes, staring upward through the elevator gate as the machine slid downward out of our view.

The three of us—Joe, Martin, and I—retreated to Joe's office, where Joe flung the windows wide. Martin pulled himself up onto his customary perch on the corner of Joe's desk.

"Are you all right?" I asked him.

In answer, Martin held out a large, long-fingered hand in front of him, seemingly studying it for any signs of a tremor. There were none.

"Yes." He sounded almost surprised. "Do you know, I can't seem to find it in myself to be angry with Powell. I should be enraged, don't you think?" He looked at me. "Does that make me heartless?"

"You're never that." I shook my head. "Perhaps you've just gone through too much today."

"You're probably right." He swallowed. "I expect I'll make it up to myself in my dreams. Dear God, if there's one thing I'd like more than anything in the world right now, it would be the anticipation of a good night's sleep."

I felt exhausted myself. "Powell's in a hell of his own making, isn't he?"

"And he'll face the noose sober, poor devil," Joe said. "I can't imagine what it's going to be like for him in jail with no bottle to save him from the horrors. I've heard that stopping the drink when you've been on it for weeks is a terrible ordeal."

"If he survives." Martin's face was bleak. "I wouldn't put it past Alex to get to him in jail. I used to wonder, every time they put a group of us together, whether one of the other prisoners didn't have a knife in wait for me."

I wanted to put my arms around him so much that my shoulders ached. Even Joe's presence might not have stopped me from doing so if there'd been anything in Martin's face to assure me he wouldn't push me away. But the terrible blankness was settling over him again. Like Powell, he was retreating inside himself somehow. I rose to my feet.

"I'm going to work," I said. "I have a dinner dress that needs to be started. The dress form has to be set up and the toile made. The customer's coming back in two days."

Martin stared at me for a moment. "You're going to keep working? *Now?* After it's all over?"

"Of course I am," I said. "After all, your name will soon be free of any taint. I want to make sure you have a thriving store to come back to in the spring."

And before he could move, I leaned over and kissed him lightly on one cheek. I exited the room with one eye on Joe, who was trying not to smile at my blush.

THIRTY-SIX

Martin had been wrong about the Gambarellis' thirst for immediate vengeance. John Powell survived to face his execution, which took place before Martin left for Europe. The oddest thing about the whole affair was that Alex Gambarelli expressly invited Martin to be present at the hanging. The event was also attended by the press and some fifty or so persons of distinction, representative of the merchant community and of the city of Chicago.

Being conducted in the courtyard between the courthouse and the jail, it was not strictly a public affair. But it was made so by being written up in the evening papers. The description of Martin standing shoulder to shoulder with the Gambarelli men in a spot with the best view of the hanging affected me strangely, and I told him so as we walked in Lake Park three days later.

"I feel that the Gambarelli family and I have reached some kind of fragile truce," Martin said, his eyes on a few leaves, shed by the spindly young trees now that October was here, that were bowling along the paths. "They're still angry with me though."

"They are?"

The path turned, and we turned with it so that the fitful gusts from the lake were now coming from our right. I could see half a dozen children in the distance, attended by a pair of ladies in black. No strangely out-of-place men of any kind. No journalists, then. The Lucetta Gambarelli murder was fast becoming stale news. What with the rehashing of Grant's scandals, the Greenbacks, and the prohibitionists, the imminent election was providing far more entertainment.

"Domenico lectured me at length about my failure to control Lucetta's— amours." Martin shook his head. "He blames me for not beating her blue and putting an end to her lovers. If I'd turned her into a good, obedient wife, she'd still be alive."

"But she had lovers before she married you," I said with indignation. "Gorton, for one."

Martin shrugged. "But they didn't know. Had they known—well, I'm not sure what would have happened had they become aware of Lucetta's behavior earlier."

I was silent. Martin, of course, had been one of Lucetta's lovers—only she'd decided to marry *him*. To untangle the threads of what might have happened was an exercise in futility that had kept me awake more than once. I was learning to accept that things had a way of happening as if they were meant to. I could hear Tess's voice reciting the verse she often repeated when I began to worry: "For I know the thoughts that I think toward you, saith the Lord, thoughts of peace, and not of evil, to give you an expected end." Was Martin my expected end? I hoped so.

I should listen to those words next time I worry about Tess, I thought. With the advent of the cooler weather, the reports of disease in Chicago had dwindled. Elizabeth had written that she would soon return to the Palmer House with her mother, bringing Tess and Sarah back to resume their lives with me. And Tess was still talking of her family as if they, not I, would provide her eventual home.

I realized that Martin had also not spoken for about five minutes. He suddenly said, as if the words were forced out of him, "The child—and then the fact that I denied I was his father—were heartbreak for them."

I nodded and then realized what Martin had really said to me. *His.* I stopped walking, tightening my grip on Martin's arm to force him to turn and face me. "How——?"

Martin closed his eyes for a moment. "I've been trying to spare you this. But I find I——I can't. Who else can I confide in? And if I don't, I fear this will be another horror that prevents me from returning to you whole and healthy."

My heart warmed for a moment at the thought that I, and nobody else, could be the person he confided in. I wrapped my hands around his, longing to do more but knowing I had to be patient. "Tell me."

"The child——the boy——was expelled from Lucetta's womb after she died." Martin's voice was steady, but he shifted the position of his hands so that they were gripping mine. "Domenico told me it was a tiny thing, smaller than the palm of his hand, but that the family midwife who inspected it——him——was certain he was a boy. It cost them a great deal of money to hide his existence." He blinked. "How they must have hated me."

"Oh, Martin." I didn't know what else to say. We stayed as we were for some minutes, our eyes on each other as Martin's breathing slowly calmed and the pain in his eyes lessened.

It was Martin who broke the contact, drawing a deep breath and tucking my arm back under his. When he spoke, his tone was light, a deliberate turning away from somber topics.

"I've been so busy I'd quite forgotten to congratulate you on your promotion."

I grinned. "I'm glad Madame Belvoix decided to make me a full couturière before you told her who I really was. Poor Madame, her face was a study."

"Don't worry about that," Martin said. "Arlette Belvoix won't give you a jot more power over her workshop than you merit, even if you have been revealed to be a shareholder. And I don't think she believed for a moment in our story that you assumed a false name to avoid accusations of favoritism."

"Yes, that 'hmmm' of hers holds a wealth of skepticism, doesn't it?"

"She told me privately that she's extremely pleased with your drawing, your cutting, and your ability to direct less experienced dressmakers. Of course, she still thinks you have much to learn."

"Of course. I have. She, on the other hand, is a true mistress of the trade. It's a privilege to learn from her. It was nice of her to tell me I could arrive and leave when I wished, but I've no intention of shirking."

"She knows that, you goose." Martin nudged me in the side as if I were a child again. "And she's taken advantage of it. Under the financial agreement she insisted on, the more you do, the more the store gains and the less you effectively earn per hour."

"But I gain when I receive my dividends," I countered. "It's no good, Martin, you can't put me off looking forward to coming to work. Although I will have to make more time for Sarah and Tess."

"You'd better. And my absence will allow you to make your own way in the store without any undue influence on my part. After all, you've climbed to the dizzy heights of couturière without my assistance. Who knows? By the time I return, you may own the store."

"I'll do my best to ensure you have no job to return to." I laughed, but I could feel a heaviness inside me. So few days remained before Martin would leave for New York, to await the sailing of the SS *Germanic*.

"Make sure you do come back though, won't you?" I couldn't help asking. "I don't want to lose you."

"Despite your previous objections to the married state?" Martin moved around to the other side of me to shelter me from the wind, which was tugging playfully at my hair. "Because, Nellie, that's the only way forward for us—once I'm properly out of mourning. I'm not going to allow you to choose any middle way. Either we part as friends and you spend your life as an independent woman, or you'll have to put up with me as your husband for the rest of your life, and have my children into the bargain."

I bit my lip. "What about the store?" I asked. "Supposing I still wish to work?"

"Oh, I don't mind you working. Plenty of women do, although no doubt the ladies of Prairie Avenue will think you completely eccentric and whisper behind your back. Wealthy ladies in general, and wealthy married ladies in particular, do charity work—but they do not work for gain."

"I thought we just determined that my wages would be pitiful?"

"And don't think you have to remain at Rutherford's either. You could take your skills and experience and work for Field or any of the others. Don't imagine I'm keeping you on because I'm in love with you."

A rush of warmth spread over me, as if I'd stepped into a hot bath. Martin and I were engaged in a strange dance of emotions, and he deliberately seemed to be giving us very few chances to express our passions in anything but the most remote and polite of ways. I lived for passing remarks like that one.

Martin cleared his throat. "We can employ as many nursemaids as you wish to feed our growing brood of sons and daughters. As long as you take care of your own health."

I squeezed his arm. "Madame Belvoix makes sure of that. She will not 'ave 'er couturières fainting from ze 'unger," I said in a fair imitation of the little woman's accent. "And shame on you, Martin Rutherford, for imagining I would want to work anywhere else than in your store."

"I just wanted to be sure you understood your position. And you do realize, don't you, that under the laws of the state of Illinois your money is yours, whether we marry or not?"

"I do know, as it happens. I asked Elizabeth. Although she wrote back to me that many men still manage to take control of their wife's money. That the law may be the law, but a man can get away with owning a woman, body and soul."

Martin hesitated for a moment. "After Lucetta, how could you ever think I'd be that sort of husband?" His voice was serious, but then he looked into my face and gave my arm a little shake. "Don't look so tragic, Nell. I think you said it yourself—we're not going to be able to avoid Lucetta. And I don't blame you for asking the question. But believe me, I have no intention of asserting control over you or your money, whether that brings me good fortune or bad." He paused. "And talking of which—"

"Lucetta's money," I said.

"I inherited it, of course, as soon as it was established that I didn't cause her death. But I've already signed the papers to hand the lot over to Domenico, along with any of Lucetta's possessions he may wish to keep. My clothes and a few personal things are to be removed from the house—the portraits too since you think we should keep them—and then it's to be sold along with its contents. No doubt at a considerable loss, given the slump in house prices, but I suppose a man can allow himself a loss once in a decade."

"You've thought of everything, haven't you?" I asked. "You're ready to leave."

Martin shook his head and took my hand in his. One of a pair of elderly ladies who were passing smiled at us, and I was sure I saw her dig an elbow into her friend's side.

"I'm not ready to leave you, Nellie. This is a temporary absence. I want to return to you healed. And I want to give you the chance to think through all the ramifications of marriage and decide if it's what you really want. I'm willing to take the risk of an answer in the negative."

"I've already made up my mind."

He shook his head. "You're an impulsive woman, my dear. And after all that's happened, you need some peace and quiet as much as I do. You just don't know it yet."

"It sounds rather tedious." The months before the spring sailings were already stretching out before me like an endless field of snow. Couldn't Martin see that?

But he smiled and kissed my hand gently. "It won't be. And just think, you've managed to survive this episode of our lives without jumping into a river or walking through a freezing snowstorm. You must be growing up."

THIRTY-SEVEN

Sarah and Tess returned in time for us all to spend a few hours together with Martin just before he left for New York. Our reunion took place at the Palmer House hotel. Martin had assiduously avoided coming to Aldine Square, had in fact never set foot in the house. I had told myself several times that he was acting out of concern for the proprieties and because he meant for me to accept him, upon his return, in the guise of a genuinely independent woman. And yet I felt uneasy. Did he anticipate that he could return from Europe so changed that it was better to stay on neutral ground?

"I wish I were sailing on a big ship too, Mama." Sarah, curled into my lap, lifted her eyes from the *First Steps in Geography* book I had just bought her. Since her return from Lake Forest, she had insisted on addressing me by the very English "Ma-MAH" I had been taught by my own mother and grandmother. Tess, I'd noticed, didn't like the change at all.

"There's nothing to stop you from sailing to Europe too, you know," said Elizabeth airily to me before turning her attention back to what she was doing. "Now look, see? You hold the dolly in one hand and the hook in the other."

She was trying to teach Tess French knitting. "Now hook the bottom loop—that's it!—and pull it over the top one."

"That bit's fun," said Tess after she'd done two or three rounds. "But it's hard to remember how to loop the yarn round the pins. You have to tell me every time."

"That's why they call it practice." Sometimes Elizabeth sounded remarkably like her mother. "See? Watch. Then loop—that's it, you do that well—and then wind. And soon you'll have a nice long knitted—thing."

"But what's it *for*?" Tess asked.

Elizabeth screwed up her brow. "Does it have to be *for* something? It's a skill, I suppose. It's what ladies do."

"I'm not a lady." Tess stuck out her chin. "Nell's a lady. *My* family is from the Back of the Yards."

A look passed between Elizabeth and me. Elizabeth had already warned me about this new theme of Tess's, which seemed to have been provoked by Miss Baker's lectures on the dignity of the working classes.

"You're ladylike, and that's what matters," said Elizabeth gamely. "After all, this is Chicago, and we don't insist on a long family pedigree here. In fact, we don't even insist on good manners most of the time. All you need is money—which you have—to buy a nice dress and a soupçon of confidence, and you'll get by just fine."

Tess stuck her lip out. "I don't know what you just said, not really. Sary, how about we walk around the garden and collect some leaves to press in the big dictionary? We'll leave the ladies to their chatter."

Sarah, who was fond of the outdoors, jumped off my lap, leaving her book behind. Tess swept out with her small nose high in the air, leaving Elizabeth and me staring at each other.

"Oh dear," I said. "I feel as if I've just been put firmly in my place. And she was rather rude to you."

"I'm sorry." Elizabeth came to sit opposite me. "She seems to have gotten much worse while she was at our house."

"It's not your fault." I closed Sarah's book and laid it on the occasional table by my elbow. "It's mine, I suppose, for hiring such a political governess. The problem is, I like the woman—and I agree with many of her views, progressive as they are. But Tess seems almost to be looking for reasons to be dissatisfied with me. I swear she blames me for Martin's going away."

"She does seem to have rather a simplistic view of you and Mr. Rutherford," Elizabeth agreed. "Poor Nell, you don't seem to do anything right in anyone else's eyes, do you?"

"If by 'anyone' you mean the dreaded ladies of Prairie Avenue, that theory has yet to be tested." Feeling something sticking into my nether regions, I investigated and pulled out a pencil Sarah had dropped. "I'll admit that between you, your mother, and Miss Baker, Sarah's company manners have come on tremendously."

"Don't be silly. She was already well behaved." Elizabeth grinned as she watched me contort myself to look for marks on my skirt. "For a child who won't be six until February, anyhow. We may have added a tiny layer of polish."

"Which Tess seems to think would be better removed."

"Do you think she's afraid of something?" Elizabeth looked thoughtful.

"Of what?"

"Of your imminent launch into Chicago society, perhaps? It is about time you paid and received some calls. Mother and I have had several talks about 'the dreaded ladies of Prairie Avenue,' as you call them. Mother even thinks she can coax some very ancient ladies out of mothballs, ones who knew your grandmother. To give you some social weight, as it were. And she'd like to know if, in introducing you into society, we may hint at your future happiness with Mr. Rutherford."

"You may not. I'm not at all sure of that happiness myself. And since we're being impertinent and I finally have you to myself, may I ask about your future happiness with Mr. Fletcher?"

Elizabeth's smile was mischievous. "We're positively on the brink of being engaged," she said. "It's been six whole weeks since David received his promotion, and I've taken every opportunity I can to hint that he should ask Father for my hand."

"And what does he say to that?"

"That I should stop hinting and let him choose the time. But he did kiss me." Elizabeth closed her eyes, a smile on her lips. "It was a very *nice* kiss."

"It's amusing to see you so keen on the idea of marriage," I said. "Given your passion for the rights of women."

Elizabeth opened her eyes. "As it happens, it's occurred to me that I can pursue that passion more effectively as a married woman than as a spinster. I'll be free of Mother's eternal committees, for one thing, and will be able to attend meetings of my own choice."

"If David allows you."

"My dear, haven't you been listening to Mother? I've been consulting her on the best ways to ensure a man stays firmly under one's thumb while reassuring him that he's the most wonderful creature on earth. And David says he's perfectly sympathetic to the women's cause—stop laughing, he's not just saying that for my sake—it's just that speaking personally, he dislikes being manipulated. He says I'll have far more success with him by being straightforward than by employing what he calls 'women's wiles.'"

"You do realize you entirely contradicted yourself just now? Besides," I sighed, "men aren't always as predictable as we'd like them to be. Even the ones we've known all our lives."

"Be that as it may," said Elizabeth, "I'm dying to become a proper suffragist, and David has no objection. I'll have an uphill battle within the ranks, of course, since I'm anti-temperance. I won't deprive Father of his post-dinner brandy. But the prize of the vote is worth the effort, even if it probably won't be won in our lifetime."

"Win it for Sarah, then." I smiled. "Personally, I'm happy not being political. I have quite enough work to do."

"Which reminds me." Elizabeth sat up straighter. "Your launch into society. How about Wednesday afternoons for giving and receiving calls? You can spare that much time from the store, can't you?"

I pursed my lips. "I could make it up on Saturdays, I suppose. But Elizabeth—what about the unavoidable fact that I have a child and no real story about my husband? I just don't seem to be able to invent one."

"You don't try hard enough," said Elizabeth severely. "Listen. Mother thinks she can get Bertha Palmer on your side, especially if she explains— privately, of course—the link between you and Mr. Rutherford. You have to realize that there's been a lot more sympathy for him among the merchants than has ever been published in the papers. And if Bertha Palmer says you're to be received, you *will* be received, with no questions asked."

I frowned. "That doesn't seem fair."

"It's the way things work. And of course Mother will make it understood that your personal wealth is considerable."

"Because, of course, being rich is the answer to everything." I knew I sounded cynical, but I couldn't help it.

"Of course it is." Elizabeth's expression turned serious. "That and knowing the right people."

"So you're telling me that the society of ladies in Chicago is every bit as political as the world of men?"

Elizabeth spread her hands wide. "My dear, *everything* in Chicago is political. What's wrong with politics? We want to see you on a sound social footing before Mr. Rutherford returns. The fact that you work will create a small obstacle, but once they see how talented a couturière you are—once one or two of them are even known to be your clients—you'll just be seen as a little eccentric. That will work splendidly."

"And I only have to give up Wednesday afternoons?"

"More or less. A few evening engagements, perhaps, but it's really time you had some fun. And—Mother doesn't know I know, but Frances told me, of course—there are several couples I can tell you about who are *not* married to each other. There's that saying about it being inadvisable for people in glass houses to throw stones."

"Good grief." I rose and crossed to the window. In the garden below, I could see the red cloud of Sarah's hair as she darted around, presumably trying to catch the few leaves that were drifting down. "You know, I remember Martin writing to me, before the financial panic in '73, that there was some shocking behavior going on."

"Yes, he's quite bourgeois at heart, isn't he?" Elizabeth's blue eyes were rounded, daring me to defend Martin, but I only smiled.

"He was strictly brought up. Very well, I will sacrifice Wednesday afternoons to the cause of establishing myself in society—but not really for my own sake."

"Agreed." Elizabeth held out her hand, which I automatically shook.

"That's settled, then." She let go of my hand and circled my waist with her arm. "Mrs. Eleanor Lillington, welcome to Chicago."

℮

"Do I have to?"

Tess's expression was obstinate. We had said good-bye to Elizabeth, settled Sarah in bed, and ensconced ourselves in the parlor with coffee and some of Mrs. Power's tiny lemon cakes. It was getting cool enough in the evenings for the fire to be lit, and the red light of the embers cast its halo onto the marble surround. The dark green velvet drapes were drawn, and the room was pleasantly warm. It would be perfect, I reflected, if only Tess were happier.

"You don't have to do anything you don't want to do." I was determined to be patient with Tess. "But it's only a few hours on a Wednesday afternoon. All we have to do is receive whomever calls from one to three and pay calls from three to five. It'll be much more fun if there are two of us."

"How do you even make calls?" Tess looked at me over the rim of her spectacles. "Don't forget, I've never done it. I didn't have your upbringing."

I sighed. "You just talk, that's all. You sit and drink tea, and eat cakes like these, and you just—talk. You like eating and drinking, and you like talking—I don't see why you should object."

"Don't you?" Tess scowled. "The rich ladies will like *you*. They won't like *me*."

"For one thing, you *are* a rich lady—compared to most people. And for another, of course they'll like you. When have you ever known somebody who knows you to not like you?"

"Plenty of people. Mr. Poulton and Mrs. Calderwood—"

"And look how they turned out to be."

"—and Martin's wife. She didn't like me, and she was a Chicago society lady."

"If any of the ladies we meet behave toward you like those people at the seminary—and as Lucetta did—I won't have them in my drawing room. It was different at the seminary, Tess. I couldn't tell any of them to leave. I was a subordinate." I saw Tess's brow furrow at the difficult word and hastened to explain. "I didn't feel I had any power. Here, I do. I'm my own mistress. Even at the store I'm now recognized as a shareholder, and I can tell you that it's making a difference to the way in which people speak to me."

"So you'll tell them to leave if they're rude to me?" Tess's lip was still protruding.

"I will. You're more important to me than any lady in Chicago society. And look at the ones you *do* know—Mrs. Parnell and Elizabeth. Have they ever excluded you from anything?"

Tess thought for a moment. "I suppose not," she conceded.

"In fact, you probably know more ladies socially than I do. Many of those women in Lake Forest have their winter homes in Chicago."

Tess shrugged. "They're still more your sort of person than my sort of person."

I felt my shoulders slump. "Tess, I don't know what your sort of person is. I don't even know what *my* sort of person is. Elizabeth, perhaps, and Madame Belvoix." I frowned. "Women who have some purpose in life, I suppose, other than repeating what they hear from their husbands, fretting about children and servants, and wearing beautiful dresses. Not that I have anything against the wearing of dresses, of course, professionally speaking. I suppose it's a question of degree."

"You see," Tess wailed. "You have a place in the world already, and I don't."

I left my chair and knelt on the floor beside Tess, putting a hand on hers. "I think you do. I think it's with me and Sarah." I paused, trying to find the right words. "But finding your family has thrown all that into doubt and confusion for you, hasn't it? You're trying to be loyal to me and to your family, and it's tearing you in two."

Tess said nothing, but a fat tear gathered in the corner of her eye and dropped into the rim of her spectacles.

"And I can't decide for you," I said. "But if there's anything I can do to help you decide—"

"There is." Tess cut across my words, but her tone was less angry than before. "Mary wrote to say I should spend a month or two with her now that I'm done spending time with the fine folk. She says I should be with the family, where I belong."

I lifted her small hand, kissing the short, stubby fingers I'd grown to love so much. "Do you want to do that?"

Tess let go of my hand to pull off her spectacles, fumbling in her skirts for the hidden pocket that held her handkerchief. "I guess I do."

I scrambled to my feet. "Then you must go, with no hard feelings on my side. But we'll miss you terribly."

THIRTY-EIGHT

I did miss her. I had my work, of course. I'd arranged my hours so that Sarah would have plenty of time with me in the late afternoon to chatter about everything she'd learned during her day spent with Miss Baker. And yet the hours stretched ahead of me after Sarah had gone to bed, with nobody to talk to. I took to retiring early so that I didn't have to face the empty parlor. Then, once I was in bed, thoughts of Martin invaded my mind and impeded my sleep.

So I was all the more delighted when Tess's brother Billy visited me just as the first month of Tess's absence was drawing to its end. The young man had recently secured a new job in the Palmer House as a junior clerk in the accounting office, and his Sunday best reflected the elevation in his status. His soft felt hat was of good quality and fairly new; his boots were of a finer leather than before, and there was a smartness about his suit that suggested that if it hadn't been tailored, it had at least been altered to fit him better.

Billy assured me that Tess was well, and we chatted for a few minutes about his new position. He shared Tess's love for columns of figures and explained that he wrote a neat hand, having always applied himself at what little schooling he'd had. "And knowing I was always of a serious disposition and never one for the drink or the larking about, they were willing to give me a chance." His grin lit up his plain, snub-nosed face. "No more dormitories for me. I've taken a room with my friend Charlie down Pilsen way, in a good tee-total boardinghouse run by a German lady who knows a bit about cooking." He patted his stomach appreciatively.

"Is there room for promotion in this office?" I asked, passing him the coffee I had just poured.

His grin widened as he dropped sugar into his cup. "Plenty. It's a good step up for me, and I'm putting a little by every week. It's a pleasure to sit in a warm, dry room and think of the day when I'll have enough saved to make something of myself and can look for a sweet little woman to marry. No broken back like Da's, only inky fingers." He spread his blunt-ended fingers wide in illustration. He had clearly scrubbed them well, but the marks of his profession could be seen like ghosts on his right hand.

"You're coming up in the world. Your parents must be so proud of you."

"Aye, they are." Billy nodded at the far end of the parlor where Sarah had made herself a nest of cushions under the windowsill and sat cross-legged, absorbed in her geography book. "There's another one who'll go far, if I'm not mistaken," he said, his voice low. "A tiny mite like that so keen on the learning—why, she's half the age of Mary's eldest, and I've never seen him stare at a book for the fun of it."

"I never did either at that age," I agreed, "unless it was one of Grandmama's fashion-plate journals. I'm glad you don't think it's unsuitable for her, being a girl."

Billy gave a dismissive shrug. "And aren't there a whole handful of colleges for women out east already? Believe you me, Mrs. Lillington, my sons and daughters will get as much learning as I can pay for. It's ignorance that leads to vice—Charlie says so. He goes to night school, and he thinks I should go too."

Sarah uncurled herself from her corner, tucked her book under her arm, and came to stand close to us. "When is Tess coming back?" she asked Billy.

"She asks me that every day," I said, looking apologetically at him. In truth, Sarah had asked the question I most wanted to hear answered. It was my besetting fear that Tess wouldn't return at all, and I couldn't imagine having to explain such a disastrous development to Sarah.

Billy rested a hand on Sarah's springy curls, a soft light in his eyes. "She'll be back when she's ready, darlin'. In fact, that's why I came to see your Ma—to encourage her, like, to try to persuade Tessie to return where she belongs."

I let out a sigh of relief. "I'm happy that you, at least, think she belongs here."

"She *does* belong here," Sarah said in a decided fashion. "She's Mama's best friend and my best Tess. We should fetch her back, Mama," she continued, her eyes on me.

"It's not as easy as that," I said. "We have to let her make her own decision—and that takes time."

"Begging your pardon," said Billy, "but if you're letting her make her own decision, you're the only one as is. There she is with Mary and Aileen and Ma talking, talking, and *talking* at her as to how she belongs with her family. And the priest besides, telling her to turn back to the faith. Not that he's having much luck." A mischievous grin lightened his homely face. "She's a marvel, our Tess. She has a verse from the Bible to answer everything they say to her."

I smiled. "Yes, she knows the Good Book almost by heart—I've even heard her quote a verse from Numbers. She's never been able to understand why I can't memorize verses. Yes, Sarah, you may have *one*—just one." This last to my daughter, whose hand had been creeping, in a hopeful fashion, nearer to the bowl of sugar lumps.

"Thank you, Mama," said Sarah prettily, claiming her prize. "May I go show Zofia the map of Africa? I know she's home because I heard her come in."

"You may, but no wheedling slice after slice of cake out of her."

"Yes, Mama." Sarah crunched her sugar with glee and skipped out of the room with cake, I had absolutely no doubt, firmly on her mind. She was an obedient child, up to a point.

"She's a sweet little poppet," proclaimed Billy once Sarah had left the room. "Tess has sung her praises to me more than once, although she won't do so in Mary's hearing. Those boys are little demons when they're shut indoors. Any comparison wouldn't be in their favor."

"Tess isn't getting too tired, is she?" I asked. "I'm anxious for her."

"She looks after herself." Billy looked sympathetic. "She tells that poor overworked maid of Mary's to mind the children when she's had enough and falls asleep in the chair." He leaned forward. "Tell me, Mrs. Lillington, do you want her back?"

"With all my heart." I could feel my voice catch on the lump in my throat. "I've never had a sister, but I couldn't love one more than I love Tess."

He nodded. "That's what I thought. Well, why don't you just go and ask her to return to you?"

I frowned. "Because, as I told Sarah, it needs to be her decision."

"And to make a proper decision, she needs to hear both sides of the story. You're not too proud to tell her you need her, are you?"

"Of course not." I knew I sounded indignant. "I've just been trying not to bother Tess with my own selfish needs."

"But that's exactly what she *does* want to hear." Billy thumped the arm of his chair. "She wants to know that you need her. She needs you to fight for her."

℘

Billy's advice warred with my own good intentions that entire week, and by Sunday had entirely beaten them down. Once church was over and a hasty Sunday lunch eaten, I bundled Sarah into her new coat—it was almost Thanksgiving, and cold—and we set off for the Back of the Yards.

Mary's house was, of course, modest compared to Aldine Square, but it looked roomier than its neighbors. It was on a more respectable-looking street than most. Now that the sharp, frosty air had robbed the stockyard smell of much of its power, I could almost have imagined myself in a small, prosperous town.

Mary herself answered my knock on the door, hastily removing her apron. "I'll tan that girl's hide," she said by way of excusing herself. "She's supposed to answer the door."

"That's quite all right." I proffered my hand. "How are you, Mrs. Sheehan?" For such was Mary's married name.

"As well as can be expected." She bent to chuck Sarah on the chin. "Look at this one, grown a whole inch since I last saw her, I swear to heaven. Would you like to play with the boys, Miss Sarah? The two youngest, at least—their brothers are at church."

"Please, may I see Tess first?" asked Sarah. "I'd love to play, but I miss Tess so much."

Mary nodded. "Of course you do, darlin'. The boys will still be there when you're ready. They're quiet for once, without their big brothers." She gave me a half smile. "Just go upstairs—the door straight in front of you when you reach the top of the first flight. Then you'll take a cup of tea with me, I hope."

I agreed willingly, and, leaving our outer clothing on a chair occupying an odd angle of the wall, we climbed the stairs and I knocked at the door.

"Tess?"

I opened the door slowly and peered around it. The bedroom was tiny, barely more than a cupboard, and mostly taken up by a short, narrow bed—which was mostly taken up by Tess. She had fallen asleep with her cheek pillowed on her hand and was snoring gently. Her spectacles sat on a chair squeezed in beside her bed, which also held her Bible and a candle in a dish. A chest of drawers made it impossible to move into the room without climbing over the bed, and it must have been impossible to open the lower drawers. Tess's dresses hung from various hooks high on the wall. Still, I reflected, it was a room of her own—and it wasn't Mary's fault that they couldn't afford bigger.

"Mama, look at the sweet room! It's like a little nest."

I inwardly blessed Sarah for the remark, she who'd spent the summer at the Parnells' sprawling mansion, where the guest quarters were bigger than this house. At her voice, Tess stirred and half opened her eyes, making an interrogative noise. Sarah needed no further encouragement.

"Tess, Tess, Tess, Tess, Tess, *Tess!*" Sarah's voice rose to a squeal as she launched herself onto the bed, which made an alarming creaking noise. "We miss you so much. Are you well? Do your spectacles need cleaning? Don't you love having all your dresses hanging on the wall? Mama, may I please hang my dresses on the wall?" Not waiting for an answer or giving Tess a chance to sit up, she burrowed into her arms and rained kisses wherever she could, which was mostly on Tess's neck.

I couldn't help laughing. "Give Tess a moment to wake up, Sarah." I insinuated myself into the corner of the room that wasn't taken up by furniture and put out my hands to help Tess assume a sitting position.

"She's right though—we miss you so much." I handed Tess her spectacles and, once she'd put them on, leaned down to hug her hard. Tess returned the hug with equal ferocity but scowled at me when I straightened myself.

"If you missed me, why didn't you come and see me?"

"Oh, Tess, that's not fair. I've written to you every week, and you know how bad I am about writing."

Tess shuffled along the bed so that she was at the end nearest the door. Behind her, Sarah curled up into the place Tess had just vacated, staring up at the walls hung with dresses.

"And it wouldn't have been fair to keep coming to see you," I continued. "You wanted to make a decision about where to live, and I didn't want to put undue pressure on you. There's no point in my vaunting my ideas about my own independence if I can't leave you yours."

"Hmph," said Tess, but then a smile broke onto her face like the sun shining through clouds. "You're funny, Nell. You're always trying to make things work for everyone."

I had to grin at that. "It's the curse of a practical mind. Anyway, it was Billy who said I should come here. He said that if I really want you to come home to us, I should fight for you."

Tess looked alarmed. "I think Mary's stronger than you."

"Not fisticuffs, silly." I made a gesture for Tess to move along and seated myself gingerly on the end of the bed, from which an ominous creak emerged. "Can this bed hold all three of us?"

"Bert says it'll break if the boys bounce on it, so don't bounce."

I fixed Sarah with a stern eye to make sure she'd heard. She only nodded, her eyes dreamy.

I wrapped an arm around Tess's shoulders, loving the warm, round, sleepy feel of her. "Billy just meant that I should come and tell you, quite plainly, that I think you belong with us. And I do. You're my sister of the heart—you have been since that first day in Prairie Haven, do you remember? You made me welcome."

"And you taught me how to sew." Tess leaned her head against my bosom, her fine hair tickling my nose.

"Do you really want to live with Mary?" I asked, laying my cheek on the top of her head. "You don't have to be my housekeeper if you don't want to.

I'll do anything you want me to. I'll even stop working at Rutherford's—or I'll get you a job there, if you want."

"You will not." Tess looked up at me, but there was a mischievous gleam in her eye. "There's much too much running up and down stairs at Rutherford's. And all that hard work."

I frowned. "It's hard work?"

"It would be for me."

"And me," came a small voice from behind Tess. "All that talking about dresses. Land sakes, Mama, you can talk about dresses till the cows come home."

"Where did you get that peculiar expression? Miss Baker, I suppose." I returned my attention to Tess. "If you want me to stop working—"

"I don't."

I hugged her tighter. "Tess, you've fought for me. With a gun, even." I felt a tiny giggle run through the small, round body next to mine and dropped a light kiss on the top of her head. "I don't have a gun, but I'm willing to argue this out with Mary and Aileen and both of your parents if necessary. If they need money, I'll supply it. I'm asking you—*begging* you—to return to us. We need you."

Tess was silent for a few moments, and I could feel the tension building inside my spine. At last, she spoke, slowly, as if she were groping for her own thoughts.

"Mary's boys are real noisy. Even if I helped her buy a bigger house, they'd still be noisy. They make me tired. And I don't want to be a Catholic, Nell, really I don't. I don't mind the church—and I like the smell of that smoky stuff—but it's not what I'm used to, and I'm happy with what I'm used to. It's the same God, after all."

"What do your parents think of the idea of you living with Mary?" I asked.

"I don't really know. Da doesn't say all that much, and you know Ma doesn't always make sense to me. She cries a lot, and she talks about the saints, and Georgie and Janet, and asks God to forgive her all the time. I keep telling her that God *does* forgive her, that He forgives all of us, but she doesn't listen, and then Da says 'hush, Tessie.'" She stuck out her lip. "I love Ma and Da, of course, but sometimes the thought of spending a whole day with them makes me feel a little bit funny."

"Why don't you ask your Ma and Da?" asked Sarah, kneeling up so that she could look at Tess. "Then we can go to the saloon and I can draw in the sawdust with my feet. I like the way it smells."

The door below banged, and the sound of running feet mingled with Mary's cry of "would you ever take off those muddy boots?" I surmised the older boys were home.

Tess looked sideways at me. "Little Robbie will start yelling in a moment because Frankie's pinched his ear. He does it every time, just to make him yell."

"So going to your parents' house might be a good idea?"

"A very good one."

※

As Tess had predicted, the arrival of the older boys soon led to mayhem. Frank, the oldest, had his mother's solid build, his father's peevish expression, and showed every sign of promise as a bully.

We drank the cup of tea Mary offered for politeness' sake, but it was a relief to climb into the rockaway and set off for the O'Dugans' saloon. There it transpired that Mr. Nutt had become accustomed to paying a trustworthy big lad to hold the horses and keep the younger children away from the carriage while he joined the O'Dugans for a cup of strong tea and a bite of cake. I wondered briefly what Mama would have said to have seen her granddaughter sitting on her carriage driver's knee, listening enraptured to tales of fur trappers and Indians—but then again, hadn't my father been a rough diamond? In any case, Sarah was occupied, and Tess and I were free to sit with the O'Dugans and bring before them the matter of where Tess should live.

I was used to Mrs. O'Dugan by now. I wasn't surprised when large tears started to roll down her face as soon as Tess began to explain that she wasn't sure where she wanted to spend her time.

"Now, Margaret." Mr. O'Dugan, who'd been sitting stolidly by as Tess had stammered her way through her confused thoughts, patted his wife's hand. "She's not saying she's up and leaving us forever, is she? Just that she might prefer a big fancy house in Aldine Square and summer in Lake Forest to living in the Back of the Yards."

"I don't think it's a question of wealth or comfort," I said hurriedly. "I don't want you to think that Tess cares about such things more than she cares about family. We lived happily together in one room in Kansas and worked hard for our living before I became rich."

Mr. O'Dugan gave me one of his rare smiles. "Don't be ashamed of your wealth, young lady. Wealth's a good thing to have. Not so much the diamonds and the paintings and all those fancy furbelows, but the wealth of a good fire whenever you want one, clean clothes on your back, and a nice piece of boiled beef for dinner. And in those things, we're equal to you, God be praised. But the way I see it, Tess has worked hard alongside you and should share in the greater comforts that your own good fortune can provide. I can see you're willing."

"I am. I promise that Tess will always have a home with me, no matter what happens. Whatever she wants will be hers. And—well, whatever happens, I guess we'll never go so far away that she can't visit you all often." Inevitably, my thoughts had strayed to Martin, and I could hear the whispers of "when Martin comes back," "if Martin comes back," and "if Martin still wants me" that always seemed to hover just above my shoulder whenever I spoke of the future.

"An unmarried daughter should live at home." Mrs. O'Dugan wiped her nose.

"And did you think that when our Deirdre went up to Winnetka to work?" Mr. O'Dugan gave a jerk of the head to indicate that his wife should pour more tea. "We gave up the right to direct our Tessie's future when we let her go to the Poor Farm." He leaned over, his movements slow and careful, and placed a large hand on Tess's shoulder. "We should never have done that, my girl."

"It's all right." Tess put her small hand on her father's. "You told me before that you didn't have enough food."

He nodded. "We had a few bad years back then. And it felt like a real godsend that you'd have a place where you'd be provided for. It seemed the right thing to do." He shook his head. "But we shouldn't have done it anyway."

"No, you shouldn't." Tess's face was serious, but there was a gleam in her almond eyes. "But you did. And maybe God wanted it that way because Nell needed me to protect her, and help her with Sary, and help her with her sewing, and tell her what it says in the Bible because she's dreadfully bad at re-membering. And I learned about housekeeping, and you know what? I miss my ledgers. Alice is keeping them in order, isn't she, Nell?"

"She is. But she'll be very happy to hand them back to you." I felt a bubble of happiness growing inside me. "So you'll come home? Before Christmas?"

"But you'll be back to spend Boxing Day with us," said her father as Tess answered my question with a hug. "Ah, well, Margaret, dry your eyes. We reap what we sow, and we've done better than we deserve."

THIRTY-NINE

Tess never mentioned my impulsive offer to stop working at Rutherford's, and I never brought up the idea again. Indeed, my fascination with my work grew daily. Rutherford's, to my mind, was the perfect balance between the old-fashioned principles of good cloth and good dressmaking, drummed into me by Grandmama, and the newfangled methods of commerce that thrived on a constantly renewed stock of sumptuous articles from all over the world. Women fond of the latest fashions could find the best and newest articles at our store while the thrifty housewives of the middle classes knew that the same articles could be had at a reduced price once the season was almost over, with the same high standard of service.

"I can never make up my mind whether this is a small department store or a very large draper's," I mused to Joe one January morning. We were standing at the railing of one of the highest galleries, watching the men on the long, hooked ladders fasten the ends of bolts of cloth to the clamps carefully hidden behind a small ledge of plaster peacock feathers. Every bolt of cloth was white, but the differences as the men unwound them were startling: the creamy sheen of a white velvet, the dazzling shine of a silk that reminded me of snow in sunshine, the astounding delicacy of a white lace that cost more per yard than most families earned in a week, the texture of a semi-translucent white linen. Down below, displays that were within reach of the customers' questing hands mounded up white clouds of more practical and affordable fabrics. Everywhere there were touches of gray and gold—gloves, perfume bottles, gilded buttons, soft gray rabbit skins for lining, and gray wolf pelts to be used on collars and cuffs.

"It's both." Joe grinned. He had assumed charge of Rutherford's with relish, making small changes here and there. His strength was in taking Martin's artistic vision and making it somehow bigger, more obvious, in a way that the customers seemed to like. "All merchants in our business are actors, of a sort," he had explained to me, "but Martin's acting style, if you will, is restrained. Mine is expansive." He had made very few changes to Martin's organizational practices, which were already excellent.

"I suppose I must take this opportunity for our regular comparison of letters from Martin," I said, my eyes on the display below. "Did yesterday's mail bring you one as well?"

"Yes, and it ended, as usual, with a brief interrogation as to your health and happiness." Joe took my arm as we turned away from the hubbub of a store readying itself for the moment of opening. "The rest was naturally about his adventures with the German and Austrian manufacturers he's visited. And about the University of Vienna." He looked at me out of the corners of his dark eyes. "Did he tell you about that?"

"No." I frowned. "What does Martin have to do with the University of Vienna?"

"Well, there are one or two doctors there who study patients who have undergone a mental shock of some kind and are having trouble shaking it off. I knew about them because one of them is my wife's cousin's husband, you see. Martin, being the methodical man he is, took the opportunity to consult them about his dreams, and about what he describes to me as a certain sense of panic when confronted with particular thoughts and images. He believes that it is possible to overcome what he sees as a weakness of the mind and is applying himself to the task. He won't tell me the nature of these consultations, but he says he thinks they will be beneficial."

I sighed. "He didn't tell me anything about this. He knows what I'd say, I suppose—that I know his weaknesses as he does mine, and that I'm happy to live with them." I paused for a moment. "But I understand this fear of his because I know where it comes from. He's afraid of becoming unstable, like his father. Only he's not a bit like him, at least not from what I recall—I was still a child when his father died, and I hadn't seen him for years before that. Martin's like his mother, in looks and character." Ruth Rutherford had been my mother's greatest friend. I remembered with fondness the tall, blond woman with an artist's eye for beauty and a huge capacity for hard work. Her greatest fault had been her tendency to hide her pain behind a stoic mask—a tendency Martin had also inherited.

"What did he write to you about?" Joe asked. "If it's not an intrusion to ask."

I smiled. "Don't worry, his letters aren't—personal, not in the way you're thinking. In many ways, they're like the ones he'd send me during my early days in Kansas, full of descriptions of places and events, as if he wanted me to see what he saw. His letters changed, of course, when Lucetta came along— but I didn't realize that until much later."

Joe nodded. "It doesn't surprise me that his letters are friendly, rather than, as you say, personal. He's trying hard to give you every possible chance to build a life without him. I suppose you could call that noble."

"I don't *want* him to be noble," I said peevishly. "He told me once that devoted love was one of my defining characteristics and that, once given, that love was steadfast. What on earth would make him think I should be any different with regard to *him*?"

"So what do you write to him?" The corner of Joe's expressive mouth twitched, as if anticipating my reply.

I couldn't help letting a rueful grin escape. "I write about the store. About what I'm doing, who our customers are, what Madame says, why I think the French cut of an evening dress will be more popular than the English this season. Very well," I said as a smile broke out over his saturnine face, "I don't exactly write words that burn the paper they're written on either. And it's hard to have a real correspondence—in the sense of a conversation—when every letter takes weeks to cross the Atlantic. But he says my letters make him feel as if he's standing beside me, and I have to admit that his descriptions make me feel I'm standing beside *him*. This time he told me about walking in the foot-hills of the Alps, with grass so green it hurt his eyes and great gray clouds that seemed to be shedding rainbows, there were so many. And then it snowed, and everything was changed overnight to dazzling white under a blue sky."

"Unlike Chicago snow, which is black with dirt half a day after it falls." We had reached Joe's office, and he flung both of his doors wide open, the one that gave onto the corridor and the one that connected with Martin's outer office. Clerks began to gather around him like ants around a sugar lump, the morning's load of correspondence in their hands. The store received hundreds of letters a week, mostly orders that were dealt with in the enormous correspondence office, but there were always some that needed a consultation. One or two of the clerks turned to me with a question about an unclear request for a style or fabric or a matter to be put before Madame Belvoix. Soon I was seated at the huge table, scribbling notes in the book I carried with me. The gradual increase in my responsibilities that had begun with the realization that I was a shareholder had become an absorbing part of my day—a great revelation to me that it was, in fact, possible to enjoy work that involved writing.

"Mrs. Lillington?" The high, flutelike voice of the messenger boy stooping over me ended in a gruff croak on the last syllable, and I hid a smile. Several of the boys were undergoing the same awkward transition into adulthood, mercilessly teased by their elders. "Madame B's compliments, Mrs. Lillington, and could you step into her room?"

I made a few more notes before closing my book and undertook the short walk to Madame's office. It was surprisingly small, which apparently was the little Alsatian woman's preference. Every available space—including the shelves lining the walls—was crammed with squares of fabric, books on dressmaking, advertisements, journals, and sheets of drawing paper on which Madame had sketched designs or made notes. Some of those sheets were fixed to the shelves with drawing pins, and I had to sit carefully to ensure they didn't come into contact with my hair.

I greeted Madame with a smile and, once seated, waited for her to begin talking. Anyone who worked with her soon learned that she preferred to direct the conversation.

"True mastery takes time," was her opening salvo. In the light of the single gas lamp, her gray irises glinted like steel.

I nodded but held my tongue, waiting for her next thought to emerge.

"You have mastered the fundamentals." Madame made an imperious movement with her head. "I have been thinking about your particular circumstances, Mrs. Lillington. You are a shareholder, and perhaps one day your share in this enterprise will be larger."

I felt myself redden. She was referring, of course, to the possibility that Martin and I might marry. This possibility was not common gossip, but it was hard to hide anything about the store from Madame Belvoix. "I can't give you any assurances about that, Madame."

"Understood. But you are, in any event, a shareholder, and I have noted a change in the attitude of the employees toward you since that fact became known. You are also a young woman of some sense and skill. I will not live forever. Taking all of these considerations into account, I come to the conclusion that it is time for you to begin your serious training. If, of course, your profession means as much to you as I think it does."

"Probably more." I smiled and was gratified to see Madame's lips curve upward.

"There are many finer points of technique that I wish to communicate to you. You will not need all of them, of course. But you must know about them sufficiently well to be able to see what is well done and what is badly done. And then there is your knowledge of fabrics, which is inadequate. It has improved since you came to work with me, of course, but you need considerable instruction."

I nodded enthusiastically, my heart beating a little faster. The greatest dressmaker I had ever met was proposing to train me—personally. It was the most exciting offer I'd ever had.

"You agree?" Madame fixed me with a severe eye.

"More than agree. I thought Tess coming home was a wonderful Christmas gift, but this is like five Christmases all rolled into one."

"Hmmm." Madame's lips compressed, but there was a twitch to them. "It will stop you from moping, anyway. Now there is something I have been meaning to ask you. We must think of spring, and the new silhouette will bring us many fresh orders. The neckline goes up, the skirt goes in, and *les fanfreluches*, the embellishments, they move lower, I think, so that the waist is more elongated." She considered my own elongated form for a moment. "I have thought of commissioning from you a number of designs that I will have our artists make up in color on large panels. They will utilize your penchant for a simpler line and not so many frills. They will show women of different ages and walks of life in a series of moments in the day, natural actions for the new, Natural Form, if you follow me."

I frowned. "Won't that run counter to our principle of designing the dress for the woman?"

Madame's eyes gleamed. "You have noticed, I am sure, that many customers come to us with an idea or two culled from the fashion journals. Why do we not shape those ideas instead? Become a leader in the fashion instead of a follower?"

"That sounds like the kind of thing Mr. Rutherford would say."

Madame shrugged. "Mr. Rutherford and I get on well for a reason. You will have to work most closely with two or three of the other couturières. Nancy, Françoise, and Anna, I think, as they all have a good feeling for what is to be fashionable in the future."

I nodded. "I agree. And as they're only designs, I suppose we can offer many variations, even if we're using some of the same pattern pieces."

"Good. Mr. Rutherford will be pleased when he returns, I think. And in due course, as your training advances, you must travel. I will write to Worth and insist you spend time in his establishment—we are old friends."

Worth! My heart skipped a beat, and I gazed at Madame Belvoix with an even greater sense of respect.

"*Eh bien.*" Madame took a folded paper down from a shelf. "I must work, and so must you. We will speak again tomorrow, when you have had a little time to think."

I found myself halfway up one of the staff staircases without quite knowing how I got there. At the corner, as the stair turned, was a large window, and I stared out of it, trying to calm my whirling thoughts. I had arrived at Rutherford's in the darkness of a winter morning, and now it was light—a pale blue sky into which a myriad of fireplaces were discharging thin streams of smoke. I clutched the railing, feeling myself suspended between the life of the building behind me and the great mass of the city below. Somewhere, so far away that my mind could not encompass the distance, was Martin. If I closed my eyes, I could imagine him returned, walking into the store to the sight of my designs, made part of his empire. We would, in that sense, be truly side by side.

"You look as if you're walking on a cloud." Joe's voice sounded in my ear, and I turned and grasped his arm.

"I think I am. I can't imagine how I'm going to work today." And then, seeing the smile on his face, "You knew about this, didn't you?"

"I had an idea. But this was entirely Arlette Belvoix's doing, you know. She is according you the signal honor of grooming you as her successor. An event that will take place far, far in the future, of course."

"True mastery takes time," I drawled in a French accent, and we both burst out laughing.

"Well, if Martin is having adventures, so are we," Joe said. "Let's see just how much we can impress him by the spring."

FORTY

"Would you sign this, please, Mrs. Lillington?"

The cash boy, one of many employed to run between the sales floor and the accounting office, or wherever else they were needed, held up a book. His name was Percival, and he was a twelve-year-old fund of practical jokes. He was also his family's only source of income and an eager student in the small school Martin had set up for the younger boys.

I took the ledger with a smile, running my finger down the columns. It was late on a Saturday evening in February, and the store had already closed, so the final accounting was taking place.

"Thirty-two corsets?" That was an unusually high number, even for a Saturday.

"And we're doing a very good trade in unmentionables, ma'am." Percival's job in the lingerie rooms had given him a familiarity beyond his years with the underpinnings of a woman's costume. "Garters as well. But they're jumping on the longer corset like ducks on a June bug."

He waited as I checked the figures and signed the page. The long, slender silhouette of the Natural Form was causing women to lace ever tighter, urged on by fashion plates featuring ladies with waists so small it was a wonder they could digest their food. Good news for corset-makers, evidently.

I rubbed my eyes, suppressing a yawn. Joe never worked on Saturdays, and as the only shareholder present, I was now in the habit of staying on Saturday evenings till the last employee had left or ascended to the dormitories on the fifth floor. I compensated by arriving at the store at three so I could spend the morning with Sarah and Tess.

Percival trotted away in the direction of the accounting office, and I walked slowly upstairs. I had been given a tiny room on the fourth floor as my own since I was accumulating papers. It was somewhat isolated, but I liked the peace and quiet. It wasn't even a year since I'd arrived at Rutherford's, and I was well aware that my greater standing was largely due to Martin, but I was content. I felt I was living the life for which I'd been born.

My paletot hung on the coat stand in the corner of my office, inviting me to leave the store. I could hear a fitful wind gusting, and from time to time a spatter of rain hit my tiny window. Good. The rain would melt the piles of snow that still lay in the alleys and on the north side of buildings. February was a short month, and March would bring in the first signs of spring, and some weeks after that, Martin would return.

I flipped up my watch. Arthur Nutt would have the rockaway outside the store's main door in twenty minutes. Plenty of time to tidy my desk and neaten my hair. Soon I'd be sharing a light supper with Tess, going over the day's small happenings and discussing our various responsibilities.

I frowned as a piece of paper caught my eye. Of course—I'd promised Mrs. Hindmarsh I'd send her the list of all the materials we'd incorporate into her summer ball gown by Monday. I'd been partway through the task earlier when I'd been called to the couture floor to talk to one of our customers.

"And now you've let her down, Nell Lillington. That's not like you," I muttered, looking at my watch again. I supposed I could finish the letter now and entrust Mr. Nutt with finding a likely boy to deliver it. He spent enough time in the vicinity of the store to know almost everyone who worked or lived on that part of State Street.

Stifling another yawn, I sat down to my task. Below, the building was becoming still. There were watchmen on duty, of course, but most of the doors were being locked on the outside as the employees left, preventing anyone but the watchmen from coming in, but not preventing anyone from going out.

I wrote steadily, all the details still in my head, my mind on a vision of silk gauze in peach and pink. I consulted my notes and drawings for the amount of hand embroidery that would be required—an expensive item, but Mrs. Hindmarsh was willing to pay. I reread my letter, imagining how the dress would look—like a Kansas sunset. I could almost smell the honey scent of the plains.

A noise from somewhere brought me out of my reverie. I glanced at my watch again. Poor Mr. Nutt had been waiting for me for a good thirty minutes.

"If you're going to daydream, do it in the carriage," I reprimanded myself, writing Mrs. Hindmarsh's address. I shrugged myself into my paletot, buttoned it quickly, pinned my hat to my hair, and turned off the gaslight. I held the letter in my hand. If I put it in one of the paletot's large pockets, I'd forget about it.

The sound of running footsteps above me made me hesitate. I'd thought there were no dormitories above me—that I was directly below the huge ateliers where we fabricated our dresses. They would most definitely have been locked hours ago, as the couturières and piece workers would be long gone.

Should I go upstairs and investigate? Five years ago, I probably would have done just that. But supposing there were thieves above? I'd learned something from putting myself into danger in the past, which was that putting myself in danger tended to lead to finding myself in danger. There were perfectly good watchmen at my disposal downstairs, and one or two of them might be making the rounds. I could run down one of the two staff staircases and find someone in three minutes.

I headed toward the nearest staircase at a fast clip, the letter clutched in my hand. I was probably wrong about the location of the dormitories, but it wouldn't hurt to check. I tugged at the heavy door to the staircase.

And shut it again hastily, coughing vigorously from the blast of smoke and heat that had hit me in the face.

I said something unladylike and set out toward the other end of the corridor. Rutherford's was on fire.

FORTY-ONE

The first coherent thought that invaded my mind as I ran was the dormitories. Rutherford's paid its employees well enough that most of them lived out. Still, row after row of tiny rooms on the fifth floor housed a number of boys, single women, and bachelors in strictly separated areas.

Before I'd run halfway down the corridor, the shrill clang of the alarm bell told me that others were aware of the fire. I pulled open the door to the staircase to the confused clamor of a large number of people coming to the realization that something was wrong. As I ran upward, they had begun to spill out of the dormitory area onto the landing.

"There's a fire at the other end of the store," I informed them. "You can't use the other staircase." I spotted a middle-aged woman I knew vaguely. "Get the children and women out of the store immediately," I told her, and she turned back instantly and without argument, her voice raised in a piercing shout. Within seconds, boys and young women, some in a state of dishabille, began to pour onto the staircase. I intercepted the first two or three young men who joined them, shouting at them that they were in no immediate danger and that they should allow the women and boys out first. I saw Percival's small, pale face turned up toward me and gave him a reassuring smile.

"Are there any watchmen down there?" I shouted as loud as I could. An answering cry brought me to the railing, looking down into the dizzying spiral of the staircase as people pushed past me. I could see the head of a watchman far below.

"Is the way out clear?" I shouted and was relieved to see him make a thumbs-up gesture. I couldn't hear his answering cry for the noise of people.

"It's all right—we'll still be able to get out." I looked around at the young men who were beginning to mass in the doorway, some looking frightened, some excited, others calm. "Does anyone have the passkey for the door into the ateliers?" I knew it existed. The building's only external fire escape was in the alley, leading from the largest workroom, and the passkey never left the dormitories.

"I do." I recognized the man who answered—Mr. Windridge from the silk department, a levelheaded and hardworking sales clerk. His expression was alert but unworried.

"Good. I swear I heard someone up there just now. And besides, if we have time to get the work in progress out, we should do so." I looked around. "Can I have volunteers? We need a handful of men to help me, and some of you should station yourselves at intervals to warn us if the fire's approaching. We'll only be a few minutes. The rest of you can leave."

To my surprise, most of them stayed. They quickly organized themselves into teams that emerged laden with the most valuable pieces of work while Mr. Windridge and I checked through every room. We found nobody.

"They could have gotten out by the staircase before the fire got too bad," I reflected.

"Not now though." Mr. Windridge wiped his brow and coughed. He'd opened a high window and stuck his head outside for two minutes. "You can see the flames coming out of the second floor. The fire escape's no good either—anyone trying to use it risks getting burned. Nobody's getting out that side of the building."

"All right. What about the pearls and gemstones?" We had a stock that was used for the most expensive dresses.

Mr. Windridge shook his head. "Locked in the safe, and I don't have the combination or keys. It's supposed to be fireproof."

"We'll have to forget them, then. I hope somebody's been sensible enough to organize getting as much stock out as possible. Although I imagine the rain will ruin what the fire doesn't destroy." I felt oddly calm, considering the circumstances. "Let's get out, Mr. Windridge. Thank you for your help."

The stairwell was still free of smoke when we arrived at the top of it. I let Mr. Windridge go ahead of me, entrusting him with the task of telling those below that the fifth floor was clear. I planned to step into each floor as I descended, just to make sure it was empty, but I wouldn't linger. I thought briefly of the day's takings, which would still be in the accounting office. But I couldn't possibly carry that amount of money, and in any case the safe they were in would be fireproof too. Chicago had learned about fire the hard way.

I had just stepped into the third-floor corridor when the explosion took place. It wasn't a large explosion, more a sort of *whoomph*, like the sound a lit oil lamp would make when dropped, only somewhat more powerful. The door I had just closed shook in its frame but held fast.

The gaslights went out. Until that moment, I hadn't realized they were still lit. But now the corridor was plunged into darkness, and I could see the glow of fire at the far end, where the building rounded the corner of State and Madison. I couldn't get out that way.

I cautiously opened the heavy doors behind me, and peered round. Below me was fire, red-orange in hue and emitting an urgent crackling sound. There was smoke, but not much.

I pulled the door shut again and hesitated, not knowing what to do for the best. I didn't think I could go down—and I couldn't jump from a third-floor window safely. Where would the fire department be? Mr. Windridge would surely check to see I'd followed him out of the building and would realize I was trapped inside. Was it the lighting gas that had exploded? Surely not—such an explosion, I thought, would have been much larger. The fire department had probably turned the gas off at the main, and that's why the lights had gone out. For a moment, I felt a bubble of panic growing inside me at finding myself alone in the dark with danger on both sides.

"And you're not here to rescue me now, are you, Martin?" I said under my breath. "So I'll just have to save myself."

I'd done it before, after all. For a split second, I wished I were back in the river. Drowning seemed infinitely preferable at that moment to the notion of being roasted alive.

"Stop that, Nell," I admonished myself. "Form a plan and follow it." The roof, perhaps? Or at least I could find a window as far away from the fire as possible and scream for help.

I had just decided to do the latter when I heard footsteps above me again. This time, of course, they were on the fourth floor. And there were shouts. Not the desperate sound of panic, but two or more men shouting instructions to one another.

If I had a plan, it changed at that moment. I didn't have much time to think in any case. The fear had left me, and I was experiencing the strange sensation of clarity that had settled on me before in times of danger. The rueful thought crossed my mind that I was, after all, going to have to rely on a man or two for my rescue, but this was no time to be particular.

I opened the door again. More smoke was billowing up, and the heat in the stairwell was increasing, but it was sufficiently far below me. I took a deep breath.

It didn't take long to climb to the next floor, but by the time I pulled open the door and stumbled into the corridor, my eyes were streaming. I released the breath I'd been holding and coughed, wiping frantically at my eyes.

"Who's there?" I shouted. "I can hear you. Are you trapped? Who's there?"

I blinked at the darkness before me, convinced I could hear running feet. If I was wrong, I was in real trouble. My thoughts strayed to the long ladders kept on hooks on the blank expanses of wall on this floor. Could I effect some kind of escape using them?

"I don't believe it."

That was the gist of it, anyway. The voice that came out of the darkness, accompanied by the sudden beam of a lantern and the smell of kerosene, was using language so colorful that I couldn't have repeated it if I'd tried. It was also a familiar voice.

A large hand grabbed my arm and began towing me along the corridor. I dug my heels in as hard as I could, resisting the movement.

"I know it's you, Crabb." I wriggled my arm out of his grasp. "And I want to know what you're doing here and where you're taking me."

"I haven't got time for explanations, you stupid bitch. I might have known it would be you, stuck in a building that's supposed to be clear. Alex!" The last word was uttered at high volume.

"Alex? Alex Gambarelli?" I could hear the high-pitched indignation in my voice. "After you told me—*promised* me—you were done with it all. Done with the spy game and done with the Gambarellis. And you have the nerve to call *me* stupid?"

"Yes, well, Alex wasn't quite done with me. And I apologize—but *will* you come on? Alex!"

The door I had come through suddenly lit up around the edges, and a tongue of flame thrust greedily at the ceiling. Crabb swore long and fluently under his breath.

"Time to get out, Crabb." There was a voice nearby, sounding mighty pleased. "Everything's ready."

I could see the bulk of a man outlined by the glow of flame behind him. The flames chasing us from the other direction flickered in his eyes. As he turned, I could see his thick beard jutting out from his chin.

"For God's sake, Alex, it's the Lillington woman." Crabb's voice held a note of urgency.

"The what?" It was getting harder to hear. The noise of the fire was rising to the roar of a beast, and despite the fact that the ceiling was made of tin, the flames were beginning to lick along it.

"Woman," bellowed Crabb. "We have to get her out. You said nobody would die."

"*Merda!*" I could see Alex clearly now, his black eyes wide as he became aware of my presence. In fact, I could see perfectly well—but this was not good news. A rolling sheet of flame was advancing toward us along the ceiling from the other end of the corridor. Feeling that this was not the time to argue, I let myself be dragged as each man seized one of my arms and towed me along the corridor.

Just as the heat became unbearable, Alex veered to the right and Crabb let go of me. This happened so suddenly that I lurched forward and hit the jamb of the door, feeling a rush of hot air on the left side of my head. Someone grasped the back of my paletot and yanked me backward so hard that I fell. A second later, I was drenched in water.

"What on earth—"

For a moment, I was in a state of utter confusion, noting only that the door was now shut and the furnace heat had abated. Then I realized that the room was lit by a lamp, and that Crabb was standing in front of me holding a metal bucket, which he had apparently just emptied over me. I could feel the water streaming down my face, accompanied by a stinging sensation on the left side of my head.

I put a hand up to the spot and yelped. A patch of skin near my left ear stung like the blazes, and the top of my ear was sore. My fingers explored a little higher. Instead of the thick, piled-up mass of curls I was used to, there was a rough patch of wet stubble.

"Your hair caught fire." Having delivered this terse explanation, Crabb dropped the bucket and turned around. I scrambled to my feet, my thick woolen paletot shedding water, and saw that he was stuffing rags into the crack under the door, from which smoke was rising.

"Get it well sealed before I open the window," Alex yelled. "Hurry up, Crabb."

I somehow found the presence of mind to unbutton my paletot and hand it to Crabb, who used his foot to jam it firmly into place under the door. A moment later, I heard a crack from behind me. I turned round to see that Alex had pushed the entire window out into the street, so that only its frame was left. The raw air of a Chicago night in winter was bliss after the heat of the corridor.

The room we were in was large, I realized, and practically empty. It contained several more buckets of water, one of which Crabb was now using to soak the rags, and—I breathed a sigh of relief—three of the long ladders. Alex was at that moment maneuvering one of those ladders out of the window.

An explosion sounded below, and flames briefly shot past the open window. I saw Crabb and Alex look at each other. Crabb's expression was fearful, Alex's oddly sardonic.

"You can go first, Crabb."

I realized, to my horror, that the ladder wasn't hanging downward as I'd thought it would be. It was sticking straight out across the alley, which was only about ten feet wide. A window on the other side of the alley was open, and I could see the white oval of a face at the other end of the ladder.

"Is that safe?" Crabb asked, eyeing our means of escape.

"My men tested it," Alex said. "Move, you idiot—it's only a few feet. They're working on the front of the building, just like we planned, so nobody's looking." Then, as Crabb hesitated, he added, "Or you can stay behind and roast if you want."

Crabb was up on the ladder in an instant, swarming over it in a sort of sliding crawl. I saw hands reach out and drag him into the other window, and somebody shouted.

"Now you." Alex Gambarelli turned to me.

"How can I—"

But he had grasped the base of my skirts and yanked them upward, freeing my lower limbs and tearing the fabric in the process. I yelled, but he picked me up—as easily as if I were Sarah—and plunked me on the ladder, holding me tight by the waist.

"Put your hands on the poles. Yes, that's it. Now slide—you saw Crabb do it—and look ahead of you. You'll be there in a few seconds. But move, because it's getting hot in here, and I'll be joining you if you're slow. The ladder should take both of us, but I can't guarantee it."

I could feel the rain-laden wind, ice-cold against my exposed face and hands. The pain on the left side of my face near my ear was torture. The ladder sloped downward slightly, I realized—and below me was empty air.

"Move." The voice behind me was laden with menace. "Or so help me, I'll push you off. And then I'll have to kill Rutherford too when he comes back. I know what you are to him."

Warm air gusted up from below, and a few sparks drifted upward. The thought that my skirts might catch fire was all the incentive I needed. I slid my hands forward on the poles, and let the rest of me follow. Slide—slither. Slide—slither. And suddenly there were hands on me, pulling me forward, and I slid painfully over a windowsill and landed on a carpet.

As I struggled to my feet, I could see Alex, moving across the ladder with the nonchalance of a circus performer. He swung himself easily into the room, then turned around and pulled the ladder forward to release the hooks. He threw it bodily into the alley and helped the other man to lift the heavy sash window back into the frame.

"Won't they suspect something?" Crabb asked. "When they see the ladder and the window, I mean."

The room was lit only by the blaze on the other side of the alley, but I could see the glint of Alex's teeth amid his beard. "Once the building's collapsed, the rubble will smolder for days. It'll burn everything to ashes."

"But they've got a witness now," the other man blurted. I wasn't sure, but I thought I recognized Jacky Gambarelli's emaciated form and plangent voice. "Why didn't you leave her to burn?"

"She won't talk." Alex turned to me. "You won't talk, because to talk would be to bring harm down upon your head and that of Martin Rutherford. And anyone else you hold dear. As it is, nobody's hurt, and Rutherford will get the insurance money."

"But why?" was all I could ask. "And how am I going to explain my face—and my hair?" I gestured to the burned side of my head. "They know I was left behind in there."

"You don't know how you got out." It was Jacky who spoke. "It must have been a miracle. You wandered away from the blaze in your confusion and fainted in a dark corner."

Anger was beginning to burn inside of me, mirroring the blaze outside. I could see we were in a pleasant, furnished room, an office of some kind, and that there were ropes coiled in front of the now-closed window. They had been planning this for some time.

"You unspeakable bastards," I said. "There were women and boys in the dormitories."

"Who do you think set off the alarm?" Alex smirked. "We gave them plenty of time to get out."

"And you set the fire so that it would be impossible to use the fire escape. For God's sake, *why?*"

Crabb spoke. "Makes it harder for the fire department to deal with the fire." He pushed back his hair. "And you control how people escape—and the fact that there are people to save creates a distraction." He shrugged.

"You've done this before."

"Not me personally," Crabb said, his eyes on Alex. "Let's just say it's done." His gaze shifted to me. "We need to get you out to the street so you can report yourself alive. Remember, you don't know how you got out."

"But that makes me complicit in your crime," I said. "And it's a crime—a terrible one. Martin's store—"

"Can be rebuilt." There was a note of satisfaction in Alex's voice. "But it will no longer be the building in which my sister died. And if you can keep your mouth shut, I give you my word that I'll never bother Rutherford again."

It was a pact with the devil, and I'd have to lie to Martin for the rest of our lives. And to Joe, and to Tess and Sarah—and I wasn't a good liar to begin with.

"If anybody was killed, I won't keep quiet," I said.

"Agreed." Alex held out a hand. "I'll take that chance." He sounded as if he were concluding an ordinary, everyday business deal.

I shook his hand, my jaw clenched.

"Time to go," said Crabb with a sudden, alert lift of his head. "I think this building's on fire now."

FORTY-TWO

It had been easier to lie than I'd thought. By the time I'd found the few men from Rutherford's who'd stayed to watch the building burn, I was exhausted and soaked through by the icy rain. I simply shook my head when they asked me about my escape. They wrapped me in something—I didn't know what—and repeatedly offered to take me to the Cook County hospital.

I refused. It had taken the arrival of Joe Salazar to tear me away from the gruesome sight of the building that had come to mean so much to me collapsing in all directions. The firemen and volunteers looked like ants in the mouth of a furnace as they did what they could to prevent the blaze from spreading.

I had collapsed myself into Joe's arms, in a flood of tears that hid my rage under my exhaustion and pain. It had been Joe who'd located Mr. Nutt, who was keeping a lonely vigil by his horses on Madison Street. The poor man almost fainted when he learned I was alive. Which had brought me to the realization that Tess would also be waiting for me. That thought forced me to agree to go home and let Mr. Nutt fetch a physician to dress my burns.

Three days later, I, who had practically never been ill in my life, succumbed to the worst fever I had ever known. I remembered little of that time except the sensation of inescapable pain punctuated by the soothing touch of female hands. Elizabeth was there, I knew that, and Tess barely left my side.

Fever turned to bronchitis, but mercifully the lung-wrenching cough was short-lived. Within a week, I was pronounced out of danger and fit enough for Sarah to be brought to see me. Two days later, I was back on my feet, physically at least. My spirits were in a black pit from which, I believed, I could never climb out again.

℮

"It doesn't look that bad."

Elizabeth's face came closer to mine. I instinctively flinched away in case she touched my burn. Beside her, Tess was straightening the blanket that covered my limbs. She looked up and smiled.

"Alice made your hair look nice, Nell. She's very clever."

"Perhaps I'll set a new fashion for wearing one's hair on the side." I knew I sounded as petulant as a spoiled child, but I had only been out of bed three days, after all. My bones still held the weakness of my fever. The scabbed-over burn by my ear felt as if a swarm of bees had landed there and were stinging me all at once.

"You need to stop feeling sorry for yourself." Elizabeth motioned for me to lean forward and inserted the pillow she'd been pounding into shape behind my back. "You're fortunate you have so much hair. If the fire had reached your scalp, you'd never have any on that side again. As it is, you're just a little stubbled—and it's growing back fast."

I grunted in reply, squirming to make myself more comfortable on the chaise longue. This had the effect of undoing Tess's work. She gave me a dour look, but said nothing as she straightened the blanket yet again.

"You're about to have visitors." Elizabeth had crossed to the window.

"I'm not at home."

"I rather think you are. It's Mr. Salazar and that funny little French woman from your store."

"I'm definitely not at home. And it's not *my* store." I barely recognized my own voice in the querulous, feeble whine. "It was Martin's, and now it's gone."

"It *is* your store, Nell," Tess said quietly. "And a little bit of it's mine too. Our money is in the store, and you work there. You can't decide you're finished with it just because you're not feeling well."

"You're going to receive them, Nell," said Elizabeth. "Now come along and sit up a bit straighter—there. This wrapper is quite the most beautiful thing I've ever seen. I must order one."

I glared downward at the rich purple silk, remembering the countless hours Chinese Mary had spent embroidering the profusion of fruits and flying insects that decorated it. How was Mary living now, without work?

I could hear Zofia answering the door and the hum of voices. I didn't want to see them. I didn't want to see anybody. There were moments when I didn't even want to see Martin—that is, to see the ruin of his dream in his eyes as he confronted the ashes of his store.

At the same time, I wanted Martin desperately. I wanted him to put his arms around me and tell me that it would be all right. I blinked furiously against the onset of tears as the door opened and Zofia announced our visitors in her soft, clear voice.

"Well, I suppose you must rest." Madame Belvoix strode into the room without any preliminary greeting and gave me what could only be described as a bracing look. "But for how long? We have no drawings, and thus no patterns and no toiles. More than half of those dresses were thought up by you. We have the few pieces that were saved, but that does not make a dress. I have the measurements of every customer, and still I must say, Mrs. Lillington, she is ill, Mrs. Lillington, she is resting. And soon the spring will be here."

The fog lifted a little from my mind. "What are you talking about? How can we fulfill our orders?"

Madame looked at Joe, who had taken my hand in greeting, and actually rolled her eyes. "How, she asks. By working, *naturellement*. Field and Leiter's have put their dress goods at our disposal at cost. I have marked the bolts I think we will need and instructed Field's to send the samples to you. I will send Françoise and Nancy to you tomorrow. They are good workers and have already begun work on the pattern pieces, but they must talk to you, *bien sûr*."

"*Where* are they working?" It suddenly occurred to me that the world had, in fact, been functioning without my presence for the last two weeks.

Joe grinned. "According to Madame, we are crammed into a miserable hovel." He looked sideways at Madame, who stuck her nose in the air. "In fact, we have three well-lit floors on Michigan Avenue. So much better than in '71, when we were all in wooden shacks. And Mr. Field will be renting us a complete store on State Street next week. Not the best part of State Street, of course, but a decent enough location." He raised his eyebrows in an expression of hopefulness. "I wish you were well enough to come and see it. Fassbinder sends his regrets, but with both of his daughters due to give birth within the month, he will not leave Saint Louis. That makes you, once again, the only shareholder present. I'd like to have your approval."

"But the stock—the money—"

Joe shrugged. "We lost a day's takings—although I'm working on the company that sold us those so-called fireproof safes to make good on its warranty—but the insurers are already paying out fifty cents on the dollar. The rest is pending the arson investigation, of course."

That got my attention. A jolt of alarm ran through me. "Arson? What makes you think that?"

"The watchmen, for one thing." Joe nodded his thanks as Tess, who had ordered tea, handed him a cup. "All but three older men who've been with us for a while have absconded and not returned for their wages. And we have Mr. Windridge's word that the explosion that trapped you happened quite independently of the fire. We spent a long time discussing whether it could have been the gas, but it seems unlikely. Putting together the sequence of events, we suspect four incendiary bombs were used."

"Then it's a criminal case, isn't it?" My fingers felt so cold I could barely grasp the handle of my cup. "The lives of those in the dormitories were put in danger."

"Hmmm." Joe looked down at the brown liquid in his cup, seeming to explore its depths, and then back up at me. "Given that no lives were lost, and given the difficulty in proving the case or even naming suspects—whatever we may think about the matter—it seems likely that the investigation may be a little cursory. And Martin will almost certainly get ninety cents on the dollar, which translates to an acceptable loss. Building costs have come down too since the store was put up in '72." He looked hard at me, and I looked away.

"You're sure no lives were lost?" I had not forgotten my vow to Alex Gambarelli.

"They've had time to go through the ashes thoroughly," Joe said, his tone gentle. "We've already started work on clearing the site. Martin's had me talking to Johnston & Edelmann about his ideas for a new store, although we can't get much done via telegraph."

Tess smiled at the mention of Martin. "How is Martin?" she asked. "Is he coming back soon?"

"He was, at one point, threatening to book passage on the first cargo steamer he could find. I told him not to be a damned fool—beg pardon, ladies, but he's been extremely trying." Joe grimaced. "There's absolutely no point in him ending up at the bottom of the ocean in an attempt to save a handful of days. The White Star Line will make the crossing much faster than a cargo ship, and it's a lot safer."

"Is he so badly upset about the store, then?" My heart fell.

Elizabeth let out her breath in a short puff. "It's not the *store* he's worrying about, goose."

"Miss Parnell is correct." Joe grinned. "Why would he worry about bricks and mortar? I just told you, the loss is acceptable. Dry goods stores burn down on a regular basis, even without incendiary bombs."

He sounded so cheerful I almost smiled. Madame Belvoix moved impatiently in her chair.

"I must know when you can return to us," she told me. "We need to begin production now that we have the necessary materials." She folded her arms across her bosom in a satisfied manner. "I even found an exact match for the green organza, and thanks to you we saved the most important pieces of that dress. We have half a dozen new customers, even, clamoring for the Natural Form." She raised her hands in the air. "It is our couturières they seek out, not the walls or the displays. And one of my more promising ladies sits here, like a mushroom."

Tess giggled, but Elizabeth looked concerned. "Nell can't work all day," she told Madame. "She's been injured and ill."

"The afternoons, perhaps?" Madame Belvoix tilted her head to one side, her coaxing, grandmotherly air betrayed by her eyes. "Your wound is slight and does not pain you too much, I hope?"

"It stings like the blazes," I said, "but I don't suppose it's going to heal any faster if I sit in this chair. Elizabeth, could I trouble you to go to my sewing room for some drawing paper? Madame and I need to spend an hour or so together."

FORTY-THREE

Naturally, the wishes of Joe and Madame Belvoix prevailed over the more sensible notion of a gradual recovery. The next day I found myself in the dusty but spacious store Joe proposed to lease from Mr. Field. He had taken me to see the site of Rutherford's, which didn't look so bad now that much of the debris had been cleared away and the good pieces of stone stacked in heaps. It was still an ugly, gaping hole on the corner of State and Madison—the more so because the adjacent buildings had also been damaged—but the activity around it was purposeful and encouraging.

The temporary store wasn't so bad either. "Does Madame approve?" I asked Joe, turning to gaze at the mahogany trim and window frames, beyond which passersby and carriages could be seen through somewhat dirty windows.

"She has given her benediction," said Joe gravely.

"Certainly, those fourth floor windows are nice and large for the workroom, although the afternoons will be a trial once the summer comes. Still, it'll have to do until Martin rebuilds. You're quite sure he's going to rebuild, aren't you?"

"I don't think he hesitated for a moment. He sent me yet another telegram today about a consignment from Paris. He's stopped worrying about you, at least. Or shall we say, he's stopped asking about you quite so often."

"Is Mr. Field charging us an exorbitant rent?"

"He's charging a fair commercial rent. I wouldn't expect any less of a New Englander. But all the dry goods merchants know the risk of fire, and a help-ing hand lent now will be repaid when Field needs it."

Joe finished his pacing and scribbled some more. "The cabinet-makers will be here this afternoon," he said. "The mahogany's coming by train tomorrow. Once we've got a date for the opening, I'll put every man and woman without a truly solid excuse on fourteen-hour days to get the place ready. Of course, we can proceed with made-to-measure without worrying about the premises. We'll keep your departments on Michigan Avenue until everything's ready for you."

"Rebirth." I watched the street outside, imagining the doors flung wide to receive our customers again.

"By the time Martin returns, we should have already counted the first few days' takings in the ready-made departments." Joe's dark eyes gleamed with enthusiasm.

"By the time Martin returns—you know when that'll be, then?" I could feel my pulse quicken.

"At this time of year, much depends on the storms and ice in the Atlantic. The *Germanic*'s scheduled sailing is on April the fifth, but there could be delays."

He blew into his fingers to warm them. The unheated building was as cold as an icebox, and I was glad of my fur muff and matching hat.

"So we'll definitely be in operation? I'd like him to see the store open and busy, with 'Rutherford & Co.' over the door."

"Don't worry. It will be." But Joe had stopped writing, regarding me with the strangest look on his face.

"What's wrong?" I asked.

"I asked Martin if I could tell you, since any letter he writes would reach you well after the fact." Joe came toward me, putting a hand on my arm. "Don't worry, there's nothing wrong. But Martin's decided on a change—or at least, he's decided to go ahead with a change he and Mr. Fassbinder have been talking about for some time."

"A change? Joe, don't beat around the bush. Just tell me straight." I was half-amused, half-alarmed. Joe's face was lit from within, and I could tell that the change, whatever it was, was no small one.

Joe put his notebook and pencil in the pocket of his overcoat and took a deep breath. "The sign will still say 'Rutherford & Co.' You know, don't you, that Mr. Fassbinder is the '& Co.,' only they thought Martin's name alone would look best."

"Yes, I know. And?"

A wide grin bisected Joe's narrow face. "The sign will stay the same, but the company's name will change very soon. To 'Rutherford, Fassbinder, Lillington—and Salazar.'"

It took me a moment to comprehend. "Lillington and Salazar? But that means—"

"Yes." Joe was still grinning. "Martin's proposal is to increase your share, taking a little out of his. He'll still be the largest shareholder, but he could, in theory, be outvoted. Friedrich Fassbinder is willing to sell a portion of his holding to me under an installment agreement. That would make me a junior partner."

I flew to Joe and hugged him tight. "Oh, *Joe!*" My eyes had filled with tears, and I had to sniff hard. "You deserve it. You've been the most loyal, trustworthy, *wonderful* friend Martin could have wished for through all of those dark days."

Joe pushed me gently away from him. "Thank you. But you're forgetting yourself—you'll be a full partner in the company too."

"And me a mere woman." I sniffed again and dug down in my reticule for a handkerchief. "Although for me, this is just a change in name only. And won't it change again when—if—I marry?"

"Only if you want it to. You could always be like Miss—or is it Mrs.?—Lucy Stoner and insist on keeping your name." Joe stamped his feet on the wooden floor. "You should cross that bridge when you come to it. Right now, let's go back to Michigan Avenue and report to Madame before we both expire from the cold."

Joe had dismissed his carriage when we arrived at the temporary store, so we headed up State Street at a brisk walk. We stopped to drink a mug of hot cocoa on the way, bought from a German whose stall was always reliably clean.

"I've had a little talk with Mr. Crabb," said Joe as we set off again.

I stared at him in alarm. "About what?"

Joe looked at me a little curiously, but the street was busy, and he needed to keep both eyes on what was ahead of us. "About unraveling the mess he and John Powell made by opening brothels near the frontier stores. I've offered him a small incentive. It's a delicate task, but I think he's clever enough to tackle it. He might end up shot, of course."

"Or he'll end up a rich man." I could see Crabb in my memory, scurrying over the ladder to safety. "I'm not at all sure if he'll pursue the endeavor in an honest fashion."

"An honest man would certainly get shot. Crabb knows how to walk the line between the dangerous elements of society and the more respectable businessmen. Perhaps people like Crabb are the price we pay for living on the grand scale we do in Chicago. It's all about money, after all. Money flowing into invention and production, money flowing in and out of business, money flooding in from women who are pursuing a dream of beauty and elegance. People like Crabb live like parasites on that money, and like some parasites, they can end up beneficial to the host."

"It's not just about money," I countered. "It's about *people*. I deal with customers one by one—I don't have your luxury of seeing them as merely a bank of open purses. It's people who matter. The Crabbs of this world feast on the misery of women who are wronged by men."

I could hear more feeling in my voice than I cared to betray. Joe and Martin would never know about the night of the fire, after all. Moreover, as I said the words, I wasn't just thinking of the poor unfortunates in the frontier pleasure houses. I was thinking of Lucetta, who might have been so much more than a society belle. She had told me she had wanted to be an opera singer, and she certainly had the voice for it. But her father would not hear of such a thing. Perhaps her lovers and her capacity for deceit had stemmed from that frustration of her deepest desires.

We arrived at the Michigan Avenue premises to find Elizabeth Parnell deep in consultation with Madame Belvoix. She grinned as she saw me.

"I'm having a wrapper like yours made. What do you think of yellow, all covered with blue motifs, like a Chinese vase?"

"Dragons in a field of intertwining leaves and flowers, I think, with some larger flowers for variety." Madame's eyes glinted—this would be an expensive item. "We have a consignment of silk on its way from San Francisco that Mademoiselle might like to inspect. I will send you a note when it arrives." She gave a small smile. "Perhaps Mrs. Lillington would like to see to the design."

"Oh, would you, Nell?" Elizabeth cried. "That would make it even more special. And if our engagement doesn't go on forever, I'll wear it . . . the morning after our wedding night." She dropped her voice on the last words so that only Madame and I could hear.

"And I've come to take Nell home," Elizabeth declared. "She's had enough excitement for a convalescent. Now, Nell, don't protest. Only yesterday you wouldn't move from your chair."

"I agree." Madame spoke emphatically. "After all, Mrs. Lillington will have a great deal to do in the coming months. We don't want her getting sick again." She looked hard at me, and I could see in her eyes that Joe's news was no news to her. She knew I was to be a partner—did the woman know everything?

"I do believe, Madame, that at heart you're a Feminist, just like Miss Parnell." I returned her look with interest. "I sometimes wonder if Mr. Rutherford makes any major decisions without consulting you."

She shrugged. "I am no Feminist, *mesdames*. Not in the sense of those silly women, always making speeches and crying about injustice. I am in a profession where women have always had power; I know how to retain and use such power. That is all."

"The power behind the throne." Elizabeth put her fur-trimmed hat back on her abundant corn-colored hair and pinned it carefully. "Just like Mother. I am so looking forward to growing into that role, Nell."

"You will learn as you get older, my young ladies, that women wield power in different ways." Madame's voice was stern. "Mrs. Lillington, for example, will have to learn to live up to the responsibilities entrusted to her."

"Well, that was a most cryptic remark," said Elizabeth after we'd bidden Madame good-bye and stood waiting for Mrs. Parnell's driver to open the carriage door and fold down the steps. "Are you going to tell me what she means?"

"I hardly know where to begin," I replied. "But I'll tell you one thing. I don't just think I found a job when I came to Chicago. I think I found a lifetime's calling."

FORTY-FOUR

The hard work of the next few weeks seemed to stoke my energy rather than deplete it. We opened the temporary store as soon as we had the first floor ready and some stock to sell. We then worked our way upward, forcing the poor clerks to shift from office to office as the improvement work was carried on. I spent my time running between the State Street and Michigan Avenue premises—or at least walking as fast as I could whenever the weather allowed. The Chicago streets that had once seemed so noisy and chaotic now felt like home. I knew automatically how to avoid their undesirable elements.

And I did find time for leisure. I kept my promise to Elizabeth to make my official debut in Chicago society—with Tess as my companion. At first, it was hard for her to remain in the parlor on Wednesday afternoons, as the ladies who called on us never quite seemed to know what to say to her. The best of them treated her more as a pet or a child initially. They soon changed their attitude once she came out of her shell and began talking naturally as subjects that interested her came up in the conversation. By the time we embarked on our first-ever outing to the novelty theater on April 16, she was quite at her ease.

"Wait till I tell Sary about the daring young man on the flying trapeze," she said as the last notes of the performance sounded, the gaslights flared into life, and the patrons began rising to their feet. "Some of the ladies and gentlemen talked much too fast, didn't they? I couldn't understand them. But I liked the songs. It was so funny that they thought that man a ghost. I could hear his footsteps quite distinctly, and ghosts don't have footsteps, do they? I liked the way he kneeled to ask the lady to marry him."

"I thought she received his proposal most coolly," Elizabeth said. "My experience was a little different." She smirked and turned to her other side. "David, did you—oh, drat the man." Her fiancé had left his seat beside her and stood at some distance, talking with animation to another couple.

"He's an independent spirit," I teased her, punning on the last speech in *A Ghost in Spite of Himself*, the short play we had just watched. It had been preceded by entertainments of all kinds—songs, jigs, and oddities—so that the evening's program had been long. Still, I'd enjoyed myself despite the frequently poor quality of the performances. It took my mind off the eternal wait for Martin, whose ship had docked at New York three days ago.

Elizabeth had been trying to attract David's attention with jerks of her pretty blond head. He steadfastly ignored her, so she turned back to me and Tess. "Ladies, let's wait for him in the lobby. I'm not going to give him the satisfaction of knowing that I care a jot for his rudeness."

"Is he coming in the carriage with us?" Tess asked. We were just a short distance from the Palmer House. Mrs. Parnell had kindly offered to send her own carriage for us to spare Mr. Nutt, who was afflicted with a particularly painful earache.

"No, he'll walk me back to the hotel and then walk himself home," said Elizabeth. She was transparently pleased at the prospect of a few minutes alone with the man she loved.

We threaded our way between the seats and reached the crowded lobby, where the better-dressed element of the audience lingered to chatter. A stout woman in a badly fitted dress pushed past me on her way out, and I instinctively put my hand up to the left side of my face.

"Does it hurt?" Elizabeth had seen the gesture.

"Just a little, but I always feel nervous when I think anything's going to touch it," I admitted. The scar extended from just above the level of my left ear in a ragged curve, a little like the f-holes on a violin, finishing in the tender skin under my earlobe. It was healing well with only a small scab left, the rest being shiny pink skin that would no doubt fade to white. I very much disliked the sensation of anything touching it and always insisted Alice sweep my hair back from the spot.

"I saw you trying to summon me with imperious looks and gestures." David's voice sounded from behind us. "You'd better get used to the fact that it won't work." He took Elizabeth's arm and turned to Tess and me. "Did you enjoy the entertainment, ladies?"

The question launched us into a discussion about future visits to the Chicago theaters, none of which, apparently, were particularly good. David had suggested one of the novelty theaters for our first outing—popular entertainment, pure and simple—and had proclaimed that Chicago could offer little more. Elizabeth, on the other hand, was highly knowledgeable about the various suggestions that had been put forward about improving Chicago's cultural offerings, this being one of Mrs. Parnell's causes. She argued with lively energy with her fiancé about the kind of establishments needed and, more to the point, who would put up the money for building them. The heated discussion provoked us to loud laughter. At a particularly outrageous suggestion on David's part, I reacted in such an exaggerated fashion that I trod on the toes of a gentleman standing behind me.

"I do beg your pardon," I exclaimed, turning. Tess turned around too, and it was she who let out a squeal of delight while I stood dumb, every nerve in my body seemingly thrown into a spasm at once.

"Martin!"

Heedless of her pretty pink-and-gold evening dress, Tess wrapped her arms around him and butted her face into his chest, the feathers of her tall headdress tickling his nose. Her exuberance caused several other patrons in the now-thinning crowd to turn to see the cause of it. A murmur arose as they recognized Martin.

If Martin's arms hadn't been occupied by Tess, I might have thrown myself into them and provided the theatergoers with more romantic entertainment than the play. The impulse wasn't helped by the look on his face, his usual inscrutability battling with—and being overcome by—an expression which mingled relief, concern, and joy as he gazed at me, clearly taking in every detail of my appearance. I couldn't help putting up a hand to my scar, but I saw no repugnance in his expression.

Martin gently pried Tess loose after depositing kisses on both of her cheeks and returning her hug with interest. He took a step toward me, turning his back on the bystanders.

"Are you sure you're all right? *Quite* all right?" He seized my hand so hard that I winced.

"I'm fine." My voice wasn't quite steady. "Just a little scorched on one side."

"You've never looked more beautiful."

A loud cough from David and Elizabeth's gleeful expression alerted both of us that several people were heading in our direction. Martin adroitly turned his grasp into a handshake while we both made an effort to rearrange our faces.

He followed suit by shaking hands with David and Elizabeth—he knew both of them, of course, albeit not well. They asked him the conventional questions about his sea voyage while I tried to gather my wits. I felt a long-fingered hand squeeze the back of my upper arm before Martin took my own hand and tucked it under his arm in a swift claiming motion that elicited another smirk from Elizabeth and was not missed, I thought, by one or two of the people waiting to get Martin's attention. I settled my fingers firmly into the sleeve of his frock coat and tried to look as if I were listening to what he was saying.

But all I really cared about was the fact of his presence, the undeniable reality of bone and muscle beneath the layers of cloth. He was really back, at last, and I hadn't felt so—*right*—for months. I tightened my grip. His response was to squeeze my arm more tightly against his side. I looked down, making a show of brushing a speck of lint from my dress so as not to betray the joy that bubbled up through me.

"I've seen the temporary store." Martin's voice cut through the chaos of my emotions, bringing me back to earth. He looked almost as dazed as I felt but was evidently forcing himself to sound normal. "You've all done an excellent job."

"You've seen it? Just from the outside, I suppose," I replied.

"No, inside as well. I went looking for you and found Joe instead. How do you think I knew where you were?"

"Homing instinct?" Elizabeth suggested in an undertone, and I felt Martin's brief jerk of laughter, saw his eyes crinkle at the corners. But the moment of amusement was quickly gone as he turned to greet two middle-aged couples who were clearly expecting to be acknowledged, letting go of me as he did so. More people joined us, expressing their commiserations at the burning of the store and their appreciation that Rutherford's was now back in business.

"We certainly are," Martin said in answer to one such remark. He had regained control of himself, although the impenetrable look of the last year had gone, replaced by an air of relaxed command. "I visited the atelier, and I've never seen such fine work as we have in hand, not in America, at least. Mr. Worth himself would be impressed." He had raised his voice a little so that everyone in the growing crowd around us could hear. *Showman,* I thought, and felt a surge of delight. Beside me, Tess gave a small squeak, her round face all smiles.

"When we rebuild on our old site," Martin was saying, "we'll have to hire more dressmakers. I'm thinking of making the new building higher."

"You'll stay on your old site, then?" asked one of the women. "Despite its terrible associations?"

A frisson ran through the crowd at the reference to the murder. But Martin answered gravely and without apparent emotion.

"Yes, I'll rebuild in the same place." His voice was clear and confident. "The unspeakable act that was perpetrated there was the fruit of one deranged mind, and it has been atoned for. I will rebuild my life on the ashes of the old as a tribute to all of the men and women who work at Rutherford's. I will make it bigger and better for the sake of the many customers who did not desert me in my darkest hour. I've been in Europe, as you know, and my business connections are more extensive than ever. Should I dare to deprive the ladies of Chicago of the best Europe has to offer, with the imaginative talents of my couturières into the bargain? Prosperity will soon come again, and we need to show New York what Chicago can do."

This last remark provoked general laughter and a few combative remarks from the men. I moved off to one side as Martin became surrounded by a small knot of people, watching him shake hands with those he knew and receive introductions to those he didn't. Seeing that Elizabeth, David, and Tess had also moved away from the crowd, I joined them.

"That was a fine speech," Elizabeth said. "And I think Europe has done Mr. Rutherford good. He doesn't look as thin as when I last saw him."

Tess yawned. "I'm tired, Nell. It's nice to see Martin, but I'm ready for my bed. Do you think we can go?"

Elizabeth fished in her reticule for her timepiece and peered at it shortsightedly.

"I don't suppose you'd better keep Randell waiting much longer," she said. "I believe it's been raining, and he catches cold easily."

"I'll get my coat and your wraps." David smiled and headed off toward the back of the lobby, now almost deserted. Even the few stragglers who'd remained to talk to Martin were making preparations to leave.

"Are you going?" Martin had freed himself and came toward us, his silk hat in his hand. "Mrs. Lillington, may I beg the indulgence of two minutes alone? I would like to make some arrangements about tomorrow."

"Be quick, then, or my mother's coachman will turn into a white mouse." Elizabeth grinned. "Of course, if you need a ride—"

"No." Martin shook his head. "I'll walk back to the Grand Pacific. I need the exercise after all that traveling." He resumed possession of my hand, patting it firmly into position on his arm. "We'll have plenty of time to talk tomorrow."

He steered me toward the front of the lobby. We stopped by a window, through which we could see the rain-slicked street. The rain had ceased, but the gaslight glinted off every wet surface and silk hat, occasionally catching the gleam of a diamond or the sheen of gold. Soon the street would be given up to the people of the night. Right now it was the province of the rich of Chicago, protected by their carriages, their servants, and the watchful police officers whose presence kept the beggars and pickpockets away.

"May I call on you tomorrow morning at your home? First thing?"

Martin released my arm and stood facing me, all trace of the showman vanished. In its place was the expression of a man balancing on a wire, calmly confident but with just a hint of fear that all might go wrong and tip him into the abyss.

"Of course." It was the first time he'd asked to come to Aldine Square, and my heart did a little skip that did my thought processes no good. "Come at seven, and we can ride to the store together."

Martin dropped his voice to a mere thread of sound. "I just want to know one thing. For heaven's sake, tell me if I'll be wasting my time tomorrow, and I'll leave you alone."

"Don't you *dare* leave me alone ever again." The vehemence in my voice surprised me, as did the sudden sting of tears in my eyes. "I've hated every moment of you being away."

Martin blinked, and the tension on his face turned to relief with such comical suddenness that I almost laughed. Only I was worried that my laughter might turn to a flood of hysterical tears. I dashed furtively at my eyes and glared at Martin.

"So you're feeling better, then," I said.

His smile was so wonderfully carefree that my knees felt weak. "Much better. It wasn't just blarney when I told those people I was ready to rebuild my life."

"Good," I said. Seeing Elizabeth and the others coming toward us, I spoke in a rapid undertone. "Because you're the only man I've ever wanted to marry—the only man I've ever loved, come to that. If you ever make me regret abandoning my principles, you'll rue the day."

And with that complete surrender, I went to take Tess's arm, and the whole group of us moved out onto the street. There was the usual confusion of good-byes and good wishes as Tess and I climbed into the carriage, Elizabeth and David preparing to take the short walk to the Palmer House hotel. The last glimpse I had of Martin was of the gaslight shining on his pale hair as he stood, hat in hand, watching our carriage with a look of baffled delight on his face.

FORTY-FIVE

Needless to say, I rose early the next morning. I chose a day dress in a muted gray with a hint of blue, with trimmings of a subtle paisley silk, silver lace, and deep blue fringe. It brought out the blue in my eyes, which, when I looked in the mirror, had an expectant yet somehow frightened look to them. I had declared myself—more or less told Martin that I would marry him—and nothing else, I supposed, could go wrong. And yet so much had happened in my life over the last six years that I feared some last-minute disaster, some startling revelation that might turn my world on end once more.

"Ridiculous," I told my reflection. "Whatever may happen, you know you can cope with it. And this is Martin, after all. He, at least, you know you can trust."

When I heard the clang of the doorbell below me at precisely seven o'clock, my heart began to beat with an odd, surging pulse, as if it were tolling the seconds. Should I stand by the fireplace? Or the window? Or sit in a chair? Should I go out into the hallway and make sure Zofia was letting him in? Supposing it were not Martin, after all?

I stood helplessly in the middle of the room, my arms dangling, feeling like a fool. But the moment the parlor door opened and Martin walked quietly into the room, the chaos in my mind ceased, like the sudden hush that falls over the audience when it realizes the play is about to begin. He smiled, and my heart gave a little hop; and when I realized that every emotion I'd been experiencing was reflected in his gray eyes, clear and sharp as a November sky, I no longer felt nervous. It *was* Martin, after all. And he'd come home to me.

"I've been up since three, terrified something might go wrong," he said as soon as Zofia shut the door behind him. "Heaven knows I've waited long enough for this moment, Nellie."

He too did not seem to know what to do with his hands. I reached out and captured one of them, reveling in its strength and solidity, and studied his face. Elizabeth was right—he was less thin, and it suited him.

"We've waited for each other most of our lives, I suppose," I said. I turned the hand I was holding over, spreading the long, capable fingers, noting how the blood seemed to gather in their tips, flushing them with warmth and life. That warmth invaded my whole body and settled somewhere in the core of my being. I looked up at Martin and felt my cheeks begin to glow, but I didn't look away.

By tacit consent we moved closer to one another, and I reached up to touch Martin's face. He was impeccably shaven, and I could still smell the faint tang of the barber's soap. The lines that the last year's trials had written around his eyes and mouth could never be erased, but they were dear to me, and I wouldn't have them otherwise. We had lived through much together, Martin and I.

"You know, I was a fool not to set my cap at you long ago," I mused, tracing the line that ran from the corner of Martin's beaky nose to the outer limit of his beautifully shaped lips. "I have been altogether a fool."

Martin captured my roving hand in his, pressing his lips to the palm. "You were always stubborn." His voice was a whisper, making my limbs soften and melt. I moved yet closer to him, even the smallest space between us unbearable. And then his mouth found mine, and I wound my arms around his neck—and there was no space between us, none at all.

❦

"We must marry soon." Martin's voice was muffled by my hair. His arms were around my waist as if they belonged there, and I was ridiculously delighted that I had to tip my head back to look up at him.

"Hmmmm?"

I was dizzy from being kissed so long and so thoroughly. My lips tingled, my face was hot, and it was remarkably difficult to summon up a coherent thought.

"We—must—marry—soon," Martin said in tones of exaggerated slowness. I could feel the laughter bubbling up inside him. "I'm most categorically tired of waiting."

I felt my eyebrows shoot up toward my hairline. "*You're* tired of waiting? At least you had Europe to keep you amused. I've had a Chicago winter, with ice and chilblains and mountains of dirty snow."

I aimed for a tone of arch crossness, but didn't succeed too well. Besides, Martin kept kissing me so that the words came out in a series of small, explosive bursts, and I finished the sentence in laughter.

"Any more scolding before I begin kissing you again?"

"Yes."

I pushed at Martin's chest; surprised, he stopped what he was doing and stared at me.

"You haven't actually asked me to marry you yet," I pointed out.

"Well—well, I suppose I haven't." One corner of his mouth twitched. "Would you prefer I propose from the traditional bended knee, or will you accept me if I remain standing?"

I hesitated, embarrassed. And then blurted out: "I know it's silly after all this time, but I would much prefer—"

"I've always thought you were a traditionalist at heart."

Martin's long body folded itself gracefully in a downward direction until he was poised on one knee on the Turkey carpet, his large hands enveloping mine. The amused look in his eyes suddenly turned serious, and his fingers tightened as if he didn't ever intend to let me go.

"Eleanor Lillington—"

"*Look!* Martin's here!"

We were gazing into each other's eyes, and it took both of us a few moments to register that we were no longer alone. Sarah ran into the room, mouth agape, but Tess stopped in the doorway. A look of dawning comprehension was on her face, mingled with glee.

"What are you doing? Why are you kneeling down? Has Mama hurt herself?" Sarah's gaze darted between us, her expression anxious.

"Sary, come back here!" cried Tess. "We mustn't interrupt—not now. I'm sorry, Nell," she continued, a small hand hovering over her mouth in an attitude somewhere betwixt dismay and mirth. "I didn't know Martin was here—we came to see where you were. I'm sorry, Martin."

Martin, who seemed to be taking the interruption with far more nonchalance than I felt, merely shifted his grounded knee into a more comfortable angle, resting his free arm on top of it. He didn't let go of my hand.

"I'm proposing marriage to your mother," he informed Sarah in a conversational tone and gave my hand a squeeze. "Don't you think it's about time?"

Sarah's eyes grew round. She took a step toward us and rested a small hand on Martin's knee, gazing at him seriously.

"You really want to marry Mama? To be Mr. Lillington?"

Martin didn't laugh, but reached out his free hand and gently pulled at one of Sarah's ringlets. "Well, I'm rather hoping your mother will become Mrs. Rutherford, or Mrs. Lillington Rutherford at the very least. It's traditional for the lady to adopt the gentleman's name. It's also traditional for the gentleman to propose on bended knee, which is why you find me sinking into the carpet."

"Oh." Sarah's brow was marked by the tiny frown she always got when trying to understand grown-ups. "But if Mama's going to be Mrs. Rutherford, how can I be called Sarah Lillington? Does my name change too?"

"If you want it to."

"So you'll be my Papa?"

"Yes." Martin's face had grown completely serious.

"For ever and ever?"

"Yes."

"Sary!" Tess hissed. "Come away and let them be private. We shouldn't be here." She then ruined the stern effect she was trying for by grinning at me and bouncing on her toes. "Just like the play. I'm awful glad."

"So am I," I said, my eyes on Martin.

Sarah reached for my hand, and I grasped hers. Her small fingers were in mine, Martin's large ones encircling my other hand. It felt wonderful.

"Your permission to continue?" Martin asked Sarah softly. She nodded and he returned his gaze to me, looking straight into my eyes with an expression that combined amusement and tenderness in such a way that my knees turned to jelly.

"Eleanor Lillington," said Martin in a voice loud enough for the others to hear, "I have loved you—well, all your life, in one way or another. In the somewhat unexpected presence of witnesses, will you do me the honor of granting me your hand in marriage?"

"Yes." The word came out as a hoarse croak, and I cleared my throat. "Yes, Martin, I will marry you. I can truthfully say you're the only man I'd ever want to marry."

Martin's eyes crinkled at the corners, but he kept a straight face as he looked at Sarah.

"Since we're being unorthodox—"

"What does that mean?" Sarah interrupted, smoothing back the lock of hair that had fallen over Martin's forehead.

"I'll explain later. Since—well, to put it more simply, Sarah, I'll be proud to be your Papa for ever and ever. May I have that privilege?"

"You certainly may." Sarah's eyes widened. "I'm going to be the daughter of Rutherford & Co.!"

Martin rose to his feet and stretched out an arm to Tess, who was still hovering in the doorway.

"You may as well join in, Tess. Will you do me the honor of continuing to live with us as my wife's—as our—best friend? As a most important member of our family?"

Tess squealed and ran to hug him, me, and Sarah in turn, setting off a positive riot of hugging all around. By the time Sarah decided she couldn't wait another moment to inform the servants of this exciting development, I felt drained of all emotion. It was only Martin's steadying hand around my waist that stopped me from collapsing on the settee in an uncharacteristically feminine bout of hysterics.

"Well, I suppose that was easier than breaking the news to them later," said Martin, shutting the door firmly as the last flounce of Tess's skirts cleared the doorway. "And now, if the future Mrs. Rutherford would indulge me, it's traditional for the gentleman to require as many kisses of his fiancée as he can get away with."

FORTY-SIX

We were wed very quietly since Martin had only been a widower for just over a year. The small ceremony merited a mere three lines or so in the press. The papers had been full of events in the South, strikes, and now the war between the Russians and the Turks, and the Rutherford murder was no longer of much interest to the Chicago populace. In some ways, Alex Gambarelli had done us a favor by removing the "murder room," as it had become known within the Rutherford's building. Before the fire, Joe had to keep it permanently locked and empty to discourage visits by curiosity-seekers.

We lived at Aldine Square after our marriage, the Katzenmeiers having informed me that they would not return till September. Our new house on Calumet Avenue would be ready by the end of the year. Martin, who was fascinated by architecture, spent much of his time traveling between the new store, the walls of which were rising fast, and the unpretentious yet spacious dwelling we would share with Sarah, Tess, and the children yet to come.

"He's also looking at land in Lake Forest," I told Elizabeth as we walked arm in arm around Aldine Square's small central garden. "He thinks we should build a summer home there, as so many of the merchants are doing.

Sarah is wild to have a pony now that she can ride—thanks to you."

"How very domestic, Mrs. Eleanor Lillington Rutherford." Elizabeth poked me playfully in the side. "It's 'he thinks' and 'he says' every minute. Adding 'Lillington' to your name may give you the illusion of independence, I suppose."

"I haven't been truly independent for years," I protested. "Since the day I decided to keep Sarah, I've had to take her welfare into account. I wasn't going to keep her, you know." I could see Sarah at a distance, walking with Tess and Miss Baker. "But then there was trouble at the Poor Farm, and I realized how vulnerable she was. I found a sense of responsibility I'd never known I possessed."

"Responsibility? Love, surely." Elizabeth's look was quizzical.

"Love, of course. But they seem to be the same thing, in many ways. And now I have to take Martin's feelings into consideration as well. And I *want* to take them into consideration, more than I'd ever realized was possible."

"There speaks the new bride." Elizabeth grinned. "A perfect slave."

"No—a partner." I bent to admire a patch of sky-blue irises, their delicate petals shining under the May sun. "I don't think Martin treats me any differently as the partner of his private life than he does as a partner in his company. He's senior in both cases—after all, he's older than me, and he built up the company in the first place. But we allot ourselves our own tasks on the basis of what we both do best. We did the same years ago when I was his guest in Victory. I should have realized back then how well a marriage between us would work. And you really do need more than romantic love in a marriage, don't you?" I looked up at Elizabeth, smiling. She and David were due to wed in the summer.

"We should enjoy the romantic love while we have it though, in my opinion." Elizabeth rolled her eyes at me. "*You* seem to be taken enough with your husband. I presume that 'brief and unsatisfactory' no longer applies."

"It doesn't, and I'll thank you to keep your pretty nose out of my personal business. I'm sure Martin and I will argue and bicker and get exasperated with one another from time to time, like all couples do. But we know each other so well that there have been no startling revelations."

And yet we discovered new, small things about each other daily. The five years we'd spent apart served to lend a certain spice to our mutual understanding. I found I was grateful for Martin's previous marriage—in ways I could perhaps discuss with Elizabeth once she was a married woman. Martin and I had found joy in the sharing of each other's secrets, building an intimate knowledge of our bodies' needs and responses, so that at times I felt we shared one skin. Yes, there were definitely aspects of marriage that were extremely pleasant.

We had some secrets still. Martin avoided telling me what happened with the doctors at the University of Vienna, and I never asked him. And I held the story of the night of the fire locked in my memories. Perhaps I would tell it years later, when it was far too late to seek any kind of recourse against Alex Gambarelli. Without the knowledge I held, Martin was safe. That was worth a small patch of burned skin.

"I've convinced David to become an ardent supporter of the Feminist cause and women's suffrage. That's one great advantage of romantic love," Elizabeth said with a toss of her head. "His only request is that I behave 'sensibly,' whatever that means. I always behave sensibly. And I can depend on you and Martin for a subscription or two, I hope?"

I watched the distant figures of Sarah, Tess, and Miss Baker as they rounded a corner. Sarah, I had no doubt, would be reading a picture book as she walked, probably munching on an apple at the same time. She would not appear to be listening to Tess and Miss Baker, but would be absorbing their conversation like a sponge. Miss Baker was probably lecturing Tess on the need for better working conditions for Chicago's poor and the justification for the strikes that were sweeping the country.

"I suppose Martin must take an interest in the rights of women now that he has a daughter," I said. "Especially one who shows every sign of growing into a complete bluestocking. Miss Baker's already telling her she must go to university, and she's only six."

"And she sees her mother working, which must have some effect on her," Elizabeth mused. "She will grow up with every advantage, including the society of active, intellectual women—and that *does* mean you, my dear. You may not care to talk about literature, but I've heard you holding forth on business matters. David says your grasp of your own investments is becoming quite respectable."

"Papa's home!"

I heard the shout from across the square, and turned to see Martin ride through the gates on Gentleman, his dappled gray. Sarah passed us in a blur of movement. I could see I'd been right about the apple—she clutched the core in one hand, eager to give it to the horse.

Every advantage, I thought, watching Sarah slow to a walk as Martin drew near. He swung one long leg over the saddle and dropped easily to the ground, bending down to kiss Sarah on the cheek as she put her hand up to caress Gentleman's soft gray nose. I too, it seemed, had ended up with every advantage, because ultimately I had been able to choose each of my ties freely. And they were bonds from which I did not wish to escape.

AUTHOR'S NOTE

The Shadow Palace is set in 1876 and 1877, pivotal—and yet often over-looked—years in American history. Reconstruction, the post-Civil War process aimed at building a slavery-free South, came to an end in ways that set the stage for future racial segregation. Big business boomed, and grow-ing inequality between the workers and their masters prepared the way for the social unrest of the late 1800s. It was a time of religious revivalism, and heightened calls for the repression of alcoholic consumption eventually led to Prohibition.

Over the century since the founding of America women had suffered a loss of rights and increasing pressure to conform to a Victorian ideal of the "little wifie" so loved by writers like Charles Dickens. By 1876-1877 the Feminists* and related groups were fighting back with calls for the right to vote, a place in the nation's political life, even the abolition of marriage in favor of a looser union that would allow them to retain control over their property and decision-making. Their granddaughters would see universal women's suffrage in 1920—but many of their ideals including free love, re-productive rights, and equal rights in the workplace didn't even begin to make real headway until almost a hundred years later. Many view the battle as far from won 130 years later.

In essence, then, those years after the Civil War saw the beginning of the America we know now, and I wish I could have put more of the historical context into *The Shadow Palace*. But my aim is to entertain you, and I can only hope that Nell's struggle to reconcile her biology with her ambitions will pique your interest over the historical background of the story. Between them, *The Year of the Century: 1876* by Dee Brown and *1877: America's Year of Living Violently* by Michael Bellesiles will give you a taste of the times.

The first two novels in the House of Closed Doors series were set in imaginary locations, which allowed me some leeway for invention. Chicago, on the other hand, is a very real place. And yet there's a dearth of information about the Reconstruction years in Chicago—historians have a tendency to leap from the Chicago Fire in 1871 to the giddy years of the 1880s and 1890s, when many of the city's iconic buildings and institutions first arose. In the latter half of the 1870s, Chicago was still suffering from the combined effect of the fire and the financial panic of 1873. Around half of its inhabitants were recent immigrants to the United States, and its society was far more fluid than that of the older Eastern cities. It was an important hub for commodities arriving from the West, including hundreds of thousands of head of livestock, which were butchered and packed in the Union Stockyards. It was a city where fortunes could be rapidly amassed by legal or illegal means. In addition to its immigrants, it drew in the young and ambitious from the old cities of the East coast and the rural Midwest. In short, it was on its way to becoming the Second City of the US—but it wasn't there yet.

If the brief glimpse I've given you of 1876-1877 Chicago fascinates you (or you want to correct a mistake I've made—I'm a storyteller, not a historian—) then I'd suggest *Challenging Chicago* by Perry R. Duis for a great overview of daily life in the growing city. *The Robber Barons* by Matthew Josephson is a lucid account of how big business was carried on during and after the Civil War, often with little regard to ethics. Herbert Asbury's classic *The Gangs of Chicago* will help you understand the Chicago underworld, with which Nell only has a minor brush.

Talking of the underworld, *The Shadow Palace*—unlike the other Nell books—features a couple of real-life characters. They are Lizzie Allen, a successful prostitute and brothel-keeper, and Christopher Columbus Crabb, who was Lizzie's "solid man" in 1878 and who pops up in later Chicago histories as a property owner. I have built a story for Crabb on these slender references, but pretty much everything about him in *The Shadow Palace* is fictional.

I also mention Marshall Field and Potter Palmer, two of Chicago's merchant princes of the era and pioneers of department stores in Chicago. Department stores, of course, were around earlier in the 19th century, especially in Europe. Yet they were still regarded as a new and innovative way of doing business. For women in particular, department stores offered a place to work and a place to shop unchaperoned. Their most startling innovations, in 19th-century eyes, were their fixed prices—no haggling—and the abundance of ready-made goods, regularly discounted to make room for new stock. The excitement of this new form of shopping was captured by French writer Emile Zola in 1883, and I recommend reading *Au Bonheur des Dames (The Ladies' Delight* or *The Ladies' Paradise)* to get a flavor of early department store life. Martin's store and the Gambarelli store are fictional, but State Street was where the major Chicago stores of the era were located.

Please visit my Pinterest board for The Shadow Palace (*https://www.pin-terest.com/janesteen/the-shadow-palace/*) to see scenes and ideas that inspired my story. And if you want to keep up with my news, please subscribe to my newsletter at *www.janesteen.com/insider.*

*I have deliberately capitalized the word in the novel. For one thing, Nell's contemporaries would have done so. For another, I wanted to make a distinction between these early Feminists and their 20th-century descendants.

Acknowledgements

I wrote *The Shadow Palace* far more quickly and efficiently than the first two books in the series. This achievement was partly due to my growing experience as an author, but it also owes much to a wonderful team of people. First and foremost, as always for this series, I would like to thank Katharine Grubb, author and critique partner extraordinaire. Nobody is better at telling me which characters stink and are best removed.

Then there are Maureen Lang and Judy Knox, fellow authors who weighed in on later drafts with frank advice and endless encouragement. Mary Walter was there to check the formatted version of the ebook, saving me another round of reading.

I couldn't produce any of these books without a team of partners whose skills contribute hugely to the final product. Jenny Quinlan, my editor, contributes a layer of polish and consistency I couldn't do without. Steve Ledell, photographer, and Derek Moore, graphic designer par excellence, turn a manuscript and a few ideas into a book. And Elizabeth Klett gives Nell a voice, adding a whole new dimension to my stories for an increasingly multi-media-conscious readership.

And there's family—Bob especially—and friends who cheer me on, come to my author events, buy my books for their friends and generally make me feel supported and loved.

And finally, all those fans I've never met who read my books, review them online, send me emails and subscribe to my newsletter. I try to read everything they write, positive or negative, and learn from their wisdom. Thank you all.

THE HOUSE OF CLOSED DOORS
SERIES

Nell's Story

"I love this series. It is exceptionally well written; the language, the historical detail. Reading it was like eating a delicious piece of rich chocolate mousse cake and wishing you had more than just the one serving."

THE HOUSE OF CLOSED DOORS

ETERNAL DECEPTION

THE SHADOW PALACE

THE HOUSE OF CLOSED DOORS

In Nell Lillington's small Midwestern town of the 1870s, marriage is the obvious fate of a young woman of some social standing. Yet Nell is determined to elude the duties and restrictions of matrimony. So when she finds herself pregnant, she refuses to divulge the name of the father.

Nell's stepfather Hiram sends Nell to live at the Poor Farm of which he is a governor, to await the day when her baby can be discreetly adopted. Nell is ready to go along with Hiram's plans until an unused padded cell is opened and two small bodies fall out.

Nell is the only resident of the Poor Farm who is convinced that the unwed mother and her baby were murdered, and the incident prompts her to rethink her decision to abandon her own child to her fate. But the revelations to which her questions lead make her realize that even if she manages to escape the Poor Farm with her baby, she may have no safe place to run to.

ℰ

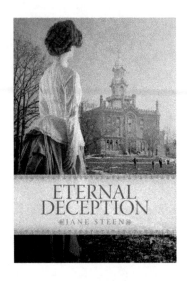

ETERNAL DECEPTION

Love or independence? Few choices remain for Nell and her new family on the Kansas frontier…

Kansas, 1872. Nell hopes to support her daughter Sarah and friend Tess by working as a seamstress in an isolated seminary. As murder and intrigue haunt the seminary and Nell attracts the attention of two suitors, she must choose between returning to her old life and remaining in charge of her destiny.

Shocking news from back home and another death at the seminary press Nell to make her decision. A disastrous winter journey, a treacherous game, and an impossible love could finally wrest control of Nell's life out of her hands for good.

The Shadow Palace

For Nell, 1876 Chicago—and her new wealth—offer the promise
of longed-for independence. She dreams of a place in society for Sarah
and contentment for Tess. Yet how can she settle in a town where she's far
too likely to run into Martin Rutherford and his glittering, faithless wife,
Lucetta? Can she resist her love for Martin for Sarah's sake?

Martin was doubtless joking when he told Nell that if she got herself mixed
up with a murderer for the third time, he'd disown her. But when Martin
himself is arrested for murder, Nell's dreams appear to be swallowed up
in the new web of secrets she constructs to help him. Secrets that threaten
to alienate Tess, Sarah, and even Martin . . .

About the Author

Jane Steen was born in England but has lived in both Belgium and the United States. Her corporate writing career included translation, editorial guidance for lawyers, contract drafting, fundraising, and marketing copy for realtors.

Jane is an independent writer of historical fiction and an active member of the Alliance of Independent Authors and the Historical Novel Society.

CPSIA information can be obtained
at www.ICGtesting.com
Printed in the USA
LVHW04s2007040718
582656LV00004B/338/P

9 780985 715083